SIX GREAT MODERN SHORT NOVELS

These half dozen short novels are as different from each other as any great works of fiction can be. From Melville we get an unforgettable tale of good and evil in conflict on the high seas. Joyce, the great genius of modern prose, gives us a touching and realistic story of lost love. Nobel Prize winner William Faulkner writes the stark drama of a young boy's savage awakening to life. From Katherine Anne Porter comes a penetrating study of Southern tragedy; from Gogol, a masterful narrative of man's quest for dignity; from Glenway Westcott, a sensitive and poignant picture of individual isolation. . . . But despite these differences, all share that one element—the unmistakable ring of human truth—that marks each of them as a masterpiece. . . .

SIX
GREAT
MODERN
SHORT
NOVELS

. . . .

Published by
Dell Publishing
a division of
Bantam Doubleday Dell Publishing Group, Inc.
666 Fifth Avenue
New York, New York 10103

ISBN: 0-440-37996-2

Previous Dell Editions #F35 and 7996
New Dell Edition
August 1967

OPM   34   33   32   31   30   29   28   27   26   25

TABLE OF CONTENTS

The Dead
   BY JAMES JOYCE
. . . . 7

Billy Budd, Foretopman
   BY HERMAN MELVILLE
. . . . 57

Noon Wine
   BY KATHERINE ANNE PORTER
. . . . 155

The Overcoat
   BY NIKOLAY GOGOL
. . . . 213

The Pilgrim Hawk
   BY GLENWAY WESCOTT
. . . . 251

The Bear
   BY WILLIAM FAULKNER
. . . . 323

THE DEAD

· ·

James Joyce

James Joyce

. . . .

James Joyce, one of the great writers of our time and one of the great masters of language, was born near Dublin in 1882. He lived most of his life, in exile, in France and Switzerland (where he died in 1941) fighting blindness and poverty and writing the books that were to influence so strongly the literature of the twentieth century. His work ranges from a slim volume of verse: *Chamber Music* (1907); to a great volume of stories: *Dubliners* (1914) (from which "The Dead" is taken); to an autobiographical novel: *A Portrait of the Artist As a Young Man* (1916); to his masterpiece of modern man: *Ulysses* (1922; 1933 in the U.S.); and, finally, to one of the great experiments in literature: *Finnegan's Wake* (1939). All of the above are published by The Viking Press, New York, except *Ulysses*, which is published by Random House, New York.

THE DEAD

LILY, the caretaker's daughter, was literally run off her feet. Hardly had she brought one gentleman into the little pantry behind the office on the ground floor and helped him off with his overcoat than the wheezy hall-door bell clanged again and she had to scamper along the bare hallway to let in another guest. It was well for her she had not to attend to the ladies also. But Miss Kate and Miss Julia had thought of that and had converted the bathroom upstairs into a ladies' dressing-room. Miss Kate and Miss Julia were there, gossiping and laughing and fussing, walking after each other to the head of the stairs, peering down over the banisters and calling down to Lily to ask her who had come.

It was always a great affair, the Misses Morkan's annual dance. Everybody who knew them came to it, members of the family, old friends of the family, the members of Julia's choir, any of Kate's pupils that were grown up enough, and even some of Mary Jane's pupils too. Never once had it fallen flat. For years and years it had gone off in splendid style, as long as anyone could remember; ever since Kate and Julia, after the death of their brother Pat, had left the house in Stoney Batter and taken Mary Jane, their only niece, to live with them in the dark, gaunt house on Usher's Island, the upper part of which they had rented from Mr. Fulham, the corn-factor on the ground floor. That was a good thirty years ago if it was a day. Mary Jane, who was then a little girl in short clothes, was now the main prop of the household, for she had the organ in Haddington Road. She had been through the Academy and gave a pupils' concert every year in the upper room of the Antient Concert Rooms. Many of her pupils be-

longed to the better-class families on the Kingstown and
Dalkey line. Old as they were, her aunts also did their
share. Julia, though she was quite grey, was still the leading soprano in Adam and Eve's, and Kate, being too feeble
to go about much, gave music lessons to beginners on the
old square piano in the back room. Lily, the caretaker's
daughter, did housemaid's work for them. Though their
life was modest, they believed in eating well; the best of
everything: diamond-bone sirloins, three-shilling tea and
the best bottled stout. But Lily seldom made a mistake in
the orders, so that she got on well with her three mistresses.
They were fussy, that was all. But the only thing they
would not stand was back answers.

Of course, they had good reason to be fussy on such a
night. And then it was long after ten o'clock and yet there
was no sign of Gabriel and his wife. Besides they were
dreadfully afraid that Freddy Malins might turn up
screwed. They would not wish for worlds that any of Mary
Jane's pupils should see him under the influence; and
when he was like that it was sometimes very hard to manage him. Freddy Malins always came late, but they wondered what could be keeping Gabriel: and that was what
brought them every two minutes to the banisters to ask
Lily had Gabriel or Freddy come.

"O, Mr. Conroy," said Lily to Gabriel when she opened
the door for him, "Miss Kate and Miss Julia thought you
were never coming. Good-night, Mrs. Conroy."

"I'll engage they did," said Gabriel, "but they forget
that my wife here takes three mortal hours to dress herself."

He stood on the mat, scraping the snow from his
goloshes, while Lily led his wife to the foot of the stairs
and called out:

"Miss Kate, here's Mrs. Conroy."

Kate and Julia came toddling down the dark stairs at
once. Both of them kissed Gabriel's wife, said she must be
perished alive, and asked was Gabriel with her.

"Here I am as right as the mail, Aunt Kate! Go on up.

I'll follow," called out Gabriel from the dark.

He continued scraping his feet vigorously while the three women went upstairs, laughing, to the ladies' dressing-room. A light fringe of snow lay like a cape on the shoulders of his overcoat and like toecaps on the toes of his goloshes; and, as the buttons of his overcoat slipped with a squeaking noise through the snow-stiffened frieze, a cold, fragrant air from out-of-doors escaped from crevices and folds.

"Is it snowing again, Mr. Conroy?" asked Lily.

She had preceded him into the pantry to help him off with his overcoat. Gabriel smiled at the three syllables she had given his surname and glanced at her. She was a slim, growing girl, pale in complexion and with hay-coloured hair. The gas in the pantry made her look still paler. Gabriel had known her when she was a child and used to sit on the lowest step nursing a rag doll.

"Yes, Lily," he answered, "and I think we're in for a night of it."

He looked up at the pantry ceiling, which was shaking with the stamping and shuffling of feet on the floor above, listened for a moment to the piano and then glanced at the girl, who was folding his overcoat carefully at the end of a shelf.

"Tell me, Lily," he said in a friendly tone, "do you still go to school?"

"O no, sir," she answered. "I'm done schooling this year and more."

"O, then," said Gabriel gaily, "I suppose we'll be going to your wedding one of these fine days with your young man, eh?"

The girl glanced back at him over her shoulder and said with great bitterness:

"The men that is now is only all palaver and what they can get out of you."

Gabriel coloured, as if he felt he had made a mistake and, without looking at her, kicked off his goloshes and flicked actively with his muffler at his patent-leather shoes.

He was a stout, tallish young man. The high colour of his cheeks pushed upwards even to his forehead, where it scattered itself in a few formless patches of pale red; and on his hairless face there scintillated restlessly the polished lenses and the bright gilt rims of the glasses which screened his delicate and restless eyes. His glossy black hair was parted in the middle and brushed in a long curve behind his ears where it curled slightly beneath the groove left by his hat.

When he had flicked lustre into his shoes he stood up and pulled his waistcoat down more tightly on his plump body. Then he took a coin rapidly from his pocket.

"O Lily," he said, thrusting it into her hands, "it's Christmas-time, isn't it? Just . . . here's a little. . . ."

He walked rapidly towards the door.

"O no, sir!" cried the girl, following him. "Really, sir, I wouldn't take it."

"Christmas-time! Christmas-time!" said Gabriel, almost trotting to the stairs and waving his hand to her in deprecation.

The girl, seeing that he had gained the stairs, called out after him:

"Well, thank you, sir."

He waited outside the drawing-room door until the waltz should finish, listening to the skirts that swept against it and to the shuffling of feet. He was still discomposed by the girl's bitter and sudden retort. It had cast a gloom over him which he tried to dispel by arranging his cuffs and the bows of his tie. He then took from his waistcoat pocket a little paper and glanced at the headings he had made for his speech. He was undecided about the lines from Robert Browning, for he feared they would be above the heads of his hearers. Some quotation that they would recognise from Shakespeare or from the Melodies would be better. The indelicate clacking of the men's heels and the shuffling of their soles reminded him that their grade of culture differed from his. He would only make himself ridiculous by quoting poetry to them which they could not understand. They would think that he was airing his superior education. He would fail with them just as he had failed with the girl in the pantry. He had taken up a wrong tone. His whole speech was a mistake from first to last, an utter failure.

Just then his aunts and his wife came out of the ladies' dressing-room. His aunts were two small, plainly dressed old women. Aunt Julia was an inch or so the taller. Her hair, drawn low over the tops of her ears, was grey; and grey also, with darker shadows, was her large flaccid face. Though she was stout in build and stood erect, her slow eyes and parted lips gave her the appearance of a woman who did not know where she was or where she was going. Aunt Kate was more vivacious. Her face, healthier than her sister's, was all puckers and creases, like a shrivelled red apple, and her hair, braided in the same old-fashioned way, had not lost its ripe nut colour.

They both kissed Gabriel frankly. He was their favourite nephew, the son of their dead elder sister, Ellen, who had married T. J. Conroy of the Port and Docks.

"Gretta tells me you're not going to take a cab back to Monkstown tonight, Gabriel," said Aunt Kate.

"No," said Gabriel, turning to his wife, "we had quite enough of that last year, hadn't we? Don't you remember, Aunt Kate, what a cold Gretta got out of it? Cab windows rattling all the way, and the east wind blowing in after we passed Merrion. Very jolly it was. Gretta caught a dreadful cold."

Aunt Kate frowned severely and nodded her head at every word.

"Quite right, Gabriel, quite right," she said. "You can't be too careful."

"But as for Gretta there," said Gabriel, "she'd walk home in the snow if she were let."

Mrs. Conroy laughed.

"Don't mind him, Aunt Kate," she said. "He's really an awful bother, what with green shades for Tom's eyes at night and making him do the dumb-bells, and forcing Eva to eat the stirabout. The poor child! And she simply hates the sight of it! . . . O, but you'll never guess what he makes me wear now!"

She broke out into a peal of laughter and glanced at her husband, whose admiring and happy eyes had been wandering from her dress to her face and hair. The two aunts laughed heartily, too, for Gabriel's solicitude was a standing joke with them.

"Goloshes!" said Mrs. Conroy. "That's the latest. Whenever it's wet underfoot I must put on my goloshes. Tonight even, he wanted me to put them on, but I wouldn't. The next thing he'll buy me will be a diving suit."

Gabriel laughed nervously and patted his tie reassuringly, while Aunt Kate nearly doubled herself, so heartily did she enjoy the joke. The smile soon faded from Aunt Julia's face and her mirthless eyes were directed towards her nephew's face. After a pause she asked:

"And what are goloshes, Gabriel?"

"Goloshes, Julia!" exclaimed her sister. "Goodness me, don't you know what goloshes are? You wear them over your . . . over your boots, Gretta, isn't it?"

"Yes," said Mrs. Conroy. "Guttapercha things. We both have a pair now. Gabriel says everyone wears them on the Continent."

"O, on the Continent," murmured Aunt Julia, nodding her head slowly.

Gabriel knitted his brows and said, as if he were slightly angered:

"It's nothing very wonderful, but Gretta thinks it very funny because she says the word reminds her of Christy Minstrels."

"But tell me, Gabriel," said Aunt Kate, with brisk tact. "Of course, you've seen about the room. Gretta was saying . . ."

"O, the room is all right," replied Gabriel. "I've taken one in the Gresham."

"To be sure," said Aunt Kate, "by far the best thing to do. And the children, Gretta, you're not anxious about them?"

"O, for one night," said Mrs. Conroy. "Besides, Bessie will look after them."

"To be sure," said Aunt Kate again. "What a comfort it is to have a girl like that, one you can depend on! There's that Lily, I'm sure I don't know what has come over her lately. She's not the girl she was at all."

Gabriel was about to ask his aunt some questions on this point, but she broke off suddenly to gaze after her sister, who had wandered down the stairs and was craning her neck over the banisters.

"Now, I ask you," she said almost testily, "where is Julia going? Julia! Julia! Where are you going?"

Julia, who had gone half way down one flight, came back and announced blandly: "Here's Freddy."

At the same moment a clapping of hands and a final flourish of the pianist told that the waltz had ended. The drawing-room door was opened from within and some couples came out. Aunt Kate drew Gabriel aside hurriedly and whispered into his ear:

"Slip down, Gabriel, like a good fellow and see if he's all right, and don't let him up if he's screwed. I'm sure he's screwed. I'm sure he is."

Gabriel went to the stairs and listened over the banisters. He could hear two persons talking in the pantry. Then he recognised Freddy Malins' laugh. He went down the stairs noisily.

"It's such a relief," said Aunt Kate to Mrs. Conroy, "that Gabriel is here. I always feel easier in my mind when he's here. . . . Julia, there's Miss Daly and Miss Power will take some refreshment. Thanks for your beautiful waltz, Miss Daly. It made lovely time."

A tall wizen-faced man, with a stiff grizzled moustache

and swarthy skin, who was passing out with his partner, said:

"And may we have some refreshment, too, Miss Morkan?"

"Julia," said Aunt Kate summarily, "and here's Mr. Browne and Miss Furlong. Take them in, Julia, with Miss Daly and Miss Power."

"I'm the man for the ladies," said Mr. Browne, pursing his lips until his moustache bristled and smiling in all his wrinkles. "You know, Miss Morkan, the reason they are so fond of me is—"

He did not finish his sentence, but, seeing that Aunt Kate was out of earshot, at once led the three young ladies into the back room. The middle of the room was occupied by two square tables placed end to end, and on these Aunt Julia and the caretaker were straightening and smoothing a large cloth. On the sideboard were arrayed dishes and plates, and glasses and bundles of knives and forks and spoons. The top of the closed square piano served also as a sideboard for viands and sweets. At a smaller sideboard in one corner two young men were standing, drinking hop-bitters.

Mr. Browne led his charges thither and invited them all, in jest, to some ladies' punch, hot, strong and sweet. As they said they never took anything strong, he opened three bottles of lemonade for them. Then he asked one of the young men to move aside, and, taking hold of the decanter, filled out for himself a goodly measure of whisky. The young men eyed him respectfully while he took a trial sip.

"God help me," he said, smiling, "it's the doctor's orders."

His wizened face broke into a broader smile, and the three young ladies laughed in musical echo to his pleasantry, swaying their bodies to and fro, with nervous jerks of their shoulders. The boldest said:

"O, now, Mr. Browne, I'm sure the doctor never ordered

anything of the kind."

Mr. Browne took another sip of his whisky and said, with sidling mimicry:

"Well, you see, I'm like the famous Mrs. Cassidy, who is reported to have said: 'Now, Mary Grimes, if I don't take it, make me take it, for I feel I want it.'"

His hot face had leaned forward a little too confidentially and he had assumed a very low Dublin accent so that the young ladies, with one instinct, received his speech in silence. Miss Furlong, who was one of Mary Jane's pupils, asked Miss Daly what was the name of the pretty waltz she had played; and Mr. Browne, seeing that he was ignored, turned promptly to the two young men who were more appreciative.

A red-faced young woman, dressed in pansy, came into the room, excitedly clapping her hands and crying:

"Quadrilles! Quadrilles!"

Close on her heels came Aunt Kate, crying:

"Two gentlemen and three ladies, Mary Jane!"

"O, here's Mr. Bergin and Mr. Kerrigan," said Mary Jane. "Mr. Kerrigan, will you take Miss Power? Miss Furlong, may I get you a partner, Mr. Bergin. O, that'll just do now."

"Three ladies, Mary Jane," said Aunt Kate.

The two young gentlemen asked the ladies if they might have the pleasure, and Mary Jane turned to Miss Daly.

"O, Miss Daly, you're really awfully good, after playing for the last two dances, but really we're so short of ladies tonight."

"I don't mind in the least, Miss Morkan."

"But I've a nice partner for you, Mr. Bartell D'Arcy, the tenor. I'll get him to sing later on. All Dublin is raving about him."

"Lovely voice, lovely voice!" said Aunt Kate.

As the piano had twice begun the prelude to the first figure Mary Jane led her recruits quickly from the room. They had hardly gone when Aunt Julia wandered slowly into the room, looking behind her at something.

"What is the matter, Julia?" asked Aunt Kate anxiously. "Who is it?"

Julia, who was carrying in a column of table-napkins, turned to her sister and said, simply, as if the question had surprised her:

"It's only Freddy, Kate, and Gabriel with him."

In fact right behind her Gabriel could be seen piloting Freddy Malins across the landing. The latter, a young man of about forty, was of Gabriel's size and build, with very round shoulders. His face was fleshy and pallid, touched with colour only at the thick hanging lobes of his ears and at the wide wings of his nose. He had coarse features, a blunt nose, a convex and receding brow, tumid and protruded lips. His heavy-lidded eyes and the disorder of his scanty hair made him look sleepy. He was laughing heartily in a high key at a story which he had been telling Gabriel on the stairs and at the same time rubbing the knuckles of his left fist backwards and forwards into his left eye.

"Good evening, Freddy," said Aunt Julia.

Freddy Malins bade the Misses Morkan good-evening in what seemed an offhand fashion by reason of the habitual catch in his voice and then, seeing that Mr. Browne was grinning at him from the sideboard, crossed the room on rather shaky legs and began to repeat in an undertone the story he had just told to Gabriel.

"He's not so bad, is he?" said Aunt Kate to Gabriel.

Gabriel's brows were dark but he raised them quickly and answered:

"O, no, hardly noticeable."

"Now, isn't he a terrible fellow!" she said. "And his poor mother made him take the pledge on New Year's Eve. But come on, Gabriel, into the drawing-room."

Before leaving the room with Gabriel she signalled to Mr. Browne by frowning and shaking her forefinger in warning to and fro. Mr. Browne nodded in answer and, when she had gone, said to Freddy Malins:

"Now, then, Teddy, I'm going to fill you out a good glass of lemonade just to buck you up."

Freddy Malins, who was nearing the climax of his story, waved the offer aside impatiently but Mr. Browne, having first called Freddy Malins' attention to a disarray in his dress, filled out and handed him a full glass of lemonade. Freddy Malins' left hand accepted the glass mechanically, his right hand being engaged in the mechanical readjustment of his dress. Mr. Browne, whose face was once more wrinkling with mirth, poured out for himself a glass of whisky while Freddy Malins exploded, before he had well reached the climax of his story, in a kink of high-pitched bronchitic laughter and, setting down his untasted and overflowing glass, began to rub the knuckles of his left fist backwards and forwards into his left eye, repeating words of his last phrase as well as his fit of laughter would allow him.

    •   •   •   •   •   •

Gabriel could not listen while Mary Jane was playing her Academy piece, full of runs and difficult passages, to the hushed drawing-room. He liked music but the piece she was playing had no melody for him and he doubted whether it had any melody for the other listeners, though they had begged Mary Jane to play something. Four young men, who had come from the refreshment-room to stand in the doorway at the sound of the piano, had gone away quietly in couples after a few minutes. The only persons who seemed to follow the music were Mary Jane herself, her hands racing along the key-board or lifted from it at the pauses like those of a priestess in momentary imprecation, and Aunt Kate standing at her elbow to turn the page.

Gabriel's eyes, irritated by the floor, which glittered with beeswax under the heavy chandelier, wandered to the wall above the piano. A picture of the balcony scene in *Romeo and Juliet* hung there and beside it was a picture

of the two murdered princes in the Tower which Aunt
Julia had worked in red, blue and brown wools when she
was a girl. Probably in the school they had gone to as girls
that kind of work had been taught for one year. His mother had worked for him as a birthday present a waistcoat
of purple tabinet, with little foxes' heads upon it, lined
with brown satin and having round mulberry buttons. It
was strange that his mother had had no musical talent
though Aunt Kate used to call her the brains carrier of
the Morkan family. Both she and Julia had always seemed
a little proud of their serious and matronly sister. Her
photograph stood before the pierglass. She held an open
book on her knees and was pointing out something in it to
Constantine who, dressed in a man-o'-war suit, lay at her
feet. It was she who had chosen the names of her sons for
she was very sensible of the dignity of family life. Thanks
to her, Constantine was now senior curate in Balbriggan
and, thanks to her, Gabriel himself had taken his degree
in the Royal University. A shadow passed over his face as
he remembered her sullen opposition to his marriage.
Some slighting phrases she had used still rankled in his
memory; she had once spoken of Gretta as being country
cute and that was not true of Gretta at all. It was Gretta
who had nursed her during all her last long illness in their
house at Monkstown.

He knew that Mary Jane must be near the end of her
piece for she was playing again the opening melody with
runs of scales after every bar and while he waited for the
end the resentment died down in his heart. The piece
ended with a trill of octaves in the treble and a final deep
octave in the bass. Great applause greeted Mary Jane as,
blushing and rolling up her music nervously, she escaped
from the room. The most vigorous clapping came from
the four young men in the doorway who had gone away
to the refreshment-room at the beginning of the piece but
had come back when the piano had stopped.

Lancers were arranged. Gabriel found himself partnered with Miss Ivors. She was a frank-mannered talkative young lady, with a freckled face and prominent brown eyes. She did not wear a low-cut bodice and the large brooch which was fixed in the front of her collar bore on it an Irish device and motto.

When they had taken their places she said abruptly:

"I have a crow to pluck with you."

"With me?" said Gabriel.

She nodded her head gravely.

"What is it?" asked Gabriel, smiling at her solemn manner.

"Who is G. C.?" answered Miss Ivors, turning her eyes upon him.

Gabriel coloured and was about to knit his brows, as if he did not understand, when she said bluntly:

"O, innocent Amy! I have found out that you write for *The Daily Express*. Now, aren't you ashamed of yourself?"

"Why should I be ashamed of myself?" asked Gabriel, blinking his eyes and trying to smile.

"Well, I'm ashamed of you," said Miss Ivors frankly. "To say you'd write for a paper like that. I didn't think you were a West Briton."

A look of perplexity appeared on Gabriel's face. It was true that he wrote a literary column every Wednesday in *The Daily Express*, for which he was paid fifteen shillings. But that did not make him a West Briton surely. The books he received for review were almost more welcome than the paltry cheque. He loved to feel the covers and turn over the pages of newly printed books. Nearly every day when his teaching in the college was ended he used to wander down the quays to the second-hand booksellers, to Hickey's on Bachelor's Walk, to Webb's or Massey's on Aston's Quay, or to O'Clohissey's in the by-street. He did not know how to meet her charge. He wanted to say that literature was above politics. But they were friends of many years' standing and their careers had been parallel, first at the University and then as teachers: he could not risk a grandiose phrase with her. He continued blinking his eyes and trying to smile and murmured lamely that he saw nothing political in writing reviews of books.

When their turn to cross had come he was still perplexed and inattentive. Miss Ivors promptly took his hand in a warm grasp and said in a soft friendly tone:

"Of course, I was only joking. Come, we cross now."

When they were together again she spoke of the University question and Gabriel felt more at ease. A friend of hers had shown her his review of Browning's poems. That was how she had found out the secret: but she liked the review immensely. Then she said suddenly:

"O, Mr. Conroy, will you come for an excursion to the Aran Isles this summer? We're going to stay there a whole month. It will be splendid out in the Atlantic. You ought to come. Mr. Clancy is coming, and Mr. Kilkelly and Kathleen Kearney. It would be splendid for Gretta too if she'd come. She's from Connacht, isn't she?"

"Her people are," said Gabriel shortly.

"But you will come, won't you?" said Miss Ivors, laying her warm hand eagerly on his arm.

"The fact is," said Gabriel, "I have just arranged to go—"

"Go where?" asked Miss Ivors.

"Well, you know, every year I go for a cycling tour with some fellows and so—"

"But where?" asked Miss Ivors.

"Well, we usually go to France or Belgium or perhaps Germany," said Gabriel awkwardly.

"And why do you go to France and Belgium," said Miss Ivors, "instead of visiting your own land?"

"Well," said Gabriel, "it's partly to keep in touch with the languages and partly for a change."

"And haven't you your own language to keep in touch with—Irish?" asked Miss Ivors.

"Well," said Gabriel, "if it comes to that, you know, Irish is not my language."

Their neighbours had turned to listen to the cross-examination. Gabriel glanced right and left nervously and tried to keep his good humour under the ordeal which was making a blush invade his forehead.

"And haven't you your own land to visit," continued Miss Ivors, "that you know nothing of, your own people, and your own country?"

"O, to tell you the truth," retorted Gabriel suddenly, "I'm sick of my own country, sick of it!"

"Why?" asked Miss Ivors.

Gabriel did not answer for his retort had heated him.

"Why?" repeated Miss Ivors.

They had to go visiting together and, as he had not answered her, Miss Ivors said warmly:

"Of course, you've no answer."

Gabriel tried to cover his agitation by taking part in the dance with great energy. He avoided her eyes for he had seen a sour expression on her face. But when they met in the long chain he was surprised to feel his hand firmly pressed. She looked at him from under her brows for a moment quizzically until he smiled. Then, just as the chain was about to start again, she stood on tiptoe and whispered into his ear:

"West Briton!"

When the lancers were over Gabriel went away to a remote corner of the room where Freddy Malins' mother was sitting. She was a stout feeble old woman with white hair. Her voice had a catch in it like her son's and she stuttered slightly. She had been told that Freddy had come and that he was nearly all right. Gabriel asked her whether she had had a good crossing. She lived with her married daughter in Glasgow and came to Dublin on a visit once a year. She answered placidly that she had had a beautiful crossing and that the captain had been most attentive to her. She spoke also of the beautiful house her daughter kept in Glasgow, and of all the friends they had there. While her tongue rambled on Gabriel tried to banish from his mind all memory of the unpleasant incident with Miss Ivors. Of course the girl or woman, or whatever she was, was an enthusiast but there was a time for all things. Perhaps he ought not to have answered her like that. But she had no right to call him a West Briton before people, even in joke. She had tried to make him ridiculous before people, heckling him and staring at him with her rabbit's eyes.

He saw his wife making her way towards him through the waltzing couples. When she reached him she said into his ear:

"Gabriel, Aunt Kate wants to know won't you carve the goose as usual. Miss Daly will carve the ham and I'll do the pudding."

"All right," said Gabriel.

"She's sending in the younger ones first as soon as this waltz is over so that we'll have the table to ourselves."

"Were you dancing?" asked Gabriel.

"Of course I was. Didn't you see me? What row had you with Molly Ivors?"

"No row. Why? Did she say so?"

"Something like that. I'm trying to get that Mr. D'Arcy to sing. He's full of conceit, I think."

"There was no row," said Gabriel moodily, "only she wanted me to go for a trip to the west of Ireland and I said I wouldn't."

His wife clasped her hands excitedly and gave a little jump.

"Ó, do go, Gabriel," she cried. "I'd love to see Galway again."

"You can go if you like," said Gabriel coldly.

She looked at him for a moment, then turned to Mrs. Malins and said:

"There's a nice husband for you, Mrs. Malins."

While she was threading her way back across the room Mrs. Malins, without adverting to the interruption, went on to tell Gabriel what beautiful places there were in Scotland and beautiful scenery. Her son-in-law brought them every year to the lakes and they used to go fishing. Her son-in-law was a splendid fisher. One day he caught a beautiful big fish and the man in the hotel cooked it for their dinner.

Gabriel hardly heard what she said. Now that supper was coming near he began to think again about his speech and about the quotation. When he saw Freddy Malins coming across the room to visit his mother Gabriel left the chair free for him and retired into the embrasure of the window. The room had already cleared and from the back room came the clatter of plates and knives. Those who still remained in the drawing-room seemed tired of dancing and were conversing quietly in little groups. Gabriel's warm trembling fingers tapped the cold pane of the window. How cool it must be outside! How pleasant it would be to walk out alone, first along by the river and then through the park! The snow would be lying on the branches of the trees and forming a bright cap on the top of the Wellington Monument. How much more pleasant it would be there than at the supper-table!

He ran over the headings of his speech: Irish hospitality, sad memories, the Three Graces, Paris, the quotation from Browning. He repeated to himself a phrase he had written in his review: "One feels that one is listening to a thought-tormented music." Miss Ivors had praised the review. Was she sincere? Had she really any life of her own behind all her propagandism? There had never been any ill-feeling between them until that night. It unnerved him to think that she would be at the supper-table, looking up at him while he spoke with her critical quizzing eyes. Perhaps she would not be sorry to see him fail in his speech. An idea came into his mind and gave him courage. He would say, alluding to Aunt Kate and Aunt Julia: "Ladies and Gentlemen, the generation which is now on the wane among us may have had its faults but for my part I think it had certain qualities of hospitality, of humour, of humanity, which the new and very serious and hypereducated gen-

eration that is growing up around us seems to me to lack."
Very good: that was one for Miss Ivors. What did he care
that his aunts were only two ignorant old women?

A murmur in the room attracted his attention. Mr.
Browne was advancing from the door, gallantly escorting
Aunt Julia, who leaned upon his arm, smiling and hanging
her head. An irregular musketry of applause escorted her
also as far as the piano and then, as Mary Jane seated herself on the stool, and Aunt Julia, no longer smiling, half
turned so as to pitch her voice fairly into the room, gradually ceased. Gabriel recognised the prelude. It was that
of an old song of Aunt Julia's—*Arrayed for the Bridal.* Her
voice, strong and clear in tone, attacked with great spirit
the runs which embellish the air and though she sang very
rapidly she did not miss even the smallest of the grace
notes. To follow the voice, without looking at the singer's
face, was to feel and share the excitement of swift and secure flight. Gabriel applauded loudly with all the others
at the close of the song and loud applause was borne in
from the invisible supper-table. It sounded so genuine that
a little colour struggled into Aunt Julia's face as she bent
to replace in the music-stand the old leather-bound song-
book that had her initials on the cover. Freddy Malins,
who had listened with his head perched sideways to hear
her better, was still applauding when everyone else had
ceased and talking animatedly to his mother who nodded
her head gravely and slowly in acquiescence. At last, when
he could clap no more, he stood up suddenly and hurried
across the room to Aunt Julia whose hand he seized and
held in both his hands, shaking it when words failed him
or the catch in his voice proved too much for him.

"I was just telling my mother," he said, "I never heard
you sing so well, never. No, I never heard your voice so
good as it is tonight. Now! Would you believe that now?
That's the truth. Upon my word and honour that's the
truth. I never heard your voice sound so fresh and so . . .
so clear and fresh, never."

Aunt Julia smiled broadly and murmured something about compliments as she released her hand from his grasp. Mr. Browne extended his open hand towards her and said to those who were near him in the manner of a showman introducing a prodigy to an audience:

"Miss Julia Morkan, my latest discovery!"

He was laughing very heartily at this himself when Freddy Malins turned to him and said:

"Well, Browne, if you're serious you might make a worse discovery. All I can say is I never heard her sing half so well as long as I am coming here. And that's the honest truth."

"Neither did I," said Mr. Browne. "I think her voice has greatly improved."

Aunt Julia shrugged her shoulders and said with meek pride:

"Thirty years ago I hadn't a bad voice as voices go."

"I often told Julia," said Aunt Kate emphatically, "that she was simply thrown away in that choir. But she never would be said by me."

She turned as if to appeal to the good sense of the others against a refractory child while Aunt Julia gazed in front of her, a vague smile of reminiscence playing on her face.

"No," continued Aunt Kate, "she wouldn't be said or led by anyone, slaving there in that choir night and day, night and day. Six o'clock on Christmas morning! And all for what?"

"Well, isn't it for the honour of God, Aunt Kate?" asked Mary Jane, twisting round on the piano-stool and smiling.

Aunt Kate turned fiercely on her niece and said:

"I know all about the honour of God, Mary Jane, but I think it's not at all honourable for the pope to turn out the women out of the choirs that have slaved there all their lives and put little whipper-snappers of boys over their heads. I suppose it is for the good of the Church if the pope does it. But it's not just, Mary Jane, and it's not right."

She had worked herself into a passion and would have continued in defence of her sister for it was a sore subject with her but Mary Jane, seeing that all the dancers had come back, intervened pacifically:

"Now, Aunt Kate, you're giving scandal to Mr. Browne who is of the other persuasion."

Aunt Kate turned to Mr. Browne, who was grinning at this allusion to his religion, and said hastily:

"O, I don't question the pope's being right. I'm only a stupid old woman and I wouldn't presume to do such a thing. But there's such a thing as common everyday politeness and gratitude. And if I were in Julia's place I'd tell that Father Healey straight up to his face . . ."

"And besides, Aunt Kate," said Mary Jane, "we really are all hungry and when we are hungry we are all very quarrelsome."

"And when we are thirsty we are also quarrelsome," added Mr. Browne.

"So that we had better go to supper," said Mary Jane, "and finish the discussion afterwards."

On the landing outside the drawing-room Gabriel found his wife and Mary Jane trying to persuade Miss Ivors to stay for supper. But Miss Ivors, who had put on her hat and was buttoning her cloak, would not stay. She did not feel in the least hungry and she had already overstayed her time.

"But only for ten minutes, Molly," said Mrs. Conroy. "That won't delay you."

"To take a pick itself," said Mary Jane, "after all your dancing."

"I really couldn't," said Miss Ivors.

"I am afraid you didn't enjoy yourself at all," said Mary Jane hopelessly.

"Ever so much, I assure you," said Miss Ivors, "but you really must let me run off now."

"But how can you get home?" asked Mrs. Conroy.

"O, it's only two steps up the quay."

Gabriel hesitated a moment and said:

"If you will allow me, Miss Ivors, I'll see you home if you are really obliged to go."

But Miss Ivors broke away from them.

"I won't hear of it," she cried. "For goodness' sake go in to your suppers and don't mind me. I'm quite well able to take care of myself."

"Well, you're the comical girl, Molly," said Mrs. Conroy frankly.

"*Beannacht libh,*" cried Miss Ivors, with a laugh, as she ran down the staircase.

Mary Jane gazed after her, a moody puzzled expression on her face, while Mrs. Conroy leaned over the banisters to listen for the hall-door. Gabriel asked himself was he the cause of her abrupt departure. But she did not seem to be in ill humour: she had gone away laughing. He stared blankly down the staircase.

At the moment Aunt Kate came toddling out of the supper-room, almost wringing her hands in despair.

"Where is Gabriel?" she cried. "Where on earth is Gabriel? There's everyone waiting in there, stage to let, and nobody to carve the goose!"

"Here I am, Aunt Kate!" cried Gabriel, with sudden animation, "ready to carve a flock of geese, if necessary."

A fat brown goose lay at one end of the table and at the other end, on a bed of creased paper strewn with sprigs of parsley, lay a great ham, stripped of its outer skin and peppered over with crust crumbs, a neat paper frill round its shin and beside this was a round of spiced beef. Between these rival ends ran parallel lines of side-dishes: two little minsters of jelly, red and yellow; a shallow dish full of blocks of blancmange and red jam, a large green leaf-shaped dish with a stalk-shaped handle, on which lay bunches of purple raisins and peeled almonds, a companion dish on which lay a solid rectangle of Smyrna figs, a dish of custard topped with grated nutmeg, a small bowl full of chocolates and sweets wrapped in gold and silver papers and a glass vase in which stood some tall celery stalks. In the centre of the table there stood, as sentries to a fruit-stand which upheld a pyramid of oranges and American apples, two squat old-fashioned decanters of cut glass, one containing port and the other dark sherry. On the closed square piano a pudding in a huge yellow dish lay in waiting and behind it were three squads of bottles of stout and ale and minerals, drawn up according to the colours of their uniforms, the first two black, with brown and red labels, the third and smallest squad white, with transverse green sashes.

Gabriel took his seat boldly at the head of the table and, having looked to the edge of the carver, plunged his fork firmly into the goose. He felt quite at ease now for he was an expert carver and liked nothing better than to find himself at the head of a well-laden table.

"Miss Furlong, what shall I send you?" he asked. "A wing or a slice of the breast?"

"Just a small slice of the breast."

"Miss Higgins, what for you?"

"O, anything at all, Mr. Conroy."

While Gabriel and Miss Daly exchanged plates of goose and plates of ham and spiced beef Lily went from guest to guest with a dish of hot floury potatoes wrapped in a white napkin. This was Mary Jane's idea and she had also suggested apple sauce for the goose but Aunt Kate had said that plain roast goose without any apple sauce had always been good enough for her and she hoped she might never eat worse. Mary Jane waited on her pupils and saw that they got the best slices and Aunt Kate and Aunt Julia opened and carried across from the piano bottles of stout and ale for the gentlemen and bottles of minerals for the ladies. There was a great deal of confusion and laughter and noise, the noise of orders and counter-orders, of knives and forks, of corks and glass-stoppers. Gabriel began to carve second helpings as soon as he had finished the first round without serving himself. Everyone protested loudly so that he compromised by taking a long draught of stout for he had found the carving hot work. Mary Jane settled down quietly to her supper but Aunt Kate and Aunt Julia were still toddling round the table, walking on each other's heels, getting in each other's way and giving each other unheeded orders. Mr. Browne begged of them to sit down and eat their suppers and so did Gabriel but they said there was time enough, so that, at last, Freddy Malins stood up and, capturing Aunt Kate, plumped her down on her chair amid general laughter.

When everyone had been well served Gabriel said, smiling:

"Now, if anyone wants a little more of what vulgar people call stuffing let him or her speak."

A chorus of voices invited him to begin his own supper and Lily came forward with three potatoes which she had reserved for him.

"Very well," said Gabriel amiably, as he took another preparatory draught, "kindly forget my existence, ladies and gentlemen, for a few minutes."

He set to his supper and took no part in the conversation with which the table covered Lily's removal of the plates. The subject of talk was the opera company which was then at the Theatre Royal. Mr. Bartell D'Arcy, the tenor, a dark-complexioned young man with a smart moustache, praised very highly the leading contralto of the company but Miss Furlong thought she had a rather vulgar style of production. Freddy Malins said there was a Negro chieftain singing in the second part of the Gaiety pantomime who had one of the finest tenor voices he had ever heard.

"Have you heard him?" he asked Mr. Bartell D'Arcy across the table.

"No," answered Mr. Bartell D'Arcy carelessly.

"Because," Freddy Malins explained, "now I'd be curious to hear your opinion of him. I think he has a grand voice."

"It takes Teddy to find out the really good things," said

Mr. Browne familiarly to the table.

"And why couldn't he have a voice too?" asked Freddy Malins sharply. "Is it because he's only a black?"

Nobody answered this question and Mary Jane led the table back to the legitimate opera. One of her pupils had given her a pass for *Mignon*. Of course it was very fine, she said, but it made her think of poor Georgina Burns. Mr. Browne could go back farther still, to the old Italian companies that used to come to Dublin— Tietjens, Ilma de Murzka, Campanini, the great Trebelli, Giuglini, Ravelli, Aramburo. Those were the days, he said, when there was something like singing to be heard in Dublin. He told too of how the top gallery of the old Royal used to be packed night after night, of how one night an Italian tenor had sung five encores to *Let me like a Soldier fall*, introducing a high C every time, and of how the gallery boys would sometimes in their enthusiasm unyoke the horses from the carriage of some great *prima donna* and pull her themselves through the streets to her hotel. Why did they never play the grand old operas now, he asked, *Dinorah, Lucrezia Borgia*? Because they could not get the voices to sing them: that was why.

"O, well," said Mr. Bartell D'Arcy, "I presume there are as good singers today as there were then."

"Where are they?" asked Mr. Browne defiantly.

"In London, Paris, Milan," said Mr. Bartell D'Arcy warmly. "I suppose Caruso, for example, is quite as good, if not better than any of the men you have mentioned."

"Maybe so," said Mr. Browne. "But I may tell you I doubt it strongly."

"O, I'd give anything to hear Caruso sing," said Mary Jane.

"For me," said Aunt Kate, who had been picking a bone, "there was only one tenor. To please me, I mean. But I suppose none of you ever heard of him."

"Who was he, Miss Morkan?" asked Mr. Bartell D'Arcy politely.

"His name," said Aunt Kate, "was Parkinson. I heard him when he was in his prime and I think he had then the purest tenor voice that was ever put into a man's throat."

"Strange," said Mr. Bartell D'Arcy. "I never even heard of him."

"Yes, yes, Miss Morkan is right," said Mr. Browne. "I remember hearing of old Parkinson but he's too far back for me."

"A beautiful, pure, sweet, mellow English tenor," said Aunt Kate with enthusiasm.

Gabriel having finished, the huge pudding was transferred to the table. The clatter of forks and spoons began again. Gabriel's wife served out spoonfuls of the pudding and passed the plates down the table. Midway down they were held up by Mary Jane, who replenished them with raspberry or orange jelly or with blancmange and jam. The pudding was of Aunt Julia's making and she received praises for it from all quarters. She herself said that it was not quite brown enough.

"Well, I hope, Miss Morkan," said Mr. Browne, "that I'm brown enough for you because, you know, I'm all brown."

All the gentlemen, except Gabriel, ate some of the pudding out of compliment to Aunt Julia. As Gabriel never ate sweets the celery had been left for him. Freddy Malins also took a stalk of celery and ate it with his pudding. He had been told that celery was a capital thing for the blood and he was just then under doctor's care. Mrs. Malins, who had been silent all through the supper, said that her son was going down to Mount Melleray in a week or so. The table then spoke of Mount Melleray, how bracing the air was down there, how hospitable the monks were and how they never asked for a penny-piece from their guests.

"And do you mean to say," asked Mr. Browne incredulously, "that a chap can go down there and put up there as if it were a hotel and live on the fat of the land and then come away without paying anything?"

"O, most people give some donation to the monastery when they leave," said Mary Jane.

"I wish we had an institution like that in our Church," said Mr. Browne candidly.

He was astonished to hear that the monks never spoke, got up at two in the morning and slept in their coffins. He asked what they did it for.

"That's the rule of the order," said Aunt Kate firmly.

"Yes, but why?" asked Mr. Browne.

Aunt Kate repeated that it was the rule, that was all. Mr. Browne still seemed not to understand. Freddy Malins explained to him, as best he could, that the monks were trying to make up for the sins committed by all the sinners in the outside world. The explanation was not very clear for Mr. Browne grinned and said:

"I like that idea very much but wouldn't a comfortable spring bed do them as well as a coffin?"

"The coffin," said Mary Jane, "is to remind them of their last end."

As the subject had grown lugubrious it was buried in a silence of the table during which Mrs. Malins could be heard saying to her neighbour in an indistinct undertone:

"They are very good men, the monks, very pious men."

The raisins and almonds and figs and apples and oranges and chocolates and sweets were now passed about the table and Aunt Julia invited all the guests to have either port or sherry. At first Mr. Bartell D'Arcy refused to take either but one of his neighbours nudged him and whispered something to him upon which he allowed his glass to be filled. Gradually as the last glasses were being filled the conversation ceased. A pause followed, broken only by the noise of the wine and by unsettlings of chairs. The Misses Morkan, all three, looked down at the tablecloth. Someone coughed once or twice and then a few gentlemen patted the table gently as a signal for silence. The silence came and Gabriel pushed back his chair and stood up.

The patting at once grew louder in encouragement and

then ceased altogether. Gabriel leaned his ten trembling
fingers on the tablecloth and smiled nervously at the company. Meeting a row of upturned faces he raised his eyes
to the chandelier. The piano was playing a waltz tune and
he could hear the skirts sweeping against the drawing-room
door. People, perhaps, were standing in the snow on the
quay outside, gazing up at the lighted windows and listening to the waltz music. The air was pure there. In the
distance lay the park where the trees were weighted with
snow. The Wellington Monument wore a gleaming cap
of snow that flashed westward over the white field of Fifteen Acres.

He began:

"Ladies and Gentlemen,

"It has fallen to my lot this evening, as in years past, to
perform a very pleasing task but a task for which I am
afraid my poor powers as a speaker are all too inadequate."

"No, no!" said Mr. Browne.

"But, however that may be, I can only ask you tonight
to take the will for the deed and to lend me your attention
for a few moments while I endeavour to express to you in
words what my feelings are on this occasion.

"Ladies and Gentlemen, it is not the first time that we
have gathered together under this hospitable roof, around
this hospitable board. It is not the first time that we have
been the recipients—or perhaps, I had better say, the victims—of the hospitality of certain good ladies."

He made a circle in the air with his arm and paused.
Everyone laughed or smiled at Aunt Kate and Aunt Julia
and Mary Jane who all turned crimson with pleasure.
Gabriel went on more boldly:

"I feel more strongly with every recurring year that our
country has no tradition which does it so much honour
and which it should guard so jealously as that of its hospitality. It is a tradition that is unique as far as my experience goes (and I have visited not a few places abroad)
among the modern nations. Some would say, perhaps, that

with us it is rather a failing than anything to be boasted
of. But granted even that, it is, to my mind, a princely
failing, and one that I trust will long be cultivated among
us. Of one thing, at least, I am sure. As long as this one
roof shelters the good ladies aforesaid—and I wish from
my heart it may do so for many and many a long year to
come—the tradition of genuine warm-hearted courteous
Irish hospitality, which our forefathers have handed down
to us and which we in turn must hand down to our descendants, is still alive among us."

A hearty murmur of assent ran round the table. It shot
through Gabriel's mind that Miss Ivors was not there and
that she had gone away discourteously: and he said with
confidence in himself:

"Ladies and Gentlemen,

"A new generation is growing up in our midst, a generation actuated by new ideas and new principles. It is
serious and enthusiastic for these new ideas and its enthusiasm, even when it is misdirected, is, I believe, in the
main sincere. But we are living in a sceptical and, if I may
use the phrase, a thought-tormented age: and sometimes
I fear that this new generation, educated or hypereducated
as it is, will lack those qualities of humanity, of hospitality,
of kindly humour which belonged to an older day. Listening tonight to the names of all those great singers of the
past it seemed to me, I must confess, that we were living
in a less spacious age. Those days might, without exaggeration, be called spacious days: and if they are gone beyond
recall let us hope, at least, that in gatherings such as this
we shall still speak of them with pride and affection, still
cherish in our hearts the memory of those dead and gone
great ones whose fame the world will not willingly let die."

"Hear, hear!" said Mr. Browne loudly.

"But yet," continued Gabriel, his voice falling into a
softer inflection, "there are always in gatherings such as
this sadder thoughts that will recur to our minds: thoughts
of the past, of youth, of changes, of absent faces that we

miss here tonight. Our path through life is strewn with many such sad memories: and were we to brood upon them always we could not find the heart to go on bravely with our work among the living. We have all of us living duties and living affections which claim, and rightly claim, our strenuous endeavours.

"Therefore, I will not linger on the past. I will not let any gloomy moralising intrude upon us here tonight. Here we are gathered together for a brief moment from the bustle and rush of our everyday routine. We are met here as friends, in the spirit of good-fellowship, as colleagues, also to a certain extent, in the true spirit of *camaraderie*, and as the guests of—what shall I call them?— the Three Graces of the Dublin musical world."

The table burst into applause and laughter at this allusion. Aunt Julia vainly asked each of her neighbours in turn to tell her what Gabriel had said.

"He says we are the Three Graces, Aunt Julia," said Mary Jane.

Aunt Julia did not understand but she looked up, smiling, at Gabriel, who continued in the same vein:

"Ladies and Gentlemen,

"I will not attempt to play tonight the part that Paris played on another occasion. I will not attempt to choose between them. The task would be an invidious one and one beyond my poor powers. For when I view them in turn, whether it be our chief hostess herself, whose good heart, whose too good heart, has become a byword with all who know her, or her sister, who seems to be gifted with perennial youth and whose singing must have been a surprise and a revelation to us all tonight, or, last but not least, when I consider our youngest hostess, talented, cheerful, hard-working and the best of nieces, I confess, Ladies and Gentlemen, that I do not know to which of them I should award the prize."

Gabriel glanced down at his aunts and, seeing the large smile on Aunt Julia's face and the tears which had risen to Aunt Kate's eyes, hastened to his close. He raised his glass of port gallantly, while every member of the company fingered a glass expectantly, and said loudly:

"Let us toast them all three together. Let us drink to their health, wealth, long life, happiness and prosperity and may they long continue to hold the proud and self-won position which they hold in their profession and the position of honour and affection which they hold in our hearts."

All the guests stood up, glass in hand, and turning towards the three seated ladies, sang in unison, with Mr. Browne as leader:

> *For they are jolly gay fellows,*
> *For they are jolly gay fellows,*
> *For they are jolly gay fellows,*
> *Which nobody can deny.*

Aunt Kate was making frank use of her handkerchief and even Aunt Julia seemed moved. Freddy Malins beat time with his pudding-fork and the singers turned towards one another, as if in melodious conference, while they sang with emphasis:

> *Unless he tells a lie,*
> *Unless he tells a lie,*

Then, turning once more towards their hostesses, they sang:

> *For they are jolly gay fellows,*
> *For they are jolly gay fellows,*
> *For they are jolly gay fellows,*
> *Which nobody can deny.*

The acclamation which followed was taken up beyond the door of the supper-room by many of the other guests and renewed time after time, Freddy Malins acting as officer with his fork on high.

•   •   •   •   •   •   •

The piercing morning air came into the hall where they were standing so that Aunt Kate said:

"Close the door, somebody. Mrs. Malins will get her death of cold."

"Browne is out there, Aunt Kate," said Mary Jane.

"Browne is everywhere," said Aunt Kate, lowering her voice.

Mary Jane laughed at her tone.

"Really," she said archly, "he is very attentive."

"He has been laid on here like the gas," said Aunt Kate in the same tone, "all during the Christmas."

She laughed herself this time good-humouredly and then added quickly:

"But tell him to come in, Mary Jane, and close the door. I hope to goodness he didn't hear me."

At that moment the hall-door was opened and Mr. Browne came in from the doorstep, laughing as if his heart would break. He was dressed in a long green overcoat with mock astrakhan cuffs and collar and wore on his head an oval fur cap. He pointed down the snow-covered quay from where the sound of shrill prolonged whistling was borne in.

"Teddy will have all the cabs in Dublin out," he said.

Gabriel advanced from the little pantry behind the office, struggling into his overcoat and, looking round the hall, said:

"Gretta not down yet?"

"She's getting on her things, Gabriel," said Aunt Kate.

"Who's playing up there?" asked Gabriel.

"Nobody. They're all gone."

"O no, Aunt Kate," said Mary Jane. "Bartell D'Arcy and Miss O'Callaghan aren't gone yet."

"Someone is fooling at the piano anyhow," said Gabriel.

Mary Jane glanced at Gabriel and Mr. Browne and said with a shiver:

"It makes me feel cold to look at you two gentlemen muffled up like that. I wouldn't like to face your journey home at this hour."

"I'd like nothing better this minute," said Mr. Browne
stoutly, "than a rattling fine walk in the country or a fast
drive with a good spanking goer between the shafts."

"We used to have a very good horse and trap at home,"
said Aunt Julia sadly.

"The never-to-be-forgotten Johnny," said Mary Jane,
laughing.

Aunt Kate and Gabriel laughed too.

"Why, what was wonderful about Johnny?" asked Mr.
Browne.

"The late lamented Patrick Morkan, our grandfather,
that is," explained Gabriel, "commonly known in his
later years as the old gentleman, was a glue-boiler."

"O, now, Gabriel," said Aunt Kate, laughing, "he had
a starch mill."

"Well, glue or starch," said Gabriel, "the old gentleman had a horse by the name of Johnny. And Johnny used
to work in the old gentleman's mill, walking round and
round in order to drive the mill. That was all very well;
but now comes the tragic part about Johnny. One fine day
the old gentleman thought he'd like to drive out with the
quality to a military review in the park."

"The Lord have mercy on his soul," said Aunt Kate
compassionately.

"Amen," said Gabriel. "So the old gentleman, as I said,
harnessed Johnny and put on his very best tall hat and his
very best stock collar and drove out in grand style from
his ancestral mansion somewhere near Back Lane, I
think."

Everyone laughed, even Mrs. Malins, at Gabriel's manner and Aunt Kate said:

"O, now, Gabriel, he didn't live in Back Lane, really.
Only the mill was there."

"Out from the mansion of his forefathers," continued
Gabriel, "he drove with Johnny. And everything went on
beautifully until Johnny came in sight of King Billy's

statue: and whether he fell in love with the horse King
Billy sits on or whether he thought he was back again in
the mill, anyhow he began to walk round the statue."

Gabriel paced in a circle round the hall in his goloshes
amid the laughter of the others.

"Round and round he went," said Gabriel, "and the
old gentleman, who was a very pompous old gentleman,
was highly indignant. 'Go on, sir! What do you mean, sir?
Johnny! Johnny! Most extraordinary conduct! Can't understand the horse!' "

The peal of laughter which followed Gabriel's imitation of the incident was interrupted by a resounding knock
at the hall door. Mary Jane ran to open it and let in Freddy
Malins. Freddy Malins, with his hat well back on his head
and his shoulders humped with cold, was puffing and
steaming after his exertions.

"I could only get one cab," he said.

"O, we'll find another along the quay," said Gabriel.

"Yes," said Aunt Kate. "Better not keep Mrs. Malins
standing in the draught."

Mrs. Malins was helped down the front steps by her son
and Mr. Browne and, after many manoeuvres, hoisted into
the cab. Freddy Malins clambered in after her and spent
a long time settling her on the seat, Mr. Browne helping
him with advice. At last she was settled comfortably and
Freddy Malins invited Mr. Browne into the cab. There
was a good deal of confused talk, and then Mr. Browne
got into the cab. The cabman settled his rug over his knees,
and bent down for the address. The confusion grew greater and the cabman was directed differently by Freddy
Malins and Mr. Browne, each of whom had his head out
through a window of the cab. The difficulty was to know
where to drop Mr. Browne along the route, and Aunt
Kate, Aunt Julia and Mary Jane helped the discussion
from the doorstep with cross-directions and contradictions
and abundance of laughter. As for Freddy Malins he was
speechless with laughter. He popped his head in and out

of the window every moment to the great danger of his
hat, and told his mother how the discussion was progressing, till at last Mr. Browne shouted to the bewildered
cabman above the din of everybody's laughter:

"Do you know Trinity College?"

"Yes, sir," said the cabman.

"Well, drive bang up against Trinity College gates,"
said Mr. Browne, "and then we'll tell you where to go.
You understand now?"

"Yes, sir," said the cabman.

"Make like a bird for Trinity College."

"Right, sir," said the cabman.

The horse was whipped up and the cab rattled off along
the quay amid a chorus of laughter and adieus.

Gabriel had not gone to the door with the others. He
was in a dark part of the hall gazing up the staircase. A
woman was standing near the top of the first flight, in the
shadow also. He could not see her face but he could see
the terra-cotta and salmon-pink panels of her skirt which
the shadow made appear black and white. It was his wife.
She was leaning on the banisters, listening to something.
Gabriel was surprised at her stillness and strained his ear
to listen also. But he could hear little save the noise of
laughter and dispute on the front steps, a few chords
struck on the piano and a few notes of a man's voice singing.

He stood still in the gloom of the hall, trying to catch
the air that the voice was singing and gazing up at his wife.
There was grace and mystery in her attitude as if she were
a symbol of something. He asked himself what is a woman
standing on the stairs in the shadow, listening to distant
music, a symbol of. If he were a painter he would paint
her in that attitude. Her blue felt hat would show off the
bronze of her hair against the darkness and the dark panels
of her skirt would show off the light ones. *Distant Music*
he would call the picture if he were a painter.

The hall-door was closed; and Aunt Kate, Aunt Julia

and Mary Jane came down the hall, still laughing.

"Well, isn't Freddy terrible?" said Mary Jane. "He's really terrible."

Gabriel said nothing but pointed up the stairs towards where his wife was standing. Now that the hall-door was closed the voice and the piano could be heard more clearly. Gabriel held up his hand for them to be silent. The song seemed to be in the old Irish tonality and the singer seemed uncertain both of his words and of his voice. The voice, made plaintive by distance and by the singer's hoarseness, faintly illuminated the cadence of the air with words expressing grief:

> *O, the rain falls on my heavy locks*
> *And the dew wets my skin,*
> *My babe lies cold . . .*

"O," exclaimed Mary Jane. "It's Bartell D'Arcy singing and he wouldn't sing all the night. O, I'll get him to sing a song before he goes."

"O, do, Mary Jane," said Aunt Kate.

Mary Jane brushed past the others and ran to the staircase, but before she reached it the singing stopped and the piano was closed abruptly.

"O, what a pity!" she cried. "Is he coming down, Gretta?"

Gabriel heard his wife answer yes and saw her come down towards them. A few steps behind her were Mr. Bartell D'Arcy and Miss O'Callaghan.

"O, Mr. D'Arcy," cried Mary Jane, "it's downright mean of you to break off like that when we were all in raptures listening to you."

"I have been at him all the evening," said Miss O'Callaghan, "and Mrs. Conroy, too, and he told us he had a dreadful cold and couldn't sing."

"O, Mr. D'Arcy," said Aunt Kate, "now that was a great fib to tell."

"Can't you see that I'm as hoarse as a crow?" said Mr.

D'Arcy roughly.

He went into the pantry hastily and put on his overcoat. The others, taken aback by his rude speech, could find nothing to say. Aunt Kate wrinkled her brows and made signs to the others to drop the subject. Mr. D'Arcy stood swathing his neck carefully and frowning.

"It's the weather," said Aunt Julia, after a pause.

"Yes, everybody has colds," said Aunt Kate readily, "everybody."

"They say," said Mary Jane, "we haven't had snow like it for thirty years; and I read this morning in the newspapers that the snow is general all over Ireland."

"I love the look of snow," said Aunt Julia sadly.

"So do I," said Miss O'Callaghan. "I think Christmas is never really Christmas unless we have the snow on the ground."

"But poor Mr. D'Arcy doesn't like the snow," said Aunt Kate, smiling.

Mr. D'Arcy came from the pantry, fully swathed and buttoned, and in a repentant tone told them the history of his cold. Everyone gave him advice and said it was a great pity and urged him to be very careful of his throat in the night air. Gabriel watched his wife, who did not join in the conversation. She was standing right under the dusty fanlight and the flame of the gas lit up the rich bronze of her hair, which he had seen her drying at the fire a few days before. She was in the same attitude and seemed unaware of the talk about her. At last she turned towards them and Gabriel saw that there was colour on her cheeks and that her eyes were shining. A sudden tide of joy went leaping out of his heart.

"Mr. D'Arcy," she said, "what is the name of that song you were singing?"

"It's called *The Lass of Aughrim*," said Mr. D'Arcy, "but I couldn't remember it properly. Why? Do you know it?"

"*The Lass of Aughrim*," she repeated. "I couldn't think of the name."

"It's a very nice air," said Mary Jane. "I'm sorry you were not in voice tonight."

"Now, Mary Jane," said Aunt Kate, "don't annoy Mr. D'Arcy. I won't have him annoyed."

Seeing that all were ready to start she shepherded them to the door, where good-night was said:

"Well, good-night, Aunt Kate, and thanks for the pleasant evening."

"Good-night, Gabriel. Good-night, Gretta!"

"Good-night, Aunt Kate, and thanks ever so much. Good-night, Aunt Julia."

"O, good-night, Gretta, I didn't see you."

"Good-night, Mr. D'Arcy. Good-night, Miss O'Callaghan."

"Good-night, Miss Morkan."

"Good-night, again."

"Good-night, all. Safe home."

"Good-night. Good night."

The morning was still dark. A dull, yellow light brooded over the houses and the river; and the sky seemed to be descending. It was slushy underfoot; and only streaks and patches of snow lay on the roofs, on the parapets of the quay and on the area railings. The lamps were still burning redly in the murky air and, across the river, the palace of the Four Courts stood out menacingly against the heavy sky.

She was walking on before him with Mr. Bartell D'Arcy, her shoes in a brown parcel tucked under one arm and her hands holding her skirt up from the slush. She had no longer any grace of attitude, but Gabriel's eyes were still bright with happiness. The blood went bounding along his veins; and the thoughts went rioting through his brain, proud, joyful, tender, valorous.

She was walking on before him so lightly and so erect that he longed to run after her noiselessly, catch her by the shoulders and say something foolish and affectionate into her ear. She seemed to him so frail that he longed to

defend her against something and then to be alone with
her. Moments of their secret life together burst like stars
upon his memory. A heliotrope envelope was lying beside
his breakfast-cup and he was caressing it with his hand.
Birds were twittering in the ivy and the sunny web of the
curtain was shimmering along the floor: he could not eat
for happiness. They were standing on the crowded platform and he was placing a ticket inside the warm palm of
her glove. He was standing with her in the cold, looking
in through a grated window at a man making bottles in a
roaring furnace. It was very cold. Her face, fragrant in
the cold air, was quite close to his; and suddenly he called
out to the man at the furnace:

"Is the fire hot, sir?"

But the man could not hear with the noise of the furnace. It was just as well. He might have answered rudely.

A wave of yet more tender joy escaped from his heart
and went coursing in warm flood along his arteries. Like
the tender fire of stars moments of their life together, that
no one knew of or would ever know of, broke upon and
illumined his memory. He longed to recall to her those
moments, to make her forget the years of their dull existence together and remember only their moments of ecstasy.
For the years, he felt, had not quenched his soul or hers.
Their children, his writing, her household cares had not
quenched all their souls' tender fire. In one letter that he
had written to her then he had said: "Why is it that words
like these seem to me so dull and cold? Is it because there
is no word tender enough to be your name?"

Like distant music these words that he had written years
before were borne towards him from the past. He longed
to be alone with her. When the others had gone away,
when he and she were in the room in the hotel, then they
would be alone together. He would call her softly:

"Gretta!"

Perhaps she would not hear at once: she would be un-
dressing. Then something in his voice would strike her.

She would turn and look at him. . . .

At the corner of Winetavern Street they met a cab. He was glad of its rattling noise as it saved him from conversation. She was looking out of the window and seemed tired. The others spoke only a few words, pointing out some building or street. The horse galloped along wearily under the murky morning sky, dragging his old rattling box after his heels, and Gabriel was again in a cab with her, galloping to catch the boat, galloping to their honeymoon.

As the cab drove across O'Connell Bridge Miss O'Callaghan said:

"They say you never cross O'Connell Bridge without seeing a white horse."

"I see a white man this time," said Gabriel.

"Where?" asked Mr. Bartell D'Arcy.

Gabriel pointed to the statue, on which lay patches of snow. Then he nodded familiarly to it and waved his hand.

"Good-night, Dan," he said gaily.

When the cab drew up before the hotel, Gabriel jumped out and, in spite of Mr. Bartell D'Arcy's protest, paid the driver. He gave the man a shilling over his fare. The man saluted and said:

"A prosperous New Year to you, sir."

"The same to you," said Gabriel cordially.

She leaned for a moment on his arm in getting out of the cab and while standing at the curbstone, bidding the others good-night. She leaned lightly on his arm, as lightly as when she had danced with him a few hours before. He had felt proud and happy then, happy that she was his, proud of her grace and wifely carriage. But now, after the kindling again of so many memories, the first touch of her body, musical and strange and perfumed, sent through him a keen pang of lust. Under cover of her silence he pressed her arm closely to his side; and, as they stood at the hotel door, he felt that they had escaped from their lives and duties, escaped from home and friends and run away together with wild and radiant hearts to a new adventure.

An old man was dozing in a great hooded chair in the hall. He lit a candle in the office and went before them to the stairs. They followed him in silence, their feet falling in soft thuds on the thickly carpeted stairs. She mounted the stairs behind the porter, her head bowed in the ascent, her frail shoulders curved as with a burden, her skirt girt tightly about her. He could have flung his arms about her hips and held her still, for his arms were trembling with desire to seize her and only the stress of his nails against the palms of his hands held the wild impulse of his body in check. The porter halted on the stairs to settle his guttering candle. They halted, too, on the steps below him. In the silence Gabriel could hear the falling of the molten wax into the tray and the thumping of his own heart against his ribs.

The porter led them along a corridor and opened a door. Then he set his unstable candle down on a toilet-table and asked at what hour they were to be called in the morning.

"Eight," said Gabriel.

The porter pointed to the tap of the electric-light and began a muttered apology, but Gabriel cut him short.

"We don't want any light. We have light enough from the street. And I say," he added, pointing to the candle, "you might remove that handsome article, like a good man."

The porter took up his candle again, but slowly, for he was surprised by such a novel idea. Then he mumbled good-night and went out. Gabriel shot the lock to.

A ghastly light from the street lamp lay in a long shaft from one window to the door. Gabriel threw his overcoat and hat on a couch and crossed the room towards the window. He looked down into the street in order that his emotion might calm a little. Then he turned and leaned against a chest of drawers with his back to the light. She had taken off her hat and cloak and was standing before a large swinging mirror, unhooking her waist. Gabriel paused for a few moments, watching her, and then said:

"Gretta!"

She turned away from the mirror slowly and walked along the shaft of light towards him. Her face looked so serious and weary that the words would not pass Gabriel's lips. No, it was not the moment yet.

"You looked tired," he said.

"I am a little," she answered.

"You don't feel ill or weak?"

"No, tired: that's all."

She went on to the window and stood there, looking out. Gabriel waited again and then, fearing that diffidence was about to conquer him, he said abruptly:

"By the way, Gretta!"

"What is it?"

"You know that poor fellow Malins?" he said quickly.

"Yes. What about him?"

"Well, poor fellow, he's a decent sort of chap, after all," continued Gabriel in a false voice. "He gave me back that sovereign I lent him, and I didn't expect it, really. It's a pity he wouldn't keep away from that Browne, because he's not a bad fellow, really."

He was trembling now with annoyance. Why did she seem so abstracted? He did not know how he could begin. Was she annoyed, too, about something? If she would only turn to him or come to him of her own accord! To take her as she was would be brutal. No, he must see some ardour in her eyes first. He longed to be master of her strange mood.

"When did you lend him the pound?" she asked, after a pause.

Gabriel strove to restrain himself from breaking out into brutal language about the sottish Malins and his pound. He longed to cry to her from his soul, to crush her body against his, to overmaster her. But he said:

"O, at Christmas, when he opened that little Christmas-card shop in Henry Street."

He was in such a fever of rage and desire that he did not

hear her come from the window. She stood before him for
an instant, looking at him strangely. Then, suddenly raising herself on tiptoe and resting her hands lightly on his
shoulders, she kissed him.

"You are a very generous person, Gabriel," she said.

Gabriel, trembling with delight at her sudden kiss and
at the quaintness of her phrase, put his hands on her hair
and began smoothing it back, scarcely touching it with his
fingers. The washing had made it fine and brilliant. His
heart was brimming over with happiness. Just when he
was wishing for it she had come to him of her own accord.
Perhaps her thoughts had been running with his. Perhaps
she had felt the impetuous desire that was in him, and then
the yielding mood had come upon her. Now that she had
fallen to him so easily, he wondered why he had been so
diffident.

He stood, holding her head between his hands. Then,
slipping one arm swiftly about her body and drawing her
towards him, he said softly:

"Gretta, dear, what are you thinking about?"

She did not answer nor yield wholly to his arm. He said
again, softly:

"Tell me what it is, Gretta. I think I know what is the
matter. Do I know?"

She did not answer at once. Then she said in an outburst
of tears:

"O, I am thinking about that song, *The Lass of Aughrim.*"

She broke loose from him and ran to the bed and, throwing her arms across the bed-rail, hid her face. Gabriel stood
stock-still for a moment in astonishment and then followed
her. As he passed in the way of the cheval-glass he caught
sight of himself in full length, his broad, well-filled shirt-
front, the face whose expression always puzzled him when
he saw it in a mirror, and his glimmering gilt-rimmed eye-
glasses. He halted a few paces from her and said:

"What about the song? Why does that make you cry?"

She raised her head from her arms and dried her eyes with the back of her hand like a child. A kinder note than he had intended went into his voice.

"Why, Gretta?" he asked.

"I am thinking about a person long ago who used to sing that song."

"And who was the person long ago?" asked Gabriel, smiling.

"It was a person I used to know in Galway when I was living with my grandmother," she said.

The smile passed away from Gabriel's face. A dull anger began to gather again at the back of his mind and the dull fires of his lust began to glow angrily in his veins.

"Someone you were in love with?" he asked ironically.

"It was a young boy I used to know," she answered, "named Michael Furey. He used to sing that song, *The Lass of Aughrim*. He was very delicate."

Gabriel was silent. He did not wish her to think that he was interested in this delicate boy.

"I can see him so plainly," she said, after a moment. "Such eyes as he had: big, dark eyes! And such an expression in them—an expression!"

"O, then, you are in love with him?" said Gabriel.

"I used to go out walking with him," she said, "when I was in Galway."

A thought flew across Gabriel's mind.

"Perhaps that was why you wanted to go to Galway with that Ivors girl?" he said coldly.

She looked at him and asked in surprise:

"What for?"

Her eyes made Gabriel feel awkward. He shrugged his shoulders and said:

"How do I know? To see him, perhaps."

She looked away from him along the shaft of light towards the window in silence.

"He is dead," she said at length. "He died when he was only seventeen. Isn't it a terrible thing to die so young as that?"

"What was he?" asked Gabriel, still ironically.

"He was in the gasworks," she said.

Gabriel felt humiliated by the failure of his irony and by the evocation of this figure from the dead, a boy in the gasworks. While he had been full of memories of their secret life together, full of tenderness and joy and desire, she had been comparing him in her mind with another. A shameful consciousness of his own person assailed him. He saw himself as a ludicrous figure, acting as a pennyboy for his aunts, a nervous, well-meaning sentimentalist, orating to vulgarians and idealising his own clownish lusts, the pitiable fatuous fellow he had caught a glimpse of in the mirror. Instinctively he turned his back more to the light lest she might see the shame that burned upon his forehead.

He tried to keep up his tone of cold interrogation, but his voice when he spoke was humble and indifferent.

"I suppose you were in love with this Michael Furey, Gretta," he said.

"I was great with him at that time," she said.

Her voice was veiled and sad. Gabriel, feeling now how vain it would be to try to lead her whither he had purposed, caressed one of her hands and said, also sadly:

"And what did he die of so young, Gretta? Consumption, was it?"

"I think he died for me," she answered.

A vague terror seized Gabriel at this answer, as if, at that hour when he had hoped to triumph, some impalpable and vindictive being was coming against him, gathering forces against him in its vague world. But he shook himself free of it with an effort of reason and continued to caress her hand. He did not question her again, for he felt that she would tell him of herself. Her hand was warm and moist: it did not respond to his touch, but he continued to caress it just as he had caressed her first letter to him that spring morning.

"It was in the winter," she said, "about the beginning of the winter when I was going to leave my grandmother's and come up here to the convent. And he was ill at the time in his lodgings in Galway and wouldn't be let out, and his people in Oughterard were written to. He was in decline, they said, or something like that. I never knew rightly."

She paused for a moment and sighed.

"Poor fellow," she said. "He was very fond of me and he was such a gentle boy. We used to go out together, walking, you know, Gabriel, like the way they do in the country. He was going to study singing only for his health. He had a very good voice, poor Michael Furey."

"Well; and then?" asked Gabriel.

"And then when it came to the time for me to leave Galway and come up to the convent he was much worse and I wouldn't be let see him so I wrote him a letter saying I was going up to Dublin and would be back in the summer, and hoping he would be better then."

She paused for a moment to get her voice under control, and then went on:

"Then the night before I left, I was in my grandmother's house in Nuns' Island, packing up, and I heard gravel thrown up against the window. The window was so wet I couldn't see, so I ran downstairs as I was and slipped out the back into the garden and there was the poor fellow at the end of the garden, shivering."

"And did you not tell him to go back?" asked Gabriel.

"I implored of him to go home at once and told him he would get his death in the rain. But he said he did not want to live. I can see his eyes as well as well! He was standing at the end of the wall where there was a tree."

"And did he go home?" asked Gabriel.

"Yes, he went home. And when I was only a week in the convent he died and he was buried in Oughterard, where his people came from. O, the day I heard that, that he was dead!"

She stopped, choking with sobs, and, overcome by emotion, flung herself face downward on the bed, sobbing in the quilt. Gabriel held her hand for a moment longer, irresolutely, and then, shy of intruding on her grief, let it fall gently and walked quietly to the window.

She was fast asleep.

Gabriel, leaning on his elbow, looked for a few moments unresentfully on her tangled hair and half-open mouth, listening to her deep-drawn breath. So she had had that romance in her life: a man had died for her sake. It hardly pained him now to think how poor a part he, her husband, had played in her life. He watched her while she slept, as though he and she had never lived together as man and wife. His curious eyes rested long upon her face and on her hair: and, as he thought of what she must have been then, in that time of her first girlish beauty, a strange, friendly pity for her entered his soul. He did not like to say even to himself that her face was no longer beautiful, but he knew that it was no longer the face for which Michael Furey had braved death.

Perhaps she had not told him all the story. His eyes moved to the chair over which she had thrown some of her clothes. A petticoat string dangled to the floor. One boot stood upright, its limp upper fallen down: the fellow of it lay upon its side. He wondered at his riot of emotions of an hour before. From what had it proceeded? From his aunt's supper, from his own foolish speech, from the wine and dancing, the merry-making when saying good-night in the hall, the pleasure of the walk along the river in the snow. Poor Aunt Julia! She, too, would soon be a shade with the shade of Patrick Morkan and his horse. He had caught that haggard look upon her face for a moment when she was singing *Arrayed for the Bridal*. Soon, perhaps, he would be sitting in that same drawing-room, dressed in black, his silk hat on his knees. The blinds would be drawn down and Aunt Kate would be sitting beside him, crying and blowing her nose and telling him how Julia had died. He would cast about in his mind for some words that might console her, and would find only lame and useless ones. Yes, yes: that would happen very soon.

The air of the room chilled his shoulders. He stretched himself cautiously along under the sheets and lay down beside his wife. One by one, they were all becoming shades. Better pass boldly into that other world, in the full glory of some passion, than fade and wither dismally with age. He thought of how she who lay beside him had locked in her heart for so many years that image of her lover's eyes when he had told her that he did not wish to live.

Generous tears filled Gabriel's eyes. He had never felt like that himself towards any woman, but he knew that such a feeling must be love. The tears gathered more thickly in his eyes and in the partial darkness he imagined he saw the form of a young man standing under a dripping tree. Other forms were near. His soul had approached that region where dwell the vast hosts of the dead. He was conscious of, but could not apprehend, their wayward and flickering existence. His own identity was fading out into a grey impalpable world: the solid world itself, which these dead had one time reared and lived in, was dissolving and dwindling.

A few light taps upon the pane made him turn to the window. It had begun to snow again. He watched sleepily the flakes, silver and dark, falling obliquely against the lamplight. The time had come for him to set out on his journey westward. Yes, the newspapers were right: snow was general all over Ireland. It was falling on every part of the dark central plain, on the treeless hills, falling softly upon the Bog of Allen and, farther westward, softly falling into the dark mutinous Shannon waves. It was falling, too, upon every part of the lonely churchyard on the hill where Michael Furey lay buried. It lay thickly drifted on the crooked crosses and headstones, on the spears of the little gate, on the barren thorns. His soul swooned slowly as he heard the snow falling faintly through the universe and faintly falling, like the descent of their last end, upon all the living and the dead.

BILLY BUDD, FORETOPMAN
What befell him in the year
of the Great Mutiny etc.

• •

Herman Melville

Herman Melville

Herman Melville was born in New York City in 1819 and died there in 1891. *Billy Budd, Foretopman* was his final work, except for a few poems. During the past ten years an extraordinary amount of critical and scholarly work has been devoted to Melville, particularly to those books which made him a failure as a selling author, and which were the best work of his life, beginning with *Mardi* and *Moby Dick* and continuing to *Billy Budd*. This Melville "revival" has caused the reappearance of much of Melville's work and has produced many interesting and valuable insights into one of America's great writers. (Three of them of particular interest are: *American Renaissance* by F. O. Matthiessen; *Herman Melville* by Newton Arvin; and *The Melville Log* edited by Jay Leyda, who also edited the fine general volume *The Portable Melville.*)

Note: The text of *Billy Budd, Foretopman* used in this book is the definitive transcription of F. Barron Freeman published by the Harvard University Press, corrected in accordance with the Corrigenda later issued with that volume. Omitted only are the editor's footnotes and indications of the editor's insertions, which make Professor Freeman's book so valuable for textual study but tend to hinder the general reader.

Dedicated to

Jack Chace

Englishman

*Wherever that great heart may now be
Here on Earth or harbored in Paradise
Captain of the main-top in the year 1843
in the U. S. Frigate "United States"*

Preface

THE YEAR 1797, the year of this narrative, belongs to a period which as every thinker now feels, involved a crisis for Christendom not exceeded in its undetermined momentousness at the time by any other era whereof there is record. The opening proposition made by the Spirit of that Age, involved the rectification of the Old World's hereditary wrongs. In France to some extent this was bloodily effected. But what then? Straightway the Revolution itself became a wrongdoer, one more oppressive than the kings. Under Napoleon it enthroned upstart Kings, and initiated that prolonged agony of continual war whose final throe was Waterloo. During those years not the wisest could have foreseen that the outcome of all would be what to some thinkers apparently it has since turned out to be, a political advance along nearly the whole line for Europeans.

Now, as elsewhere hinted, it was something caught from the Revolutionary Spirit that at Spithead emboldened the man-of-war's men to rise against real abuses, long-standing ones, and afterwards at the Nore to make inordinate and aggressive demands, successful resistance to which was confirmed only when the ringleaders were hung for an admonitory spectacle to the anchored fleet. Yet in a way analogous to the operation of the Revolution at large the Great Mutiny, though by Englishmen naturally deemed monstrous at the time, doubtless gave the first latent prompting to most important reforms in the British Navy.

BILLY BUDD
SAILOR
(An inside narrative.)

1

IN THE TIME before steamships, or then more frequently than now, a stroller along the docks of any considerable sea-port would occasionally have his attention arrested by a group of bronzed mariners, man-of-war's men or merchant-sailors in holiday attire ashore on liberty. In certain instances they would flank, or, like a body-guard quite surround some superior figure of their own class, moving along with them like Aldebaran among the lesser lights of his constellation. That signal object was the "Handsome Sailor" of the less prosaic time alike of the military and merchant navies. With no perceptible trace of the vainglorious about him, rather with the off-hand unaffectedness of natural regality, he seemed to accept the spontaneous homage of his shipmates. A somewhat remarkable instance recurs to me. In Liverpool, now half a century ago I saw under the shadow of the great dingy street-wall of Prince's Dock (an obstruction long since removed) a common sailor, so intensely black that he must needs have been a native African of the unadulterate blood of Ham. A symmetric figure much above the average height. The two ends of a gay silk handkerchief thrown loose about the neck danced upon the displayed ebony of his chest; in his ears were big hoops of gold, and a Scotch

Highland bonnet with a tartan band set off his shapely
head.

It was a hot noon in July; and his face, lustrous with
perspiration, beamed with barbaric good humor. In jovial
sallies right and left his white teeth flashing into view, he
rollicked along, the centre of a company of his shipmates.
These were made up of such an assortment of tribes and
complexions as would have well fitted them to be marched
up by Anacharsis Cloots before the bar of the first French
Assembly as Representatives of the Human Race. At each
spontaneous tribute rendered by the wayfarers to this black
pagod of a fellow—the tribute of a pause and stare, and
less frequent an exclamation,—the motley retinue showed
that they took that sort of pride in the evoker of it which
the Assyrian priests doubtless showed for their grand
sculptured Bull when the faithful prostrated themselves.

To return.

If in some cases a bit of a nautical Murat in setting forth
his person ashore, the handsome sailor of the period in
question evinced nothing of the dandified Billy-be-Dam,
an amusing character all but extinct now, but occasionally
to be encountered, and in a form yet more amusing than
the original, at the tiller of the boats on the tempestuous
Erie Canal or, more likely, vaporing in the groggeries along
the tow-path. Invariably a proficient in his perilous calling,
he was also more or less of a mighty boxer or wrestler. It
was strength and beauty. Tales of his prowess were re-
cited. Ashore he was the champion; afloat the spokesman;
on every suitable occasion always foremost. Close-reefing
topsails in a gale, there he was, astride the weather yard-
arm-end, foot in the Flemish horse as "stirrup," both hands
tugging at the "earring" as at a bridle, in very much the
attitude of young Alexander curbing the fiery Bucephalus.
A superb figure, tossed up as by the horns of Taurus against
the thunderous sky, cheerily hallooing to the strenuous
file along the spar.

The moral nature was seldom out of keeping with the

physical make. Indeed, except as toned by the former, the comeliness and power, always attractive in masculine conjunction, hardly could have drawn the sort of honest homage the Handsome Sailor in some examples received from his less gifted associates.

Such a cynosure, at least in aspect, and something such too in nature, though with important variations made apparent as the story proceeds, was welkin-eyed Billy Budd, or Baby Budd as more familiarly under circumstances hereafter to be given he at last came to be called aged twenty-one, a foretopman of the British fleet toward the close of the last decade of the eighteenth century. It was not very long prior to the time of the narration that follows that he had entered the King's Service, having been impressed on the Narrow Seas from a homeward-bound English merchantman into a seventy-four outward-bound, H.M.S. *Indomitable;* which ship, as was not unusual in those hurried days having been obliged to put to sea short of her proper complement of men. Plump upon Billy at first sight in the gangway the boarding officer Lieutenant Ratcliffe pounced, even before the merchantman's crew was formally mustered on the quarter-deck for his deliberate inspection. And him only he elected. For whether it was because the other men when ranged before him showed to ill advantage after Billy, or whether he had some scruples in view of the merchantman being rather short-handed, however it might be, the officer contented himself with his first spontaneous choice. To the surprise of the ship's company, though much to the Lieutenant's satisfaction Billy made no demur. But, indeed, any demur would have been as idle as the protest of a goldfinch popped into a cage.

Noting this uncomplaining acquiescence, all but cheerful one might say, the shipmates turned a surprised glance of silent reproach at the sailor. The shipmaster was one of those worthy mortals found in every vocation even the humbler ones—the sort of person whom everybody agrees

in calling "a respectable man." And—nor so strange to report as it may appear to be—though a ploughman of the
troubled waters, life-long contending with the intractable
elements, there was nothing this honest soul at heart loved
better than simple peace and quiet. For the rest, he was
fifty or thereabouts, a little inclined to corpulence, a pre-
possessing face, unwhiskered, and of an agreeable color—
a rather full face, humanely intelligent in expression. On
a fair day with a fair wind and all going well, a certain
musical chime in his voice seemed to be the veritable unobstructed outcome of the innermost man. He had much
prudence, much conscientiousness, and there were occasions when these virtues were the cause of overmuch disquietude in him. On a passage, so long as his craft was in
any proximity to land, no sleep for Captain Graveling. He
took to heart those serious responsibilities not so heavily
borne by some shipmasters.

Now while Billy Budd was down in the forecastle getting his kit together, the *Indomitable's* lieutenant, burly
and bluff, nowise disconcerted by Captain Graveling's
omitting to proffer the customary hospitalities on an occasion so unwelcome to him, an omission simply caused by
preoccupation of thought, unceremoniously invited himself into the cabin, and also to a flask from the spirit-locker,
a receptacle which his experienced eye instantly discovered. In fact he was one of those sea-dogs in whom all the
hardship and peril of naval life in the great prolonged
wars of his time never impaired the natural instinct for
sensuous enjoyment. His duty he always faithfully did; but
duty is sometimes a dry obligation, and he was for irri-
gating its aridity, whensoever possible, with a fertilizing
decoction of strong waters. For the cabin's proprietor there
was nothing left but to play the part of the enforced host
with whatever grace and alacrity were practicable. As necessary adjuncts to the flask, he silently placed tumbler and
water-jug before the irrepressible guest. But excusing himself from partaking just then, he dismally watched the

unembarrassed officer deliberately diluting his grog a little, then tossing it off in three swallows, pushing the empty tumbler away, yet not so far as to be beyond easy reach, at the same time settling himself in his seat and smacking his lips with high satisfaction, looking straight at the host.

These proceedings over, the Master broke the silence; and there lurked a rueful reproach in the tone of his voice: "Lieutenant, you are going to take my best man from me, the jewel of 'em."

"Yes, I know" rejoined the other, immediately drawing back the tumbler preliminary to a replenishing; "Yes, I know. Sorry."

"Beg pardon, but you don't understand, Lieutenant. See here now. Before I shipped that young fellow, my forecastle was a rat-pit of quarrels. It was black times, I tell you, aboard the *Rights* here. I was worried to that degree my pipe had no comfort for me. But Billy came; and it was like a Catholic priest striking peace in an Irish shindy. Not that he preached to them or said or did anything in particular; but a virtue went out of him, sugaring the sour ones. They took to him like hornets to treacle; all but the buffer of the gang, the big shaggy chap with the fire-red whiskers. He indeed out of envy, perhaps, of the newcomer, and thinking such a 'sweet and pleasant fellow,' as he mockingly designated him to the others, could hardly have the spirit of a game-cock, must needs bestir himself in trying to get up an ugly row with him. Billy forebore with him and reasoned with him in a pleasant way—he is something like myself, lieutenant, to whom aught like a quarrel is hateful—but nothing served. So, in the second dog-watch one day the Red Whiskers in presence of the others, under pretence of showing Billy just whence a sirloin steak was cut—for the fellow had once been a butcher—insultingly gave him a dig under the ribs. Quick as lightning Billy let fly his arm. I dare say he never meant to do quite as much as he did, but anyhow he gave the burly fool a terrible drubbing. It took about half a minute,

I should think. And, lord bless you, the lubber was astonished at the celerity. And will you believe it, Lieutenant, the Red Whiskers now really loves Billy—loves him, or is the biggest hypocrite that ever I heard of. But they all love him. Some of 'em do his washing, darn his old trousers for him; the carpenter is at odd times making a pretty little chest of drawers for him. Anybody will do anything for Billy Budd; and it's the happy family here. But now Lieutenant, if that young fellow goes—I know how it will be aboard the *'Rights.'* Not again very soon shall I, coming up from dinner, lean over the capstan smoking a quiet pipe—no, not very soon again, I think. Ay, Lieutenant, you are going to take away the jewel of 'em; you are going to take away my peacemaker!" And with that the good soul had really some ado in checking a rising sob.

"Well," said the officer who had listened with amused interest to all this, and now waxing merry with his tipple; "Well, blessed are the peacemakers especially the fighting peacemakers! And such are the seventy-four beauties some of which you see poking their noses out at the port-holes of yonder war-ship lying-to for me" pointing through the cabin window of the *Indomitable.* "But courage! don't look so downhearted, man. Why, I pledge you in advance the royal approbation. Rest assured that His Majesty will be delighted to know that in a time when his hard tack is not sought for by sailors with such avidity as should be; a time also when some shipmasters privily resent the borrowing from them a tar or two for the service; His Majesty, I say, will be delighted to learn that *one* shipmaster at least cheerfully surrenders to the King, the flower of his flock, a sailor who with equal loyalty makes no dissent.— But where's my beauty? Ah," looking through the cabin's open door "Here he comes; and, by Jove—lugging along his chest—Apollo with his portmanteau!—My man," stepping out to him, "you can't take that big box aboard a war-ship. The boxes there are mostly shot-boxes. Put your duds in a bag, lad. Boot and saddle for the cavalryman, bag and hammock for the man-of-war's man."

The transfer from chest to bag was made. And, after seeing his man into the cutter and then following him down, the lieutenant pushed off from the *Rights-of-Man*. That was the merchant-ship's name; though by her master and crew abbreviated in sailor fashion into *The Rights*. The hard-headed Dundee owner was a staunch admirer of Thomas Paine whose book in rejoinder to Burke's arraignment of the French Revolution had then been published for some time and had gone everywhere. In christening his vessel after the title of Paine's volume the man of Dundee was something like his contemporary shipowner, Stephen Girard of Philadelphia, whose sympathies, alike with his native land and its liberal philosophers, he evinced by naming his ships after Voltaire, Diderot, and so forth.

But now, when the boat swept under the merchantman's stern, and officer and oarsmen were noting—some bitterly and others with a grin,—the name emblazoned there; just then it was that the new recruit jumped up from the bow where the coxswain had directed him to sit, and waving his hat to his silent shipmates sorrowfully looking over at him from the taffrail, bade the lads a genial good-bye. Then, making a salutation as to the ship herself, "And good bye to you too, old *Rights of Man*."

"Down, Sir!" roared the lieutenant, instantly assuming all the rigor of his rank, though with difficulty repressing a smile.

To be sure Billy's action was a terrible breach of naval decorum. But in that decorum he had never been instructed; in consideration of which the lieutenant would hardly have been so energetic in reproof but for the concluding farewell to the ship. This he rather took as meant to convey a covert sally on the new recruit's part, a sly slur at impressment in general, and that of himself in especial. And yet, more likely, if satire it was in effect, it was hardly so by intention, for Billy though happily en-

dowed with the gayety of high health, youth, and a free
heart, was yet by no means of a satirical turn. The will to
it and the sinister dexterity were alike wanting. To deal
in double meanings and insinuations of any sort was
quite foreign to his nature.

As to his enforced enlistment, that he seemed to take
pretty much as he was wont to take any vicissitude of
weather. Like the animals, though no philosopher, he was,
without knowing it, practically a fatalist. And, it may be,
that he rather liked this adventurous turn in his affairs,
which promised an opening into novel scenes and martial
excitements.

Aboard the *Indomitable* our merchant-sailor was forthwith rated as an able-seaman and assigned to the starboard
watch of the fore-top. He was soon at home in the service,
not at all disliked for his unpretentious good looks and a
sort of genial happy-go-lucky air. No merrier man in his
mess: in marked contrast to certain other individuals included like himself among the impressed portion of the
ship's company; for these when not actively employed were
sometimes, and more particularly in the last dog-watch
when the drawing near of twilight induced revery, apt to
fall into a saddish mood which in some partook of sullen-
ness. But they were not so young as our foretopman, and
no few of them must have known a hearth of some sort,
others may have had wives and children left, too probably,
in uncertain circumstances, and hardly any but must have
had acknowledged kith and kin, while for Billy, as will
shortly be seen, his entire family was practically invested
in himself.

2

Though our new-made foretopman was well received in
the top and on the gun-decks, hardly here was he that
cynosure he had previously been among those minor ship's

companies of the merchant marine, with which companies only had he hitherto consorted.

He was young; and despite his all but fully developed frame in aspect looked even younger than he really was, owing to a lingering adolescent expression in the as yet smooth face all but feminine in purity of natural complexion but where, thanks to his seagoing, the lily was quite suppressed and the rose had some ado visibly to flush through the tan.

To one essentially such a novice in the complexities of factitious life, the abrupt transition from his former and simpler sphere to the ampler and more knowing world of a great war-ship; this might well have abashed him had there been any conceit or vanity in his composition. Among her miscellaneous multitude, the *Indomitable* mustered several individuals who however inferior in grade were of no common natural stamp, sailors more signally susceptive of that air which continuous martial discipline and repeated presence in battle can in some degree impart even to the average man. As the *handsome sailor* Billy Budd's position aboard the seventy-four was something analogous to that of a rustic beauty transplanted from the provinces and brought into competition with the high-born dames of the court. But this change of circumstances he scarce noted. As little did he observe that something about him provoked an ambiguous smile in one or two harder faces among the blue-jackets. Nor less unaware was he of the peculiar favorable effect his person and demeanor had upon the more intelligent gentlemen of the quarter-deck. Nor could this well have been otherwise. Cast in a mould peculiar to the finest physical examples of those Englishmen in whom the Saxon strain would seem not at all to partake of any Norman or other admixture, he showed in face that humane look of reposeful good nature which the Greek sculptor in some instances gave to his heroic strong man, Hercules. But this again was subtly modified by another and pervasive qual-

ity. The ear, small and shapely, the arch of the foot, the
curve in mouth and nostril, even the indurated hand dyed
to the orange-tawny of the toucan's bill, a hand telling
alike of the halyards and tar-bucket; but, above all, something in the mobile expression, and every chance attitude
and movement, something suggestive of a mother eminent-
ly favored by Love and the Graces; all this strangely indicated a lineage in direct contradiction to his lot. The
mysteriousness here, became less mysterious through a mat-
ter-of-fact elicited when Billy at the capstan was being
formally mustered into the service. Asked by the officer, a
small brisk little gentleman as it chanced among other
questions, his place of birth, he replied, "Please, Sir, I
don't know."

"Don't know where you were born?—Who was your
father?"

"God knows, Sir."

Struck by the straightforward simplicity of these replies,
the officer next asked "Do you know anything about your
beginning?"

"No, Sir. But I have heard that I was found in a pretty
silk-lined basket hanging one morning from the knocker
of a good man's door in Bristol."

"*Found* say you? Well," throwing back his head and
looking up and down the new recruit; "Well it turns out
to have been a pretty good find. Hope they'll find some
more like you, my man; the fleet sadly needs them."

Yes, Billy Budd was a foundling, a presumable bye-blow,
and, evidently, no ignoble one. Noble descent was as evident in him as in a blood horse.

For the rest, with little or no sharpness of faculty or any
trace of the wisdom of the serpent, nor yet quite a dove,
he possessed that kind and degree of intelligence going
along with the unconventional rectitude of a sound human creature, one to whom not yet has been proffered the
questionable apple of knowledge. He was illiterate; he
could not read, but he could sing, and like the illiterate

nightingale was sometimes the composer of his own song.

Of self-consciousness he seemed to have little or none, or about as much as we may reasonably impute to a dog of Saint Bernard's breed.

Habitually living with the elements and knowing little more of the land than as a beach, or, rather, that portion of the terraqueous globe providentially set apart for dance-houses doxies and tapsters, in short what sailors call a "fiddlers' green," his simple nature remained unsophisticated by those moral obliquities which are not in every case incompatible with that manufacturable thing known as respectability. But are sailors, frequenters of "fiddlers'-greens", without vices? No; but less often than with landsmen do their vices, so called, partake of crookedness of heart, seeming less to proceed from viciousness than exuberance of vitality after long constraint; frank manifestations in accordance with natural law. By his original constitution aided by the cooperating influences of his lot, Billy in many respects was little more than a sort of upright barbarian, much such perhaps as Adam presumably might have been ere the urbane Serpent wriggled himself into his company.

And here be it submitted that apparently going to corroborate the doctrine of man's fall, a doctrine now popularly ignored, it is observable that where certain virtues pristine and unadulterate peculiarly characterize anybody in the external uniform of civilization, they will upon scrutiny seem not to be derived from custom or convention, but rather to be out of keeping with these, as if indeed exceptionally transmitted from a period prior to Cain's city and citified man. The character marked by such qualities has to an unvitiated taste an untampered-with flavor like that of berries, while the man thoroughly civilized even in a fair specimen of the breed has to the same moral palate a questionable smack as of a compounded wine. To any stray inheritor of these primitive qualities found, like Caspar Hauser, wandering dazed in any Christian capital

of our time the good-natured poet's famous invocation,
near two thousand years ago, of the good rustic out of his
latitude in the Rome of the Cesars, still appropriately
holds:—

> "Honest and poor, Faithful in word and thought
> What has thee, Fabian, to the city brought."

Though our Handsome Sailor had as much of masculine
beauty as one can expect anywhere to see; nevertheless,
like the beautiful woman in one of Hawthorne's minor
tales, there was just one thing amiss in him. No visible
blemish indeed, as with the lady; no, but an occasional
liability to a vocal defect. Though in the hour of elemental
uproar or peril, he was everything that a sailor should be,
yet under sudden provocation of strong heart-feeling his
voice otherwise singularly musical, as if expressive of the
harmony within, was apt to develop an organic hesitancy,
in fact more or less of a stutter or even worse. In this particular Billy was a striking instance that the arch inter-
ferer, the envious marplot of Eden still has more or less to
do with every human consignment to this planet of earth.
In every case, one way or another he is sure to slip in his
little card, as much as to remind us—I too have a hand
here.

The avowal of such an imperfection in the Handsome
Sailor should be evidence not alone that he is not presented
as a conventional hero, but also that the story in which he
is the main figure is no romance.

3

At the time of Billy Budd's arbitrary enlistment into the
Indomitable that ship was on her way to join the Mediterranean fleet. No long time elapsed before the junction
was effected. As one of that fleet the seventy-four partici-

pated in its movements, though at times on account of her superior sailing qualities, in the absence of frigates, despatched on separate duty as a scout and at times on less temporary service. But with all this the story has little concernment, restricted as it is to the inner life of one particular ship and the career of an individual sailor.

It was the summer of 1797. In the April of that year had occurred the commotion at Spithead followed in May by a second and yet more serious outbreak in the fleet at the Nore. The latter is known, and without exaggeration in the epithet, as the Great Mutiny. It was indeed a demonstration more menacing to England than the contemporary manifestoes and conquering and proselyting armies of the French Directory.

To the British Empire the Nore Mutiny was what a strike in the fire-brigade would be to London threatened by general arson. In a crisis when the kingdom might well have anticipated the famous signal that some years later published along the naval line of battle what it was that upon occasion England expected of Englishmen; *that* was the time when at the mast-heads of the three-deckers and seventy-fours moored in her own roadstead—a fleet, the right arm of a Power then all but the sole free conservative one of the Old World, the blue-jackets, to be numbered by thousands ran up with huzzas the British colors with the union and cross wiped out; by that cancellation transmuting the flag of founded law and freedom defined, into the enemy's red meteor of unbridled and unbounded revolt. Reasonable discontent growing out of practical grievances in the fleet had been ignited into irrational combustion as by live cinders blown across the Channel from France in flames.

The event converted into irony for a time those spirited strains of Dibdin—as a song-writer no mean auxiliary to the English Government at the European conjuncture—strains celebrating, among other things, the patriotic devotion of the British tar:

"And as for my life, 'tis the King's!"

Such an episode in the Island's grand naval story her naval historians naturally abridge; one of them (G. P. R. James) candidly acknowledging that fain would he pass it over did not "impartiality forbid fastidiousness." And yet his mention is less a narration than a reference, having to do hardly at all with details. Nor are these readily to be found in the libraries. Like some other events in every age befalling states everywhere including America the Great Mutiny was of such character that national pride along with views of policy would fain shade it off into the historical background. Such events can not be ignored, but there is a considerate way of historically treating them. If a well-constituted individual refrains from blazoning aught amiss or calamitous in his family; a nation in the like circumstance may without reproach be equally discreet.

Though after parleyings between Government and the ringleaders, and concessions by the former as to some glaring abuses, the first uprising—that at Spithead—with difficulty was put down, or matters for the time pacified; yet at the Nore the unforeseen renewal of insurrection on a yet larger scale, and emphasized in the conferences that ensued by demands deemed by the authorities not only inadmissible but aggressively insolent, indicated—if the Red Flag did not sufficiently do so, what was the spirit animating the men. Final suppression, however, there was; but only made possible perhaps by the unswerving loyalty of the marine corps a voluntary resumption of loyalty among influential sections of the crews.

To some extent the Nore Mutiny may be regarded as analogous to the distempering irruption of contagious fever in a frame constitutionally sound, and which anon throws it off.

At all events, of these thousands of mutineers were some of the tars who not so very long afterwards—whether wholly prompted thereto by patriotism, or pugnacious instinct, or by both,—helped to win a coronet for Nelson at the Nile, and the naval crown of crowns for him at Trafalgar. To the mutineers those battles and especially Trafalgar were a plenary absolution and a grand one: For all that goes to make up scenic naval display, and heroic magnificence in arms those battles especially Trafalgar stand unmatched in human annals.

4

Concerning "The greatest sailor since the world began." Tennyson?

In this matter of writing, resolve as one may to keep to the main road, some by-paths have an enticement not readily to be withstood. I am going to err into such a by-path. If the reader will keep me company I shall be glad. At the least we can promise ourselves that pleasure which is wickedly said to be in sinning, for a literary sin the divergence will be.

Very likely it is no new remark that the inventions of our time have at last brought about a change in sea-warfare in degree corresponding to the revolution in all warfare effected by the original introduction from China into Europe of gunpowder. The first European fire-arm, a clumsy contrivance, was, as is well known, scouted by no few of the knights as a base implement, good enough peradventure for weavers too craven to stand up crossing steel with steel in frank fight. But as ashore knightly valor though shorn of its blazonry did not cease with the knights, neither on the seas though nowadays in encounters there a certain kind of displayed gallantry be fallen out of date as hardly applicable under changed circumstances, did the nobler qualities of such naval magnates as Don John of Austria, Doria, Van Tromp, Jean Bart, the long line of British Admirals and the American Decaturs of 1812 become obsolete with their wooden walls.

Nevertheless, to anybody who can hold the Present at its worth without being inappreciative of the Past, it may be forgiven, if to such an one the solitary old hulk at Portsmouth, Nelson's *Victory*, seems to float there, not alone as the decaying monument of a fame incorruptible, but also as a poetic reproach, softened by its picturesqueness, to the *Monitors* and yet mightier hulls of the European iron-clads. And this not altogether because such craft are unsightly, unavoidably lacking the symmetry and grand lines of the old battle-ships, but equally for other reasons.

There are some, perhaps, who while not altogether inaccessible to that poetic reproach just alluded to, may yet on behalf of the new order, be disposed to parry it; and this to the extent of iconoclasm, if need be. For example, prompted by the sight of the star inserted in the *Victory's* quarter-deck designating the spot where the Great Sailor fell, these martial utilitarians may suggest considerations implying that Nelson's ornate publication of his person in battle was not only unnecessary, but not military, nay savored of foolhardiness and vanity. They may add, too, that at Trafalgar it was in effect nothing less than a challenge to death; and death came; and that but for his bravado the victorious Admiral might possibly have survived the battle, and so, instead of having his sagacious dying injunctions overruled by his immediate successor in command he himself when the contest was decided might have brought his shattered fleet to anchor, a proceeding which might have averted the deplorable loss of life by shipwreck in the elemental tempest that followed the martial one.

Well, should we set aside the more disputable point whether for various reasons it was possible to anchor the fleet, then plausibly enough the Benthamites of war may urge the above.

But the *might-have-been* is but boggy ground to build on. And certainly, in foresight as to the larger issue of an

encounter, and anxious preparations for it—buoying the
deadly way and mapping it out, as at Copenhagen—few
commanders have been so painstakingly circumspect as
this same reckless declarer of his person in fight.

Personal prudence even when dictated by quite other
than selfish considerations surely is no special virtue in a
military man; while an excessive love of glory, impassion-
ing a less burning impulse the honest sense of duty, is the
first. If the name *Wellington* is not so much of a trumpet
to the blood as the simpler name *Nelson,* the reason for this
may perhaps be inferred from the above. Alfred in his
funeral ode on the victor of Waterloo ventures not to call
him the greatest soldier of all time, though in the same
ode he invokes Nelson as "the greatest sailor since the
world began."

At Trafalgar Nelson on the brink of opening the fight
sat down and wrote his last brief will and testament. If
under the presentiment of the most magnificent of all victories to be crowned by his own glorious death, a sort of
priestly motive led him to dress his person in the jewelled
vouchers of his own shining deeds; if thus to have adorned
himself for the altar and the sacrifice were indeed vainglory, then affectation and fustian is each more heroic line
in the great epics and dramas, since in such lines the poet
but embodies in verse those exaltations of sentiment that
a nature like Nelson, the opportunity being given, vitalizes
into acts.

5

Yes, the outbreak at the Nore was put down. But not every
grievance was redressed. If the contractors, for example,
were no longer permitted to ply some practices peculiar
to their tribe everywhere, such as providing shoddy cloth,
rations not sound, or false in the measure; not the less
impressment, for one thing, went on. By custom sanctioned

for centuries, and judicially maintained by a Lord Chancellor as late as Mansfield, that mode of manning the fleet, a mode now fallen into a sort of abeyance but never formally renounced, it was not practicable to give up in those years. Its abrogation would have crippled the indispensable fleet, one wholly under canvas, no steam-power, its innumerable sails and thousands of cannon, everything in short, worked by muscle alone; a fleet the more insatiate in demand for men, because then multiplying its ships of all grades against contingencies present and to come of the convulsed Continent.

Discontent foreran the Two Mutinies, and more or less it lurkingly survived them. Hence it was not unreasonable to apprehend some return of trouble sporadic or general. One instance of such apprehensions: In the same year with this story, Nelson, then Vice Admiral Sir Horatio, being with the fleet off the Spanish coast, was directed by the Admiral in command to shift his pennant from the *Captain* to the *Theseus;* and for this reason: that the latter ship having newly arrived on the station from home where it had taken part in the Great Mutiny, danger was apprehended from the temper of the men; and it was thought that an officer like Nelson was the one, not indeed to terrorize the crew into base subjection, but to win them, by force of his mere presence back to an allegiance if not as enthusiastic as his own, yet as true. So it was that for a time on more than one quarter-deck anxiety did exist. At sea precautionary vigilance was strained against relapse. At short notice an engagement might come on. When it did, the lieutenants assigned to batteries felt it incumbent on them, in some instances to stand with drawn swords behind the men working the guns.

6

But on board the seventy-four in which Billy now swung his hammock, very little in the manner of the men and nothing obvious in the demeanor of the officers would have suggested to an ordinary observer that the Great Mutiny was a recent event. In their general bearing and conduct the commissioned officers of a war-ship naturally take their tone from the commander, that is if he have that ascendancy of character that ought to be his.

Captain the Honorable Edward Fairfax Vere, to give his full title, was a bachelor of forty or thereabouts, a sailor of distinction even in a time prolific of renowned seamen. Though allied to the higher nobility his advancement had not been altogether owing to influences connected with that circumstance. He had seen much service, been in various engagements, always acquitting himself as an officer mindful of the welfare of his men, but never tolerating an infraction of discipline; thoroughly versed in the science of his profession, and intrepid to the verge of temerity, though never injudiciously so. For his gallantry in the West Indian waters as flag-lieutenant under Rodney in that Admiral's crowning victory over De Grasse, he was made a post-captain.

Ashore in the garb of a civilian scarce anyone would have taken him for a sailor, more especially that he never garnished unprofessional talk with nautical terms, and grave in his bearing, evinced little appreciation of mere humor. It was not out of keeping with these traits that on a passage when nothing demanded his paramount action, he was the most undemonstrative of men. Any landsman observing this gentleman not conspicuous by his stature and wearing no pronounced insignia, emerging from his cabin retreat to the open deck, and noting the silent deference of the officers retiring to leeward, might have taken him for the King's guest, a civilian aboard the King's-ship, some highly honorable discreet envoy on his way to an important post. But in fact this unobtrusiveness of demeanor may have proceeded from a certain unaffected modesty of manhood sometimes accompanying a resolute nature, a modesty evinced at all times not calling for pronounced action, and which shown in any rank of life suggests a virtue aristocratic in kind.

As with some others engaged in various departments of the world's more heroic activities, Captain Vere though practical enough upon occasion would at times betray a certain dreaminess of mood. Standing alone on the weather-side of the quarter deck, one hand holding by the rigging he would absently gaze off at the blank sea. At the presentation to him then of some minor matter interrupting the current of his thoughts he would show more or less irascibility; but instantly he would control it.

In the navy he was popularly known by the appellation—Starry Vere. How such a designation happened to fall upon one who whatever his sterling qualities was without any brilliant ones was in this wise: A favorite kinsman, Lord Denton, a free-hearted fellow, had been the first to meet and congratulate him upon his return to England from his West Indian cruise; and but the day previous turning over a copy of Andrew Marvell's poems had lighted, not for the first time however, upon the lines entitled *Appleton House,* the name of one of the seats of their common ancestor, a hero in the German wars of the seventeenth century, in which poem occur the lines,

> "This 'tis to have been from the first
> In a domestic heaven nursed,
> Under the discipline severe
> Of Fairfax and the starry Vere."

And so, upon embracing his cousin fresh from Rodney's great victory wherein he had played so gallant a part, brimming over with just family pride in the sailor of their house, he exuberantly exclaimed, "Give ye joy, Ed; give ye joy, my starry Vere!" This got currency, and the novel prefix serving in familiar parlance readily to distinguish the *Indomitable's* Captain from another Vere his senior, a distant relative an officer of like rank in the navy, it remained permanently attached to the surname.

7

In view of the part that the commander of the *Indomitable* plays in scenes shortly to follow, it may be well to fill out that sketch of him outlined in the previous chapter.

Aside from his qualities as a sea-officer Captain Vere was an exceptional character. Unlike no few of England's renowned sailors, long and arduous service with signal devotion to it, had not resulted in absorbing and *salting* the entire man. He had a marked leaning toward everything intellectual. He loved books, never going to sea without a newly replenished library, compact but of the best. The isolated leisure, in some cases so wearisome, falling at intervals to commanders even during a war-cruise, never was tedious to Captain Vere. With nothing of that literary taste which less heeds the thing conveyed than the vehicle, his bias was toward those books to which every serious mind of superior order occupying any active post of authority in the world, naturally inclines: books treating of actual men and events no matter of what era—history, biography and unconventional writers, who, free from cant and convention, like Montaigne, honestly and in the spirit of common sense philosophize upon realities.

In this love of reading he found confirmation of his own more reserved thoughts—confirmation which he had vainly sought in social converse, so that as touching most fundamental topics, there had got to be established in him some positive convictions, which he forfelt would abide in him essentially unmodified so long as his intelligent part remained unimpaired. In view of the troubled period in which his lot was cast this was well for him. His settled convictions were as a dyke against those invading waters of novel opinion social political and otherwise, which carried away as in a torrent no few minds in those days, minds by nature not inferior to his own. While other members of that aristocracy to which by birth he belonged were incensed at the innovators mainly because their theories were inimical to the privileged classes, not alone Captain Vere disinterestedly opposed them because they seemed to him incapable of embodiment in lasting institutions, but at war with the peace of the world and the true welfare of mankind.

With minds less stored than his and less earnest, some officers of his rank, with whom at times he would necessarily consort, found him lacking in the companionable quality, a dry and bookish gentleman, as they deemed. Upon any chance withdrawal from their company one would be apt to say to another, something like this: "Vere is a noble fellow, Starry Vere. Spite the gazettes, Sir Horatio" meaning him with the Lord title "is at bottom scarce a better seaman or fighter. But between you and me now don't you think there is a queer streak of the pedantic running through him? Yes, like the King's yarn in a coil of navy-rope?"

Some apparent ground there was for this sort of confidential criticism; since not only did the Captain's discourse never fall into the jocosely familiar, but in illustrating of any point touching the stirring personages and events of the time he would be as apt to cite some historic character or incident of antiquity as that he would cite from the moderns. He seemed unmindful of the circumstance that to his bluff company such remote allusions however pertinent they might really be were altogether alien to men whose reading was mainly confined to the journals. But considerateness in such matters is not easy to natures constituted like Captain Vere's. Their honesty prescribes to them directness, sometimes far-reaching like that of a migratory fowl that in its flight never heeds when it crosses a frontier.

8

The lieutenants and other commissioned gentlemen forming Captain Vere's staff it is not necessary here to particularize, nor needs it to make any mention of any of the warrant-officers. But among the petty-officers was one who having much to do with the story, may as well be forthwith introduced. His portrait I essay, but shall never hit it. This was John Claggart, the Master-at-arms. But that sea-title may to landsmen seem somewhat equivocal. Originally doubtless that petty-officer's function was the instruction of the men in the use of arms, sword or cutlas. But very long ago, owing to the advance in gunnery making hand-to-hand encounters less frequent and giving to nitre and sulphur the preeminence over steel, that function ceased; the Master-at-arms of a great war-ship becoming a sort of Chief of Police charged among other matters with the duty of preserving order on the populous lower gun-decks.

Claggart was a man of about five and thirty, somewhat spare and tall, yet of no ill figure upon the whole. His hand was too small and shapely to have been accustomed to hard toil. The face was a notable one; the features all except the chin cleanly cut as those on a Greek medallion; yet the chin, beardless as Tecumseh's, had something of strange protuberant heaviness in its make that recalled the prints of the Rev. Dr. Titus Oates, the historic deponent with the clerical drawl in the time of Charles II and the fraud of the alleged Popish Plot. It served Claggart in his office that his eye could cast a tutoring glance. His brow was of the sort phrenologically associated with more than average intellect; silken jet curls partly clustering over it, making a foil to the pallor below, a pallor tinged with a faint shade of amber akin to the hue of time-tinted marbles of old. This complexion, singularly contrasting with the red or deeply bronzed visages of the sailors, and in part the result of his official seclusion from the sunlight, though it was not exactly displeasing, nevertheless seemed to hint of something defective or abnormal in the constitution and blood. But his general aspect and manner were so suggestive of an education and career incongruous with his naval function that when not actively engaged in it he looked like a man of high quality, social and moral, who for reasons of his own was keeping incog. Nothing was known of his former life. It might be that he was an Englishman; and yet there lurked a bit of accent in his speech suggesting that possibly he was not such by birth, but through naturalization in early childhood. Among certain grizzled sea-gossips of the gun-decks and forecastle went a rumor perdue that the master-at-arms was a *chevalier* who had volunteered into the King's navy by way of compounding for some mysterious swindle whereof he had been arraigned at the King's Bench. The fact that nobody could substantiate this report was, of course, nothing against its secret currency. Such a rumor once started on the gun-decks in reference to almost anyone below the rank of a commissioned officer would, during the period assigned to this narrative, have seemed not altogether wanting in credibility to the tarry old wiseacres of a man-of-war crew. And indeed a man of Claggart's accomplishments, without prior nautical experience entering the navy at mature life, as he did, and necessarily allotted at the start to the lowest grade in it; a man too who never made allusion to his previous life ashore; these were circumstances which in the dearth of exact knowledge as to his true antecedents opened to the invidious a vague field for unfavorable surmise.

But the sailors' dog-watch gossip concerning him derived a vague plausibility from the fact that now for some period the British Navy could so little afford to be squeamish in the matter of keeping up the muster-rolls, that not only were press-gangs notoriously abroad both afloat and ashore, but there was little or no secret about another matter, namely that the London police were at liberty to capture any able-bodied suspect, any questionable fellow at large and summarily ship him to the dock-yard or fleet. Furthermore, even among voluntary enlistments there were instances where the motive thereto partook neither of patriotic impulse nor yet of a random desire to experience a bit of sea-life and martial adventure. Insolvent debtors of minor grade, together with the promiscuous lame ducks of morality found in the Navy a convenient and secure refuge. Secure, because once enlisted aboard a King's-Ship, they were as much in sanctuary, as the transgressor of the Middle Ages harboring himself under the shadow of the altar. Such sanctioned irregularities which for obvious reasons the Government would hardly think to parade at the time and which consequently, and as affecting the least influential class of mankind, have all but dropped into oblivion, lend color to something for the truth whereof I do not vouch, and hence have some scruple in stating; something I remember having seen in print though the book I can not recall; but the same thing was personally communicated to me now more than forty years ago by an old pensioner in a cocked hat with whom I had a most interesting talk on the terrace at Greenwich, a Baltimore negro, a Trafalgar man. It was to this effect: In the case of a warship short of hands whose speedy sailing was imperative, the deficient quota in lack of any other way of making it good, would be eked out by draughts culled direct from the jails. For reasons previously suggested it would not perhaps be easy at the present day directly to prove or disprove the allegation. But allowed as a verity, how significant would it be of England's straits at the time confronted by those wars which like a flight of harpies rose shrieking from the din and dust of the fallen Bastille. That era appears measurably clear to us who look back

at it, and but read of it. But to the grandfathers of us gray-
beards, the more thoughtful of them, the genius of it presented an aspect like that of Camoens' Spirit of the Cape,
an eclipsing menace mysterious and prodigious. Not America was exempt from apprehension. At the height of Napoleon's unexampled conquests, there were Americans
who had fought at Bunker Hill who looked forward to the
possibility that the Atlantic might prove no barrier against
the ultimate schemes of this French portentous upstart
from the revolutionary chaos who seemed in act of fulfill-
ing judgment prefigured in the Apocalypse.

But the less credence was to be given to the gun-deck
talk touching Claggart, seeing that no man holding his
office in a man-of-war can ever hope to be popular with the
crew. Besides, in derogatory comments upon anyone
against whom they have a grudge, or for any reason or no
reason mislike, sailors are much like landsmen, they are
apt to exaggerate or romance it.

About as much was really known to the *Indomitable's*
tars of the master-at-arms' career before entering the service as an astronomer knows about a comet's travels prior
to its first observable appearance in the sky. The verdict
of the sea quidnuncs has been cited only by way of showing
what sort of moral impression the man made upon rude
uncultivated natures whose conceptions of human wicked-
ness were necessarily of the narrowest, limited to ideas of
vulgar rascality,—a thief among the swinging hammocks
during a night-watch, or the man-brokers and land-sharks
of the sea-ports.

It was no gossip, however, but fact, that though, as before hinted, Claggart upon his entrance into the navy was,
as a novice, assigned to the least honorable section of a
man-of-war's crew, embracing the drudgery, he did not
long remain there.

The superior capacity he immediately evinced, his con-
stitutional sobriety, ingratiating deference to superiors,
together with a peculiar ferreting genius manifested on a

singular occasion, all this capped by a certain austere patriotism abruptly advanced him to the position of master-at-arms.

Of this maritime Chief of Police the ship's-corporals, so called, were the immediate subordinates, and compliant ones; and this, as is to be noted in some business departments ashore, almost to a degree inconsistent with entire moral volition. His place put various converging wires of underground influence under the Chief's control, capable when astutely worked through his understrappers of operating to the mysterious discomfort if nothing worse, of any of the sea-commonalty.

9

Life in the fore-top well agreed with Billy Budd. There, when not actually engaged on the yards yet higher aloft, the topmen, who as such had been picked out for youth and activity, constituted an aerial club lounging at ease against the smaller stun'sails rolled up into cushions, spinning yarns like the lazy gods, and frequently amused with what was going on in the busy world of the decks below. No wonder then that a young fellow of Billy's disposition was well content in such society. Giving no cause of offence to anybody, he was always alert at a call. So in the merchant service it had been with him. But now such a punctiliousness in duty was shown that his topmates would sometimes good-naturedly laugh at him for it. This heightened alacrity had its cause, namely, the impression made upon him by the first formal gangway-punishment he had ever witnessed, which befell the day following his impressment. It had been incurred by a little fellow, young, a novice an after-guardsman absent from his assigned post when the ship was being put about; a dereliction resulting in a rather serious hitch to that manœuvre, one demanding instantaneous promptitude in letting go and making fast.

When Billy saw the culprit's naked back under the scourge gridironed with red welts, and worse; when he marked the dire expression on the liberated man's face as with his woolen shirt flung over him by the executioner he rushed forward from the spot to bury himself in the crowd, Billy was horrified. He resolved that never through remissness would he make himself liable to such a visitation or do or omit aught that might merit even verbal reproof. What then was his surprise and concern when ultimately he found himself getting into petty trouble occasionally about such matters as the stowage of his bag or something amiss in his hammock, matters under the police oversight of the ship's-corporals of the lower decks, and which brought down on him a vague threat from one of them.

So heedful in all things as he was, how could this be? He could not understand it, and it more than vexed him. When he spoke to his young topmates about it they were either lightly incredulous or found something comical in his unconcealed anxiety. "Is it your bag, Billy?" said one "well, sew yourself up in it, bully boy, and then you'll be sure to know if anybody meddles with it."

Now there was a veteran aboard who because his years began to disqualify him for more active work had been recently assigned duty as main-mast-man in his watch, looking to the gear belayed at the rail roundabout that great spar near the deck. At off-times the foretopman had picked up some acquaintance with him, and now in his trouble it occurred to him that he might be the sort of person to go to for wise counsel. He was an old Dansker long anglicized in the service, of few words, many wrinkles and some honorable scars. His wizened face, time-tinted and weather-stained to the complexion of an antique parchment, was here and there peppered blue by the chance explosion of a gun-cartridge in action. He was an *Agamemnon*-man; some two years prior to the time of this story having served under Nelson when but Sir Horatio in that ship immortal in naval memory, and which dis-

mantled and in part broken up to her bare ribs is seen a
grand skeleton in Haydon's etching. As one of a boarding-
party from the *Agamemnon* he had received a cut slant-
wise along one temple and cheek leaving a long pale scar
like a streak of dawn's light falling athwart the dark visage.
It was on account of that scar and the affair in which it was
known that he had received it, as well as from his blue-
peppered complexion that the Dansker went among the
Indomitable's crew by the name of "Board-her-in-the-
smoke."

Now the first time that his small weazel-eyes happened
to light on Billy Budd, a certain grim internal merriment
set all his ancient wrinkles into antic play. Was it that
his eccentric unsentimental old sapience primitive in its
kind saw or thought it saw something which in contrast
with the war-ship's environment looked oddly incongruous
in the handsome sailor? But after slyly studying him at
intervals, the old Merlin's equivocal merriment was modified; for now when the twain would meet, it would start
in his face a quizzing sort of look, but it would be but momentary and sometimes replaced by an expression of spec-
ulative query as to what might eventually befall a nature
like that, dropped into a world not without some man-
traps and against whose subtleties simple courage lacking
experience and address and without any touch of defensive
ugliness, is of little avail; and where such innocence as
man is capable of does yet in a moral emergency not always
sharpen the faculties or enlighten the will.

However it was the Dansker in his ascetic way rather
took to Billy. Nor was this only because of a certain philosophic interest in such a character. There was another
cause. While the old man's eccentricities, sometimes bordering on the ursine, repelled the juniors, Billy, unde-
terred thereby, revering him as a salt hero would make
advances, never passing the old Agamemnon-man without
a salutation marked by that respect which is seldom lost
on the aged however crabbed at times or whatever their

station in life.

There was a vein of dry humor, or what not, in the mast-
man; and, whether in freak of patriarchal irony touching
Billy's youth and athletic frame, or for some other and
more recondite reason, from the first in addressing him
he always substituted Baby for Billy. The Dansker in fact
being the originator of the name by which the foretopman
eventually became known aboard ship.

Well then, in his mysterious little difficulty going in
quest of the wrinkled one, Billy found him off duty in a
dog-watch ruminating by himself seated on a shot-box of
the upper gun-deck now and then surveying with a somewhat cynical regard certain of the more swaggering promenaders there. Billy recounted his trouble, again wondering how it all happened. The salt seer attentively listened,
accompanying the foretopman's recital with queer twitch-
ings of his wrinkles and problematical little sparkles of
his small ferret eyes. Making an end of his story, the foretopman asked, "And now, Dansker, do tell me what you
think of it."

The old man, shoving up the front of his tarpaulin and
deliberately rubbing the long slant scar at the point where
it entered the thin hair, laconically said, "Baby Budd,
Jimmy Legs" (meaning the master-at-arms) "is down on
you."

"*Jemmy Legs!*" ejaculated Billy his welkin eyes expanding; "what for? Why he calls me *the sweet and pleasant
young fellow,* they tell me."

"Does he so?" grinned the grizzled one; then said "Ay
Baby Lad a sweet voice has *Jimmy Legs.*"

"No, not always. But to me he has. I seldom pass him
but there comes a pleasant word."

"And that's because he's down upon you, Baby Budd."

Such reiteration along with the manner of it, incomprehensible to a novice, disturbed Billy almost as much as the
mystery for which he had sought explanation. Something
less unpleasingly oracular he tried to extract; but the old

sea-Chiron thinking perhaps that for the nonce he had
sufficiently instructed his young Achilles, pursed his lips,
gathered all his wrinkles together and would commit himself to nothing further.

Years, and those experiences which befall certain
shrewder men subordinated life-long to the will of superiors, all this had developed in the Dansker the pithy
guarded cynicism that was his leading characteristic.

10

The next day an incident served to confirm Billy Budd in
his incredulity as to the Dansker's strange summing up of
the case submitted. The ship at noon going large before the
wind was rolling on her course, and he below at dinner and
engaged in some sportful talk with the members of his
mess, chanced in a sudden lurch to spill the entire contents
of his soup-pan upon the new scrubbed deck. Claggart, the
Master-at-arms, official rattan in hand, happened to be passing along the battery in a bay of which the mess was lodged,
and the greasy liquid streamed just across his path. Stepping over it, he was proceeding on his way without comment, since the matter was nothing to take notice of under
the circumstances, when he happened to observe who
it was that had done the spilling. His countenance
changed. Pausing, he was about to ejaculate something
hasty at the sailor, but checked himself, and pointing down
to the streaming soup, playfully tapped him from behind
with his rattan, saying in a low musical voice peculiar to
him at times "Handsomely done, my lad! And handsome
is as handsome did it too!" And with that passed on. Not
noted by Billy as not coming within his view was the involuntary smile, or rather grimace, that accompanied Claggart's equivocal words. Aridly it drew down the thin corners of his shapely mouth. But everybody taking his re-

mark as meant for humorous, and at which therefore as
coming from a superior they were bound to laugh, "with
counterfeited glee" acted accordingly; and Billy tickled,
it may be, by the allusion to his being the handsome sailor,
merrily joined in; then addressing his messmates exclaimed
"There now, who says that Jimmy Legs is down on me!"
"And who said he was, Beauty?" demanded one Donald
with some surprise. Whereat the foretopman looked a
little foolish recalling that it was only one person, Board-
her-in-the-smoke who had suggested what to him was
the smoky idea that this master-at-arms was in any peculiar way hostile to him. Meantime that functionary
resuming his path must have momentarily worn some
expression less guarded than that of the bitter smile, and,
usurping the face from the heart, some distorting expression perhaps, for a drummer-boy heedlessly frolicking
along from the opposite direction and chancing to come
into light collision with his person was strangely disconcerted by his aspect. Nor was the impression lessened
when the official impulsively giving him a sharp cut with
the rattan, vehemently exclaimed "Look where you go!"

11

What was the matter with the master-at-arms? And, be
the matter what it might, how could it have direct relation
to Billy Budd with whom prior to the affair of the spilled
soup he had never come into any special contact official or
otherwise? What indeed could the trouble have to do with
one so little inclined to give offence as the merchant-ship's
peacemaker, even him who in Claggart's own phrase was
"the sweet and pleasant young fellow?" Yes, why should
Jemmy Legs, to borrow the Dansker's expression, be *down*
on the Handsome Sailor? But, at heart and not for nothing,
as the late chance encounter may indicate to the discern-

ing, down on him, secretly down on him, he assuredly was.

Now to invent something touching the more private career of Claggart, something involving Billy Budd, of which something the latter should be wholly ignorant, some romantic incident implying that Claggart's knowledge of the young blue-jacket began at some period anterior to catching sight of him on board the seventy-four—all this, not so difficult to do, might avail in a way more or less interesting to account for whatever of enigma may appear to lurk in the case. But in fact there was nothing of the sort. And yet the cause, necessarily to be assumed as the sole one assignable, is in its very realism as much charged with that prime element of Radcliffian romance, *the mysterious,* as any that the ingenuity of the author of the *Mysteries of Udolpho* could devise. For what can more partake of the mysterious than an antipathy spontaneous and profound such as is evoked in certain exceptional mortals by the mere aspect of some other mortal, however harmless he may be? if not called forth by this very harmlessness itself.

Now there can exist no irritating juxtaposition of dissimilar personalities comparable to that which is possible aboard a great war-ship fully manned and at sea. There, every day among all ranks almost every man comes into more or less of contact with almost every other man. Wholly there to avoid even the sight of an aggravating object one must needs give it Jonah's toss or jump overboard himself. Imagine how all this might eventually operate on some peculiar human creature the direct reverse of a saint?

But for the adequate comprehending of Claggart by a normal nature these hints are insufficient. To pass from a normal nature to him one must cross "the deadly space between." And this is best done by indirection.

Long ago an honest scholar my senior, said to me in reference to one who like himself is now no more, a man so unimpeachably respectable that against him nothing

was ever openly said though among the few something
was whispered, "Yes, X— is a nut not to be cracked by
the tap of a lady's fan. You are aware that I am the ad-
herent of no organized religion much less of any philos-
ophy built into a system. Well, for all that, I think that to
try and get into X—, enter his labyrinth and get out
again, without a clue derived from some source other than
what is known as *knowledge of the world*—that were hardly possible, at least for me."

"Why," said I, "X— however singular a study to some,
is yet human, and knowledge of the world assuredly im-
plies the knowledge of human nature, and in most of its
varieties."

"Yes, but a superficial knowledge of it, serving ordinary
purposes. But for anything deeper, I am not certain whether to know the world and to know human nature be not
two distinct branches of knowledge, which while they may
coexist in the same heart, yet either may exist with little
or nothing of the other. Nay, in an average man of the
world, his constant rubbing with it blunts that fine spiritual insight indispensable to the understanding of the essential in certain exceptional characters, whether evil ones
or good. In a matter of some importance I have seen a girl
wind an old lawyer about her little finger. Nor was it the
dotage of senile love. Nothing of the sort. But he knew
law better than he knew the girl's heart. Coke and Black-
stone hardly shed so much light into obscure spiritual
places as the Hebrew prophets. And who were they? Mostly recluses."

At the time my inexperience was such that I did not
quite see the drift of all this. It may be that I see it now.
And, indeed, if that lexicon which is based on Holy Writ
were any longer popular, one might with less difficulty
define and denominate certain phenomenal men. As it is,
one must turn to some authority not liable to the charge
of being tinctured with the Biblical element.

In a list of definitions included in the authentic translation of Plato, a list attributed to him, occurs this: "Natural Depravity: a depravity according to nature." A definition which though savoring of Calvinism, by no means involves Calvin's dogma as to total mankind. Evidently its intent makes it applicable but to individuals. Not many are the examples of this depravity which the gallows and jail supply. At any rate for notable instances, since these have no vulgar alloy of the brute in them, but invariably are dominated by intellectuality, one must go elsewhere. Civilization, especially if of the austerer sort, is auspicious to it. It folds itself in the mantle of respectability. It has its certain negative virtues serving as silent auxiliaries. It never allows wine to get within its guard. It is not going too far to say that it is without vices or small sins. There is a phenomenal pride in it that excludes them from anything mercenary or avaricious. In short the depravity here meant partakes nothing of the sordid or sensual. It is serious, but free from acerbity. Though no flatterer of mankind it never speaks ill of it.

But the thing which in eminent instances signalizes so exceptional a nature is this: though the man's even temper and discreet bearing would seem to intimate a mind peculiarly subject to the law of reason, not the less in his heart he would seem to riot in complete exemption from that law having apparently little to do with reason further than to employ it as an ambidexter implement for effecting the irrational. That is to say: Toward the accomplishment of an aim which in wantonness of malignity would seem to partake of the insane, he will direct a cool judgement sagacious and sound.

These men are true madmen, and of the most dangerous sort, for their lunacy is not continuous but occasional evoked by some special object; it is probably secretive, which is as much to say it is self-contained, so that when moreover, most active it is to the average mind not distinguishable from sanity, and for the reason above suggested that whatever its aims may be, and the aim is never de-

clared—the method and the outward proceeding are always
perfectly rational.

Now something such an one was Claggart, in whom was
the mania of an evil nature, not engendered by vicious
training or corrupting books or licentious living, but born
with him and innate, in short "a depravity according to
nature."

12

Lawyers, Experts, Clergy
An Episode

By the way, can it be the phenomenon, disowned or at
least concealed, that in some criminal cases puzzles the
courts? For this cause have our juries at times not only to
endure the prolonged contentions of lawyers with their
fees, but also the yet more perplexing strife of the medical
experts with theirs?—But why leave it to them? why not
subpoena (?) as well the clerical proficients? Their vocation bringing them into peculiar contact with so many
human beings, and sometimes in their least guarded hour,
in interviews very much more confidential than those of
physician and patient; this would seem to qualify them
to know something about those intricacies involved in the
question of moral responsibility; whether in a given case,
say, the crime proceeded from mania in the brain or rabies
of the heart. As to any differences among themselves these
clerical proficients might develop on the stand, these could
hardly be greater than the direct contradictions exchanged
between the remunerated medical experts.

Dark sayings are these, some will say. But why? Is it because they somewhat savor of Holy Writ in its phrase
"mysteries of iniquity"? If they do, such savor was far
enough from being intended for little will it commend
these pages to many a reader of to-day.

The point of the present story turning on the hidden nature of the master-at-arms has necessitated this chapter. With an added hint or two in connection with the incident at the mess, the resumed narrative must be left to vindicate, as it may, its own credibility.

13

Pale ire, envy and despair

That Claggart's figure was not amiss, and his face, save the chin, well moulded, has already been said. Of these favorable points he seemed not insensible, for he was not only neat but careful in his dress. But the form of Billy Budd was heroic; and if his face was without the intellectual look of the pallid Claggart's, not the less was it lit, like his, from within, though from a different source. The bonfire in his heart made luminous the rose-tan in his cheek.

In view of the marked contrast between the persons of the twain, it is more than probable that when the master-at-arms in the scene last given applied to the sailor the proverb *Handsome is as handsome does;* he there let escape an ironic inkling, not caught by the young sailors who heard it, as to what it was that had first moved him against Billy, namely, his significant personal beauty.

Now envy and antipathy passions irreconcilable in reason, nevertheless in fact may spring conjoined like Chang and Eng in one birth. Is Envy then such a monster? Well, though many an arraigned mortal has in hopes of mitigated penalty pleaded guilty to horrible actions, did ever anybody seriously confess to envy? Something there is in it universally felt to be more shameful than even felonious crime. And not only does everybody disown it but the better sort are inclined to incredulity when it is in earnest imputed to an intelligent man. But since its lodgement is in the heart not the brain, no degree of intellect supplies

a guarantee against it. But Claggart's was no vulgar form
of the passion. Nor, as directed toward Billy Budd did it
partake of that streak of apprehensive jealousy that marred
Saul's visage perturbedly brooding on the comely young
David. Claggart's envy struck deeper. If askance he eyed
the good looks, cheery health and frank enjoyment of
young life in Billy Budd, it was because these went along
with a nature that as Claggart magnetically felt, had in
its simplicity never willed malice or experienced the reac-
tionary bite of that serpent. To him, the spirit lodged
within Billy, and looking out from his welkin eyes as from
windows, that ineffability it was which made the dimple
in his dyed cheek, suppled his joints, and dancing in his
yellow curls made him preeminently the Handsome Sailor.
One person excepted the master-at-arms was perhaps the
only man in the ship intellectually capable of adequately
appreciating the moral phenomenon presented in Billy
Budd. And the insight but intensified his passion, which
assuming various secret forms within him, at times assumed that of cynic disdain—disdain of innocence—To be
nothing more than innocent! Yet in an aesthetic way he
saw the charm of it, the courageous free-and-easy temper
of it, and fain would have shared it, but he despaired of it.

With no power to annul the elemental evil in him,
though readily enough he could hide it; apprehending
the good, but powerless to be it; a nature like Claggart's
surcharged with energy as such natures almost invariably
are, what recourse is left to it but to recoil upon itself and
like the scorpion for which the Creator alone is responsible, act out to the end the part allotted it.

14

Passion, and passion in its profoundest, is not a thing demanding a palatial stage whereon to play its part. Down
among the groundlings, among the beggars and rakers of

the garbage, profound passion is enacted. And the circumstances that provoke it, however trivial or mean, are no measure of its power. In the present instance the stage is a scrubbed gun-deck, and one of the external provocations a man-of-war's-man's spilled soup.

Now when the Master-at-arms noticed whence came that greasy fluid streaming before his feet, he must have taken it—to some extent wilfully, perhaps—not for the mere accident it assuredly was, but for the sly escape of a spontaneous feeling on Billy's part more or less answering to the antipathy on his own. In effect a foolish demonstration he must have thought, and very harmless, like the futile kick of a heifer, which yet were the heifer a shod stallion, would not be so harmless. Even so was it that into the gall of Claggart's envy he infused the vitriol of his contempt. But the incident confirmed to him certain tell-tale reports purveyed to his ear by *Squeak,* one of his more cunning Corporals, a grizzled little man, so nicknamed by the sailors on account of his squeaky voice, and sharp visage ferreting about the dark corners of the lower decks after interlopers, satirically suggesting to them the idea of a rat in a cellar.

From his Chief's employing him as an implicit tool in laying little traps for the worriment of the Foretopman—for it was from the Master-at-arms that the petty persecutions heretofore adverted to had proceeded—the corporal having naturally enough concluded that his master could have no love for the sailor, made it his business, faithful understrapper that he was, to foment the ill blood by perverting to his Chief certain innocent frolics of the good natured Foretopman, besides inventing for his mouth sundry contumelious epithets he claimed to have overheard him let fall. The Master-at-arms never suspected the veracity of these reports, more especially as to the epithets, for he well knew how secretly unpopular may become a master-at-arms at least a master-at-arms of those days zealous in his function, and how the blue-jackets shoot at him in

private their raillery and wit; the nickname by which he
goes among them *(Jimmy Legs)* implying under the form
of merriment their cherished disrespect and dislike.

But in view of the greediness of hate for patrolmen it
hardly needed a purveyor to feed Claggart's passion. An
uncommon prudence is habitual with the subtler depravity, for it has everything to hide. And in case of an injury
but suspected, its secretiveness voluntarily cuts it off from
enlightenment or disillusion; and, not unreluctantly, action is taken upon surmise as upon certainty. And the re-
taliation is apt to be in monstrous disproportion to the
supposed offence; for when in anybody was revenge in its
exactions aught else but an inordinate usurer. But how
with Claggart's conscience? for though consciences are unlike as foreheads, every intelligence, not excluding the
Scriptural devils who "believe and tremble," has one. But
Claggart's conscience being but the lawyer to his will, made
ogres of trifles, probably arguing that the motive imputed
to Billy in spilling the soup just when he did, together
with the epithets alleged, these, if nothing more, made a
strong case against him; nay, justified animosity into a sort
of retributive righteousness. The Pharisee is the Guy
Fawkes prowling in the hid chambers underlying the Clag-
garts. And they can really form no conception of an unre-
ciprocated malice. Probably, the master-at-arms' clandestine persecution of Billy was started to try the temper of
the man; but it had not developed any quality in him that
enmity could make official use of or even pervert into even
plausible self-justification; so that the occurrence at the
mess, petty if it were, was a welcome one to that peculiar
conscience assigned to be the private mentor of Claggart;
And, for the rest, not improbably it put him upon new
experiments.

15

Not many days after the last incident narrated something befell Billy Budd that more gravelled him than aught that had previously occurred.

It was a warm night for the latitude; and the Foretopman, whose watch at the time was properly below, was dozing on the uppermost deck whither he had ascended from his hot hammock one of hundreds suspended so closely wedged together over a lower gun-deck that there was little or no swing to them. He lay as in the shadow of a hill-side, stretched under the lee of the *booms,* a piled ridge of spare spars amidships between foremast and mainmast and among which the ship's largest boat, the launch, was stowed. Alongside of three other slumberers from below, he lay near that end of the booms which approaches the foremast; his station aloft on duty as a foretopman being just over the deck-station of the forecastlemen, entitling him according to usage to make himself more or less at home in that neighborhood.

Presently he was stirred into semi-consciousness by somebody, who must have previously sounded the sleep of the others, touching his shoulder, and then as the Foretopman raised his head, breathing into his ear in a quick whisper, "Slip into the lee forechains, Billy; there is something in the wind. Don't speak. Quick I will meet you there;" and disappeared.

Now Billy like sundry other essentially good natured ones had some of the weaknesses inseparable from essential good nature; and among these was a reluctance, almost an incapacity of plumply saying *no* to an abrupt proposition not obviously absurd, on the face of it, nor obviously unfriendly, nor iniquitous. And being of warm blood he had not the phlegm tacitly to negative any proposition by unresponsive inaction. Like his sense of fear, his apprehension as to aught outside of the honest and natural was seldom very quick. Besides, upon the present occasion, the drowse from his sleep still hung upon him.

However it was, he mechanically rose, and sleepily wondering what could be in the wind, betook himself to the designated place, a narrow platform, one of six, outside of the high bulwarks and screened by the great dead-eyes and multiple columned lanyards of the shrouds and back-stays; and, in a great war-ship of that time, of dimensions commensurate to the hull's magnitude; a tarry balcony in short overhanging the sea, and so secluded that one mariner of the *Indomitable,* a non-conformist old tar of a serious turn, made it even in daytime his private oratory.

In this retired nook the stranger soon joined Billy Budd. There was no moon as yet; a haze obscured the star-light. He could not distinctly see the stranger's face. Yet from something in the outline and carriage, Billy took him to be, and correctly, for one of the afterguard.

"Hist! Billy," said the man in the same quick cautionary whisper as before; "You were impressed, weren't you? Well, so was I;" and he paused, as to mark the effect. But Billy not knowing exactly what to make of this said nothing. Then the other: "We are not the only impressed ones, Billy. There's a gang of us.—Couldn't you—help—at a pinch?"

"What do you mean?" demanded Billy here shaking off his drowse.

"Hist, hist!" the hurried whisper now growing husky, "see here;" and the man held up two small objects faintly twinkling in the nightlight; "see, they are yours, Billy, if you'll only—"

But Billy broke in, and in his resentful eagerness to deliver himself his vocal infirmity somewhat intruded: "D-D-Damme, I don't know what you are d-d-driving at, or what you mean, but you had better g-g-go where you belong!" For the moment the fellow, as confounded, did not stir; and Billy, springing to his feet, said "If you d-don't start I'll t-t-toss you back over the r-rail!" There was no mistaking this and the mysterious emissary decamped, disappearing in the direction of the mainmast in the shadow of the booms.

"Hallo, what's the matter?" here came growling from a forecastleman awakened from his deck-doze by Billy's raised voice. And as the foretopman reappeared and was recognized by him; "Ah, *Beauty*, is it you? Well, something must have been the matter for you st-st-stuttered."

"O," rejoined Billy, now mastering the impediment; "I found an afterguardsman in our part of the ship here and I bid him be off where he belongs."

"And is that all you did about it, foretopman?" gruffly demanded another, an irascible old fellow of brick-colored visage and hair, and who was known to his associate forecastlemen as *Red Pepper;* "Such sneaks I should like to marry to the gunner's daughter!" by that expression meaning that he would like to subject them to disciplinary castigation over a gun.

However, Billy's rendering of the matter satisfactorily accounted to these inquirers for the brief commotion, since of all the sections of a ship's company the forecastlemen, veterans for the most part and bigoted in their sea-prejudices, are the most jealous in resenting territorial encroachments, especially on the part of any of the afterguard, of whom they have but a sorry opinion, chiefly landsmen, never going aloft except to reef or furl the mainsail, and in no wise competent to handle a marlinspike or turn in a *dead-eye*, say.

16

This incident sorely puzzled Billy Budd. It was an entirely new experience; the first time in his life that he had ever been personally approached in underhand intriguing fash-

ion. Prior to this encounter he had known nothing of the
afterguardsman, the two men being stationed wide apart,
one forward and aloft during his watch, the other on deck
and aft.

What could it mean? And could they really be guineas,
those two glittering objects the interloper had held up to
his (Billy's) eyes? Where could the fellow get guineas?
Why even buttons spare buttons are not so plentiful at sea.
The more he turned the matter over, the more he was
non-plussed, and made uneasy and discomforted. In his
disgustful recoil from an overture which though he but
ill comprehended he instinctively knew must involve evil
of some sort, Billy Budd was like a young horse fresh from
the pasture suddenly inhaling a vile whiff from some chem-
ical factory and by repeated snortings tries to get it out of
his nostrils and lungs. This frame of mind barred all desire
of holding further parley with the fellow, even were it but
for the purpose of gaining some enlightenment as to his
design in approaching him. And yet he was not without
natural curiosity to see how such a visitor in the dark
would look in broad day.

He espied him the following afternoon in his first dog-
watch below one of the smokers on that forward part of
the upper gun deck allotted to the pipe. He recognized
him by his general cut and build, more than by his round
freckled face and glassy eyes of pale blue, veiled with lashes
all but white. And yet Billy was a bit uncertain whether
indeed it were he—yonder chap about his own age chatting
and laughing in free-hearted way, leaning against a gun;
a genial young fellow enough to look at, and something
of a rattle-brain, to all appearance. Rather chubby too
for a sailor even an afterguardsman. In short the last man
in the world, one would think, to be overburthened with
thoughts, especially those perilous thoughts that must
needs belong to a conspirator in any serious project, or
even to the underling of such a conspirator.

Although Billy was not aware of it, the fellow, with a

sidelong watchful glance had perceived Billy first, and then noting that Billy was looking at him, thereupon nodded a familiar sort of friendly recognition as to an old acquaintance, without interrupting the talk he was engaged in with the group of smokers. A day or two afterwards chancing in the evening promenade on a gun deck, to pass Billy, he offered a flying word of good-fellowship as it were, which by its unexpectedness, and equivocalness under the circumstances so embarrassed Billy that he knew not how to respond to it, and let it go unnoticed.

Billy was now left more at a loss than before. The ineffectual speculations into which he was led were so disturbingly alien to him that he did his best to smother them. It never entered his mind that here was a matter which from its extreme questionableness, it was his duty as a loyal blue-jacket to report in the proper quarter. And, probably, had such a step been suggested to him, he would have been deterred from taking it by the thought, one of novice-magnanimity, that it would savor overmuch of the dirty work of a tell-tale. He kept the thing to himself. Yet upon one occasion, he could not forbear a little disburdening himself to the old Dansker, tempted thereto perhaps by the influence of a balmy night when the ship lay becalmed; the twain, silent for the most part, sitting together on deck, their heads propped against the bulwarks. But it was only a partial and anonymous account that Billy gave, the unfounded scruples above referred to preventing full disclosure to anybody. Upon hearing Billy's version, the sage Dansker seemed to divine more than he was told; and after a little meditation during which his wrinkles were pursed as into a point, quite effacing for the time that quizzing expression his face sometimes wore,—"Didn't I say so, Baby Budd?"

"Say what?" demanded Billy.

"Why, *Jemmy Legs* is *down* on you."

"And what" rejoined Billy in amazement, "has *Jemmy Legs* to do with that cracked afterguardsman?"

"Ho, it was an afterguardsman then. A cat's-paw, a cat's-paw!" And with that exclamation, which, whether it had reference to a light puff of air just then coming over the calm sea, or subtler relation to the afterguardsman, there is no telling, the old Merlin gave a twisting wrench with his black teeth at his plug of tobacco, vouchsafing no reply to Billy's impetuous question, though now repeated, for it was his wont to relapse into grim silence when interrogated in skeptical sort as to any of his sententious oracles, not always very clear ones, rather partaking of that obscurity which invests most Delphic deliverances from any quarter.

Long experience had very likely brought this old man to that bitter prudence which never interferes in aught and never gives advice.

17

Yes, despite the Dansker's pithy insistence as to the Master-at-arms being at the bottom of these strange experiences of Billy on board the *Indomitable,* the young sailor was ready to ascribe them to almost anybody but the man who, to use Billy's own expression, "always had a pleasant word for him." This is to be wondered at. Yet not so much to be wondered at. In certain matters, some sailors even in mature life remain unsophisticated enough. But a young seafarer of the disposition of our athletic Foretopman, is much of a child-man. And yet a child's utter innocence is but its blank ignorance, and the innocence more or less wanes as intelligence waxes. But in Billy Budd intelligence, such as it was, had advanced, while yet his simplemindedness remained for the most part unaffected. Experience is a teacher indeed; yet did Billy's years make his experience small. Besides, he had none of that intuitive knowledge of the bad which in natures not good or incompletely so foreruns experience, and therefore may pertain, as in some instances it too clearly does pertain, even to youth.

And what could Billy know of man except of man as a mere sailor? And the old-fashioned sailor, the veritable man-before-the-mast, the sailor from boyhood up, he, though indeed of the same species as a landsman is in some respects singularly distinct from him. The sailor is frankness, the landsman is finesse. Life is not a game with the sailor, demanding the long head; no intricate game of chess where few moves are made in straightforwardness, and ends are attained by indirection; an oblique, tedious, barren game hardly worth that poor candle burnt out in playing it.

Yes, as a class, sailors are in character a juvenile race. Even their deviations are marked by juvenility. And this more especially holding true with the sailors of Billy's time. Then, too, certain things which apply to all sailors, do more pointedly operate here and there, upon the junior one. Every sailor, too is accustomed to obey orders without debating them; his life afloat is externally ruled for him; he is not brought into that promiscuous commerce with mankind where unobstructed free agency on equal terms—equal superficially, at least—soon teaches one that unless upon occasion he exercise a distrust keen in proportion to the fairness of the appearance, some foul turn may be served him. A ruled undemonstrative distrustfulness is so habitual, not with business-men so much, as with men who know their kind in less shallow relations than business, namely, certain men-of-the-world, that they come at last to employ it all but unconsciously; and some of them would very likely feel real surprise at being charged with it as one of their general characteristics.

18

But after the little matter at the mess Billy Budd no more
found himself in strange trouble at times about his hammock or his clothes-bag or what not. While, as to that
smile that occasionally sunned him, and the pleasant passing word, these were if not more frequent, yet if anything
more pronounced than before.

But for all that, there were certain other demonstrations
now. When Claggart's unobserved glance happened to
light on belted Billy rolling along the upper gun-deck in
the leisure of the second dog-watch exchanging passing
broadsides of fun with other young promenaders in the
crowd; that glance would follow the cheerful sea-Hyperion
with a settled meditative and melancholy expression, his
eyes strangely suffused with incipient feverish tears. Then
would Claggart look like the man of sorrows. Yes, and
sometimes the melancholy expression would have in it a
touch of soft yearning, as if Claggart could even have loved
Billy but for fate and ban. But this was an evanescence,
and quickly repented of, as it were, by an immitigable
look, pinching and shrivelling the visage into the momentary semblance of a wrinkled walnut. But sometimes catching sight in advance of the foretopman coming in his direction, he would, upon their nearing, step aside a little to
let him pass, dwelling upon Billy for the moment with the
glittering dental satire of a Guise. But upon any abrupt
unforeseen encounter a red light would flash forth from
his eye like a spark from an anvil in a dusk smithy. That
quick fierce light was a strange one, darted from orbs which
in repose were of a color nearest approaching a deeper
violet, the softest of shades.

Though some of these caprices of the pit could not but
be observed by their object, yet were they beyond the con-
struing of such a nature. And the *thews* of Billy were hard-

ly compatible with that sort of sensitive spiritual organisation which in some cases instinctively conveys to ignorant innocence an admonition of the proximity of the malign. He thought the Master-at-arms acted in a manner rather queer at times. That was all. But the occasional frank air and pleasant word went for what they purported to be, the young sailor never having heard as yet of the "too fair-spoken man."

Had the foretopman been conscious of having done or said anything to provoke the ill will of the official, it would have been different with him, and his sight might have been purged if not sharpened. As it was innocence was his blinder.

So was it with him in yet another matter. Two minor officers—the Armorer and Captain of the Hold, with whom he had never exchanged a word, his position in the ship not bringing him into contact with them; these men now for the first began to cast upon Billy when they chanced to encounter him, that peculiar glance which evidences that the man from whom it comes has been some way tampered with and to the prejudice of him upon whom the glance lights. Never did it occur to Billy as a thing to be noted or a thing suspicious, though he well knew the fact, that the Armorer and Captain of the Hold, with the ship's-yeoman, apothecary, and others of that grade, were by naval usage, mess-mates of the master-at-arms, men with ears convenient to his confidential tongue.

But the general popularity that our *Handsome Sailor's* manly forwardness upon occasion, and irresistible good nature indicating no mental superiority tending to excite an invidious feeling; this good will on the part of most of his shipmates made him the less to concern himself about such mute aspects toward him as those whereto allusion has just been made.

As to the afterguardsman, though Billy for reasons already given necessarily saw little of him, yet when the two did happen to meet, invariably came the fellow's off-hand

cheerful recognition, sometimes accompanied by a passing
pleasant word or two. Whatever that equivocal young person's original design may really have been, or the design
of which he might have been the deputy, certain it was
from his manner upon these occasions, that he had wholly
dropped it.

It was as if his precocity of crookedness (and every vulgar
villain is precocious) had for once deceived him, and the
man he had sought to entrap as a simpleton had, through
his very simplicity ignominiously baffled him.

But shrewd ones may opine that it was hardly possible
for Billy to refrain from going up to the afterguardsman
and bluntly demanding to know his purpose in the initial
interview, so abruptly closed in the fore-chains. Shrewd
ones may also think it but natural in Billy to set about
sounding some of the other impressed men of the ship in
order to discover what basis, if any, there was for the emissary's obscure suggestions as to plotting disaffection
aboard. Yes, the shrewd may so think. But something more,
or rather, something else than mere shrewdness is perhaps
needful for the due understanding of such a character as
Billy Budd's.

As to Claggart, the monomania in the man—if that indeed it were—as involuntarily disclosed by starts in the
manifestations detailed, yet in general covered over by his
self-contained and rational demeanor; this, like a subter-
ranean fire was eating its way deeper and deeper in him.
Something decisive must come of it.

19

After the mysterious interview in the fore-chains, the one
so abruptly ended there by Billy, nothing especially German to the story occurred until the events now about to
be narrated.

Elsewhere it has been said that in the lack of frigates (of

course better sailers than line-of-battle ships) in the English squadron up the Straits at that period, the *Indomitable* was occasionally employed not only as an available substitute for a scout, but at times on detached service of more important kind. This was not alone because of her sailing qualities, not common in a ship of her rate, but quite as much, probably, that the character of her commander, it was thought, specially adapted him for any duty where under unforeseen difficulties a prompt initiative might have to be taken in some matter demanding knowledge and ability in addition to those qualities implied in good seamanship. It was on an expedition of the latter sort, a somewhat distant one, and when the *Indomitable* was almost at her furthest remove from the fleet that in the latter part of an afternoon-watch she unexpectedly came in sight of a ship of the enemy. It proved to be a frigate. The latter perceiving through the glass that the weight of men and metal would be heavily against her, invoking her light heels crowded sail to get away. After a chace urged almost against hope and lasting until about the middle of the first dog-watch, she signally succeeded in effecting her escape.

Not long after the pursuit had been given up, and ere the excitement incident thereto had altogether waned away, the Master-at-Arms ascending from his cavernous sphere made his appearance cap in hand by the mainmast respectfully waiting the notice of Captain Vere then solitary walking the weather-side of the quarter-deck, doubtless somewhat chafed at the failure of the pursuit. The spot where Claggart stood was the place allotted to men of lesser grades seeking some more particular interview either with the officer-of-the-deck or the Captain himself. But from the latter it was not often that a sailor or petty-officer of those days would seek a hearing; only some exceptional cause, would, according to established custom, have warranted that.

Presently, just as the Commander absorbed in his reflections was on the point of turning aft in his promenade, he became sensible of Claggart's presence, and saw the doffed cap held in deferential expectancy. Here be it said that Captain Vere's personal knowledge of this petty-officer had only begun at the time of the ship's last sailing from home, Claggart then for the first, in transfer from a ship detained for repairs, supplying on board the *Indomitable* the place of a previous master-at-arms disabled and ashore.

No sooner did the Commander observe who it was that now deferentially stood awaiting his notice, than a peculiar expression came over him. It was not unlike that which uncontrollably will flit across the countenance of one at unawares encountering a person who though known to him indeed has hardly been long enough known for thorough knowledge, but something in whose aspect nevertheless now for the first provokes a vaguely repellent distaste. But coming to a stand, and resuming much of his wonted official manner, save that a sort of impatience lurked in the intonation of the opening word, he said, "Well? what is it, Master-at-Arms?"

With the air of a subordinate grieved at the necessity of being a messenger of ill tidings, and while conscientiously determined to be frank, yet equally resolved upon shunning overstatement, Claggart at this invitation or rather summons to disburthen, spoke up. What he said, conveyed in the language of no uneducated man, was to the effect following if not altogether in these words, namely, that during the chace and preparations for the possible encounter he had seen enough to convince him that at least one sailor aboard was a dangerous character in a ship mustering some who not only had taken a guilty part in the late serious troubles, but others also who, like the man in question, had entered His Majesty's service under another form than enlistment.

At this point Captain Vere with some impatience interrupted him: "Be direct, man; say impressed men."

Claggart made a gesture of subservience, and proceeded. Quite lately, he (Claggart) had begun to suspect that on the gun-decks some sort of movement prompted by the sailor in question was covertly going on, but he had not thought himself warranted in reporting the suspicion so long as it remained indistinct. But from what he had that afternoon observed in the man referred to the suspicion of something clandestine going on had advanced to a point less removed from certainty. He deeply felt, he added, the serious responsibility assumed in making a report involving such possible consequences to the individual mainly concerned, besides tending to augment those natural anxieties which every naval commander must feel in view of extraordinary outbreaks so recent as those which, he sorrowfully said it, it needed not to name.

Now at the first broaching of the matter Captain Vere taken by surprise could not wholly dissemble his disquietude. But as Claggart went on, the former's aspect changed into restiveness under something in the witness' manner in giving his testimony. However, he refrained from interrupting him. And Claggart, continuing, concluded with this:

"God forbid, your honor, that the *Indomitable's* should be the experience of the ——"

"Never mind that!" here peremptorily broke in the superior, his face altering with anger, instinctively divining the ship that the other was about to name, one in which the Nore Mutiny had assumed a singularly tragical character that for a time jeopardized the life of its commander. Under the circumstances he was indignant at the purposed allusion. When the commissioned officers themselves were on all occasions very heedful how they referred to the recent events, for a petty-officer unnecessarily to allude to them in the presence of his Captain, this struck him as a most immodest presumption. Besides, to his quick sense of self-respect, it even looked under the circumstances something like an attempt to alarm him. Nor at first was he without some surprise that one who so far as he had hitherto come under his notice had shown considerable

tact in his function should in this particular evince such
lack of it.

But these thoughts and kindred dubious ones flitting
across his mind were suddenly replaced by an intuitional
surmise which though as yet obscure in form served practically to affect his reception of the ill tidings. Certain it
is, that long versed in everything pertaining to the compli-
cated gun-deck life, which like every other form of life,
has its secret mines and dubious side, the side popularly
disclaimed, Captain Vere did not permit himself to be
unduly disturbed by the general tenor of his subordinate's
report. Furthermore, if in view of recent events prompt
action should be taken at the first palpable sign of recurring insubordination, for all that, not judicious would
it be, he thought, to keep the idea of lingering disaffection
alive by undue forwardness in crediting an informer even
if his own subordinate and charged among other things
with police surveillance of the crew. This feeling would
not perhaps have so prevailed with him were it not that
upon a prior occasion the patriotic zeal officially evinced
by Claggart had somewhat irritated him as appearing rather supersensible and strained. Furthermore something even
in the official's self-possessed and somewhat ostentatious
manner in making his specifications strangely reminded
him of a bandsman, a perjurous witness in a capital case
before a court-martial ashore of which when a lieutenant
he Captain Vere had been a member.

Now the peremptory check given to Claggart in the matter of the arrested allusion was quickly followed up by
this: "You say that there is at least one dangerous man
aboard. Name him."

"William Budd. A foretopman, your honor—"

"William Budd" repeated Captain Vere with unfeigned
astonishment; "and mean you the man that Lieutenant
Ratcliff took from the merchantman not very long ago—
the young fellow who seems to be so popular with the men
—Billy, the Handsome Sailor, as they call him?"

"The same, your honor; but for all his youth and good looks, a deep one. Not for nothing does he insinuate himself into the good will of his shipmates, since at the least all hands will at a pinch say a good word for him at all hazards. Did Lieutenant Ratcliffe happen to tell your honor of that adroit fling of Budd's, jumping up in the cutter's bow under the merchantman's stern when he was being taken off? It is even masqued by that sort of good humored air that at heart he resents his impressment. You have but noted his fair cheek. A man-trap may be under his ruddy-tipped daisies."

Now the *Handsome Sailor* as a signal figure among the crew had naturally enough attracted the Captain's attention from the first. Though in general not very demonstrative to his officers, he had congratulated Lieutenant Ratcliffe upon his good fortune in lighting on such a fine specimen of the genus homo, who in the nude might have posed for a statue of young Adam before the Fall. As to Billy's adieu to the ship *Rights-of-Man,* which the boarding lieutenant had indeed reported to him, but in a deferential way more as a good story than aught else, Captain Vere, though mistakenly understanding it as a satiric sally, had but thought so much the better of the impressed man for it; as a military sailor, admiring the spirit that could take an arbitrary enlistment so merrily and sensibly. The foretopman's conduct, too, so far as it had fallen under the Captain's notice had confirmed the first happy augury, while the new recruit's qualities as a *sailor-man* seemed to be such that he had thought of recommending him to the executive officer for promotion to a place that would more frequently bring him under his own observation, namely, the captaincy of the mizzen-top, replacing there in the starboard watch a man not so young whom partly for that reason he deemed less fitted for the post. Be it parenthesized here that since the mizzen-top-men having not to handle such breadths of heavy canvas as the lower sails on the main-mast and fore-mast, a young

man if of the right stuff not only seems best adapted to
duty there, but in fact is generally selected for the captaincy of that top, and the company under him are light
hands and often but striplings. In sum, Captain Vere had
from the beginning deemed Billy Budd to be what in the
naval parlance of the time was called a *"King's bargain"*
that is to say, for His Britannic Majesty's navy a capital
investment at small outlay or none at all.

After a brief pause during which the reminiscences
above mentioned passed vividly through his mind and he
weighed the import of Claggart's last suggestion conveyed
in the phrase "pitfall under the clover," and the more he
weighed it the less reliance he felt in the informer's good
faith. Suddenly he turned upon him and in a low voice:
"Do you come to me, Master-at-Arms, with so foggy a tale?
As to Budd, cite me an act or spoken word of his confirma-
tory of what you in general charge against him. Stay,"
drawing nearer to him "heed what you speak. Just now,
and in a case like this, there is a yard-arm-end for the false-
witness."

"Ah, your honor!" sighed Claggart mildly shaking his
shapely head as in sad deprecation of such unmerited
severity of tone. Then, bridling—erecting himself as in
virtuous self-assertion, he circumstantially alleged certain
words and acts, which collectively, if credited, led to pre-
sumptions mortally inculpating Budd. And for some of
these averments, he added, substantiating proof was not
far.

With gray eyes impatient and distrustful essaying to
fathom to the bottom Claggart's calm violet ones, Captain
Vere again heard him out; then for the moment stood
ruminating. The mood he evinced, Claggart—himself for
the time liberated from the other's scrutiny—steadily regarded with a look difficult to render,—a look curious of
the operation of his tactics, a look such as might have been
that of the spokesman of the envious children of Jacob
deceptively imposing upon the troubled patriarch the

blood-dyed coat of young Joseph.

Though something exceptional in the moral quality of Captain Vere made him, in earnest encounter with a fellow-man, a veritable touch-stone of that man's essential nature, yet now as to Claggart and what was really going on in him his feeling partook less of intuitional conviction than of strong suspicion clogged by strange dubieties. The perplexity he evinced proceeded less from aught touching the man informed against—as Claggart doubtless opined—than from considerations how best to act in regard to the informer. At first indeed he was naturally for summoning that substantiation of his allegations which Claggart said was at hand. But such a proceeding would result in the matter at once getting abroad, which in the present stage of it, he thought, might undesirably affect the ship's company. If Claggart was a false witness,—that closed the affair. And therefore before trying the accusation, he would first practically test the accuser; and he thought this could be done in a quiet undemonstrative way.

The measure he determined upon involved a shifting of the scene, a transfer to a place less exposed to observation than the broad quarter-deck. For although the few gun-room officers there at the time had, in due observance of naval etiquette, withdrawn to leeward the moment Captain Vere had begun his promenade on the deck's weather-side; and though during the colloquy with Claggart they of course ventured not to diminish the distance; and though throughout the interview Captain Vere's voice was far from high, and Claggart's silvery and low; and the wind in the cordage and the wash of the sea helped the more to put them beyond ear-shot; nevertheless, the interview's continuance already had attracted observation from some topmen aloft and other sailors in the waist or further forward.

Having determined upon his measures, Captain Vere forthwith took action. Abruptly turning to Claggart he asked "Master-at-arms, is it now Budd's watch aloft?"

"No, your honor." Whereupon, "Mr. Wilkes!" summoning the nearest midshipman, "tell Albert to come to me." Albert was the Captain's hammock-boy, a sort of sea-valet in whose discretion and fidelity his master had much confidence. The lad appeared. "You know Budd the foretopman?"

"I do, Sir."

"Go find him. It is his watch off. Manage to tell him out of earshot that he is wanted aft. Contrive it that he speaks to nobody. Keep him in talk yourself. And not till you get well aft here, not till then let him know that the place where he is wanted is my cabin. You understand. Go.— Master-at-Arms, show yourself on the decks below, and when you think it time for Albert to be coming with his man, stand by quietly to follow the sailor in."

20

Now when the foretopman found himself closeted there, as it were, in the cabin with the Captain and Claggart, he was surprised enough. But it was a surprise unaccompanied by apprehension or distrust. To an immature nature essentially honest and humane, forewarning intimations of subtler danger from one's kind come tardily if at all. The only thing that took shape in the young sailor's mind was this: Yes, the Captain, I have always thought, looks kindly upon me. Wonder if he's going to make me his coxswain. I should like that. And maybe now he is going to ask the master-at-arms about me.

"Shut the door there, sentry," said the commander; "stand without, and let nobody come in.—Now, master-at-arms, tell this man to his face what you told of him to me;" and stood prepared to scrutinize the mutually confronting visages.

With the measured step and calm collected air of an asylum-physician approaching in the public hall some patient beginning to show indications of a coming paroxysm, Claggart deliberately advanced within short range of Billy, and mesmerically looking him in the eye, briefly recapitulated the accusation.

Not at first did Billy take it in. When he did, the rose-tan of his cheek looked struck as by white leprosy. He stood like one impaled and gagged. Meanwhile the accuser's eyes removing not as yet from the blue dilated ones, underwent a phenomenal change, their wonted rich violet color blurring into a muddy purple. Those lights of human intelligence losing human expression, gelidly protruding like the alien eyes of certain uncatalogued creatures of the deep. The first mesmeric glance was one of serpent fascination; the last was as the hungry lurch of the torpedo-fish.

"Speak, man!" said Captain Vere to the transfixed one struck by his aspect even more than by Claggart's, "Speak! defend yourself." Which appeal caused but a strange dumb gesturing and gurgling in Billy; amazement at such an accusation so suddenly sprung on inexperienced nonage; this, and, it may be, horror of the accuser, serving to bring out his lurking defect and in this instance for the time intensifying it into a convulsed tongue-tie; while the intent head and entire form straining forward in an agony of ineffectual eagerness to obey the injunction to speak and defend himself, gave an expression to the face like that of a condemned Vestal priestess in the moment of being buried alive, and in the first struggle against suffocation.

Though at the time Captain Vere was quite ignorant of Billy's liability to vocal impediment, he now immediately divined it, since vividly Billy's aspect recalled to him that of a bright young schoolmate of his whom he had once seen struck by much the same startling impotence in the act of eagerly rising in the class to be foremost in response to a testing question put to it by the master. Going close up to the young sailor, and laying a soothing hand on his shoulder, he said: "There is no hurry, my boy. Take your

time, take your time." Contrary to the effect intended,
these words so fatherly in tone, doubtless touching Billy's
heart to the quick, prompted yet more violent efforts at
utterance—efforts soon ending for the time in confirming
the paralysis, and bringing to his face an expression which
was as a crucifixion to behold. The next instant, quick as
the flame from a discharged cannon at night, his right arm
shot out, and Claggart dropped to the deck. Whether in-
tentionally or but owing to the young athlete's superior
height, the blow had taken effect full upon the forehead,
so shapely and intellectual-looking a feature in the master-
at-arms; so that the body fell over lengthwise, like a heavy
plank tilted from erectness. A gasp or two, and he lay
motionless.

"Fated boy," breathed Captain Vere in tone so low as
to be almost a whisper, "what have you done! But here,
help me."

The twain raised the felled one from the loins up into a
sitting position. The spare form flexibly acquiesced, but
inertly. It was like handling a dead snake. They lowered
it back. Regaining erectness Captain Vere with one hand
covering his face stood to all appearance as impassive as
the object at his feet. Was he absorbed in taking in all the
bearings of the event and what was best not only now at
once to be done, but also in the sequel? Slowly he uncov-
ered his face; and the effect was as if the moon emerging
from eclipse should reappear with quite another aspect
than that which had gone into hiding. The father in him,
manifested towards Billy thus far in the scene, was replaced by the military disciplinarian. In his official tone
he bade the foretopman retire to a state-room aft (pointing
it out) and there remain till thence summoned. This order
Billy in silence mechanically obeyed. Then going to the
cabin-door where it opened on the quarter-deck, Captain
Vere said to the sentry without, "Tell somebody to send
Albert here." When the lad appeared his master so con-
trived it that he should not catch sight of the prone one.

"Albert," he said to him, "tell the Surgeon I wish to see him. You need not come back till called." When the Surgeon entered—a self-poised character of that grave sense and experience that hardly anything could take him aback,—Captain Vere advanced to meet him, thus unconsciously intercepting his view of Claggart and interrupting the other's wonted ceremonious salutation, said, "Nay, tell me how it is with yonder man," directing his attention to the prostrate one.

The Surgeon looked, and for all his self-command, somewhat started at the abrupt revelation. On Claggart's always pallid complexion, thick black blood was now oozing from nostril and ear. To the gazer's professional eye it was unmistakably no living man that he saw.

"Is it so then?" said Captain Vere intently watching him. "I thought it. But verify it." Whereupon the customary tests confirmed the Surgeon's first glance, who now looking up in unfeigned concern, cast a look of intense inquisitiveness upon his superior. But Captain Vere, with one hand to his brow, was standing motionless. Suddenly, catching the Surgeon's arm convulsively, he exclaimed, pointing down to the body—"It is the divine judgment on Ananias! Look!"

Disturbed by the excited manner he had never before observed in the *Indomitable's* Captain, and as yet wholly ignorant of the affair, the prudent Surgeon nevertheless held his peace, only again looking an earnest interrogation as to what it was that had resulted in such a tragedy.

But Captain Vere was now again motionless standing absorbed in thought. But again starting, he vehemently exclaimed—"Struck dead by an angel of God! Yet the angel must hang!"

At these passionate interjections, mere incoherences to the listener as yet unapprised of the antecedents, the Surgeon was profoundly discomposed. But now as recollecting himself, Captain Vere in less passionate tone briefly related the circumstances leading up to the event.

"But come; we must despatch" he added. "Help me to
remove him (meaning the body) to yonder compartment,"
designating one opposite that where the foretopman remained immured. Anew disturbed by a request that as
implying a desire for secrecy, seemed unaccountably
strange to him, there was nothing for the subordinate to
do but comply.

"Go now" said Captain Vere with something of his
wonted manner—"Go now. I shall presently call a drum-
head court. Tell the lieutenants what has happened, and
tell Mr. Mordant," meaning the captain of marines, "and
charge them to keep the matter to themselves."

21

Full of disquietude and misgiving the Surgeon left the
cabin. Was Captain Vere suddenly affected in his mind, or
was it but a transient excitement, brought about by so
strange and extraordinary a happening? As to the drum-
head court, it struck the Surgeon as impolitic, if nothing
more. The thing to do, he thought, was to place Billy
Budd in confinement and in a way dictated by usage, and
postpone further action in so extraordinary a case, to such
time as they should rejoin the squadron, and then refer it
to the Admiral. He recalled the unwonted agitation of
Captain Vere and his excited exclamations so at variance
with his normal manner. Was he unhinged? But assuming
that he is, it is not so susceptible of proof. What then can
he do? No more trying situation is conceivable than that
of an officer subordinate under a Captain whom he sus-
pects to be, not mad indeed, but yet not quite unaffected
in his intellect. To argue his order to him would be insolence. To resist him would be mutiny.

In obedience to Captain Vere he communicated what
had happened to the lieutenants and captain of marines;
saying nothing as to the Captain's state. They fully shared

his own surprise and concern. Like him too they seemed to think that such a matter should be referred to the Admiral.

22

Who in the rainbow can show the line where the violet tint ends and the orange tint begins? Distinctly we see the difference of the colors, but when exactly does the one first blendingly enter into the other? So with sanity and insanity. In pronounced cases there is no question about them. But in some supposed cases, in various degrees supposedly less pronounced, to draw the exact line of demarkation few will undertake though for a fee some professional experts will. There is nothing namable but that some men will undertake to do it for pay.

Whether Captain Vere, as the Surgeon professionally and privately surmised, was really the sudden victim of any degree of aberration, one must determine for himself by such light as this narrative may afford.

That the unhappy event which has been narrated could not have happened at a worse juncture was but too true. For it was close on the heel of the suppressed insurrections, an after-time very critical to naval authority, demanding from every English sea-commander two qualities not readily interfusable—prudence and rigor. Moreover there was something crucial in the case.

In the jugglery of circumstances preceding and attending the event on board the *Indomitable* and in the light of that martial code whereby it was formally to be judged, innocence and guilt personified in Claggart and Budd in effect changed places. In a legal view the apparent victim of the tragedy was he who had sought to victimize a man blameless; and the indisputable deed of the latter, navally regarded, constituted the most heinous of military crimes. Yet more. The essential right and wrong involved in the matter, the clearer that might be, so much the worse for the responsibility of a loyal sea-commander inasmuch as he was not authorized to determine the matter on that primitive basis.

Small wonder then that the *Indomitable's* Captain though in general a man of rapid decision, felt that circumspectness not less than promptitude was necessary. Until he could decide upon his course, and in each detail; and not only so, but until the concluding measure was upon the point of being enacted, he deemed it advisable, in view of all the circumstances to guard as much as possible against publicity. Here he may or may not have erred. Certain it is however that subsequently in the confidential talk of more than one or two gun-rooms and cabins he was not a little criticized by some officers, a fact imputed by his friends and vehemently by his cousin Jack Denton to professional jealousy of *Starry Vere*. Some imaginative ground for invidious comment there was. The maintenance of secrecy in the matter, the confining all knowledge of it for a time to the place where the homicide occurred, the quarter-deck cabin; in these particulars lurked some resemblance to the policy adopted in those tragedies of the palace which have occurred more than once in the capital founded by Peter the Barbarian.

The case indeed was such that fain would the *Indomitable's* captain have deferred taking any action whatever respecting it further than to keep the foretopman a close prisoner till the ship rejoined the squadron and then submitting the matter to the judgement of his Admiral.

But a true military officer is in one particular like a true monk. Not with more of self-abnegation will the latter keep his vows of monastic obedience than the former his vows of allegiance to martial duty.

Feeling that unless quick action was taken on it, the deed of the foretopman, so soon as it should be known on the gun-decks would tend to awaken any slumbering embers of the Nore among the crew, a sense of the urgency of the case overruled in Captain Vere every other consideration. But though a conscientious disciplinarian he was no lover of authority for mere authority's sake. Very far was he from embracing opportunities for monopolizing to himself the perils of moral responsibility none at least that could properly be referred to an official superior or shared with him by his official equals or even subordinates. So thinking he was glad it would not be at variance with usage to turn the matter over to a summary court of his own officers, reserving to himself as the one on whom the ultimate accountability would rest, the right of maintaining a supervision of it, or formally or informally interposing at need. Accordingly a drum-head court was summarily convened, he electing the individuals composing it, the First Lieutenant, the Captain of marines, and the Sailing Master.

In associating an officer of marines with the sea-lieutenants in a case having to do with a sailor the Commander perhaps deviated from general custom. He was prompted thereto by the circumstance that he took that soldier to be a judicious person, thoughtful, and not altogether incapable of grappling with a difficult case unprecedented in his prior experience. Yet even as to him he was not without some latent misgiving, for withal he was an extremely good-natured man, an enjoyer of his dinner, a sound sleeper, and inclined to obesity. A man who though he would always maintain his manhood in battle might not prove altogether reliable in a moral dilemma involving aught of the tragic. As to the First Lieutenant and the Sailing Master Captain Vere could not but be aware that though honest natures, of approved gallantry upon occasion their intelligence was mostly confined to the matter of active seamanship and the fighting demands of their profession. The court was held in the same cabin where the unfortunate affair had taken place. This cabin, the Commander's, embraced the entire area under the poop-deck. Aft, and on either side was a small state-room the one room temporarily a jail and the other a dead-house and a yet smaller compartment leaving a space between, expanding forward into a goodly oblong of length coinciding with the ship's beam. A skylight of moderate dimension was overhead and at each end of the oblong space were two sashed port-hole windows easily convertible back into embrasures for short carronades.

All being quickly in readiness, Billy Budd was arraigned, Captain Vere necessarily appearing as the sole witness in the case, and as such temporarily sinking his rank, though singularly maintaining it in a matter apparently trivial, namely, that he testified from the ship's weather-side with that object having caused the court to sit on the lee-side. Concisely he narrated all that had led up to the catastrophe, omitting nothing in Claggart's accusation and deposing as to the manner in which the prisoner had received it. At this testimony the three officers glanced with no little surprise at Billy Budd, the last man they would have suspected either of the mutinous design alleged by Claggart or the undeniable deed he himself had done.

The First Lieutenant taking judicial primacy and turning toward the prisoner, said, "Captain Vere has spoken. Is it or is it not as Captain Vere says?" In response came syllables not so much impeded in the utterance as might have been anticipated. They were these: "Captain Vere tells the truth. It is just as Captain Vere says, but it is not as the Master-in-Arms said. I have eaten the King's bread and I am true to the King."

"I believe you, my man," said the witness his voice indicating a suppressed emotion not otherwise betrayed.

"God will bless you for that, Your Honor!" not without stammering said Billy, and all but broke down. But immediately was recalled to self-control by another question, to which with the same emotional difficulty of utterance he said "No, there was no malice between us. I never bore malice against the Master-at-arms. I am sorry that he is dead. I did not mean to kill him. Could I have used my tongue I would not have struck him. But he foully lied to my face and in presence of my Captain, and I had to say something, and I could only say it with a blow, God help me!"

In the impulsive above-board manner of the frank one the court saw confirmed all that was implied in words that just previously had perplexed them coming as they did from the testifier to the tragedy and promptly following Billy's impassioned disclaimer of mutinous intent—Captain Vere's words, "I believe you, my man."

Next it was asked of him whether he knew of or suspected aught savoring of incipient trouble (meaning mutiny, though the explicit term was avoided) going on in any section of the ship's company.

The reply lingered. This was naturally imputed by the court to the same vocal embarrassment which had retarded or obstructed previous answers. But in main it was otherwise here; the question immediately recalling to Billy's mind the interview with the afterguardsman in the forechains. But an innate repugnance to playing a part at all approaching that of an informer against one's own shipmates—the same erring sense of uninstructed honor which had stood in the way of his reporting the matter at the time though as a loyal man-of-war-man it was incumbent on him and failure so to do if charged against him and proven, would have subjected him to the heaviest of penalties; this, with the blind feeling now his, that nothing really was being hatched, prevailed with him. When the answer came it was a negative.

"One question more," said the officer of marines now first speaking and with a troubled earnestness, "You tell us that what the Master-at-arms said against you was a lie. Now why should he have so lied, so maliciously lied, since you declare there was no malice between you?"

At that question unintentionally touching on a spiritual sphere wholly obscure to Billy's thoughts, he was non-plussed, evincing a confusion indeed that some observers, such as can readily be imagined, would have construed into involuntary evidence of hidden guilt. Nevertheless he strove some way to answer, but all at once relinquished the vain endeavor, at the same time turning an appealing glance towards Captain Vere as deeming him his best helper and friend. Captain Vere who had been seated for a time rose to his feet, addressing the interrogator. "The question you put to him comes naturally enough. But how can he rightly answer it? or anybody else? unless indeed it be he who lies within there" designating the compartment where lay the corpse. "But the prone one there will not rise to our summons. In effect, though, as it seems to me, the point you make is hardly material. Quite aside from any conceivable motive actuating the Master-at-arms, and irrespective of the provocation to the blow, a martial court must needs in the present case confine its attention to the blow's consequence, which consequence justly is to be deemed not otherwise than as the striker's deed."

This utterance the full significance of which it was not at all likely that Billy took in, nevertheless caused him to turn a wistful interrogative look toward the speaker, a look in its dumb expressiveness not unlike that which a dog of generous breed might turn upon his master seeking in his face some elucidation of a previous gesture ambiguous to the canine intelligence. Nor was the same utterance without marked effect upon the three officers, more especially the soldier. Couched in it seemed to them a meaning unanticipated, involving a prejudgement on the speaker's part. It served to augment a mental disturbance previously evident enough.

The soldier once more spoke; in a tone of suggestive dubiety addressing at once his associates and Captain Vere: "Nobody is present—none of the ship's company, I mean, who might shed lateral light, if any is to be had, upon what remains mysterious in this matter."

"That is thoughtfully put" said Captain Vere; "I see

your drift. Ay, there is a mystery; but, to use a Scriptural phrase, it is 'a mystery of iniquity,' a matter for psychologic theologians to discuss. But what has a military court to do with it? Not to add that for us any possible investigation of it is cut off by the lasting tongue-tie of—him—in yonder," again designating the mortuary state-room. "The prisoner's deed,—with that alone we have to do."

To this, and particularly the closing reiteration, the marine soldier knowing not how aptly to reply, sadly abstained from saying aught. The First Lieutenant who at the outset had not unnaturally assumed primacy in the court, now overrulingly instructed by a glance from Captain Vere, a glance more effective than words, resumed that primacy. Turning to the prisoner, "Budd," he said, and scarce in equable tones, "Budd, if you have aught further to say for yourself, say it now."

Upon this the young sailor turned another quick glance toward Captain Vere; then, as taking a hint from that aspect, a hint confirming his own instinct that silence was now best, replied to the Lieutenant, "I have said all, Sir."

The marine—the same who had been the sentinel without the cabin-door at the time that the foretopman followed by the master-at-arms, entered it—he, standing by the sailor throughout these judicial proceedings, was now directed to take him back to the after compartment originally assigned to the prisoner and his custodian. As the twain disappeared from view, the three officers as partially liberated from some inward constraint associated with Billy's mere presence, simultaneously stirred in their seats. They exchanged looks of troubled indecision, yet feeling that decide they must and without long delay. For Captain Vere, he for the time stood unconsciously with his back toward them, apparently in one of his absent fits, gazing out from a sashed port-hole to windward upon the monotonous blank of the twilight sea. But the court's silence continuing, broken only at moments by brief consultations in low earnest tones, this seemed to assure him and encourage

him. Turning, he to-and-fro paced the cabin athwart; in
the returning ascent to windward, climbing the slant deck
in the ship's lee roll; without knowing it symbolizing thus
in his action a mind resolute to surmount difficulties even
if against primitive instincts strong as the wind and the
sea. Presently he came to a stand before the three. After
scanning their faces he stood less as mustering his thoughts
for expression, than as one inly deliberating how best to
put them to well-meaning men not intellectually mature,
men with whom it was necessary to demonstrate certain
principles that were axioms to himself. Similar impatience
as to talking is perhaps one reason that deters some minds
from addressing any popular assemblies.

When speak he did, something both in the substance of
what he said and his manner of saying it, showed the influence of unshared studies modifying and tempering the
practical training of an active career. This, along with his
phraseology now and then was suggestive of the grounds
whereon rested that imputation of a certain pedantry socially alleged against him by certain naval men of wholly
practical cast, captains who nevertheless would frankly
concede that His Majesty's navy mustered no more efficient
officer of their grade than *Starry Vere*.

What he said was to this effect: "Hitherto I have been
but the witness, little more; and I should hardly think
now to take another tone, that of your coadjutor, for the
time, did I not perceive in you,—at the crisis too—a troubled hesitancy, proceeding, I doubt not from the clash of
military duty with moral scruple—scruple vitalized by
compassion. For the compassion how can I otherwise than
share it. But, mindful of paramount obligations I strive
against scruples that may tend to enervate decision. Not,
gentlemen, that I hide from myself that the case is an exceptional one. Speculatively regarded, it well might be
referred to a jury of casuists. But for us here acting not
as casuists or moralists, it is a case practical, and under
martial law practically to be dealt with.

"But your scruples: do they move as in a dusk? Challenge them. Make them advance and declare themselves. Come now: do they import something like this: If, mindless of palliating circumstances, we are bound to regard the death of the Master-at-arms as the prisoner's deed, then does that deed constitute a capital crime whereof the penalty is a mortal one. But in natural justice is nothing but the prisoner's overt act to be considered? How can we adjudge to summary and shameful death a fellow-creature innocent before God, and whom we feel to be so?—Does that state it aright? You sign sad assent. Well, I too feel that, the full force of that. It is Nature. But do these buttons that we wear attest that our allegiance is to Nature? No, to the King. Though the ocean, which is inviolate Nature primeval, though this be the element where we move and have our being as sailors, yet as the King's officers lies our duty in a sphere correspondingly natural? So little is that true, that in receiving our commissions we in the most important regards ceased to be natural free-agents. When war is declared are we the commissioned fighters previously consulted? We fight at command. If our judgements approve the war, that is but coincidence. So in other particulars. So now. For suppose condemnation to follow these present proceedings. Would it be so much we ourselves that would condemn as it would be martial law operating through us? For that law and the rigour of it, we are not responsible. Our vowed responsibility is in this: That however pitilessly that law may operate, we nevertheless adhere to it and administer it.

"But the exceptional in the matter moves the hearts within you. Even so too is mine moved. But let not warm hearts betray heads that should be cool. Ashore in a criminal case will an upright judge allow himself off the bench to be waylaid by some tender kinswoman of the accused seeking to touch him with her tearful plea? Well the heart here denotes the feminine in man, is as that piteous woman, and hard though it be, she must here be ruled out."

He paused, earnestly studying them for a moment; then resumed.

"But something in your aspect seems to urge that it is not solely the heart that moves in you, but also the conscience, the private conscience. But tell me whether or not, occupying the position we do, private conscience should not yield to that imperial one formulated in the code under which alone we officially proceed?"

Here the three men moved in their seats, less convinced than agitated by the course of an argument troubling but the more the spontaneous conflict within.

Perceiving which, the speaker paused for a moment; then abruptly changing his tone, went on.

"To steady us a bit, let us recur to the facts.—In wartime at sea a man-of-war's-man strikes his superior in grade, and the blow kills. Apart from its effect the blow itself is, according to the Articles of War, a capital crime. Furthermore—"

"Ay, Sir," emotionally broke in the officer of marines, "in one sense it was. But surely Budd purposed neither mutiny nor homicide."

"Surely not, my good man. And before a court less arbitrary and more merciful than a martial one, that plea would largely extenuate. At the Last Assizes it shall acquit. But how here? We proceed under the law of the Mutiny Act. In feature no child can resemble his father more than that Act resembles in spirit the thing from which it derives—War. In His Majesty's service—in this ship indeed—there are Englishmen forced to fight for the King against their will. Against their conscience, for aught we know. Though as their fellow-creatures some of us may appreciate their position, yet as navy officers, what reck we of it? Still less recks the enemy. Our impressed men he would fain cut down in the same swath with our volunteers. As regards the enemy's naval conscripts, some of whom may even share our own abhorrence of the regicidal French Directory, it is the same on our side. War looks but to the frontage, the appearance. And the Mutiny Act, War's child, takes after the father. Budd's intent or non-intent is nothing to the purpose.

"But while, put to it by those anxieties in you which I can not but respect, I only repeat myself—while thus strangely we prolong proceedings that should be summary —the enemy may be sighted and an engagement result. We must do; and one of two things must we do—condemn or let go."

"Can we not convict and yet mitigate the penalty?" asked the junior Lieutenant here speaking, and falteringly, for the first.

"Lieutenant, were that clearly lawful for us under the circumstances consider the consequences of such clemency. The people" (meaning the ship's company) "have native-sense; most of them are familiar with our naval usage and tradition; and how would they take it? Even could you explain to them—which our official position forbids—they, long moulded by arbitrary discipline have not that kind of intelligent responsiveness that might qualify them to comprehend and discriminate. No, to the people the fore-topman's deed however it be worded in the announcement will be plain homicide committed in a flagrant act of mutiny. What penalty for that should follow, they know. But it does not follow. *Why?* they will ruminate. You know what sailors are. Will they not revert to the recent outbreak at the Nore? Ay. They know the well-founded alarm—the panic it struck throughout England. Your clement sentence they would account pusillanimous. They would think that we flinch, that we are afraid of them—afraid of practising a lawful rigor singularly demanded at this juncture lest it should provoke new troubles. What shame to us such a conjecture on their part, and how deadly to discipline. You see then, whither prompted by duty and the law I steadfastly drive. But I beseech you, my friends, do not take me amiss. I feel as you do for this unfortunate boy. But did he know our hearts, I take him to be of that generous nature that he would feel even for us on whom in this military necessity so heavy a compulsion is laid."

With that, crossing the deck he resumed his place by the sashed port-hole, tacitly leaving the three to come to a decision. On the cabin's opposite side the troubled court sat silent. Loyal lieges, plain and practical, though at bottom they dissented from some points Captain Vere had put to them, they were without the faculty, hardly had the inclination to gainsay one whom they felt to be an earnest man, one too not less their superior in mind than in naval rank. But it is not improbable that even such of his words as were not without influence over them, less came home to them than his closing appeal to their instinct as sea-officers in the forethought he threw out as to the practical consequences to discipline, considering the unconfirmed tone of the fleet at the time, should a man-of-war's-man's violent killing at sea of a superior in grade be allowed to pass for aught else than a capital crime demanding prompt infliction of the penalty.

Not unlikely they were brought to something more or less akin to that harassed frame of mind which in the year 1842 actuated the commander of the U.S. brig-of-war *Somers* to resolve, under the so-called Articles of War, Articles modelled upon the English Mutiny Act, to resolve upon the execution at sea of a midshipman and two petty-officers as mutineers designing the seizure of the brig. Which resolution was carried out though in a time of peace and within not many days sail of home. An act vindicated by a naval court of inquiry subsequently convened ashore. History, and here cited without comment. True, the circumstances on board the *Somers* were different from those on board the *Indomitable*. But the urgency felt, well-warranted or otherwise, was much the same.

Says a writer whom few know, "Forty years after a battle it is easy for a non-combatant to reason about how it ought to have been fought. It is another thing personally and under fire to direct the fighting while involved in the obscuring smoke of it. Much so with respect to other emergencies involving considerations both practical and moral, and when it is imperative promptly to act. The greater the fog the more it imperils the steamer, and speed is put on though at the hazard of running somebody down. Little ween the snug card-players in the cabin of the responsibilities of the sleepless man on the bridge."

In brief, Billy Budd was formally convicted and sentenced to be hung at the yard-arm in the early morning-watch, it being now night. Otherwise, as is customary in such cases, the sentence would forthwith have been carried out. In war-time on the field or in the fleet, a mortal punishment decreed by a drum-head court—on the field sometimes decreed by but a nod from the General—follows without delay on the heel of conviction without appeal.

23

It was Captain Vere himself who of his own motion communicated the finding of the court to the prisoner; for that purpose going to the compartment where he was in custody and bidding the marine there to withdraw for the time.

Beyond the communication of the sentence what took place at this interview was never known. But in view of the character of the twain briefly closeted in that stateroom, each radically sharing in the rarer qualities of our nature—so rare indeed as to be all but incredible to average minds however much cultivated—some conjectures may be ventured.

It would have been in consonance with the spirit of Captain Vere should he on this occasion have concealed nothing from the condemned one—should he indeed have frankly disclosed to him the part he himself had played in bringing about the decision, at the same time revealing his actuating motives. On Billy's side it is not improbable

that such a confession would have been received in much
the same spirit that prompted it. Not without a sort of joy
indeed he might have appreciated the brave opinion of
him implied in his Captain making such a confidant of
him. Nor, as to the sentence itself could he have been insensible that it was imparted to him as to one not afraid
to die. Even more may have been. Captain Vere in the
end may have developed the passion sometimes latent
under an exterior stoical or indifferent. He was old enough
to have been Billy's father. The austere devotee of military
duty letting himself melt back into what remains primeval
in our formalized humanity may in the end have caught
Billy to his heart even as Abraham may have caught young
Isaac on the brink of resolutely offering him up in obedience to the exacting behest. But there is no telling the sacra-
ment, seldom if in any case revealed to the gadding world
wherever under circumstances at all akin to those here
attempted to be set forth two of great Nature's nobler
order embrace. There is privacy at the time, inviolable
to the survivor, and holy oblivion the sequel to each di-
viner magnanimity, providentially covers all at last.

The first to encounter Captain Vere in act of leaving the
compartment was the senior Lieutenant. The fact he beheld, for the moment one expressive of the agony of the
strong, was to that officer, though a man of fifty, a startling
revelation. That the condemned one suffered less than he
who mainly had effected the condemnation was apparently
indicated by the former's exclamation in the scene soon
perforce to be touched upon.

24

Of a series of incidents within a brief term rapidly following each other, the adequate narration may take up a term
less brief, especially if explanation or comment here and
there seem requisite to the better understanding of such

incidents. Between the entrance into the cabin of him who never left it alive, and him who when he did leave it left it as one condemned to die; between this and the closeted interview just given less than an hour and a half had elapsed. It was an interval long enough however to awaken speculations among no few of the ship's company as to what it was that could be detaining in the cabin the master-at-arms and the sailor; for a rumor that both of them had been seen to enter it and neither of them had been seen to emerge, this rumor had got abroad upon the gun-decks and in the tops; the people of a great warship being in one respect like villagers taking microscopic note of every outward movement or non-movement going on. When therefore in weather not at all tempestuous all hands were called in the second dog-watch, a summons under such circumstances not usual in those hours, the crew were not wholly unprepared for some announcement extraordinary, one having connection too with the continued absence of the two men from their wonted haunts.

There was a moderate sea at the time; and the moon, newly risen and near to being at its full, silvered the white spar-deck wherever not blotted by the clear-cut shadows horizontally thrown of fixtures and moving men. On either side the quarter-deck the marine guard under arms was drawn up; and Captain Vere standing in his place surrounded by all the ward-room officers, addressed his men. In so doing his manner showed neither more nor less than that properly pertaining to his supreme position aboard his own ship. In clear terms and concise he told them what had taken place in the cabin; that the master-at-arms was dead; that he who had killed him had been already tried by a summary court and condemned to death; and that the execution would take place in the early morning watch. The word *mutiny* was not named in what he said. He refrained too from making the occasion an opportunity for any preachment as to the maintenance of discipline, thinking perhaps that under existing circumstances in the navy the consequence of violating discipline should be made to speak for itself.

Their captain's announcement was listened to by the throng of standing sailors in a dumbness like that of a seated congregation of believers in hell listening to the clergyman's announcement of his Calvinistic text.

At the close, however, a confused murmur went up. It began to wax. All but instantly, then, at a sign, it was pierced and suppressed by shrill whistles of the Boatswain and his Mates piping down one watch.

To be prepared for burial Claggart's body was delivered to certain petty-officers of his mess. And here, not to clog the sequel with lateral matters, it may be added that at a suitable hour, the Master-at-Arms was committed to the sea with every funeral honor properly belonging to his naval grade.

In this proceeding as in every public one growing out of the tragedy strict adherence to usage was observed. Nor in any point could it have been at all deviated from, either with respect to Claggart or Billy Budd without begetting undesirable speculations in the ship's company, sailors, and more particularly men-of-war's men, being of all men the greatest sticklers for usage.

For similar cause, all communication between Captain Vere and the condemned one ended with the closeted interview already given, the latter being now surrendered to the ordinary routine preliminary to the end. This transfer under guard from the Captain's quarters was effected without unusual precautions—at least no visible ones.

If possible not to let the men so much as surmise that their officers anticipate aught amiss from them is the tacit rule in a military ship. And the more that some sort of trouble should really be apprehended the more do the officers keep that apprehension to themselves; though not the less unostentatious vigilance may be augmented.

In the present instance the sentry placed over the prisoner had strict orders to let no one have communication with him but the Chaplain. And certain unobtrusive measures were taken absolutely to insure this point.

25

In a seventy-four of the old order the deck known as the upper gun-deck was the one covered over by the spar-deck which last though not without its armament was for the most part exposed to the weather. In general it was at all hours free from hammocks; those of the crew swinging on the lower gun-deck, and berth-deck, the latter being not only a dormitory but also the place for the stowing of the sailors' bags, and on both sides lined with the large chests or movable pantries of the many messes of the men.

On the starboard side of the *Indomitable's* upper gun-deck, behold Billy Budd under sentry lying prone in irons in one of the bays formed by the regular spacing of the guns comprising the batteries on either side. All these pieces were of the heavier calibre of that period. Mounted on lumbering wooden carriages they were hampered with cumbersome harness of breechen and strong side-tackles for running them out. Guns and carriages, together with the long rammers and shorter lintstocks lodged in loops overhead—all these, as customary, were painted black; and the heavy hempen breechens tarred to the same tint, wore the like livery of the undertakers. In contrast with the funereal hue of these surroundings the prone sailor's exterior apparel, white *jumper* and white duck trousers, each more or less soiled, dimly glimmered in the obscure light of the bay like a patch of discolored snow in early April lingering at some upland cave's black mouth. In effect he is already in his shroud or the garments that shall serve him in lieu of one. Over him but scarce illuminating him, two battle-lanterns swing from two massive beams of the deck above. Fed with the oil supplied by the war-contractors (whose gains, honest or otherwise, are in every land

an anticipated portion of the harvest of death) with flickering splashes of dirty yellow light they pollute the pale
moonshine all but ineffectually struggling in obstructed
flecks through the open ports from which the tompioned
cannon protrude. Other lanterns at intervals serve but to
bring out somewhat the obscurer bays which like small
confessionals or side-chapels in a cathedral branch from
the long dim-vistaed broad aisle between the two batteries
of that covered tier.

Such was the deck where now lay the Handsome Sailor.
Through the rose-tan of his complexion, no pallor could
have shown. It would have taken days of sequestration
from the winds and the sun to have brought about the
effacement of that. But the skeleton in the cheek-bone at
the point of its angle was just beginning delicately to be
defined under the warm-tinted skin. In fervid hearts self-
contained some brief experiences devour our human tissue
as secret fire in a ship's hold consumes cotton in the bale.

But now lying between the two guns, as nipped in the
vice of fate, Billy's agony, mainly proceeding from a generous young heart's virgin experience of the diabolical
incarnate and effective in some men—the tension of that
agony was over now. It survived not the something healing
in the closeted interview with Captain Vere. Without
movement, he lay as in a trance. That adolescent expression previously noted as his, taking on something akin to
the look of a slumbering child in the cradle when the
warm hearth-glow of the still chamber at night plays on
the dimples that at whiles mysteriously form in the cheek,
silently coming and going there. For now and then in the
gyved one's trance a serene happy light born of some wandering reminiscence or dream would diffuse itself over his
face, and then wane away only anew to return.

The Chaplain coming to see him and finding him thus,
and perceiving no sign that he was conscious of his presence, attentively regarded him for a space, then slipping
aside, withdrew for the time, peradventure feeling that

even he the minister of Christ though receiving his stipend from Mars had no consolation to proffer which could result in a peace transcending that which he beheld. But in the small hours he came again. And the prisoner now awake to his surroundings noticed his approach and civilly, all but cheerfully, welcomed him. But it was to little purpose that in the interview following the good man sought to bring Billy Budd to some godly understanding that he must die, and at dawn. True, Billy himself freely referred to his death as a thing close at hand; but it was something in the way that children will refer to death in general, who yet among their other sports will play a funeral with hearse and mourners.

Not that like children Billy was incapable of conceiving what death really is. No, but he was wholly without irrational fear of it, a fear more prevalent in highly civilized communities than those so-called barbarous ones which in all respects stand nearer to unadulterate Nature. And, as elsewhere said, a barbarian Billy radically was; as much so, for all the costume, as his countrymen the British captives, living trophies, made to march in the Roman triumph of Germanicus. Quite as much so as those later barbarians, young men probably, and picked specimens among the earlier British converts to Christianity, at least nominally such and taken to Rome (as today converts from lesser isles of the sea may be taken to London) of whom the Pope of that time, admiring the strangeness of their personal beauty so unlike the Italian stamp, their clear ruddy complexion and curled flaxen locks, exclaimed, "Angles" (meaning *English* the modern derivative) "Angles do you call them? And is it because they look so like angels?" Had it been later in time one would think that the Pope had in mind Fra Angelico's seraphs some of whom, plucking apples in gardens of the Hesperides have the faint rose-bud complexion of the more beautiful English girls.

If in vain the good Chaplain sought to impress the young

barbarian with ideas of death akin to those conveyed in
the skull, dial, and cross-bones on old tombstones; equally
futile to all appearance were his efforts to bring home to
him the thought of salvation and a Saviour. Billy listened,
but less out of awe or reverence perhaps than from a certain natural politeness; doubtless at bottom regarding all
that in much the same way that most mariners of his class
take any discourse abstract or out of the common tone of
the work-a-day world. And this sailor-way of taking clerical
discourse is not wholly unlike the way in which the pioneer
of Christianity full of transcendent miracles was received
long ago on tropic isles by any superior *savage* so called—
a Tahitian say of Captain Cook's time or shortly after that
time. Out of natural courtesy he received, but did not appropriate. It was like a gift placed in the palm of an out-
reached hand upon which the fingers do not close.

But the *Indomitable's* Chaplain was a discreet man possessing the good sense of a good heart. So he insisted not
in his vocation here. At the instance of Captain Vere, a
lieutenant had apprised him of pretty much everything as
to Billy; and since he felt that innocence was even a better
thing than religion wherewith to go to Judgement, he
reluctantly withdrew; but in his emotion not without first
performing an act strange enough in an Englishman, and
under the circumstances yet more so in any regular priest.
Stooping over, he kissed on the fair cheek his fellow-man,
a felon in martial law, one who though on the confines of
death he felt he could never convert to a dogma; nor for all
that did he fear for his future.

Marvel not that having been made acquainted with the
young sailor's essential innocence (an irruption of heretic
thought hard to suppress) the worthy man lifted not a
finger to avert the doom of such a martyr to martial discipline. So to do would not only have been as idle as invoking the desert, but would also have been an audacious
transgression of the bounds of his function, one as exactly
prescribed to him by military law as that of the boatswain

or any other naval officer. Bluntly put, a chaplain, is the
minister of the Prince of Peace serving in the host of the
God of War—Mars. As such, he is as incongruous as that
musket of Blücher etc. at Christmas. Why then is he there?
Because he indirectly subserves the purpose attested by the
cannon; because too he lends the sanction of the religion
of the meek to that which practically is the abrogation of
everything but brute Force.

26

The night so luminous on the spar-deck but otherwise on
the cavernous ones below, levels so like the tiered galleries
in a coal-mine—the luminous night passed away. But, like
the prophet in the chariot disappearing in heaven and
dropping his mantle to Elisha, the withdrawing night
transferred its pale robe to the breaking day. A meek shy
light appeared in the East, where stretched a diaphanous
fleece of white furrowed vapor. That light slowly waxed.
Suddenly *eight bells* was struck aft, responded to by one
louder metallic stroke from forward. It was four o'clock
in the morning. Instantly the silver whistles were heard
summoning all hands to witness punishment. Up through
the great hatchways rimmed with racks of heavy shot, the
watch below came pouring overspreading with the watch
already on deck the space between the mainmast and fore-
mast including that occupied by the capacious *launch* and
the black booms tiered on either side of it, boat and booms
making a summit of observation for the powder-boys and
younger tars. A different group comprising one watch of
topmen leaned over the rail of that sea-balcony, no small
one in a seventy-four, looking down on the crowd below.
Man or boy none spake but in whisper, and few spake at
all. Captain Vere—as before, the central figure among the
assembled commissioned officers—stood nigh the break of
the poop-deck facing forward. Just below him on the

quarter-deck the marines in full equipment were drawn up much as at the scene of the promulgated sentence.

At sea in the old time, the execution by halter of a military sailor was generally from the fore-yard. In the present instance, for special reasons the main-yard was assigned. Under an arm of that weather or lee ? yard the prisoner was presently brought up, the Chaplain attending him. It was noted at the time and remarked upon afterwards, that in this final scene the good man evinced little or nothing of the perfunctory. Brief speech indeed he had with the condemned one, but the genuine Gospel was less on his tongue than in his aspect and manner towards him. The final preparations personal to the latter being speedily brought to an end by two boatswain's-mates, the consummation impended. Billy stood facing aft. At the penultimate moment, his words, his only ones, words wholly unobstructed in the utterance were these—"God bless Captain Vere!" Syllables so unanticipated coming from one with the ignominious hemp about his neck—a conventional felon's benediction directed aft towards the quarters of honor; syllables too delivered in the clear melody of a singing-bird on the point of launching from the twig, had a phenomenal effect, not unenhanced by the rare personal beauty of the young sailor spiritualized now through late experiences so poignantly profound.

Without volition as it were, as if indeed the ship's populace were but the vehicles of some vocal current electric, with one voice from alow and aloft came a resonant sympathetic echo—"God bless Captain Vere!" And yet at that instant Billy alone must have been in their hearts, even as he was in their eyes.

At the pronounced words and the spontaneous echo that voluminously rebounded them, Captain Vere, either through stoic self-control or a sort of momentary paralysis induced by emotional shock, stood erectly rigid as a musket in the ship-armorer's rack.

The hull deliberately recovering from the periodic roll

to leeward was just regaining an even keel, when the last signal a preconcerted dumb one was given. At the same moment it chanced that the vapory fleece hanging low in the East, was shot through with a soft glory as of the fleece of the Lamb of God seen in mystical vision and simultaneously therewith, watched by the wedged mass of upturned faces, Billy ascended; and, ascending, took the full rose of the dawn.

In the pinioned figure, arrived at the yard-end, to the wonder of all no motion was apparent, none save that created by the ship's motion, in moderate weather so majestic in a great ship ponderously cannoned.

27

A Digression

When some days afterward in reference to the singularity just mentioned, the Purser a rather ruddy rotund person more accurate as an accountant than profound as a philosopher, said at mess to the Surgeon, "What testimony to the force lodged in will-power" the latter, saturnine, spare and tall, one in whom a discreet causticity went along with a manner less genial than polite, replied, "Your pardon, Mr. Purser. In a hanging scientifically conducted—and under special orders I myself directed how Budd's was to be effected—any movement following the completed suspension and originating in the body suspended, such movement indicates mechanical spasm in the muscular system. Hence the absence of that is no more attributable to will-power as you call it than to horse-power—begging your pardon."

"But this muscular spasm you speak of, is not that in a degree more or less invariable in these cases?"

"Assuredly so, Mr. Purser."

"How then, my good sir, do you account for its absence

in this instance?"

"Mr. Purser, it is clear that your sense of the singularity in this matter equals not mine. You account for it by what you call will-power a term not yet included in the lexicon of science. For me I do not, with my present knowledge pretend to account for it at all. Even should we assume the hypothesis that at the first touch of the halyards the action of Budd's heart, intensified by extraordinary emotion at its climax, abruptly stopt—much like a watch when in carelessly winding it up you strain at the finish, thus snapping the chain—even under that hypothesis how account for the phenomenon that followed?"

"You admit then that the absence of spasmodic movement was phenomenal."

"It was phenomenal, Mr. Purser, in the sense that it was an appearance the cause of which is not immediately to be assigned."

"But tell me, my dear Sir," pertinaciously continued the other, "was the man's death effected by the halter, or was it a species of euthanasia?"

"*Euthanasia,* Mr. Purser, is something like your *will-power*: I doubt its authenticity as a scientific term—begging your pardon again. It is at once imaginative and metaphysical,—in short, Greek. But" abruptly changing his tone "there is a case in the sick-bay that I do not care to leave to my assistants. Beg your pardon, but excuse me." And rising from the mess he formally withdrew.

28

The silence at the moment of execution and for a moment or two continuing thereafter, a silence but emphasized by the regular wash of the sea against the hull or the flutter of a sail caused by the helmsman's eyes being tempted astray, this emphasized silence was gradually disturbed by a sound not easily to be verbally rendered. Whoever has heard the freshet-wave of a torrent suddenly swelled by pouring showers in tropical mountains, showers not shared by the plain; whoever has heard the first muffled murmur of its sloping advance through precipitous woods, may form some conception of the sound now heard. The seeming remoteness of its source was because of its murmurous indistinctness since it came from close-by, even from the men massed on the ship's open deck. Being inarticulate, it was dubious in significance further than it seemed to indicate some capricious revulsion of thought or feeling such as mobs ashore are liable to, in the present instance possibly implying a sullen revocation on the men's part of their involuntary echoing of Billy's benediction. But ere the murmur had time to wax into clamor it was met by a strategic command, the more telling that it came with abrupt unexpectedness.

"Pipe down the starboard watch Boatswain, and see that they go."

Shrill as the shriek of the sea-hawk the whistles of the Boatswain and his Mates pierced that ominous low sound, dissipating it; and yielding to the mechanism of discipline the throng was thinned by one half. For the remainder most of them were set to temporary employments connected with trimming the yards and so forth, business readily to be got up to serve occasion by any officer-of-the-deck.

Now each proceeding that follows a mortal sentence pronounced at sea by a drum-head court is characterised by promptitude not perceptibly merging into hurry, though bordering that. The hammock, the one which had been Billy's bed when alive, having already been ballasted with shot and otherwise prepared to serve for his canvas coffin, the last offices of the sea-undertakers, the Sail-maker's Mates, were now speedily completed. When everything was in readiness a second call for all hands made necessary by the strategic movement before mentioned was sounded and now to witness burial.

The details of this closing formality it needs not to give. But when the tilted plank let slide its freight into the sea, a second strange human murmur was heard, blended now with another inarticulate sound proceeding from certain larger sea-fowl whose attention having been attracted by the peculiar commotion in the water resulting from the heavy sloped dive of the shotted hammock into the sea, flew screaming to the spot. So near the hull did they come, that the stridor or bony creak of their gaunt double-jointed pinions was audible. As the ship under light airs passed on, leaving the burial-spot astern, they still kept circling it low down with the moving shadow of their outstretched wings and the croaked requiem of their cries.

Upon sailors as superstitious as those of the age preceding ours, men-of-war's men too who had just beheld the prodigy of repose in the form suspended in air and now foundering in the deeps; to such mariners the action of the sea-fowl though dictated by mere animal greed for prey, was big with no prosaic significance. An uncertain movement began among them, in which some encroachment was made. It was tolerated but for a moment. For suddenly the drum beat to quarters, which familiar sound happening at least twice every day, had upon the present occasion a signal peremptoriness in it. True martial discipline long continued superinduces in average man a sort of impulse of docility whose operation at the official sound of command much resembles in its promptitude the effect of an instinct.

The drum-beat dissolved the multitude, distributing most of them along the batteries of the two covered gun-decks. There, as wont, the guns' crews stood by their respective cannon erect and silent. In due course the First Officer, sword under arm and standing in his place on the quarter-deck formally received the successive reports of the sworded Lieutenants commanding the sections of batteries below; the last of which reports being made the summed report he delivered with the customary salute to the Commander. All this occupied time, which in the present case, was the object of beating to quarters at an hour prior to the customary one. That such variance from usage was authorized by an officer like Captain Vere, a martinet as some deemed him, was evidence of the necessity for unusual action implied in what he deemed to be temporarily the mood of his men. "With mankind" he would say "forms, measured forms are everything; and that is the import couched in the story of Orpheus with his lyre spell-binding the wild denizens of the wood." And this he once applied to the disruption of forms going on across the Channel and the consequences thereof.

At this unwonted muster at quarters, all proceeded as at the regular hour. The band on the quarter-deck played a sacred air. After which the Chaplain went through the customary morning service. That done, the drum beat the retreat, and toned by music and religious rites subserving the discipline and purpose of war, the men in their wonted orderly manner, dispersed to the places allotted them when not at the guns.

And now it was full day. The fleece of low-hanging vapor had vanished, licked up by the sun that late had so glorified it. And the circumambient air in the clearness of its serenity was like smooth white marble in the polished block not yet removed from the marble-dealer's yard.

29

The symmetry of form attainable in pure fiction can not so readily be achieved in a narration essentially having less to do with fable than with fact. Truth uncompromisingly told will always have its ragged edges; hence the conclusion of such a narration is apt to be less finished than an architectural finial.

How it fared with the Handsome Sailor during the year of the Great Mutiny has been faithfully given. But though properly the story ends with his life, something in way of sequel will not be amiss. Three brief chapters will suffice.

In the general re-christening under the Directory of the craft originally forming the navy of the French monarchy, the *St. Louis* line-of-battle ship was named the *Athéiste.* Such a name, like some other substituted ones in the Revolutionary fleet while proclaiming the infidel audacity of the ruling power was yet, though not so intended to be, the aptest name, if one consider it, ever given to a war-ship; far more so indeed than the *Devastation,* the *Erebus* (the *Hell*) and similar names bestowed upon fighting-ships.

On the return-passage to the English fleet from the detached cruise during which occurred the events already recorded, the *Indomitable* fell in with the *Athéiste.* An engagement ensued; during which Captain Vere in the act of putting his ship alongside the enemy with a view of throwing his boarders across her bulwarks, was hit by a musket-ball from a port-hole of the enemy's main cabin. More than disabled he dropped to the deck and was carried below to the same cock-pit where some of his men already lay. The senior Lieutenant took command. Under him the enemy was finally captured and though much crippled was by rare good fortune successfully taken into Gibraltar, an English port not very distant from the scene of the fight. There, Captain Vere with the rest of the wounded was put ashore. He lingered for some days, but the end came. Unhappily he was cut off too early for the Nile and Trafalgar. The spirit that spite its philosophic austerity may yet have indulged in the most secret of all passions, ambition, never attained to the fulness of fame.

Not long before death while lying under the influence of that magical drug which soothing the physical frame mysteriously operates on the subtler element in man, he was heard to murmur words inexplicable to his attendant—"Billy Budd, Billy Budd." That these were not the accents of remorse, would seem clear from what the attendant said to the *Indomitable's* senior officer of marines who as the most reluctant to condemn of the members of the drumhead court, too well knew though here he kept the knowledge to himself, who Billy Budd was.

30

Some few weeks after the execution, among other matters under the head of *News from the Mediterranean,* there appeared in a naval chronicle of the time, an authorized weekly publication, an account of the affair. It was doubtless for the most part written in good faith, though the medium, partly rumor, through which the facts must have reached the writer, served to deflect and in part falsify them. The account was as follows:—

"On the tenth of the last month a deplorable occurrence took place on board H.M.S. *Indomitable.* John Claggart, the ship's master-at-arms, discovering that some sort of plot was incipient among an inferior section of the ship's company, and that the ringleader was one William Budd; he, Claggart in the act of arraigning the man before the Captain was vindictively stabbed to the heart by the suddenly drawn sheath-knife of Budd.

"The deed and the implement employed, sufficiently suggest that though mustered into the service under an English name the assassin was no Englishman, but one of those aliens adopting English cognomens whom the present extraordinary necessities of the Service have caused to be admitted into it in considerable numbers.

"The enormity of the crime and the extreme depravity of the criminal, appear the greater in view of the character of the victim, a middle-aged man respectable and discreet, belonging to that minor official grade, the petty-officers, upon whom, as none know better than the commissioned gentlemen, the efficiency of His Majesty's navy so largely depends. His function was a responsible one; at once

onerous and thankless and his fidelity in it the greater
because of his strong patriotic impulse. In this instance as
in so many other instances in these days, the character of
this unfortunate man signally refutes, if refutation were
needed, that peevish saying attributed to the late Dr. John-
son, that patriotism is the last refuge of a scoundrel.

"The criminal paid the penalty of his crime. The promptitude of the punishment has proved salutary. Nothing
amiss is now apprehended aboard H.M.S. *Indomitable.*"

The above appearing in a publication now long ago
superannuated and forgotten is all that hitherto has stood
in human record to attest what manner of men respectively
were John Claggart and Billy Budd.

31

Everything is for a term remarkable in navies. Any tangi-
ble object associated with some striking incident of the
service is converted into a monument. The spar from
which the Foretopman was suspended, was for some few
years kept trace of by the blue-jackets. Their knowledge
followed it from ship to dock-yard and again from dock-
yard to ship, still pursuing it even when at last reduced
to a mere dock-yard boom. To them a chip of it was as a
piece of the Cross. Ignorant though they were of the secret
facts of the tragedy, and not thinking but that the penalty
was somehow unavoidably inflicted from the naval point
of view, for all that they instinctively felt that Billy was a
sort of man as incapable of mutiny as of wilful murder.
They recalled the fresh young image of the Handsome
Sailor, that face never deformed by a sneer or subtler vile
freak of the heart within. Their impression of him was
doubtless deepened by the fact that he was gone, and in a
measure mysteriously gone. On the gun-decks of the *Indomitable* the general estimate of his nature and its unconscious simplicity eventually found rude utterance from

another foretopman one of his own watch gifted, as some sailors are, with an artless poetic temperament. The tarry hands made some lines which after circulating among the shipboard crew for a while, finally got rudely printed at Portsmouth as a ballad. The title given to it was the sailor's.

BILLY IN THE DARBIES

Good of the Chaplain to enter Lone Bay
And down on his marrow-bones here and pray
For the likes just o' me, Billy Budd.—But look:
Through the port comes the moon-shine astray!
It tips the guard's cutlas and silvers this nook;
But 'twill die in the dawning of Billy's last day.
A jewel-block they'll make of me tomorrow,
Pendant pearl from the yard-arm-end
Like the ear-drop I gave to Bristol Molly—
O, 'tis me, not the sentence they'll suspend.
Ay, Ay, all is up; and I must up too
Early in the morning, aloft from alow.
On an empty stomach, now, never it would do.
They'll give me a nibble—bit o' biscuit ere I go.
Sure, a messmate will reach me the last parting cup;
But, turning heads away from the hoist and the belay,
Heaven knows who will have the running of me up!
No pipe to those halyards.—But aren't it all sham?
A blur's in my eyes; it is dreaming that I am.
A hatchet to my hawser? all adrift to go?
The drum roll to grog, and Billy never know?
But Donald he has promised to stand by the plank;
So I'll shake a friendly hand ere I sink.
But—no! It is dead then I'll be, come to think.—
I remember Taff the Welshman when he sank.
And his cheek it was like the budding pink.

But me they'll lash me in hammock, drop me deep.
Fathoms down, fathoms down, how I'll dream fast asleep.
I feel it stealing now. Sentry, are you there?
Just ease this darbies at the wrist,
And roll me over fair,
I am sleepy, and the oozy weeds about me twist.

END OF BOOK

April 19th
1891

NOON WINE

Katherine Anne Porter

Katherine Anne Porter

• •

Katherine Anne Porter was born in Indian Creek, Texas, in 1894. She has worked on a newspaper, she has taught, and she has traveled extensively in America, Mexico, and Europe. Her considerable reputation as a first-rate writer is based on a comparatively small number of books and some fragments of others; but this reputation is richly deserved. Her first volume, *Flowering Judas and Other Stories*, was published in 1930. When it appeared Miss Porter seemed, as a writer, to have sprung full grown out of the head of Zeus, so superb was the work. This assumption discounted the care and the patience involved in the writing of and the decision to publish each story. *Pale Horse, Pale Rider*, a volume of three short novels, appeared as a book in 1939; *The Leaning Tower and Other Stories* was published in 1944; and *The Days Before*, a collection of essays and critical writing, appeared in 1953. All of these books are published by Harcourt, Brace & Company, New York; *Flowering Judas* and *Pale Horse, Pale Rider* are available in the Modern Library. Miss Porter can be heard on records reading *Pale Horse, Pale Rider* and "*The Downward Path to Wisdom*."

NOON WINE

Time: 1896-1905
Place: Small South Texas Farm

THE TWO grubby small boys with tow-colored hair who were digging among the ragweed in the front yard sat back on their heels and said, "Hello," when the tall bony man with straw-colored hair turned in at their gate. He did not pause at the gate; it had swung back, conveniently half open, long ago, and was now sunk so firmly on its broken hinges no one thought of trying to close it. He did not even glance at the small boys, much less give them good-day. He just clumped down his big square dusty shoes one after the other steadily, like a man following a plow, as if he knew the place well and knew where he was going and what he would find there. Rounding the right-hand corner of the house under the row of chinaberry trees, he walked up to the side porch where Mr. Thompson was pushing a big swing churn back and forth.

Mr. Thompson was a tough weather-beaten man with stiff black hair and a week's growth of black whiskers. He was a noisy proud man who held his neck so straight his whole face stood level with his Adam's apple, and the whiskers continued down his neck and disappeared into a black thatch under his open collar. The churn rumbled and swished like the belly of a trotting horse, and Mr. Thompson seemed somehow to be driving a horse with one hand, reining it in and urging it forward; and every now and then he turned halfway around and squirted a tremendous spit of tobacco juice out over the steps. The door stones were brown and gleaming with fresh tobacco juice. Mr. Thompson had been churning quite a while and he was tired of it. He was just fetching a mouthful of juice to squirt again when the stranger came around the corner and stopped. Mr. Thompson saw a narrow-chested man with blue eyes so pale they were almost white, looking and not looking at him from a long gaunt face, under white eyebrows. Mr. Thompson judged him to be another of these Irishmen, by his long upper lip.

"Howdy do, sir," said Mr. Thompson politely, swinging his churn.

"I need work," said the man, clearly enough but with some kind of foreign accent Mr. Thompson couldn't place. It wasn't Cajun and it wasn't Nigger and it wasn't Dutch, so it had him stumped. "You need a man here?"

Mr. Thompson gave the churn a great shove and it swung back and forth several times on its own momentum. He sat on the steps, shot his quid into the grass, and said, "Set down. Maybe we can make a deal. I been kinda lookin' round for somebody. I had two niggers but they got into a cutting scrape up the creek last week, one of 'em dead now and the other in the hoosegow at Cold Springs. Neither one of 'em worth killing, come right down to it. So it looks like I'd better get somebody. Where'd you work last?"

"North Dakota," said the man, folding himself down on the other end of the steps, but not as if he were tired. He folded up and settled down as if it would be a long time before he got up again. He never had looked at Mr. Thompson, but there wasn't anything sneaking in his eye, either. He didn't seem to be looking anywhere else. His eyes sat in his head and let things pass by them. They didn't seem to be expecting to see anything worth looking at. Mr. Thompson waited a long time for the man to say something more, but he had gone into a brown study.

"North Dakota," said Mr. Thompson, trying to remember where that was. "That's a right smart distance off, seems to me."

"I can do everything on farm," said the man; "cheap. I need work."

Mr. Thompson settled himself to get down to business. "My name's Thompson, Mr. Royal Earle Thompson," he said.

"I'm Mr. Helton," said the man, "Mr. Olaf Helton." He did not move.

"Well, now," said Mr. Thompson in his most carrying voice, "I guess we'd better talk turkey."

When Mr. Thompson expected to drive a bargain he always grew very hearty and jovial. There was nothing wrong with him except that he hated like the devil to pay wages. He said so himself. "You furnish grub and a shack," he said, "and then you got to pay 'em besides. It ain't right. Besides the wear and tear on your implements," he said, "they just let everything go to rack and ruin." So he began to laugh and shout his way through the deal.

"Now, what I want to know is, how much you fixing to gouge outa me?" he brayed, slapping his knee. After he had kept it up as long as he could, he quieted down, feeling a little sheepish, and cut himself a chew. Mr. Helton was staring out somewhere between the barn and the orchard, and seemed to be sleeping with his eyes open.

"I'm good worker," said Mr. Helton as from the tomb. "I get dollar a day."

Mr. Thompson was so shocked he forgot to start laughing again at the top of his voice until it was nearly too late to do any good. "Haw, haw," he bawled. "Why, for a dollar a day I'd hire out myself. What kinda work is it where they pay you a dollar a day?"

"Wheatfields, North Dakota," said Mr. Helton, not even smiling.

Mr. Thompson stopped laughing. "Well, this ain't any wheatfield by a long shot. This is more of a dairy farm," he said, feeling apologetic. "My wife, she was set on a dairy, she seemed to like working around with cows and calves, so I humored her. But it was a mistake," he said. "I got nearly everything to do, anyhow. My wife ain't very strong. She's sick today, that's a fact. She's been porely for the last few days. We plant a little feed, and a corn patch, and there's the orchard, and a few pigs and chickens, but our main hold is the cows. Now just speakin' as one man to another, there ain't any money in it. Now I can't give you no dollar a day because ackshally I don't make that much out of it. No, sir, we get along on a lot less than a dollar a day, I'd say, if we figger up everything in the long run. Now, I paid seven dollars a month to the two niggers, three-fifty each, and grub, but what I say is, one middlin'-good white man ekals a whole passel of niggers any day in the week, so I'll give you seven dollars and you eat at the table with us, and you'll be treated like a white man, as the feller says—"

"That's all right," said Mr. Helton. "I take it."

"Well, now I guess we'll call it a deal, hey?" Mr. Thompson jumped up as if he had remembered important business. "Now, you just take hold of that churn and give it a few swings, will you, while I ride to town on a coupla little errands. I ain't been able to leave the place all week. I guess you know what to do with butter after you get it, don't you?"

"I know," said Mr. Helton without turning his head. "I know butter business." He had a strange drawling voice, and even when he spoke only two words his voice waved slowly up and down and the emphasis was in the wrong place. Mr. Thompson wondered what kind of foreigner Mr. Helton could be.

"Now just where did you say you worked last?" he asked, as if he expected Mr. Helton to contradict himself.

"North Dakota," said Mr. Helton.

"Well, one place is good as another once you get used to it," said Mr. Thompson, amply. "You're a forriner, ain't you?"

"I'm a Swede," said Mr. Helton, beginning to swing the churn.

Mr. Thompson let forth a booming laugh, as if this was the best joke on somebody he'd ever heard. "Well, I'll be damned," he said at the top of his voice. "A Swede: well, now, I'm afraid you'll get pretty lonesome around here. I never seen any Swedes in this neck of the woods."

"That's all right," said Mr. Helton. He went on swinging the churn as if he had been working on the place for years.

"In fact, I might as well tell you, you're practically the first Swede I ever laid eyes on."

"That's all right," said Mr. Helton.

Mr. Thompson went into the front room where Mrs. Thompson was lying down, with the green shades drawn. She had a bowl of water by her on the table and a wet cloth over her eyes. She took the cloth off at the sound of Mr. Thompson's boots and said, "What's all the noise out there? Who is it?"

"Got a feller out there says he's a Swede, Ellie," said Mr. Thompson; "says he knows how to make butter."

"I hope it turns out to be the truth," said Mrs. Thompson. "Looks like my head never will get any better."

"Don't you worry," said Mr. Thompson. "You fret too much. Now I'm gointa ride into town and get a little order of groceries."

"Don't you linger, now, Mr. Thompson," said Mrs. Thompson. "Don't go to the hotel." She meant the saloon; the proprietor also had rooms for rent upstairs.

"Just a coupla little toddies," said Mr. Thompson, laughing loudly, "never hurt anybody."

"I never took a dram in my life," said Mrs. Thompson, "and what's more I never will."

"I wasn't talking about the womenfolks," said Mr. Thompson.

The sound of the swinging churn rocked Mrs. Thompson first into a gentle doze, then a deep drowse from which she waked suddenly knowing that the swinging had stopped a good while ago. She sat up shading her weak eyes from the flat strips of late summer sunlight between

the sill and the lowered shades. There she was, thank
God, still alive, with supper to cook but no churning on
hand, and her head still bewildered, but easy. Slowly she
realized she had been hearing a new sound even in her
sleep. Somebody was playing a tune on the harmonica,
not merely shrilling up and down making a sickening
noise, but really playing a pretty tune, merry and sad.

She went out through the kitchen, stepped off the porch,
and stood facing the east, shading her eyes. When her
vision cleared and settled, she saw a long, pale-haired man
in blue jeans sitting in the doorway of the hired man's
shack, tilted back in a kitchen chair, blowing away at the
harmonica with his eyes shut. Mrs. Thompson's heart flut-
tered and sank. Heavens, he looked lazy and worthless, he
did, now. First a lot of no-count fiddling darkies and then
a no-count white man. It was just like Mr. Thompson to
take on that kind. She did wish he would be more considerate, and take a little trouble with his business. She
wanted to believe in her husband, and there were too
many times when she couldn't. She wanted to believe that
tomorrow, or at least the day after, life, such a battle at
best, was going to be better.

She walked past the shack without glancing aside, stepping carefully, bent at the waist because of the nagging
pain in her side, and went to the springhouse, trying to
harden her mind to speak very plainly to that new hired
man if he had not done his work.

The milk house was only another shack of weather-
beaten boards nailed together hastily years before because
they needed a milk house; it was meant to be temporary,
and it was; already shapeless, leaning this way and that
over a perpetual cool trickle of water that fell from a little
grot, almost choked with pallid ferns. No one else in the
whole countryside had such a spring on his land. Mr. and
Mrs. Thompson felt they had a fortune in that spring, if
ever they got around to doing anything with it.

Rickety wooden shelves clung at hazard in the square

around the small pool where the larger pails of milk and butter stood, fresh and sweet in the cold water. One hand supporting her flat, pained side, the other shading her eyes, Mrs. Thompson leaned over and peered into the pails. The cream had been skimmed and set aside, there was a rich roll of butter, the wooden molds and shallow pans had been scrubbed and scalded for the first time in who knows when, the barrel was full of buttermilk ready for the pigs and the weanling calves, the hard packed-dirt floor had been swept smooth. Mrs. Thompson straightened up again, smiling tenderly. She had been ready to scold him, a poor man who needed a job, who had just come there and who might not have been expected to do things properly at first. There was nothing she could do to make up for the injustice she had done him in her thoughts but to tell him how she appreciated his good clean work, finished already, in no time at all. She ventured near the door of the shack with her careful steps; Mr. Helton opened his eyes, stopped playing, and brought his chair down straight, but did not look at her, or get up. She was a little frail woman with long thick brown hair in a braid, a suffering patient mouth and diseased eyes which cried easily. She wove her fingers into an eyeshade, thumbs on temples, and, winking her tearful lids, said with a polite little manner, "Howdy do, sir. I'm Miz Thompson, and I wanted to tell you I think you did real well in the milk house. It's always been a hard place to keep."

He said, "That's all right," in a slow voice, without moving.

Mrs. Thompson waited a moment. "That's a pretty tune you're playing. Most folks don't seem to get much music out of a harmonica."

Mr. Helton sat humped over, long legs sprawling, his spine in a bow, running his thumb over the square mouth-stops; except for his moving hand he might have been asleep. The harmonica was a big shiny new one, and Mrs. Thompson, her gaze wandering about, counted five others, all good and expensive, standing in a row on the shelf beside his cot. "He must carry them around in his jumper pocket," she thought, and noted there was not a sign of any other possession lying about. "I see you're mighty fond of music," she said. "We used to have an old accordion, and Mr. Thompson could play it right smart, but the little boys broke it up."

Mr. Helton stood up rather suddenly, the chair clattered under him, his knees straightened though his shoulders did not, and he looked at the floor as if he were listening carefully. "You know how little boys are," said Mrs. Thompson. "You'd better set them harmonicas on a high shelf or they'll be after them. They're great hands for getting into things. I try to learn 'em, but it don't do much good."

Mr. Helton, in one wide gesture of his long arms, swept his harmonicas up against his chest, and from there transferred them in a row to the ledge where the roof joined to the wall. He pushed them back almost out of sight.

"That'll do, maybe," said Mrs. Thompson. "Now I wonder," she said, turning and closing her eyes helplessly against the stronger western light, "I wonder what became of them little tads. I can't keep up with them." She had a way of speaking about her children as if they were rather troublesome nephews on a prolonged visit.

"Down by the creek," said Mr. Helton, in his hollow voice. Mrs. Thompson, pausing confusedly, decided he had answered her question. He stood in silent patience, not exactly waiting for her to go, perhaps, but pretty plainly not waiting for anything else. Mrs. Thompson was perfectly accustomed to all kinds of men full of all kinds of cranky ways. The point was, to find out just how Mr. Helton's crankiness was different from any other man's, and then get used to it, and let him feel at home. Her father had been cranky, her brothers and uncles had all been set in their ways and none of them alike; and every hired man she'd ever seen had quirks and crotchets of his own. Now here was Mr. Helton, who was a Swede, who wouldn't talk, and who played the harmonica besides.

"They'll be needing something to eat," said Mrs. Thompson in a vague friendly way, "pretty soon. Now I wonder what I ought to be thinking about for supper? Now what do you like to eat, Mr. Helton? We always have plenty of good butter and milk and cream, that's a blessing. Mr. Thompson says we ought to sell all of it, but I say my family comes first." Her little face went all out of shape in a pained blind smile.

"I eat anything," said Mr. Helton, his words wandering up and down.

He *can't* talk, for one thing, thought Mrs. Thompson, it's a shame to keep at him when he don't know the language good. She took a slow step away from the shack, looking back over her shoulder. "We usually have cornbread except on Sundays," she told him. "I suppose in your part of the country you don't get much good cornbread."

Not a word from Mr. Helton. She saw from her eye-corner that he had sat down again, looking at his harmonica, chair tilted. She hoped he would remember it was getting near milking time. As she moved away, he started playing again, the same tune.

Milking time came and went. Mrs. Thompson saw Mr. Helton going back and forth between the cow barn and the milk house. He swung along in an easy lope, shoulders bent, head hanging, the big buckets balancing like a pair of scales at the ends of his bony arms. Mr. Thompson rode in from town sitting straighter than usual, chin in, a towsack full of supplies swung behind the saddle. After a trip to the barn, he came into the kitchen full of good will, and gave Mrs. Thompson a hearty smack on the cheek after dusting her face off with his tough whiskers. He had been to the hotel, that was plain. "Took a look around the premises, Ellie," he shouted. "That Swede sure is

grinding out the labor. But he is the closest mouthed
feller I ever met up with in all my days. Looks like he's
scared he'll crack his jaw if he opens his front teeth."

Mrs. Thompson was stirring up a big bowl of buttermilk cornbread. "You smell like a toper, Mr. Thompson,"
she said with perfect dignity. "I wish you'd get one of the
little boys to bring me in an extra load of firewood. I'm
thinking about baking a batch of cookies tomorrow."

Mr. Thompson, all at once smelling the liquor on his
own breath, sneaked out, justly rebuked, and brought in
the firewood himself. Arthur and Herbert, grubby from
thatched head to toes, from skin to shirt, came stamping
in yelling for supper. "Go wash your faces and comb your
hair," said Mrs. Thompson, automatically. They retired
to the porch. Each one put his hand under the pump and
wet his forelock, combed it down with his fingers, and
returned at once to the kitchen, where all the fair pros-
pects of life were centered. Mrs. Thompson set an extra
plate and commanded Arthur, the eldest, eight years old,
to call Mr. Helton for supper.

Arthur, without moving from the spot, bawled like a
bull calf, "Saaaaaay, Helllllllton, suuuuuupper's ready!"
and added in a lower voice, "You big Swede!"

"Listen to me," said Mrs. Thompson, "that's no way to
act. Now you go out there and ask him decent, or I'll get
your daddy to give you a good licking."

Mr. Helton loomed, long and gloomy, in the doorway.
"Sit right there," boomed Mr. Thompson, waving his arm.
Mr. Helton swung his square shoes across the kitchen in
two steps, slumped onto the bench and sat. Mr. Thompson occupied his chair at the head of the table, the two
boys scrambled into place opposite Mr. Helton, and Mrs.
Thompson sat at the end nearest the stove. Mrs. Thompson clasped her hands, bowed her head and said aloud
hastily, "Lord, for all these and Thy other blessings we
thank Thee in Jesus' name, amen," trying to finish before
Herbert's rusty little paw reached the nearest dish. Other-

wise she would be duty-bound to send him away from the table, and growing children need their meals. Mr. Thompson and Arthur always waited, but Herbert, aged six, was too young to take training yet.

Mr. and Mrs. Thompson tried to engage Mr. Helton in conversation, but it was a failure. They tried first the weather, and then the crops, and then the cows, but Mr. Helton simply did not reply. Mr. Thompson then told something funny he had seen in town. It was about some of the other old grangers at the hotel, friends of his, giving beer to a goat, and the goat's subsequent behavior. Mr. Helton did not seem to hear. Mrs. Thompson laughed dutifully, but she didn't think it was very funny. She had heard it often before, though Mr. Thompson, each time he told it, pretended it had happened that self-same day. It must have happened years ago if it ever happened at all, and it had never been a story that Mrs. Thompson thought suitable for mixed company. The whole thing came of Mr. Thompson's weakness for a dram too much now and then, though he voted for local option at every election. She passed the food to Mr. Helton, who took a helping of everything, but not much, not enough to keep him up to his full powers if he expected to go on working the way he had started.

At last, he took a fair-sized piece of cornbread, wiped his plate up as clean as if it had been licked by a hound dog, stuffed his mouth full, and, still chewing, slid off the bench and started for the door.

"Good night, Mr. Helton," said Mrs. Thompson, and the other Thompsons took it up in a scattered chorus. "Good night, Mr. Helton!"

"Good night," said Mr. Helton's wavering voice grudgingly from the darkness.

"Gude not," said Arthur, imitating Mr. Helton.

"Gude not," said Herbert, the copy-cat.

"You don't do it right," said Arthur. "Now listen to me. Guuuuuude naht," and he ran a hollow scale in a luxury

of successful impersonation. Herbert almost went into a
fit with joy.

"Now you *stop* that," said Mrs. Thompson. "He can't
help the way he talks. You ought to be ashamed of yourselves, both of you, making fun of a poor stranger like
that. How'd you like to be a stranger in a strange land?"

"I'd like it," said Arthur. "I think it would be fun."

"They're both regular heathens, Ellie," said Mr.
Thompson. "Just plain ignoramuses." He turned the face
of awful fatherhood upon his young. "You're both going
to get sent to school next year, and that'll knock some
sense into you."

"I'm going to git sent to the 'formatory when I'm old
enough," piped up Herbert. "That's where I'm goin'."

"Oh, you are, are you?" asked Mr. Thompson. "Who
says so?"

"The Sunday School Supintendant," said Herbert, a
bright boy showing off.

"You see?" said Mr. Thompson, staring at his wife.
"What did I tell you?" He became a hurricane of wrath.
"Get to bed, you two," he roared until his Adam's apple
shuddered. "Get now before I take the hide off you!" They
got, and shortly from their attic bedroom the sounds of
scuffling and snorting and giggling and growling filled
the house and shook the kitchen ceiling.

Mrs. Thompson held her head and said in a small uncertain voice, "It's no use picking on them when they're
so young and tender. I can't stand it."

"My goodness, Ellie," said Mr. Thompson, "we've got
to raise 'em. We can't just let 'em grow up hog wild."

She went on in another tone. "That Mr. Helton seems
all right, even if he can't be made to talk. Wonder how
he comes to be so far from home."

"Like I said, he isn't no whamper-jaw," said Mr.
Thompson, "but he sure knows how to lay out the work.
I guess that's the main thing around here. Country's full
of fellers trampin' round looking for work."

Mrs. Thompson was gathering up the dishes. She now gathered up Mr. Thompson's plate from under his chin. "To tell you the honest truth," she remarked, "I think it's a mighty good change to have a man round the place who knows how to work and keep his mouth shut. Means he'll keep out of our business. Not that we've got anything to hide, but it's convenient."

"That's a fact," said Mr. Thompson. "Haw, haw," he shouted suddenly. "Means you can do all the talking, huh?"

"The only thing," went on Mrs. Thompson, "is this: he don't eat hearty enough to suit me. I like to see a man set down and relish a good meal. My granma used to say it was no use putting dependence on a man who won't set down and make out his dinner. I hope it won't be that way this time."

"Tell *you* the truth, Ellie," said Mr. Thompson, picking his teeth with a fork and leaning back in the best of good humors, "I always thought your granma was a ter'ble ole fool. She'd just say the first thing that popped into her head and call it God's wisdom."

"My granma wasn't anybody's fool. Nine times out of ten she knew what she was talking about. I always say, the first thing you think is the best thing you can say."

"Well," said Mr. Thompson, going into another shout, "you're so re*e*fined about that goat story, you just try speaking out in mixed comp'ny sometime! You just try it. S'pose you happened to be thinking about a hen and a rooster, hey? I reckon you'd shock the Babtist preacher!" He gave her a good pinch on her thin little rump. "No more meat on you than a rabbit," he said, fondly. "Now I like 'em cornfed."

Mrs. Thompson looked at him open-eyed and blushed. She could see better by lamplight. "Why, Mr. Thompson, sometimes I think you're the evilest-minded man that ever lived." She took a handful of hair on the crown of his head and gave it a good, slow pull. "That's to show you how it feels, pinching so hard when you're supposed to be playing," she said, gently.

In spite of his situation in life, Mr. Thompson had never been able to outgrow his deep conviction that running a dairy and chasing after chickens was woman's work. He was fond of saying that he could plow a furrow, cut sorghum, shuck corn, handle a team, build a corn crib, as well as any man. Buying and selling, too, were man's work. Twice a week he drove the spring wagon to market with the fresh butter, a few eggs, fruits in their proper season, sold them, pocketed the change, and spent it as seemed best, being careful not to dig into Mrs. Thompson's pin money.

But from the first the cows worried him, coming up regularly twice a day to be milked, standing there reproaching him with their smug female faces. Calves worried him, fighting the rope and strangling themselves until their eyes bulged, trying to get at the teat. Wrestling with a calf unmanned him, like having to change a baby's diaper. Milk worried him, coming bitter sometimes, drying up, turning sour. Hens worried him, cackling, clucking, hatching out when you least expected it and leading their broods into the barnyard where the horses could step on them; dying of roup and wryneck and getting plagues of chicken lice; laying eggs all over God's creation so that half of them were spoiled before a man could find them, in spite of a rack of nests Mrs. Thompson had set out for them in the feed room. Hens were a blasted nuisance.

Slopping hogs was hired man's work, in Mr. Thompson's opinion. Killing hogs was a job for the boss, but scraping them and cutting them up was for the hired man again; and again woman's proper work was dressing meat, smoking, pickling, and making lard and sausage. All his carefully limited fields of activity were related somehow to Mr. Thompson's feeling for the appearance of things, his own appearance in the sight of God and man. "It don't *look* right," was his final reason for not doing anything he did not wish to do.

It was his dignity and his reputation that he cared about, and there were only a few kinds of work manly enough for Mr. Thompson to undertake with his own hands. Mrs. Thompson, to whom so many forms of work would have been becoming, had simply gone down on him early. He saw, after a while, how short-sighted it had been of him to expect much from Mrs. Thompson; he had fallen in love with her delicate waist and lace-trimmed petticoats and big blue eyes, and, though all those charms had disappeared, she had in the meantime become Ellie to him, not at all the same person as Miss Ellen Bridges, popular Sunday School teacher in the Mountain City First Baptist Church, but his dear wife, Ellie, who was not strong. Deprived as he was, however, of the main support in life which a man might expect in marriage, he had almost without knowing it resigned himself to failure. Head erect, a prompt payer of taxes, yearly subscriber to the preacher's salary, land owner and father of a family, employer, a hearty good fellow among men, Mr. Thompson knew, without putting it into words, that he had been going steadily down hill. God amighty, it did look like somebody around the place might take a rake in hand now and then and clear up the clutter around the barn and the kitchen steps. The wagon shed was so full of broken-down machinery and ragged harness and old wagon wheels and battered milk pails and rotting lumber you could hardly drive in there any more. Not a soul on the place would raise a hand to it, and as for him, he had all he could do with his regular work. He would sometimes in the slack season sit for hours worrying about it, squirting tobacco on the ragweeds growing in a thicket against the wood pile, wondering what a fellow could do, handicapped as he was. He looked forward to the boys growing up soon; he was going to put them through the mill just as his own father had done with him when he was a boy; they were

going to learn how to take hold and run the place right.
He wasn't going to overdo it, but those two boys were going to earn their salt, or he'd know why. Great big lubbers
sitting around whittling! Mr. Thompson sometimes grew
quite enraged with them, when imagining their possible
future, big lubbers sitting around whittling or thinking
about fishing trips. Well, he'd put a stop to that, mighty
damn quick.

As the seasons passed, and Mr. Helton took hold more
and more, Mr. Thompson began to relax in his mind a
little. There seemed to be nothing the fellow couldn't do,
all in the day's work and as a matter of course. He got up
at five o'clock in the morning, boiled his own coffee and
fried his own bacon and was out in the cow lot before Mr.
Thompson had even begun to yawn, stretch, groan, roar
and thump around looking for his jeans. He milked the
cows, kept the milk house, and churned the butter;
rounded the hens up and somehow persuaded them to lay
in the nests, not under the house and behind the hay-
stacks; he fed them regularly and they hatched out until
you couldn't set a foot down for them. Little by little the
piles of trash around the barns and house disappeared.
He carried buttermilk and corn to the hogs, and curried
cockleburs out of the horses' manes. He was gentle with
the calves, if a little grim with the cows and hens; judging
by his conduct, Mr. Helton had never heard of the difference between man's and woman's work on a farm.

In the second year, he showed Mr. Thompson the picture of a cheese press in a mail order catalogue, and said,
"This is a good thing. You buy this, I make cheese." The
press was bought and Mr. Helton did make cheese, and
it was sold, along with the increased butter and the crates
of eggs. Sometimes Mr. Thompson felt a little contemp-
tuous of Mr. Helton's ways. It did seem kind of picayune
for a man to go around picking up half a dozen ears of
corn that had fallen off the wagon on the way from the
field, gathering up fallen fruit to feed to the pigs, storing

up old nails and stray parts of machinery, spending good time stamping a fancy pattern on the butter before it went to market. Mr. Thompson, sitting up high on the spring-wagon seat, with the decorated butter in a five-gallon lard can wrapped in wet towsack, driving to town, chirruping to the horses and snapping the reins over their backs, sometimes thought that Mr. Helton was a pretty meeching sort of fellow; but he never gave way to these feelings, he knew a good thing when he had it. It was a fact the hogs were in better shape and sold for more money. It was a fact that Mr. Thompson stopped buying feed, Mr. Helton managed the crops so well. When beef- and hog-slaughtering time came, Mr. Helton knew how to save the scraps that Mr. Thompson had thrown away, and wasn't above scraping guts and filling them with sausages that he made by his own methods. In all, Mr. Thompson had no grounds for complaint. In the third year, he raised Mr. Helton's wages, though Mr. Helton had not asked for a raise. The fourth year, when Mr. Thompson was not only out of debt but had a little cash in the bank, he raised Mr. Helton's wages again, two dollars and a half a month each time.

"The man's worth it, Ellie," said Mr. Thompson, in a glow of self-justification for his extravagance. "He's made this place pay, and I want him to know I appreciate it."

Mr. Helton's silence, the pallor of his eyebrows and hair, his long, glum jaw and eyes that refused to see anything, even the work under his hands, had grown perfectly familiar to the Thompsons. At first, Mrs. Thompson complained a little. "It's like sitting down at the table with a disembodied spirit," she said. "You'd think he'd find something to say, sooner or later."

"Let him alone," said Mr. Thompson. "When he gets ready to talk, he'll talk."

The years passed, and Mr. Helton never got ready to talk. After his work was finished for the day, he would come up from the barn or the milk house or the chicken house, swinging his lantern, his big shoes clumping like

pony hoofs on the hard path. They, sitting in the kitchen
in the winter, or on the back porch in summer, would hear
him drag out his wooden chair, hear the creak of it tilted
back, and then for a little while he would play his single
tune on one or another of his harmonicas. The harmonicas
were in different keys, some lower and sweeter than the
others, but the same changeless tune went on, a strange
tune, with sudden turns in it, night after night, and sometimes even in the afternoons when Mr. Helton sat down
to catch his breath. At first the Thompsons liked it very
much, and always stopped to listen. Later there came a
time when they were fairly sick of it, and began to wish to
each other that he would learn a new one. At last they did
not hear it any more, it was as natural as the sound of the
wind rising in the evenings, or the cows lowing, or their
own voices.

Mrs. Thompson pondered now and then over Mr. Helton's soul. He didn't seem to be a church-goer, and worked
straight through Sunday as if it were any common day of
the week. "I think we ought to invite him to go to hear
Dr. Martin," she told Mr. Thompson. "It isn't very Christian of us not to ask him. He's not a forward kind of man.
He'd wait to be asked."

"Let him alone," said Mr. Thompson. "The way I look
at it, his religion is every man's own business. Besides, he
ain't got any Sunday clothes. He wouldn't want to go to
church in them jeans and jumpers of his. I don't know
what he does with his money. He certainly don't spend it
foolishly."

Still, once the notion got into her head, Mrs. Thompson
could not rest until she invited Mr. Helton to go to church
with the family next Sunday. He was pitching hay into
neat little piles in the field back of the orchard. Mrs.
Thompson put on smoked glasses and a sunbonnet and
walked all the way down there to speak to him. He
stopped and leaned on his pitchfork, listening, and for a
moment Mrs. Thompson was almost frightened at his face.

The pale eyes seemed to glare past her, the eyebrows frowned, the long jaw hardened. "I got work," he said bluntly, and lifting his pitchfork he turned from her and began to toss the hay. Mrs. Thompson, her feelings hurt, walked back thinking that by now she should be used to Mr. Helton's ways, but it did seem like a man, even a foreigner, could be just a little polite when you gave him a Christian invitation. "He's not polite, that's the only thing I've got against him," she said to Mr. Thompson. "He just can't seem to behave like other people. You'd think he had a grudge against the world," she said. "I sometimes don't know what to make of it."

In the second year something had happened that made Mrs. Thompson uneasy, the kind of thing she could not put into words, hardly into thoughts, and if she had tried to explain to Mr. Thompson it would have sounded worse than it was, or not bad enough. It was that kind of queer thing that seems to be giving a warning, and yet, nearly always nothing comes of it. It was on a hot, still spring day, and Mrs. Thompson had been down to the garden patch to pull some new carrots and green onions and string beans for dinner. As she worked, sunbonnet low over her eyes, putting each kind of vegetable in a pile by itself in her basket, she noticed how neatly Mr. Helton weeded, and how rich the soil was. He had spread it all over with manure from the barns, and worked it in, in the fall, and the vegetables were coming up fine and full. She walked back under the nubbly little fig trees where the unpruned branches leaned almost to the ground, and the thick leaves made a cool screen. Mrs. Thompson was always looking for shade to save her eyes. So she, looking idly about, saw through the screen a sight that struck her as very strange. If it had been a noisy spectacle, it would have been quite natural. It was the silence that struck her. Mr. Helton was shaking Arthur by the shoulders, ferociously, his face most terribly fixed and pale. Arthur's head snapped back and forth and he had not stiffened in

resistance, as he did when Mrs. Thompson tried to shake
him. His eyes were rather frightened, but surprised, too,
probably more surprised than anything else. Herbert stood
by meekly, watching. Mr. Helton dropped Arthur, and
seized Herbert, and shook him with the same methodical
ferocity, the same face of hatred. Herbert's mouth crum-
pled as if he would cry, but he made no sound. Mr. Helton
let him go, turned and strode into the shack, and the little
boys ran, as if for their lives, without a word. They disappeared around the corner to the front of the house.

Mrs. Thompson took time to set her basket on the
kitchen table, to push her sunbonnet back on her head
and draw it forward again, to look in the stove and make
certain the fire was going, before she followed the boys.
They were sitting huddled together under a clump of
chinaberry trees in plain sight of her bedroom window, as
if it were a safe place they had discovered.

"What are you doing?" asked Mrs. Thompson.

They looked hang-dog from under their foreheads and
Arthur mumbled, "Nothin'."

"Nothing *now*, you mean," said Mrs. Thompson, severely. "Well, I have plenty for you to do. Come right in here
this minute and help me fix vegetables. This minute."

They scrambled up very eagerly and followed her close.
Mrs. Thompson tried to imagine what they had been up
to; she did not like the notion of Mr. Helton taking it on
himself to correct her little boys, but she was afraid to
ask them for reasons. They might tell her a lie, and she
would have to overtake them in it, and whip them. Or she
would have to pretend to believe them, and they would
get in the habit of lying. Or they might tell her the truth,
and it would be something she would have to whip them
for. The very thought of it gave her a headache. She supposed she might ask Mr. Helton, but it was not her place
to ask. She would wait and tell Mr. Thompson, and let
him get at the bottom of it. While her mind ran on, she
kept the little boys hopping. "Cut those carrot tops closer,

Herbert, you're just being careless. Arthur, stop breaking up the beans so little. They're little enough already. Herbert, you go get an armload of wood. Arthur, you take these onions and wash them under the pump. Herbert, as soon as you're done here, you get a broom and sweep out this kitchen. Arthur, you get a shovel and take up the ashes. Stop picking your nose, Herbert. How often must I tell you? Arthur, you go look in the top drawer of my bureau, left-hand side, and bring me the vaseline for Herbert's nose. Herbert, come here to me. . . ."

They galloped through their chores, their animal spirits rose with activity, and shortly they were out in the front yard again, engaged in a wrestling match. They sprawled and fought, scrambled, clutched, rose and fell shouting, as aimlessly, noisily, montonously as two puppies. They imitated various animals, not a human sound from them, and their dirty faces were streaked with sweat. Mrs. Thompson, sitting at her window, watched them with baffled pride and tenderness, they were so sturdy and healthy and growing so fast; but uneasily, too, with her pained little smile and the tears rolling from her eyelids that clinched themselves against the sunlight. They were so idle and careless, as if they had no future in this world, and no immortal souls to save, and oh, what had they been up to that Mr. Helton had shaken them, with his face positively dangerous?

In the evening before supper, without a word to Mr. Thompson of the curious fear the sight had caused her, she told him that Mr. Helton had shaken the little boys for some reason. He stepped out to the shack and spoke to Mr. Helton. In five minutes he was back, glaring at his young. "He says them brats been fooling with his harmonicas, Ellie, blowing in them and getting them all dirty and full of spit and they don't play good."

"Did he say all that?" asked Mrs. Thompson. "It doesn't seem possible."

"Well, that's what he meant, anyhow," said Mr. Thompson. "He didn't say it just that way. But he acted pretty worked up about it."

"That's a shame," said Mrs. Thompson, "a perfect shame. Now we've got to do something so they'll remember they mustn't go into Mr. Helton's things."

"I'll tan their hides for them," said Mr. Thompson. "I'll take a calf rope to them if they don't look out."

"Maybe you'd better leave the whipping to me," said Mrs. Thompson. "You haven't got a light enough hand for children."

"That's just what's the matter with them now," shouted Mr. Thompson, "rotten spoiled and they'll wind up in the penitentiary. You don't half whip 'em. Just little love taps. My pa used to knock me down with a stick of stove wood or anything else that came handy."

"Well, that's not saying it's right," said Mrs. Thompson. "I don't hold with that way of raising children. It makes them run away from home. I've seen too much of it."

"I'll break every bone in 'em," said Mr. Thompson, simmering down, "if they don't mind you better and stop being so bull-headed."

"Leave the table and wash your face and hands," Mrs. Thompson commanded the boys, suddenly. They slunk out and dabbled at the pump and slunk in again, trying to make themselves small. They had learned long ago that their mother always made them wash when there was trouble ahead. They looked at their plates. Mr. Thompson opened up on them.

"Well, now, what you got to say for yourselves about going into Mr. Helton's shack and ruining his harmonicas?"

The two little boys wilted, their faces drooped into the grieved hopeless lines of children's faces when they are brought to the terrible bar of blind adult justice; their eyes telegraphed each other in panic, "Now we're really going to catch a licking"; in despair, they dropped their buttered cornbread on their plates, their hands lagged on the edge of the table.

"I ought to break your ribs," said Mr. Thompson, "and I'm a good mind to do it."

"Yes, sir," whispered Arthur, faintly.

"Yes, sir," said Herbert, his lip trembling.

"Now, papa," said Mrs. Thompson in a warning tone. The children did not glance at her. They had no faith in her good will. She had betrayed them in the first place. There was no trusting her. Now she might save them and she might not. No use depending on her.

"Well, you ought to get a good thrashing. You deserve it, don't you, Arthur?"

Arthur hung his head. "Yes, sir."

"And the next time I catch either of you hanging around Mr. Helton's shack, I'm going to take the hide off *both* of you, you hear me, Herbert?"

Herbert mumbled and choked, scattering his cornbread. "Yes, sir."

"Well, now sit up and eat your supper and not another word out of you," said Mr. Thompson, beginning on his own food. The little boys perked up somewhat and started chewing, but every time they looked around they met their parents' eyes, regarding them steadily. There was no telling when they would think of something new. The boys ate warily, trying not to be seen or heard, the cornbread sticking, the buttermilk gurgling, as it went down their gullets.

"And something else, Mr. Thompson," said Mrs. Thompson after a pause. "Tell Mr. Helton he's to come straight to us when they bother him, and not to trouble shaking them himself. Tell him we'll look after that."

"They're so mean," answered Mr. Thompson, staring at them. "It's a wonder he don't just kill 'em off and be done with it." But there was something in the tone that told Arthur and Herbert that nothing more worth worrying about was going to happen this time. Heaving deep sighs, they sat up, reaching for the food nearest them.

"Listen," said Mrs. Thompson, suddenly. The little
boys stopped eating. "Mr. Helton hasn't come for his supper. Arthur, go and tell Mr. Helton he's late for supper.
Tell him nice, now."

Arthur, miserably depressed, slid out of his place and
made for the door, without a word.

There were no miracles of fortune to be brought to pass
on a small dairy farm. The Thompsons did not grow rich,
but they kept out of the poor house, as Mr. Thompson
was fond of saying, meaning he had got a little foothold
in spite of Ellie's poor health, and unexpected weather,
and strange declines in market prices, and his own mysterious handicaps which weighed him down. Mr. Helton was
the hope and the prop of the family, and all the Thompsons became fond of him, or at any rate they ceased to regard him as in any way peculiar, and looked upon him,
from a distance they did not know how to bridge, as a
good man and a good friend. Mr. Helton went his way,
worked, played his tune. Nine years passed. The boys grew
up and learned to work. They could not remember the
time when Ole Helton hadn't been there: a grouchy cuss,
Brother Bones; Mr. Helton, the dairymaid; that Big
Swede. If he had heard them, he might have been annoyed at some of the names they called him. But he did
not hear them, and besides they meant no harm—or at
least such harm as existed was all there, in the names; the
boys referred to their father as the Old Man, or the Old
Geezer, but not to his face. They lived through by main
strength all the grimy, secret, oblique phases of growing
up and got past the crisis safely if anyone does. Their parents could see they were good solid boys with hearts of
gold in spite of their rough ways. Mr. Thompson was re-
lieved to find that, without knowing how he had done it,
he had succeeded in raising a set of boys who were not
trifling whittlers. They were such good boys Mr. Thompson began to believe they were born that way, and that he

had never spoken a harsh word to them in their lives, much less thrashed them. Herbert and Arthur never disputed his word.

Mr. Helton, his hair wet with sweat, plastered to his dripping forehead, his jumper streaked dark and light blue and clinging to his ribs, was chopping a little firewood. He chopped slowly, struck the ax into the end of the chopping log, and piled the wood up neatly. He then disappeared round the house into his shack, which shared with the wood pile a good shade from a row of mulberry trees. Mr. Thompson was lolling in a swing chair on the front porch, a place he had never liked. The chair was new, and Mrs. Thompson had wanted it on the front porch, though the side porch was the place for it, being cooler; and Mr. Thompson wanted to sit in the chair, so there he was. As soon as the new wore off of it, and Ellie's pride in it was exhausted, he would move it round to the side porch. Meantime the August heat was almost unbearable, the air so thick you could poke a hole in it. The dust was inches thick on everything, though Mr. Helton sprinkled the whole yard regularly every night. He even shot the hose upward and washed the tree tops and the roof of the house. They had laid waterpipes to the kitchen and an outside faucet. Mr. Thompson must have dozed, for he opened his eyes and shut his mouth just in time to save his face before a stranger who had driven up to the front gate. Mr. Thompson stood up, put on his hat, pulled up his jeans, and watched while the stranger tied his team, attached to a light spring wagon, to the hitching post. Mr. Thompson recognized the team and wagon. They were from a livery stable in Buda. While the stranger was opening the gate, a strong gate that Mr. Helton had built and set firmly on its hinges several years back, Mr. Thompson strolled down the path to greet him and find out what in God's world a man's business might be that would bring him out at this time of day, in all this dust and welter.

He wasn't exactly a fat man. He was more like a man who had been fat recently. His skin was baggy and his clothes were too big for him, and he somehow looked like a man who should be fat, ordinarily, but who might have just got over a spell of sickness. Mr. Thompson didn't take to his looks at all, he couldn't say why.

The stranger took off his hat. He said in a loud hearty voice, "Is this Mr. Thompson, Mr. Royal Earle Thompson?"

"That's my name," said Mr. Thompson, almost quietly, he was so taken aback by the free manner of the stranger.

"My name is Hatch," said the stranger, "Mr. Homer T. Hatch, and I've come to see you about buying a horse."

"I reckon you've been misdirected," said Mr. Thompson. "I haven't got a horse for sale. Usually if I've got anything like that to sell," he said, "I tell the neighbors and tack up a little sign on the gate."

The fat man opened his mouth and roared with joy, showing rabbit teeth brown as shoeleather. Mr. Thompson saw nothing to laugh at, for once. The stranger shouted, "That's just an old joke of mine." He caught one of his hands in the other and shook hands with himself heartily. "I always say something like that when I'm calling on a stranger, because I've noticed that when a feller says he's come to buy something nobody takes him for a suspicious character. You see? Haw, haw, haw."

His joviality made Mr. Thompson nervous, because the expression in the man's eyes didn't match the sounds he was making. "Haw, haw," laughed Mr. Thompson obligingly, still not seeing the joke. "Well, that's all wasted on me because I never take any man for a suspicious character 'til he shows hisself to be one. Says or does something," he explained. "Until that happens, one man's as good as another, so far's *I'm* concerned."

"Well," said the stranger, suddenly very sober and sensible, "I ain't come neither to buy nor sell. Fact is, I want to see you about something that's of interest to us both.

Yes, sir, I'd like to have a little talk with you, and it won't cost you a cent."

"I guess that's fair enough," said Mr. Thompson, reluctantly. "Come on around the house where there's a little shade."

They went round and seated themselves on two stumps under a chinaberry tree.

"Yes, sir, Homer T. Hatch is my name and America is my nation," said the stranger. "I reckon you must know the name? I used to have a cousin named Jameson Hatch lived up the country a ways."

"Don't think I know the name," said Mr. Thompson. "There's some Hatchers settled somewhere around Mountain City."

"Don't know the old Hatch family," cried the man in deep concern. He seemed to be pitying Mr. Thompson's ignorance. "Why, we came over from Georgia fifty years ago. Been here long yourself?"

"Just all my whole life," said Mr. Thompson, beginning to feel peevish. "And my pa and my grampap before me. Yes, sir, we've been right here all along. Anybody wants to find a Thompson knows where to look for him. My grampap immigrated in 1836."

"From Ireland, I reckon?" said the stranger.

"From Pennsylvania," said Mr. Thompson. "Now what makes you think we came from Ireland?"

The stranger opened his mouth and began to shout with merriment, and he shook hands with himself as if he hadn't met himself for a long time. "Well, what I always says is, a feller's got to come from *somewhere*, ain't he?"

While they were talking, Mr. Thompson kept glancing at the face near him. He certainly did remind Mr. Thompson of somebody, or maybe he really had seen the man himself somewhere. He couldn't just place the features. Mr. Thompson finally decided it was just that all rabbit-teethed men looked alike.

"That's right," acknowledged Mr. Thompson, rather

sourly, "but what I always say is, Thompsons have been
settled here for so long it don't make much difference any
more *where* they come from. Now a course, this is the slack
season, and we're all just laying round a little, but nevertheless we've all got our chores to do, and I don't want to
hurry you, and so if you've come to see me on business
maybe we'd better get down to it."

"As I said, it's not in a way, and again in a way it is,"
said the fat man. "Now I'm looking for a man named
Helton, Mr. Olaf Eric Helton, from North Dakota, and
I was told up around the country a ways that I might find
him here, and I wouldn't mind having a little talk with
him. No, siree, I sure wouldn't mind, if it's all the same
to you."

"I never knew his middle name," said Mr. Thompson,
"but Mr. Helton is right here, and been here now for going
on nine years. He's a mighty steady man, and you can tell
anybody I said so."

"I'm glad to hear that," said Mr. Homer T. Hatch. "I
like to hear of a feller mending his ways and settling down.
Now when I knew Mr. Helton he was pretty wild, yes, sir,
wild is what he was, he didn't know his own mind atall.
Well, now, it's going to be a great pleasure to me to meet
up with an old friend and find him all settled down and
doing well by hisself."

"We've all got to be young once," said Mr. Thompson.
"It's like the measles, it breaks out all over you, and you're
a nuisance to yourself and everybody else, but it don't
last, and it usually don't leave no ill effects." He was so
pleased with this notion he forgot and broke into a guffaw.
The stranger folded his arms over his stomach and went
into a kind of fit, roaring until he had tears in his eyes.
Mr. Thompson stopped shouting and eyed the stranger
uneasily. Now he liked a good laugh as well as any man,
but there ought to be a little moderation. Now this feller
laughed like a perfect lunatic, that was a fact. And he
wasn't laughing because he really thought things were

funny, either. He was laughing for reasons of his own. Mr. Thompson fell into a moody silence, and waited until Mr. Hatch settled down a little.

Mr. Hatch got out a very dirty blue cotton bandanna and wiped his eyes. "That joke just about caught me where I live," he said, almost apologetically. "Now I wish I could think up things as funny as that to say. It's a gift. It's . . ."

"If you want to speak to Mr. Helton, I'll go and round him up," said Mr. Thompson, making motions as if he might get up. "He may be in the milk house and he may be setting in his shack this time of day." It was drawing towards five o'clock. "It's right around the corner," he said.

"Oh, well, there ain't no special hurry," said Mr. Hatch. "I've been wanting to speak to him for a good long spell now and I guess a few minutes more won't make no difference. I just more wanted to locate him, like. That's all."

Mr. Thompson stopped beginning to stand up, and unbuttoned one more button of his shirt, and said, "Well, he's here, and he's this kind of man, that if he had any business with you he'd like to get it over. He don't dawdle, that's one thing you can say for him."

Mr. Hatch appeared to sulk a little at these words. He wiped his face with the bandanna and opened his mouth to speak, when round the house there came the music of Mr. Helton's harmonica. Mr. Thompson raised a finger. "There he is," said Mr. Thompson. "Now's your time."

Mr. Hatch cocked an ear towards the east side of the house and listened for a few seconds, a very strange expression on his face.

"I know that tune like I know the palm of my own hand," said Mr. Thompson, "but I never heard Mr. Helton say what it was."

"That's a kind of Scandahoovian song," said Mr. Hatch. "Where I come from they sing it a lot. In North Dakota, they sing it. It says something about starting out in the morning feeling so good you can't hardly stand it, so you

drink up all your likker before noon. All the likker, y'
understand, that you was saving for the noon lay-off. The
words ain't much, but it's a pretty tune. It's a kind of
drinking song." He sat there drooping a little, and Mr.
Thompson didn't like his expression. It was a satisfied
expression, but it was more like the cat that et the canary.

"So far as I know," said Mr. Thompson, "he ain't
touched a drop since he's been on the place, and that's
nine years this coming September. Yes, sir, nine years, so
far as I know, he ain't wetted his whistle once. And that's
more than I can say for myself," he said, meekly proud.

"Yes, that's a drinking song," said Mr. Hatch. "I used
to play 'Little Brown Jug' on the fiddle when I was younger
than I am now," he went on, "but this Helton, he just
keeps it up. He just sits and plays it by himself."

"He's been playing it off and on for nine years right
here on the place," said Mr. Thompson, feeling a little
proprietary.

"And he was certainly singing it as well, fifteen years
before that, in North Dakota," said Mr. Hatch. "He used
to sit up in a straitjacket, practically, when he was in the
asylum—"

"What's that you say?" said Mr. Thompson. "What's
that?"

"Shucks, I didn't mean to tell you," said Mr. Hatch, a
faint leer of regret in his drooping eyelids. "Shucks, that
just slipped out. Funny, now I'd made up my mind I
wouldn' say a word, because it would just make a lot of
excitement, and what I say is, if a man has lived harmless
and quiet for nine years it don't matter if he *is* loony, does
it? So long's he keeps quiet and don't do nobody harm."

"You mean they had him in a straitjacket?" asked Mr.
Thompson, uneasily. "In a lunatic asylum?"

"They sure did," said Mr. Hatch. "That's right where
they had him, from time to time."

"They put my Aunt Ida in one of them things in the
State asylum," said Mr. Thompson. "She got vi'lent, and

they put her in one of these jackets with long sleeves and tied her to an iron ring in the wall, and Aunt Ida got so wild she broke a blood vessel and when they went to look after her she was dead. I'd think one of them things was dangerous."

"Mr. Helton used to sing his drinking song when he was in a straitjacket," said Mr. Hatch. "Nothing ever bothered him, except if you tried to make him talk. That bothered him, and he'd get vi'lent, like your Aunt Ida. He'd get vi'lent and then they'd put him in the jacket and go off and leave him, and he'd lay there perfickly contented, so far's you could see, singing his song. Then one night he just disappeared. Left, you might say, just went, and nobody ever saw hide or hair of him again. And then I come along and find him here," said Mr. Hatch, "all settled down and playing the same song."

"He never acted crazy to me," said Mr. Thompson. "He always acted like a sensible man, to me. He never got married, for one thing, and he works like a horse, and I bet he's got the first cent I paid him when he landed here, and he don't drink, and he never says a word, much less swear, and he don't waste time runnin' around Saturday nights, and if he's crazy," said Mr. Thompson, "why, I think I'll go crazy myself for a change."

"Haw, ha," said Mr. Hatch, "heh, he, that's good! Ha, ha, ha, I hadn't thought of it jes like that. Yeah, that's right! Let's all go crazy and get rid of our wives and save our money, hey?" He smiled unpleasantly, showing his little rabbit teeth.

Mr. Thompson felt he was being misunderstood. He turned around and motioned toward the open window back of the honeysuckle trellis. "Let's move off down here a little," he said. "I oughta thought of that before." His visitor bothered Mr. Thompson. He had a way of taking the words out of Mr. Thompson's mouth, turning them around and mixing them up until Mr. Thompson didn't know himself what he had said. "My wife's not very

strong," said Mr. Thompson. "She's been kind of invalid
now goin' on fourteen years. It's mighty tough on a poor
man, havin' sickness in the family. She had four opera-
tions," he said proudly, "one right after the other, but
they didn't do any good. For five years handrunnin', I just
turned every nickel I made over to the doctors. Upshot
is, she's a mighty delicate woman."

"My old woman," said Mr. Homer T. Hatch, "had a
back like a mule, yes, sir. That woman could have moved
the barn with her bare hands if she'd ever took the notion.
I used to say, it was a good thing she didn't know her own
stren'th. She's dead now, though. That kind wear out
quicker than the puny ones. I never had much use for a
woman always complainin'. I'd get rid of her mighty quick,
yes, sir, mighty quick. It's just as you say: a dead loss,
keepin' one of 'em up."

This was not at all what Mr. Thompson had heard
himself say; he had been trying to explain that a wife as
expensive as his was a credit to a man. "She's a mighty
reasonable woman," said Mr. Thompson, feeling baffled,
"but I wouldn't answer for what she'd say or do if she
found out we'd had a lunatic on the place all this time."
They had moved away from the window; Mr. Thompson
took Mr. Hatch the front way, because if he went the back
way they would have to pass Mr. Helton's shack. For some
reason he didn't want the stranger to see or talk to Mr.
Helton. It was strange, but that was the way Mr. Thompson felt.

Mr. Thompson sat down again, on the chopping log,
offering his guest another tree stump. "Now, I mighta
got upset myself at such a thing, once," said Mr. Thompson, "but now I *deefy* anything to get me lathered up."
He cut himself an enormous plug of tobacco with his horn-
handled pocketknife, and offered it to Mr. Hatch, who
then produced his own plug and, opening a huge bowie
knife with a long blade sharply whetted, cut off a large
wad and put it in his mouth. They then compared plugs

and both of them were astonished to see how different men's ideas of good chewing tobacco were.

"Now, for instance," said Mr. Hatch, "mine is lighter colored. That's because, for one thing, there ain't any sweetenin' in this plug. I like it dry, natural leaf, medium strong."

"A little sweetenin' don't do no harm so far as I'm concerned," said Mr. Thompson, "but it's got to be mighty little. But with me, now, I want a strong leaf, I want it heavy-cured, as the feller says. There's a man near here, named Williams, Mr. John Morgan Williams, who chews a plug—well, sir, it's black as your hat and soft as melted tar. It fairly drips with molasses, jus' plain molasses, and it chews like licorice. Now, I don't call that a good chew."

"One man's meat," said Mr. Hatch, "is another man's poison. Now, such a chew would simply gag me. I couldn't begin to put it in my mouth."

"Well," said Mr. Thompson, a tinge of apology in his voice, "I jus' barely tasted it myself, you might say. Just took a little piece in my mouth and spit it out again."

"I'm dead sure I couldn't even get that far," said Mr. Hatch. "I like a dry natural chew without any artificial flavorin' of any kind."

Mr. Thompson began to feel that Mr. Hatch was trying to make out he had the best judgment in tobacco, and was going to keep up the argument until he proved it. He began to feel seriously annoyed with the fat man. After all, who was he and where did he come from? Who was he to go around telling other people what kind of tobacco to chew?

"Artificial flavorin'," Mr. Hatch went on, doggedly, "is jes put in to cover up a cheap leaf and make a man think he's gettin' somethin' more than he *is* gettin'. Even a little sweetenin' is a sign of a cheap leaf, you can mark my words."

"I've always paid a fair price for my plug," said Mr. Thompson, stiffly. "I'm not a rich man and I don't go round settin' myself up for one, but I'll say this, when it comes to such things as tobacco, I buy the best on the market."

"Sweetenin', even a little," began Mr. Hatch, shifting his plug and squirting tobacco juice at a dry-looking little rose bush that was having a hard enough time as it was, standing all day in the blazing sun, its roots clenched in the baked earth, "is the sign of—"

"About this Mr. Helton, now," said Mr. Thompson, determinedly, "I don't see no reason to hold it against a man because he went loony once or twice in his lifetime and so I don't expect to take no steps about it. Not a step. I've got nothin' against the man, he's always treated me fair. They's things and people," he went on, " 'nough to drive any man loony. The wonder to me is, more men don't wind up in straitjackets, the way things are going these days and times."

"That's right," said Mr. Hatch, promptly, entirely too promptly, as if he were turning Mr. Thompson's meaning back on him. "You took the words right out of my mouth. There ain't every man in a straitjacket that ought to be there. Ha, ha, you're right all right. You got the idea."

Mr. Thompson sat silent and chewed steadily and stared at a spot on the ground about six feet away and felt a slow muffled resentment climbing from somewhere deep down in him, climbing and spreading all through him. What was this fellow driving at? What was he trying to say? It wasn't so much his words, but his looks and his way of talking: that droopy look in the eye, that tone of voice, as if he was trying to mortify Mr. Thompson about something. Mr. Thompson didn't like it, but he couldn't get hold of it either. He wanted to turn around and shove the fellow off the stump, but it wouldn't look reasonable. Suppose something happened to the fellow when he fell off the stump, just for instance, if he fell on the ax and cut himself, and then someone should ask Mr. Thompson why he shoved him, and what could a man say? It would look mighty funny, it would sound mighty strange to say, Well, him and me fell out over a plug of tobacco. He might just shove him anyhow and then tell people he was a fat man not used to the heat and while he was talking he got dizzy and fell off by himself, or something like that, and it wouldn't be the truth either, because it wasn't the heat and it wasn't the tobacco. Mr. Thompson made up his mind to get the fellow off the place pretty quick, without seeming to be anxious, and watch him sharp till he was out of sight. It doesn't pay to be friendly with strangers from another part of the country. They're always up to something, or they'd stay at home where they belong.

"And they's some people," said Mr. Hatch, "would jus' as soon have a loonatic around their house as not, they can't see no difference between them and anybody else. I always say, if that's the way a man feels, don't care who he associates with, why, why, that's his business, not mine. I don't wanta have a thing to do with it. Now back home in North Dakota, we don't feel that way. I'd like to a seen anybody hiring a loonatic there, aspecially after what he done."

"I didn't understand your home was North Dakota," said Mr. Thompson. "I thought you said Georgia."

"I've got a married sister in North Dakota," said Mr. Hatch, "married a Swede, but a white man if ever I saw one. So I say *we* because we got into a little business together out that way. And it seems like home, kind of."

"What did he do?" asked Mr. Thompson, feeling very uneasy again.

"Oh, nothin' to speak of," said Mr. Hatch, jovially, "jus' went loony one day in the hayfield and shoved a pitchfork right square through his brother, when they was makin' hay. They was goin' to execute him, but they found out he had went crazy with the heat, as the feller says, and so they put him in the asylum. That's all he done. Nothin' to get lathered up about, ha, ha, ha!" he said, and taking out his sharp knife he began to slice off a chew as carefully as if he were cutting cake.

"Well," said Mr. Thompson, "I don't deny that's news. Yes, sir, news. But I still say somethin' must have drove him to it. Some men make you feel like giving 'em a good killing just by lookin' at you. His brother may a been a mean ornery cuss."

"Brother was going to get married," said Mr. Hatch; "used to go courtin' his girl nights. Borrowed Mr. Helton's harmonica to give her a serenade one evenin', and lost it. Brand new harmonica."

"He thinks a heap of his harmonicas," said Mr. Thompson. "Only money he ever spends, now and then he buys hisself a new one. Must have a dozen in that shack, all kinds and sizes."

"Brother wouldn't buy him a new one," said Mr. Hatch, "so Mr. Helton just ups, as I says, and runs his pitchfork through his brother. Now you know he musta been crazy to get all worked up over a little thing like that."

"Sounds like it," said Mr. Thompson, reluctant to agree in anything with this intrusive and disagreeable fellow. He kept thinking he couldn't remember when he had taken such a dislike to a man on first sight.

"Seems to me you'd get pretty sick of hearin' the same tune year in, year out," said Mr. Hatch.

"Well, sometimes I think it wouldn't do no harm if he learned a new one," said Mr. Thompson, "but he don't, so there's nothin' to be done about it. It's a pretty good tune, though."

"One of the Scandahoovians told me what it meant, that's how I come to know," said Mr. Hatch. "Especially that part about getting so gay you jus' go ahead and drink up all the likker you got on hand before noon. It seems like up in them Swede countries a man carries a bottle of wine around with him as a matter of course, at least that's the way I understood it. Those fellers will tell you anything, though—" He broke off and spat.

The idea of drinking any kind of liquor in this heat

made Mr. Thompson dizzy. The idea of anybody feeling good on a day like this, for instance, made him tired. He felt he was really suffering from the heat. The fat man looked as if he had grown to the stump; he slumped there in his damp, dark clothes too big for him, his belly slack in his pants, his wide black felt hat pushed off his narrow forehead red with prickly heat. A bottle of good cold beer, now, would be a help, thought Mr. Thompson, remembering the four bottles sitting deep in the pool at the springhouse, and his dry tongue squirmed in his mouth. He wasn't going to offer this man anything, though, not even a drop of water. He wasn't even going to chew any more tobacco with him. He shot out his quid suddenly, and wiped his mouth on the back of his hand, and studied the head near him attentively. The man was no good, and he was there for no good, but what was he up to? Mr. Thompson made up his mind he'd give him a little more time to get his business, whatever it was, with Mr. Helton over, and then if he didn't get off the place he'd kick him off.

Mr. Hatch, as if he suspected Mr. Thompson's thoughts, turned his eyes, wicked and pig-like, on Mr. Thompson. "Fact is," he said, as if he had made up his mind about something, "I might need your help in the little matter I've got on hand, but it won't cost you any trouble. Now, this Mr. Helton here, like I tell you, he's a dangerous escaped loonatic, you might say. Now fact is, in the last twelve years or so I musta rounded up twenty-odd escaped loonatics, besides a couple of escaped convicts that I just run into by accident, like. I don't make a business of it, but if there's a reward, and there usually is a reward, of course, I get it. It amounts to a tidy little sum in the long run, but that ain't the main question. Fact is, I'm for law and order, I don't like to see lawbreakers and loonatics at large. It ain't the place for them. Now I reckon you're bound to agree with me on that, aren't you?"

Mr. Thompson said, "Well, circumstances alters cases,

as the feller says. Now, what I know of Mr. Helton, he ain't dangerous, as I told you." Something serious was going to happen, Mr. Thompson could see that. He stopped thinking about it. He'd just let this fellow shoot off his head and then see what could be done about it. Without thinking he got out his knife and plug and started to cut a chew, then remembered himself and put them back in his pocket.

"The law," said Mr. Hatch, "is solidly behind me. Now this Mr. Helton, he's been one of my toughest cases. He's kept my record from being practically one hundred per cent. I knew him before he went loony, and I know the fam'ly, so I undertook to help out rounding him up. Well, sir, he was gone slick as a whistle, for all we knew the man was as good as dead long while ago. Now we never might have caught up with him, but do you know what he did? Well, sir, about two weeks ago his old mother gets a letter from him, and in that letter, what do you reckon she found? Well, it was a check on that little bank in town for eight hundred and fifty dollars, just like that; the letter wasn't nothing much, just said he was sending her a few little savings, she might need something, but there it was, name, postmark, date, everything. The old woman practically lost her mind with joy. She's gettin' childish, and it looked like she kinda forgot that her only living son killed his brother and went loony. Mr. Helton said he was getting along all right, and for her not to tell nobody. Well, natchally, she couldn't keep it to herself, with that check to cash and everything. So that's how I come to know." His feelings got the better of him. "You coulda knocked me down with a feather." He shook hands with himself and rocked, wagging his head, going "Heh, heh," in his throat. Mr. Thompson felt the corners of his mouth turning down. Why, the dirty low-down hound, sneaking around spying into other people's business like that. Collecting blood money, that's what it was! Let him talk!

"Yea, well, that musta been a surprise all right," he said,

trying to hold his voice even. "I'd say a surprise."

"Well, siree," said Mr. Hatch, "the more I got to thinking about it, the more I just come to the conclusion that
I'd better look into the matter a little, and so I talked to
the old woman. She's pretty decrepit, now, half blind and
all, but she was all for taking the first train out and going
to see her son. I put it up to her square—how she was too
feeble for the trip, and all. So, just as a favor to her, I told
her for my expenses I'd come down and see Mr. Helton
and bring her back all the news about him. She gave me a
new shirt she made herself by hand, and a big Swedish
kind of cake to bring to him, but I musta mislaid them
along the road somewhere. It don't reely matter, though,
he prob'ly ain't in any state of mind to appreciate 'em."

Mr. Thompson sat up and turning round on the log
looked at Mr. Hatch and asked as quietly as he could, "And
now what are you aiming to do? That's the question."

Mr. Hatch slouched up to his feet and shook himself.
"Well, I come all prepared for a little scuffle," he said. "I
got the handcuffs," he said, "but I don't want no violence
if I can help it. I didn't want to say nothing around the
countryside, making an uproar. I figured the two of us
could overpower him." He reached into his big inside
pocket and pulled them out. Handcuffs, for God's sake,
thought Mr. Thompson. Coming round on a peaceable
afternoon worrying a man, and making trouble, and fishing handcuffs out of his pocket on a decent family home-
stead, as if it was all in the day's work.

Mr. Thompson, his head buzzing, got up too. "Well,"
he said, roundly, "I want to tell you I think you've got a
mighty sorry job on hand, you sure must be hard up for
something to do, and now I want to give you a good piece
of advice. You just drop the idea that you're going to
come here and make trouble for Mr. Helton, and the
quicker you drive that hired rig away from my front gate
the better I'll be satisfied."

Mr. Hatch put one handcuff in his outside pocket, the

other dangling down. He pulled his hat down over his eyes, and reminded Mr. Thompson of a sheriff, somehow. He didn't seem in the least nervous, and didn't take up Mr. Thompson's words. He said, "Now listen just a minute, it ain't reasonable to suppose that a man like yourself is going to stand in the way of getting an escaped loonatic back to the asylum where he belongs. Now I know it's enough to throw you off, coming sudden like this, but fact is I counted on your being a respectable man and helping me out to see that justice is done. Now a course, if you won't help, I'll have to look around for help somewheres else. It won't look very good to your neighbors that you was harboring an escaped loonatic who killed his own brother, and then you refused to give him up. It will look mighty funny."

Mr. Thompson knew almost before he heard the words that it would look funny. It would put him in a mighty awkward position. He said, "But I've been trying to tell you all along that the man ain't loony now. He's been perfectly harmless for nine years. He's—he's—"

Mr. Thompson couldn't think how to describe how it was with Mr. Helton. "Why, he's been like one of the family," he said, "the best standby a man ever had." Mr. Thompson tried to see his way out. It was a fact Mr. Helton might go loony again any minute, and now this fellow talking around the country would put Mr. Thompson in a fix. It was a terrible position. He couldn't think of any way out. "You're crazy," Mr. Thompson roared suddenly, "you're the crazy one around here, you're crazier than he ever was! You get off this place or I'll handcuff you and turn you over to the law. You're trespassing," shouted Mr. Thompson. "Get out of here before I knock you down!"

He took a step towards the fat man, who backed off, shrinking, "Try it, try it, go ahead!" and then something happened that Mr. Thompson tried hard afterwards to piece together in his mind, and in fact it never did come straight. He saw the fat man with his long bowie knife in his hand, he saw Mr. Helton come round the corner on the run, his long jaw dropped, his arms swinging, his eyes wild. Mr. Helton came in between them, fists doubled up, then stopped short, glaring at the fat man, his big frame seemed to collapse, he trembled like a shied horse; and then the fat man drove at him, knife in one hand, handcuffs in the other. Mr. Thompson saw it coming, he saw the blade going into Mr. Helton's stomach, he knew he had the ax out of the log in his own hands, felt his arms go up over his head and bring the ax down on Mr. Hatch's head as if he were stunning a beef.

Mrs. Thompson had been listening uneasily for some time to the voices going on, one of them strange to her, but she was too tired at first to get up and come out to see what was going on. The confused shouting that rose so suddenly brought her up to her feet and out across the front porch without her slippers, hair half-braided. Shading her eyes, she saw first Mr. Helton, running all stooped over through the orchard, running like a man with dogs after him; and Mr. Thompson supporting himself on the ax handle was leaning over shaking by the shoulder a man Mrs. Thompson had never seen, who lay doubled up with the top of his head smashed and the blood running away in a greasy-looking puddle. Mr. Thompson without taking his hand from the man's shoulder, said in a thick voice, "He killed Mr. Helton, he killed him, I saw him do it. I had to knock him out," he called loudly, "but he won't come to."

Mrs. Thompson said in a faint scream, "Why, yonder goes Mr. Helton," and she pointed. Mr. Thompson pulled himself up and looked where she pointed. Mrs. Thompson sat down slowly against the side of the house and began to slide forward on her face; she felt as if she were drowning, she couldn't rise to the top somehow, and her only thought was she was glad the boys were not there, they

were out, fishing at Halifax, oh, God, she was glad the
boys were not there.

Mr. and Mrs. Thompson drove up to their barn about sunset. Mr. Thompson handed the reins to his wife, got out
to open the big door, and Mrs. Thompson guided old Jim
in under the roof. The buggy was gray with dust and age,
Mrs. Thompson's face was gray with dust and weariness,
and Mr. Thompson's face, as he stood at the horse's head
and began unhitching, was gray except for the dark blue
of his freshly shaven jaws and chin, gray and blue and
caved in, but patient, like a dead man's face.

Mrs. Thompson stepped down to the hard packed manure of the barn floor, and shook out her light flower-
sprigged dress. She wore her smoked glasses, and her wide
shady leghorn hat with the wreath of exhausted pink and
blue forget-me-nots hid her forehead, fixed in a knot of
distress.

The horse hung his head, raised a huge sigh and flexed
his stiffened legs. Mr. Thompson's words came up muffled
and hollow. "Poor ole Jim," he said, clearing his throat,
"he looks pretty sunk in the ribs. I guess he's had a hard
week." He lifted the harness up in one piece, slid it off and
Jim walked out of the shafts halting a little. "Well, this is
the last time," Mr. Thompson said, still talking to Jim.
"Now you can get a good rest."

Mrs. Thompson closed her eyes behind her smoked
glasses. The last time, and high time, and they should
never have gone at all. She did not need her glasses any
more, now the good darkness was coming down again, but
her eyes ran full of tears steadily, though she was not crying, and she felt better with the glasses, safer, hidden away
behind them. She took out her handkerchief with her
hands shaking as they had been shaking ever since *that day*,
and blew her nose. She said, "I see the boys have lighted
the lamps. I hope they've started the stove going."

She stepped along the rough path holding her thin dress

and starched petticoats around her, feeling her way between the sharp small stones, leaving the barn because she could hardly bear to be near Mr. Thompson, advancing slowly towards the house because she dreaded going there. Life was all one dread, the faces of her neighbors, of her boys, of her husband, the face of the whole world, the shape of her own house in the darkness, the very smell of the grass and the trees were horrible to her. There was no place to go, only one thing to do, bear it somehow—but how? She asked herself that question often. How was she going to keep on living now? Why had she lived at all? She wished now she had died one of those times when she had been so sick, instead of living on for this.

The boys were in the kitchen; Herbert was looking at the funny pictures from last Sunday's newspapers, the Katzenjammer Kids and Happy Hooligan. His chin was in his hands and his elbows on the table, and he was really reading and looking at the pictures, but his face was unhappy. Arthur was building the fire, adding kindling a stick at a time, watching it catch and blaze. His face was heavier and darker than Herbert's, but he was a little sullen by nature; Mrs. Thompson thought, he takes things harder, too. Arthur said, "Hello, Momma," and went on with his work. Herbert swept the papers together and moved over on the bench. They were big boys—fifteen and seventeen, and Arthur as tall as his father. Mrs. Thompson sat down beside Herbert, taking off her hat. She said, "I guess you're hungry. We were late today. We went the Log Hollow road, it's rougher than ever." Her pale mouth drooped with a sad fold on either side.

"I guess you saw the Mannings, then," said Herbert.

"Yes, and the Fergusons, and the Allbrights, and that new family McClellan."

"Anybody say anything?" asked Herbert.

"Nothing much, you know how it's been all along, some of them keeps saying, yes, they know it was a clear case and a fair trial and they say how glad they are your papa came

out so well, and all that, some of 'em do, anyhow, but it
looks like they don't really take sides with him. I'm about
wore out," she said, the tears rolling again from under
her dark glasses. "I don't know what good it does, but your
papa can't seem to rest unless he's telling how it happened.
I don't know."

"I don't think it does any good, not a speck," said
Arthur, moving away from the stove. "It just keeps the
whole question stirred up in people's minds. Everybody
will go round telling what he heard, and the whole thing
is going to get worse mixed up than ever. It just makes
matters worse. I wish you could get Papa to stop driving
round the country talking like that."

"Your papa knows best," said Mrs. Thompson. "You
oughtn't to criticize him. He's got enough to put up with
without that."

Arthur said nothing, his jaw stubborn. Mr. Thompson
came in, his eyes hollowed out and dead-looking, his thick
hands gray white and seamed from washing them clean
every day before he started out to see the neighbors to tell
them his side of the story. He was wearing his Sunday
clothes, a thick pepper-and-salt-colored suit with a black
string tie.

Mrs. Thompson stood up, her head swimming. "Now
you-all get out of the kitchen, it's too hot in here and I
need room. I'll get us a little bite of supper, if you'll just
get out and give me some room."

They went as if they were glad to go, the boys outside,
Mr. Thompson into his bedroom. She heard him groaning
to himself as he took off his shoes, and heard the bed creak
as he lay down. Mrs. Thompson opened the icebox and
felt the sweet coldness flow out of it; she had never expected to have an icebox, much less did she hope to afford
to keep it filled with ice. It still seemed like a miracle, after
two or three years. There was the food, cold and clean, all
ready to be warmed over. She would never have had that
icebox if Mr. Helton hadn't happened along one day, just

by the strangest luck; so saving, and so managing, so good, thought Mrs. Thompson, her heart swelling until she feared she would faint again, standing there with the door open and leaning her head upon it. She simply could not bear to remember Mr. Helton, with his long sad face and silent ways, who had always been so quiet and harmless, who had worked so hard and helped Mr. Thompson so much, running through the hot fields and woods, being hunted like a mad dog, everybody turning out with ropes and guns and sticks to catch and tie him. Oh, God, said Mrs. Thompson in a long dry moan, kneeling before the icebox and fumbling inside for the dishes, even if they did pile mattresses all over the jail floor and against the walls, and five men there to hold him to keep him from hurting himself any more, he was already hurt too badly, he couldn't have lived anyway. Mr. Barbee, the sheriff, told her about it. He said, well, they didn't aim to harm him but they had to catch him, he was crazy as a loon; he picked up rocks and tried to brain every man that got near him. He had two harmonicas in his jumper pocket, said the sheriff, but they fell out in the scuffle, and Mr. Helton tried to pick 'em up again, and that's when they finally got him. "They *had* to be rough, Miz Thompson, he fought like a wildcat." Yes, thought Mrs. Thompson again with the same bitterness, of course, they had to be rough. They always have to be rough. Mr. Thompson can't argue with a man and get him off the place peaceably; no, she thought, standing up and shutting the icebox, he has to kill somebody, he has to be a murderer and ruin his boys' lives and cause Mr. Helton to be killed like a mad dog.

Her thoughts stopped with a little soundless explosion, cleared and began again. The rest of Mr. Helton's harmonicas were still in the shack, his tune ran in Mrs. Thompson's head at certain times of the day. She missed it in the evenings. It seemed so strange she had never known the name of that song, nor what it meant, until after Mr. Helton was gone. Mrs. Thompson, trembling in

the knees, took a drink of water at the sink and poured
the red beans into the baking dish, and began to roll the
pieces of chicken in flour to fry them. There was a time,
she said to herself, when I thought I had neighbors and
friends, there was a time when we could hold up our heads,
there was a time when my husband hadn't killed a man
and I could tell the truth to anybody about anything.

Mr. Thompson, turning on his bed, figured that he had
done all he could, he'd just try to let the matter rest from
now on. His lawyer, Mr. Burleigh, had told him right at
the beginning, "Now you keep calm and collected. You've
got a fine case, even if you haven't got witnesses. Your wife
must sit in court, she'll be a powerful argument with the
jury. You just plead not guilty and I'll do the rest.
The trial is going to be a mere formality, you haven't
got a thing to worry about. You'll be clean out of this before you know it." And to make talk Mr. Burleigh had
got to telling about all the men he knew around the country who for one reason or another had been forced to kill
somebody, always in self-defense, and there just wasn't
anything to it at all. He even told about how his own
father in the old days had shot and killed a man just for
setting foot inside his gate when he told him not to. "Sure,
I shot the scoundrel," said Mr. Burleigh's father, "in self-
defense; I *told* him I'd shoot him if he set his foot in my
yard, and he did, and I did." There had been bad blood
between them for years, Mr. Burleigh said, and his father
had waited a long time to catch the other fellow in the
wrong, and when he did he certainly made the most of his
opportunity.

"But Mr. Hatch, as I told you," Mr. Thompson had
said, "made a pass at Mr. Helton with his bowie knife.
That's why I took a hand."

"All the better," said Mr. Burleigh. "That stranger
hadn't any right coming to your house on such an errand.
Why, hell," said Mr. Burleigh, "that wasn't even man-

slaughter you committed. So now you just hold your horses and keep your shirt on. And don't say one word without I tell you."

Wasn't even manslaughter. Mr. Thompson had to cover Mr. Hatch with a piece of wagon canvas and ride to town to tell the sheriff. It had been hard on Ellie. When they got back, the sheriff and the coroner and two deputies, they found her sitting beside the road, on a low bridge over a gulley, about half a mile from the place. He had taken her up behind his saddle and got her back to the house. He had already told the sheriff that his wife had witnessed the whole business, and now he had time, getting her to her room and in bed, to tell her what to say if they asked anything. He had left out the part about Mr. Helton being crazy all along, but it came out at the trial. By Mr. Burleigh's advice Mr. Thompson had pretended to be perfectly ignorant; Mr. Hatch hadn't said a word about that. Mr. Thompson pretended to believe that Mr. Hatch had just come looking for Mr. Helton to settle old scores, and the two members of Mr. Hatch's family who had come down to try to get Mr. Thompson convicted didn't get anywhere at all. It hadn't been much of a trial, Mr. Burleigh saw to that. He had charged a reasonable fee, and Mr. Thompson had paid him and felt grateful, but after it was over Mr. Burleigh didn't seem pleased to see him when he got to dropping into the office to talk it over, telling him things that had slipped his mind at first: trying to explain what an ornery low hound Mr. Hatch had been, anyhow. Mr. Burleigh seemed to have lost his interest; he looked sour and upset when he saw Mr. Thompson at the door. Mr. Thompson kept saying to himself that he'd got off, all right, just as Mr. Burleigh had predicted, but, but—and it was right there that Mr. Thompson's mind stuck, squirming like an angleworm on a fishhook: he had killed Mr. Hatch, and he was a murderer. That was the truth about himself that Mr. Thompson couldn't grasp, even when he said the word to himself. Why, he had not even once *thought* of killing anybody, much less Mr. Hatch, and if Mr. Helton hadn't come out so unexpectedly, hearing the row, why, then—but then, Mr. Helton had come on the run that way to help him. What he couldn't understand was what happened next. He had seen Mr. Hatch go after Mr. Helton with the knife, he had seen the point, blade up, go into Mr. Helton's stomach and slice up like you slice a hog, but when they finally caught Mr. Helton there wasn't a knife scratch on him. Mr. Thompson knew he had the ax in his own hands and felt himself lifting it, but he couldn't remember hitting Mr. Hatch. He couldn't remember it. He couldn't. He remembered only that he had been determined to stop Mr. Hatch from cutting Mr. Helton. If he was given a chance he could explain the whole matter. At the trial they hadn't let him talk. They just asked questions and he answered yes or no, and they never did get to the core of the matter. Since the trial, now, every day for a week he had washed and shaved and put on his best clothes and had taken Ellie with him to tell every neighbor he had that he never killed Mr. Hatch on purpose, and what good did it do? Nobody believed him. Even when he turned to Ellie and said, "You was there, you saw it, didn't you?" and Ellie spoke up, saying, "Yes, that's the truth. Mr. Thompson was trying to save Mr. Helton's life," and he added, "If you don't believe me, you can believe my wife. She won't lie," Mr. Thompson saw something in all their faces that disheartened him, made him feel empty and tired out. They didn't believe he was not a murderer.

Even Ellie never said anything to comfort him. He hoped she would say finally, "I remember now, Mr. Thompson, I really did come round the corner in time to see everything. It's not a lie, Mr. Thompson. Don't you worry." But as they drove together in silence, with the days still hot and dry, shortening for fall, day after day, the buggy jolting in the ruts, she said nothing; they grew to dread the sight of another house, and the people in it:

all houses looked alike now, and the people—old neighbors or new—had the same expression when Mr. Thompson told them why he had come and began his story. Their eyes looked as if someone had pinched the eyeball at the back; they shriveled and the light went out of them. Some of them sat with fixed tight smiles trying to be friendly. "Yes, Mr. Thompson, we know how you must feel. It must be terrible for you, Mrs. Thompson. Yes, you know, I've about come to the point where I believe in such a thing as killing in self-defense. Why, certainly, we believe you, Mr. Thompson, why shouldn't we believe you? Didn't you have a perfectly fair and above-board trial? Well, now, natchally, Mr. Thompson, we think you done right."

Mr. Thompson was satisfied they didn't think so. Sometimes the air around him was so thick with their blame he fought and pushed with his fists, and the sweat broke out all over him, he shouted his story in a dust-choked voice, he would fairly bellow at last: "My wife, here, you know her, she was there, she saw and heard it all, if you don't believe me, ask her, she won't lie!" and Mrs. Thompson, with her hands knotted together, aching, her chin trembling, would never fail to say: "Yes, that's right, that's the truth—"

The last straw had been laid on today, Mr. Thompson decided. Tom Allbright, an old beau of Ellie's, why, he had squired Ellie around a whole summer, had come out to meet them when they drove up, and standing there bareheaded had stopped them from getting out. He had looked past them with an embarrassed frown on his face, telling them his wife's sister was there with a raft of young ones, and the house was pretty full and everything upset, or he'd ask them to come in. "We've been thinking of trying to get up to your place one of these days," said Mr. Allbright, moving away trying to look busy, "we've been mighty occupied up here of late." So they had to say, "Well, we just happened to be driving this way," and go on. "The Allbrights," said Mrs. Thompson, "always was fair-weather friends." "They look out for number one, that's a fact," said Mr. Thompson. But it was cold comfort to them both.

Finally Mrs. Thompson had given up. "Let's go home," she said. "Old Jim's tired and thirsty, and we've gone far enough."

Mr. Thompson said, "Well, while we're out this way, we might as well stop at the McClellans'." They drove in, and asked a little cotton-haired boy if his mamma and papa were at home. Mr. Thompson wanted to see them. The little boy stood gazing with his mouth open, then galloped into the house shouting, "Mommer, Popper, come out hyah. That man that kilt Mr. Hatch has come ter see yer!"

The man came out in his sock feet, with one gallus up, the other broken and dangling, and said, "Light down, Mr. Thompson, and come in. The ole woman's washing, but she'll git here." Mrs. Thompson, feeling her way, stepped down and sat in a broken rocking-chair on the porch that sagged under her feet. The woman of the house, barefooted, in a calico wrapper, sat on the edge of the porch, her fat sallow face full of curiosity. Mr. Thompson began, "Well, as I reckon you happen to know, I've had some strange troubles lately, and, as the feller says, it's not the kind of trouble that happens to a man every day in the year, and there's some things I don't want no misunderstanding about in the neighbors' minds, so—" He halted and stumbled forward, and the two listening faces took on a mean look, a greedy, despising look, a look that said plain as day, "My, you must be a purty sorry feller to come round worrying about what *we* think, *we* know you wouldn't be here if you had anybody else to turn to—my, I wouldn't lower myself that much, myself." Mr. Thompson was ashamed of himself, he was suddenly in a rage, he'd like to knock their dirty skunk heads together, the low-down white trash—but he held himself down and went on to the end. "My wife will tell you," he said, and this was the hardest place, because Ellie always without moving a muscle seemed to stiffen as if somebody had threatened to hit her; "ask my wife, she won't lie."

"It's true, I saw it—"

"Well, now," said the man, drily, scratching his ribs inside his shirt, "that sholy is too bad. Well, now, I kaint see what we've got to do with all this here, however. I kaint see no good reason for us to git mixed up in these murder matters, I shore kaint. Whichever way you look at it, it ain't none of my business. However, it's mighty nice of you-all to come around and give us the straight of it, fur we've heerd some mighty queer yarns about it, mighty queer, I golly you couldn't hardly make head ner tail of it."

"Evvybody goin' round shootin' they heads off," said the woman. "Now we don't hold with killin'; the Bible says—"

"Shet yer trap," said the man, "and keep it shet 'r I'll shet it fer yer. Now it shore looks like to me—"

"We mustn't linger," said Mrs. Thompson, unclasping her hands. "We've lingered too long now. It's getting late, and we've far to go." Mr. Thompson took the hint and followed her. The man and the woman lolled against their rickety porch poles and watched them go.

Now lying on his bed, Mr. Thompson knew the end had come. Now, this minute, lying in the bed where he had slept with Ellie for eighteen years; under this roof where he had laid the shingles when he was waiting to get married; there as he was with his whiskers already sprouting since his shave that morning; with his fingers feeling his bony chin, Mr. Thompson felt he was a dead man. He was dead to his other life, he had got to the end of something without knowing why, and he had to make a fresh start, he did not know how. Something different was going to begin, he didn't know what. It was in some way not his business. He didn't feel he was going to have much to do with it. He got up, aching, hollow, and went out to the

kitchen where Mrs. Thompson was just taking up the
supper.

"Call the boys," said Mrs. Thompson. They had been
down to the barn, and Arthur put out the lantern before
hanging it on a nail near the door. Mr. Thompson didn't
like their silence. They had hardly said a word about anything to him since that day. They seemed to avoid him,
they ran the place together as if he wasn't there, and at-
tended to everything without asking him for any advice.
"What you boys been up to?" he asked, trying to be hearty.
"Finishing your chores?"

"No, sir," said Arthur, "there ain't much to do. Just
greasing some axles." Herbert said nothing. Mrs. Thompson bowed her head: "For these and all Thy blessings. . . .
Amen," she whispered weakly, and the Thompsons sat
there with their eyes down and their faces sorrowful, as if
they were at a funeral.

Every time he shut his eyes, trying to sleep, Mr. Thompson's mind started up and began to run like a rabbit. It
jumped from one thing to another, trying to pick up a
trail here or there that would straighten out what had happened that day he killed Mr. Hatch. Try as he might, Mr.
Thompson's mind would not go anywhere that it had not
already been, he could not see anything but what he had
seen once, and he knew that was not right. If he had not
seen straight that first time, then everything about his
killing Mr. Hatch was wrong from start to finish, and there
was nothing more to be done about it, he might just as
well give up. It still seemed to him that he had done, maybe not the right thing, but the only thing he could do, that
day, but had he? *Did he have to kill Mr. Hatch?* He had
never seen a man he hated more, the minute he laid eyes
on him. He knew in his bones the fellow was there for
trouble. What seemed so funny now was this: Why hadn't
he just told Mr. Hatch to get out before he ever even got
in?

Mrs. Thompson, her arms crossed on her breast, was lying beside him, perfectly still, but she seemed awake, somehow. "Asleep, Ellie?"

After all, he might have got rid of him peaceably, or maybe he might have had to overpower him and put those handcuffs on him and turn him over to the sheriff for disturbing the peace. The most they could have done was to lock Mr. Hatch up while he cooled off for a few days, or fine him a little something. He would try to think of things he might have said to Mr. Hatch. Why, let's see, I could just have said, Now look here, Mr. Hatch, I want to talk to you as man to man. But his brain would go empty. What could he have said or done? But if he *could* have done anything else almost except kill Mr. Hatch, then nothing would have happened to Mr. Helton. Mr. Thompson hardly ever thought of Mr. Helton. His mind just skipped over him and went on. If he stopped to think about Mr. Helton he'd never in God's world get anywhere. He tried to imagine how it might all have been, this very night even, if Mr. Helton were still safe and sound out in his shack playing his tune about feeling so good in the morning, drinking up all the wine so you'd feel even better; and Mr. Hatch safe in jail somewhere, mad as hops, maybe, but out of harm's way and ready to listen to reason and to repent of his meanness, the dirty, yellow-livered hound coming around persecuting an innocent man and ruining a whole family that never harmed him! Mr. Thompson felt the veins of his forehead start up, his fists clutched as if they seized an ax handle, the sweat broke out on him, he bounded up from the bed with a yell smothered in his throat, and Ellie started up after him, crying out, "Oh, oh, don't! Don't! Don't!" as if she were having a nightmare. He stood shaking until his bones rattled in him, crying hoarsely, "Light the lamp, light the lamp, Ellie."

Instead, Mrs. Thompson gave a shrill weak scream, almost the same scream he had heard on that day she came

around the house when he was standing there with the
ax in his hand. He could not see her in the dark, but she
was on the bed, rolling violently. He felt for her in horror,
and his groping hands found her arms, up, and her own
hands pulling her hair straight out from her head, her
neck strained back, and the tight screams strangling her.
He shouted out for Arthur, for Herbert. "Your mother!"
he bawled, his voice cracking. As he held Mrs. Thompson's
arms, the boys came tumbling in, Arthur with the lamp
above his head. By this light Mr. Thompson saw Mrs.
Thompson's eyes, wide open, staring dreadfully at him,
the tears pouring. She sat up at sight of the boys, and held
out one arm towards them, the hand wagging in a crazy
circle, then dropped on her back again, and suddenly
went limp. Arthur set the lamp on the table and turned
on Mr. Thompson. "She's scared," he said, "she's scared
to death." His face was in a knot of rage, his fists were
doubled up, he faced his father as if he meant to strike
him. Mr. Thompson's jaw fell, he was so surprised he
stepped back from the bed. Herbert went to the other side.
They stood on each side of Mrs. Thompson and watched
Mr. Thompson as if he were a dangerous wild beast. "What
did you do to her?" shouted Arthur, in a grown man's
voice. "You touch her again and I'll blow your heart out!"
Herbert was pale and his cheek twitched, but he was on
Arthur's side; he would do what he could to help Arthur.

Mr. Thompson had no fight left in him. His knees bent
as he stood, his chest collapsed. "Why, Arthur," he said,
his words crumbling and his breath coming short. "She's
fainted again. Get the ammonia." Arthur did not move.
Herbert brought the bottle, and handed it, shrinking, to
his father.

Mr. Thompson held it under Mrs. Thompson's nose.
He poured a little in the palm of his hand and rubbed it
on her forehead. She gasped and opened her eyes and
turned her head away from him. Herbert began a doleful
hopeless sniffling. "Mamma," he kept saying, "Mamma,

don't die."

"I'm all right," Mrs. Thompson said. "Now don't you worry around. Now Herbert, you mustn't do that. I'm all right." She closed her eyes. Mr. Thompson began pulling on his best pants; he put on his socks and shoes. The boys sat on each side of the bed, watching Mrs. Thompson's face. Mr. Thompson put on his shirt and coat. He said, "I reckon I'll ride over and get the doctor. Don't look like all this fainting is a good sign. Now you just keep watch until I get back." They listened, but said nothing. He said, "Don't you get any notions in your head. I never did your mother any harm in my life, on purpose." He went out, and, looking back, saw Herbert staring at him from under his brows, like a stranger. "You'll know how to look after her," said Mr. Thompson.

Mr. Thompson went through the kitchen. There he lighted the lantern, took a thin pad of scratch paper and a stub pencil from the shelf where the boys kept their schoolbooks. He swung the lantern on his arm and reached into the cupboard where he kept the guns. The shotgun was there to his hand, primed and ready, a man never knows when he may need a shotgun. He went out of the house without looking around, or looking back when he had left it, passed his barn without seeing it, and struck out to the farthest end of his fields, which ran for half a mile to the east. So many blows had been struck at Mr. Thompson and from so many directions he couldn't stop any more to find out where he was hit. He walked on, over plowed ground and over meadow, going through barbed wire fences cautiously, putting his gun through first; he could almost see in the dark, now his eyes were used to it. Finally he came to the last fence; here he sat down, back against a post, lantern at his side, and, with the pad on his knee, moistened the stub pencil and began to write:

"Before Almighty God, the great judge of all before who I am about to appear, I do hereby solemnly swear that I did not take the life of Mr. Homer T. Hatch on

purpose. It was done in defense of Mr. Helton. I did not
aim to hit him with the ax but only to keep him off Mr.
Helton. He aimed a blow at Mr. Helton who was not looking for it. It was my belief at the time that Mr. Hatch
would of taken the life of Mr. Helton if I did not interfere.
I have told all this to the judge and the jury and they let
me off but nobody believes it. This is the only way I can
prove I am not a cold blooded murderer like everybody
seems to think. If I had been in Mr. Helton's place he
would of done the same for me. I still think I done the
only thing there was to do. My wife—"

Mr. Thompson stopped here to think a while. He wet
the pencil point with the tip of his tongue and marked
out the last two words. He sat a while blacking out the
words until he had made a neat oblong patch where they
had been, and started again:

"It was Mr. Homer T. Hatch who came to do wrong to
a harmless man. He caused all this trouble and he deserved
to die but I am sorry it was me who had to kill him."

He licked the point of his pencil again, and signed his
full name carefully, folded the paper and put it in his outside pocket. Taking off his right shoe and sock, he set the
butt of the shotgun along the ground with the twin barrels
pointed towards his head. It was very awkward. He
thought about this a little, leaning his head against the
gun mouth. He was trembling and his head was drumming
until he was deaf and blind, but he lay down flat on the
earth on his side, drew the barrel under his chin and
fumbled for the trigger with his great toe. That way he
could work it.

THE OVERCOAT

· ·

Nikolay Gogol

Nikolay Gogol

. . . .

Nikolay Gogol, born in 1809, not only wrote at least one of the masterpieces of Russian literature but helped to influence that literature—so much so that Dostoievsky once remarked that all Russian writers were descended from Gogol's *Overcoat.* Gogol's two other most famous works are *The Inspector General,* a hilarious play lampooning bureaucracy; and *Dead Souls,* a classic novel presenting a penetrating insight into life in the Russian provinces. In these works humor and symbol and message are combined into superb stories. They are the imaginative works of a genius. But it was "message" that Gogol tragically mistook to be his most important task. And he died, finally, with his faith in his imagination destroyed, in 1852.

THE OVERCOAT

IN THE department of . . . but I had better not mention in what department. There is nothing in the world more readily moved to wrath than a department, a regiment, a government office, and in fact any sort of official body. Nowadays every private individual considers all society insulted in his person. I have been told that very lately a petition was handed in from a police-captain of what town I don't recollect, and that in this petition he set forth clearly that the institutions of the State were in danger and that its sacred name was being taken in vain; and, in proof thereof, he appended to his petition an enormously long volume of some work of romance in which a police-captain appeared on every tenth page, occasionally, indeed, in an intoxicated condition. And so, to avoid any unpleasantness, we had better call the department of which we are speaking a certain department.

And so, in a certain department there was a government clerk; a clerk of whom it cannot be said that he was very remarkable; he was short, somewhat pock-marked, with rather reddish hair and rather dim, bleary eyes, with a small bald patch on the top of his head, with wrinkles on both sides of his cheeks and the sort of complexion which is usually associated with hæmorrhoids . . . no help for that, it is the Petersburg climate. As for his grade in the service (for among us the grade is what must be put first), he was what is called a perpetual titular councillor, a class at which, as we all know, various writers who indulge in the praiseworthy habit of attacking those who cannot defend themselves jeer and jibe to their hearts' content. This clerk's surname was Bashmatchkin. From the very name it is clear that it must have been derived from a shoe *(bashmak);* but when and under what circumstances it was derived from a shoe, it is impossible to say. Both his father and his grandfather and even his brother-in-law, and all the Bashmatchkins without exception wore boots, which they simply re-soled two or three times a year. His name was Akaky Akakyevitch. Perhaps it may strike the reader as a rather strange and far-fetched name, but I can assure him that it was not far-fetched at all, that the circumstances were such that it was quite out of the question to give him any other name. Akaky Akakyevitch was born towards nightfall, if my memory does not deceive me, on the twenty-third of March. His mother, the wife of a government clerk, a very good woman, made arrangements in due course to christen the child. She was still lying in bed, facing the door, while on her right hand stood the godfather, an excellent man called Ivan Ivanovitch Yeroshkin, one of the head clerks in the Senate, and the godmother, the wife of a police official, and a woman of rare qualities, Arina Semyonovna Byelobryushkov. Three names were offered to the happy mother for selection—Moky, Sossy, or the name of the martyr Hozdazat. "No," thought the poor lady, "they are all such names!" To satisfy her, they opened the calendar at another place, and the names which turned up were: Trifily, Dula, Varahasy. "What an infliction!" said the mother. "What names they all are! I really never heard such names. Varadat or Varuh would be bad enough, but Trifily and Varahasy!" They turned over another page and the names were: Pavsikahy and Vahtisy. "Well, I see," said the mother, "it is clear that it is his fate. Since that is how it is, he had better be called after his father, his father is Akaky, let the son be Akaky, too:" This was how he came to be Akaky Akakyevitch. The baby was christened and cried and made wry faces during the ceremony, as though he foresaw that he would be a titular councillor. So that was how it all came to pass. We have recalled it here so that the reader may see for himself that it happened quite inevitably and that

to give him any other name was out of the question. No
one has been able to remember when and how long ago he
entered the department, nor who gave him the job. However many directors and higher officials of all sorts came
and went, he was always seen in the same place, in the same
position, at the very same duty, precisely the same copying
clerk, so that they used to declare that he must have been
born a copying clerk in uniform all complete and with a
bald patch on his head. No respect at all was shown him
in the department. The porters, far from getting up from
their seats when he came in, took no more notice of him
than if a simple fly had flown across the vestibule. His superiors treated him with a sort of domineering chilliness.
The head clerk's assistant used to throw papers under his
nose without even saying: "Copy this" or "Here is an interesting, nice little case" or some agreeable remark of the
sort, as is usually done in well-behaved offices. And he
would take it, gazing only at the paper without looking
to see who had put it there and whether he had the right
to do so; he would take it and at once set to work to copy
it. The young clerks jeered and made jokes at him to the
best of their clerkly wit, and told before his face all sorts
of stories of their own invention about him; they would
say of his landlady, an old woman of seventy, that she beat
him, would enquire when the wedding was to take place,
and would scatter bits of paper on his head, calling them
snow. Akaky Akakyevitch never answered a word, however, but behaved as though there were no one there. It
had no influence on his work even; in the midst of all this
teasing, he never made a single mistake in his copying.
Only when the jokes were too unbearable, when they
jolted his arm and prevented him from going on with his
work, he would bring out: "Leave me alone! Why do you
insult me?" and there was something strange in the words
and in the voice in which they were uttered. There was a
note in it of something that aroused compassion, so that
one young man, new to the office, who, following the ex-

ample of the rest, had allowed himself to mock at him, suddenly stopped as though cut to the heart, and from that time forth, everything was, as it were, changed and appeared in a different light to him. Some unnatural force seemed to thrust him away from the companions with whom he had become acquainted, accepting them as well-bred, polished people. And long afterwards, at moments of the greatest gaiety, the figure of the humble little clerk with a bald patch on his head rose before him with his heart-rending words: "Leave me alone! Why do you insult me?" and in those heart-rending words he heard others: "I am your brother." And the poor young man hid his face in his hands, and many times afterwards in his life he shuddered, seeing how much inhumanity there is in man, how much savage brutality lies hidden under refined, cultured politeness, and, my God! even in a man whom the world accepts as a gentleman and a man of honor. . . .

It would be hard to find a man who lived in his work as did Akaky Akakyevitch. To say that he was zealous in his work is not enough; no, he loved his work. In it, in that copying, he found a varied and agreeable world of his own. There was a look of enjoyment on his face; certain letters were favorites with him, and when he came to them he was delighted; he chuckled to himself and winked and moved his lips, so that it seemed as though every letter his pen was forming could be read in his face. If rewards had been given according to the measure of zeal in the service, he might to his amazement have even found himself a civil councillor; but all he gained in the service, as the wits, his fellow-clerks expressed it, was a buckle in his button-hole and a pain in his back. It cannot be said, however, that no notice had ever been taken of him. One director, being a good-natured man and anxious to reward him for his long service, sent him something a little more important than his ordinary copying; he was instructed from a finished document to make some sort of report for another office; the work consisted only of altering the headings and in places changing the first person into the third. This cost him such an effort that it threw him into a regular perspiration: he mopped his brow and said at last, "No, better let me copy something."

From that time forth they left him to go on copying for ever. It seemed as though nothing in the world existed for him outside his copying. He gave no thought at all to his clothes; his uniform was—well, not green but some sort of rusty, muddy color. His collar was very short and narrow, so that, although his neck was not particularly long, yet, standing out of the collar, it looked as immensely long as those of the plaster kittens that wag their heads and are carried about on trays on the heads of dozens of foreigners living in Russia. And there were always things sticking to his uniform, either bits of hay or threads; moreover, he had a special art of passing under a window at the very moment when various rubbish was being flung out into the street, and so was continually carrying off bits of melon rind and similar litter on his hat. He had never once in his life noticed what was being done and going on in the street, all those things at which, as we all know, his colleagues, the young clerks, always stare, carrying their sharp sight so far even as to notice anyone on the other side of the pavement with a trouser strap hanging loose—a detail which always calls forth a sly grin. Whatever Akaky Akakyevitch looked at, he saw nothing anywhere but his clear, evenly written lines, and only perhaps when a horse's head suddenly appeared from nowhere just on his shoulder, and its nostrils blew a perfect gale upon his cheek, did he notice that he was not in the middle of his writing, but rather in the middle of the street.

On reaching home, he would sit down at once to the table, hurriedly sup his soup and eat a piece of beef with an onion; he did not notice the taste at all, but ate it all up together with the flies and anything else that Providence chanced to send him. When he felt that his stomach was beginning to be full, he would rise up from the table, get

out a bottle of ink and set to copying the papers he had
brought home with him. When he had none to do, he
would make a copy expressly for his own pleasure, particularly if the document were remarkable not for the
beauty of its style but for the fact of its being addressed
to some new or important personage.

Even at those hours when the grey Petersburg sky is
completely overcast and the whole population of clerks
have dined and eaten their fill, each as best he can, according to the salary he receives and his personal tastes; when
they are all resting after the scratching of pens and bustle
of the office, their own necessary work and other people's,
and all the tasks that an over-zealous man voluntarily sets
himself even beyond what is necessary; when the clerks
are hastening to devote what is left of their time to pleasure; some more enterprising are flying to the theatre, others to the street to spend their leisure, staring at women's
hats, some to spend the evening paying compliments to
some attractive girl, the star of a little official circle, while
some—and this is the most frequent of all—go simply to a
fellow-clerk's flat on the third or fourth storey, two little
rooms with an entry or a kitchen, with some pretentions
to style, with a lamp or some such article that has cost
many sacrifices of dinners and excursions—at the time
when all the clerks are scattered about the little flats of
their friends, playing a tempestuous game of whist, sipping
tea out of glasses to the accompaniment of farthing rusks,
sucking in smoke from long pipes, telling, as the cards are
dealt, some scandal that has floated down from higher
circles, a pleasure which the Russian can never by any
possibility deny himself, or, when there is nothing better
to talk about, repeating the everlasting anecdote of the
commanding officer who was told that the tail had been cut
off his horse on the Falconet monument—in short, even
when every one was eagerly seeking entertainment, Akaky
Akakyevitch did not give himself up to any amusement.
No one could say that they had ever seen him at an evening

party. After working to his heart's content, he would go to bed, smiling at the thought of the next day and wondering what God would send him to copy. So flowed on the peaceful life of a man who knew how to be content with his fate on a salary of four hundred roubles, and so perhaps it would have flowed on to extreme old age, had it not been for the various calamities that bestrew the path through life, not only of titular, but even of privy, actual court and all other councillors, even those who neither give counsel to others nor accept it themselves.

There is in Petersburg a mighty foe of all who receive a salary of four hundred roubles or about that sum. That foe is none other than our northern frost, although it is said to be very good for the health. Between eight and nine in the morning, precisely at the hour when the streets are full of clerks going to their departments, the frost begins giving such sharp and stinging flips at all their noses indiscriminately that the poor fellows don't know what to do with them. At that time, when even those in the higher grade have a pain in their brows and tears in their eyes from the frost, the poor titular councillors are sometimes almost defenceless. Their only protection lies in running as fast as they can through five or six streets in a wretched, thin little overcoat and then warming their feet thoroughly in the porter's room, till all their faculties and qualifications for their various duties thaw again after being frozen on the way. Akaky Akakyevitch had for some time been feeling that his back and shoulders were particularly nipped by the cold, although he did try to run the regular distance as fast as he could. He wondered at last whether there were any defects in his overcoat. After examining it thoroughly in the privacy of his home, he discovered that in two or three places, to wit on the back and the shoulders, it had become a regular sieve; the cloth was so worn that you could see through it and the lining was coming out. I must observe that Akaky Akakyevitch's overcoat had also served as a butt for the jibes of the clerks.

It had even been deprived of the honorable name of overcoat and had been referred to as the "dressing jacket." It was indeed of rather a strange make. Its collar had been growing smaller year by year as it served to patch the other parts. The patches were not good specimens of the tailor's art, and they certainly looked clumsy and ugly. On seeing what was wrong, Akaky Akakyevitch decided that he would have to take the overcoat to Petrovitch, a tailor who lived on a fourth storey up a back staircase, and, in spite of having only one eye and being pock-marked all over his face, was rather successful in repairing the trousers and coats of clerks and others—that is, when he was sober, be it understood, and had no other enterprise in his mind. Of this tailor I ought not, of course, to say much, but since it is now the rule that the character of every person in a novel must be completely drawn, well, there is no help for it, here is Petrovitch too. At first he was called simply Grigory, and was a serf belonging to some gentleman or other. He began to be called Petrovitch from the time that he got his freedom and began to drink rather heavily on every holiday, at first only on the chief holidays, but afterwards on all church holidays indiscriminately, wherever there is a cross in the calendar. On that side he was true to the customs of his forefathers, and when he quarrelled with his wife used to call her "a worldly woman and a German." Since we have now mentioned the wife, it will be necessary to say a few words about her too, but unfortunately not much is known about her, except indeed that Petrovitch had a wife and that she wore a cap and not a kerchief, but apparently she could not boast of beauty; anyway, none but soldiers of the Guards peeped under her cap when they met her, and they twitched their moustaches and gave vent to a rather peculiar sound.

As he climbed the stairs, leading to Petrovitch's—which, to do them justice, were all soaked with water and slops and saturated through and through with that smell of spirits which makes the eyes smart, and is, as we all know,

inseparable from the backstairs of Petersburg houses—
Akaky Akakyevitch was already wondering how much
Petrovitch would ask for the job, and inwardly resolving
not to give more than two roubles. The door was open, for
Petrovitch's wife was frying some fish and had so filled the
kitchen with smoke that you could not even see the black-
beetles. Akaky Akakyevitch crossed the kitchen unnoticed
by the good woman, and walked at last into a room where
he saw Petrovitch sitting on a big, wooden, unpainted
table with his legs tucked under him like a Turkish Pasha.
The feet, as is usual with tailors when they sit at work,
were bare; and the first object that caught Akaky Akakyevitch's eye was the big toe, with which he was already familiar, with a misshapen nail as thick and strong as the
shell of a tortoise. Round Petrovitch's neck hung a skein
of silk and another of thread and on his knees was a rag
of some sort. He had for the last three minutes been trying
to thread his needle, but could not get the thread into the
eye and so was very angry with the darkness and indeed
with the thread itself, muttering in an undertone: "It
won't go in, the savage! You wear me out, you rascal."
Akaky Akakyevitch was vexed that he had come just at
the minute when Petrovitch was in a bad humor; he liked
to give him an order when he was a little "elevated," or,
as his wife expressed it, "had fortified himself with fizz, the
one-eyed devil." In such circumstances Petrovitch was as
a rule very ready to give way and agree, and invariably
bowed and thanked him, indeed. Afterwards, it is true,
his wife would come wailing that her husband had been
drunk and so had asked too little, but adding a single ten-
kopeck piece would settle that. But on this occasion Petrovitch was apparently sober and consequently curt, unwill-
ing to bargain, and the devil knows what price he would
be ready to lay on. Akaky Akakyevitch perceived this, and
was, as the saying is, beating a retreat, but things had gone
too far, for Petrovitch was screwing up his solitary eye
very attentively at him and Akaky Akakyevitch involun-

tarily brought out: "Good day, Petrovitch!" "I wish you a good day, sir," said Petrovitch, and squinted at Akaky Akakyevitch's hands, trying to discover what sort of goods he had brought.

"Here I have come to you, Petrovitch, do you see . . . !"

It must be noticed that Akaky Akakyevitch for the most part explained himself by apologies, vague phrases, and particles which have absolutely no significance whatever. If the subject were a very difficult one, it was his habit indeed to leave his sentences quite unfinished, so that very often after a sentence had begun with the words, "It really is, don't you know . . ." nothing at all would follow and he himself would be quite oblivious, supposing he had said all that was necessary.

"What is it?" said Petrovitch, and at the same time with his solitary eye he scrutinized his whole uniform from the collar to the sleeves, the back, the skirts, the button-holes—with all of which he was very familiar, they were all his own work. Such scrutiny is habitual with tailors, it is the first thing they do on meeting one.

"It's like this, Petrovitch . . . the overcoat, the cloth . . . you see everywhere else it is quite strong; it's a little dusty and looks as though it were old, but it is new and it is only in one place just a little . . . on the back, and just a little worn on one shoulder and on this shoulder, too, a little . . . do you see? that's all, and it's not much work. . . ."

Petrovitch took the "dressing jacket," first spread it out over the table, examined it for a long time, shook his head and put his hand out to the window for a round snuff-box with a portrait on the lid of some general—which precisely I can't say, for a finger had been thrust through the spot where a face should have been, and the hole had been pasted up with a square bit of paper. After taking a pinch of snuff, Petrovitch held the "dressing jacket" up in his hands and looked at it against the light, and again he shook his head; then he turned it with the lining upwards and once more shook his head; again he took off the lid

with the general pasted up with paper and stuffed a pinch
into his nose, shut the box, put it away and at last said:
"No, it can't be repaired; a wretched garment!" Akaky
Akakyevitch's heart sank at those words.

"Why can't it, Petrovitch?" he said, almost in the imploring voice of a child. "Why, the only thing is it is a bit
worn on the shoulders; why, you have got some little
pieces. . . ."

"Yes, the pieces will be found all right," said Petrovitch,
"but it can't be patched, the stuff is quite rotten; if you
put a needle in it, it would give way."

"Let it give way, but you just put a patch on it."

"There is nothing to put a patch on. There is nothing
for it to hold on to; there is a great strain on it, it is not
worth calling cloth, it would fly away at a breath of wind."

"Well, then, strengthen it with something—upon my
word, really, this is . . . !"

"No," said Petrovitch resolutely, "there is nothing to
be done, the thing is no good at all. You had far better,
when the cold winter weather comes, make yourself leg
wrappings out of it, for there is no warmth in stockings,
the Germans invented them just to make money." (Petrovitch was fond of a dig at the Germans occasionally.) "And
as for the overcoat, it is clear that you will have to have a
new one."

At the word "new" there was a mist before Akaky
Akakyevitch's eyes, and everything in the room seemed
blurred. He could see nothing clearly but the general with
the piece of paper over his face on the lid of Petrovitch's
snuff-box.

"A new one?" he said, still feeling as though he were in a
dream; "why, I haven't the money for it."

"Yes, a new one," Petrovitch repeated with barbarous
composure.

"Well, and if I did have a new one, how much would
it . . . ?"

"You mean what will it cost?"

"Yes."

"Well, three fifty-rouble notes or more," sad Petrovitch, and he compressed his lips significantly. He was very fond of making an effect, he was fond of suddenly disconcerting a man completely and then squinting sideways to see what sort of a face he made.

"A hundred and fifty roubles for an overcoat," screamed poor Akaky Akakyevitch—it was perhaps the first time he had screamed in his life, for he was always distinguished by the softness of his voice.

"Yes," said Petrovitch, "and even then it's according to the coat. If I were to put marten on the collar, and add a hood with silk linings, it would come to two hundred."

"Petrovitch, please," said Akaky Akakyevitch in an imploring voice, not hearing and not trying to hear what Petrovitch said, and missing all his effects, "do repair it somehow, so that it will serve a little longer."

"No, that would be wasting work and spending money for nothing," said Petrovitch, and after that Akaky Akakyevitch went away completely crushed, and when he had gone Petrovitch remained standing for a long time with his lips pursed up significantly before he took up his work again, feeling pleased that he had not demeaned himself nor lowered the dignity of the tailor's art.

When he got into the street, Akaky Akakyevitch was as though in a dream. "So that is how it is," he said to himself. "I really did not think it would be so . . ." and then after a pause he added, "So there it is! so that's how it is at last! and I really could never have supposed it would have been so. And there . . ." There followed another long silence, after which he brought out: "So there it is! well, it really is so utterly unexpected . . . who would have thought . . . what a circumstance. . . ." Saying this, instead of going home he walked off in quite the opposite direction without suspecting what he was doing. On the way a clumsy sweep brushed the whole of his sooty side against him and blackened all his shoulder; a regular hatful of plaster scattered upon him from the top of a house that was being built. He noticed nothing of this, and only after he had jostled against a sentry who had set his halberd down beside him and was shaking some snuff out of his horn into his rough fist, he came to himself a little and then only because the sentry said: "Why are you poking yourself right in one's face, haven't you the pavement to yourself?" This made him look round and turn homeward; only there he began to collect his thoughts, to see his position in a clear and true light and began talking to himself no longer incoherently but reasonably and openly as with a sensible friend with whom one can discuss the most intimate and vital matters. "No, indeed," said Akaky Akakyevitch, "it is no use talking to Petrovitch now; just now he really is ... his wife must have been giving it to him. I had better go to him on Sunday morning; after the Saturday evening he will be squinting and sleepy, so he'll want a little drink to carry it off and his wife won't give him a penny. I'll slip ten kopecks into his hand and then he will be more accommodating and maybe take the overcoat. . . ."

So reasoning with himself, Akaky Akakyevitch cheered up and waited until the next Sunday; then, seeing from a distance Petrovitch's wife leaving the house, he went straight in. Petrovitch certainly was very tipsy after the Saturday. He could hardly hold his head up and was very drowsy: but, for all that, as soon as he heard what he was speaking about, it seemed as though the devil had nudged him. "I can't," he said, "you must kindly order a new one." Akaky Akakyevitch at once slipped a ten-kopeck piece into his hand. "I thank you, sir, I will have just a drop to your health, but don't trouble yourself about the overcoat; it is not a bit of good for anything. I'll make you a fine new coat, you can trust me for that."

Akaky Akakyevitch would have said more about repairs, but Petrovitch, without listening, said: "A new one now I'll make you without fail; you can rely upon that, I'll do my best. It could even be like the fashion that has come in with the collar to button with silver claws under appliqué."

Then Akaky Akakyevitch saw that there was no escape from a new overcoat and he was utterly depressed. How indeed, for what, with what money could he get it? Of course he could to some extent rely on the bonus for the coming holiday, but that money had long ago been appropriated and its use determined beforehand. It was needed for new trousers and to pay the cobbler an old debt for putting some new tops to some old boot-legs, and he had to order three shirts from a seamstress as well as two specimens of an under-garment which it is improper to mention in print; in short, all that money absolutely must be spent, and even if the director were to be so gracious as to assign him a gratuity of forty-five or even fifty, instead of forty roubles, there would be still left a mere trifle, which would be but as a drop in the ocean beside the fortune needed for an overcoat. Though, of course, he knew that Petrovitch had a strange craze for suddenly putting on the devil knows what enormous price, so that at times his own wife could not help crying out: "Why, you are out of your wits, you idiot! Another time he'll undertake a job for nothing, and here the devil has bewitched him to ask more than he is worth himself." Though, of course, he knew that Petrovitch would undertake to make it for eighty roubles, still where would he get those eighty roubles? He might manage half of that sum; half of it could be found, perhaps even a little more; but where could he get the other half? . . . But, first of all, the reader ought to know where that first half was to be found. Akaky Akakyevitch had the habit every time he spent a rouble of putting aside two kopecks in a little locked-up box with a slit in the lid for slipping the money in. At the end of every half-year he would inspect the pile of coppers there and change them for small silver. He had done this for a long time, and in the course of many years the sum had mounted up to forty roubles and so he had half the money in his hands, but where was he to get the other half, where was he to get another forty roubles? Akaky Akakyevitch pondered and pondered and decided at last that he would have to diminish his ordinary expenses, at least for a year; give up burning candles in the evening, and if he had to do anything he must go into the landlady's room and work by her candle; that as he walked along the streets he must walk as lightly and carefully as possible, almost on tiptoe, on the cobbles and flagstones, so that his soles might last a little longer than usual; that he must send his linen to the wash less frequently, and that, to preserve it from being worn, he must take it off every day when he came home and sit in a thin cotton-shoddy dressing-gown, a very ancient garment which Time itself had spared. To tell the truth, he found it at first rather hard to get used to these privations, but after a while it became a habit and went smoothly enough—he even became quite accustomed to being hungry in the evening; on the other hand, he had spiritual nourishment, for he carried ever in his thoughts the idea of his future overcoat. His whole existence had in a sense become fuller, as though he had married, as though some other person were present with him, as though he were no longer alone, but an agreeable companion had consented to walk the path of life hand in hand with him, and that companion was no other than the new overcoat with its thick wadding and its strong, durable lining. He became, as it were, more alive, even more strong-willed, like a man who has set before himself a definite aim. Uncertainty, indecision, in fact all the hesitating and vague characteristics vanished from his face and his manners. At times there was a gleam in his eyes, indeed, the most bold and audacious ideas flashed through his mind. Why not really have marten on the collar? Meditation on the subject always made him absent-minded. On one occasion when he was copying a document, he very nearly made a mistake, so that he almost cried out "ough" aloud and crossed himself. At least once every month he went to

Petrovitch to talk about the overcoat, where it would be best to buy the cloth, and what color it should be, and what price, and, though he returned home a little anxious, he was always pleased at the thought that at last the time was at hand when everything would be bought and the overcoat would be made. Things moved even faster than he had anticipated. Contrary to all expectations, the director bestowed on Akaky Akakyevitch a gratuity of no less than sixty roubles. Whether it was that he had an inkling that Akaky Akakyevitch needed a greatcoat, or whether it happened so by chance, owing to this he found he had twenty roubles extra. This circumstance hastened the course of affairs. Another two or three months of partial fasting and Akaky Akakyevitch had actually saved up nearly eighty roubles. His heart, as a rule very tranquil, began to throb. The very first day he set off in company with Petrovitch to the shops. They bought some very good cloth, and no wonder, since they had been thinking of it for more than six months before, and scarcely a month had passed without their going to the shop to compare prices; now Petrovitch himself declared that there was no better cloth to be had. For the lining they chose calico, but of a stout quality, which in Petrovitch's words was even better than silk, and actually as strong and handsome to look at. Marten they did not buy, because it certainly was dear, but instead they chose cat fur, the best to be found in the shop—cat which in the distance might almost be taken for marten. Petrovitch was busy over the coat for a whole fortnight, because there were a great many button-holes, otherwise it would have been ready sooner. Petrovitch asked twelve roubles for the work; less than that it hardly could have been, everything was sewn with silk, with fine double seams, and Petrovitch went over every seam afterwards with his own teeth imprinting various figures with them. It was . . . it is hard to say precisely on what day, but probably on the most triumphant day of the life of Akaky Akakyevitch that Petrovitch at last brought the overcoat. He brought it in the morning, just before it was time to set off for the department. The overcoat could not have arrived more in the nick of time, for rather sharp frosts were just beginning and seemed threatening to be even more severe. Petrovitch brought the greatcoat himself as a good tailor should. There was an expression of importance on his face, such as Akaky Akakyevitch had never seen there before. He seemed fully conscious of having completed a work of no little moment and of having shown in his own person the gulf that separates tailors who only put in linings and do repairs from those who make up new materials. He took the greatcoat out of the pocket-handkerchief in which he had brought it (the pocket-handkerchief had just come home from the wash), he then folded it up and put it in his pocket for future use. After taking out the overcoat, he looked at it with much pride and, holding it in both hands, threw it very deftly over Akaky Akakyevitch's shoulders, then pulled it down and smoothed it out behind with his hands; then draped it about Akaky Akakyevitch with somewhat jaunty carelessness. The latter, as a man advanced in years, wished to try it with his arms in the sleeves. Petrovitch helped him to put it on, and it appeared that it looked splendid too with his arms in the sleeves. In fact it turned out that the overcoat was completely and entirely successful. Petrovitch did not let slip the occasion for observing that it was only because he lived in a small street and had no signboard, and because he had known Akaky Akakyevitch so long, that he had done it so cheaply, but on the Nevsky Prospect they would have asked him seventy-five roubles for the work alone. Akaky Akakyevitch had no inclination to discuss this with Petrovitch, besides he was frightened of the big sums that Petrovitch was fond of flinging airily about in conversation. He paid him, thanked him, and went off on the spot, with his new overcoat on, to the department. Petrovitch followed him out and stopped in the street, staring for a good time at the coat from a distance and then purposely turned off and, taking a short cut by a side street, came back into the street and got another view of the coat from the other side, that is, from the front.

Meanwhile Akaky Akakyevich walked along with every emotion in its most holiday mood. He felt every second that he had a new overcoat on his shoulders, and several times he actually laughed from inward satisfaction. Indeed, it had two advantages, one that it was warm and the other that it was good. He did not notice the way at all and found himself all at once at the department; in the porter's room he took off the overcoat, looked it over and put it in the porter's special care. I cannot tell how it happened, but all at once every one in the department learned that Akaky Akakyevitch had a new overcoat and that the "dressing jacket" no longer existed. They all ran out at once into the porter's room to look at Akaky Akakyevitch's new overcoat, they began welcoming him and congratulating him so that at first he could do nothing but smile and afterwards felt positively abashed. When, coming up to him, they all began saying that he must "sprinkle" the new overcoat and that he ought at least to stand them all a supper, Akaky Akakyevitch lost his head completely and did not know what to do, how to get out of it, nor what to answer. A few minutes later, flushing crimson, he even began assuring them with great simplicity that it was not a new overcoat at all, that it was just nothing, that it was an old overcoat. At last one of the clerks, indeed the assistant of the head clerk of the room, probably in order to show that he was not proud and was able to get on with those beneath him, said: "So be it, I'll give a party instead of Akaky Akakyevitch and invite you all to tea with me this evening; as luck would have it, it is my nameday." The clerks naturally congratulated the assistant head clerk and eagerly accepted the invitation. Akaky Akakyevitch was beginning to make excuses, but they all declared that it was uncivil of him, that it was simply a shame and a disgrace and that he could not possibly refuse. However, he felt pleased about it afterwards when he remembered that through this he would have the opportunity of going out in the evening, too, in his new overcoat. That whole day was for Akaky Akakyevitch the most triumphant and festive day in his life. He returned home in the happiest frame of mind, took off the overcoat and hung it carefully on the wall, admiring the cloth and lining once more, and then pulled out his old "dressing jacket," now completely coming to pieces, on purpose to compare them. He glanced at it and positively laughed, the difference was so immense! And long afterwards he went on laughing at dinner, as the position in which the "dressing jacket" was placed recurred to his mind. He dined in excellent spirits and after dinner wrote nothing, no papers at all, but just took his ease for a little while on his bed, till it got dark, then, without putting things off, he dressed, put on his overcoat, and went out into the street. Where precisely the clerk who had invited him lived we regret to say that we cannot tell; our memory is beginning to fail sadly, and everything there is in Petersburg, all the streets and houses, are so blurred and muddled in our head that it is a very difficult business to put anything in orderly fashion. However that may have been, there is no doubt that the clerk lived in the better part of the town and consequently a very long distance from Akaky Akakyevitch. At first the latter had to walk through deserted streets, scantily lighted, but as he approached his destination the streets became more lively, more full of people, and more brightly lighted; passers-by began to be more frequent, ladies began to appear, here and there, beautifully dressed, beaver collars were to be seen on the men. Cabmen with wooden trellis-work sledges, studded with gilt nails, were less frequently to be met; on the other hand, jaunty drivers in raspberry colored velvet caps with varnished sledges and bearskin rugs appeared, and carriages with decorated boxes dashed along the streets, their wheels crunching through the snow.

Akaky Akakyevitch looked at all this as a novelty; for several years he had not gone out into the streets in the evening. He stopped with curiosity before a lighted shop-window to look at a picture in which a beautiful woman was represented in the act of taking off her shoe and displaying as she did so the whole of a very shapely leg, while behind her back a gentleman with whiskers and a handsome imperial on his chin was putting his head in at the door. Akaky Akakyevitch shook his head and smiled and then went on his way. Why did he smile? Was it because he had come across something quite unfamiliar to him, though every man retains some instinctive feeling on the subject, or was it that he reflected, like many other clerks, as follows: "Well, upon my soul, those Frenchmen! it's beyond anything! if they try on anything of the sort, it really is . . . !" Though possibly he did not even think that; there is no creeping into a man's soul and finding out all that he thinks. At last he reached the house in which the assistant head clerk lived in fine style; there was a lamp burning on the stairs, and the flat was on the second floor. As he went into the entry Akaky Akakyevitch saw whole rows of goloshes. Amongst them in the middle of the room stood a samovar hissing and letting off clouds of steam. On the walls hung coats and cloaks, among which some actually had beaver collars or velvet revers. The other side of the wall there was noise and talk, which suddenly became clear and loud when the door opened and the footman came out with a tray full of empty glasses, a jug of cream, and a basket of biscuits. It was evident that the clerks had arrived long before and had already drunk their first glass of tea. Akaky Akakyevitch, after hanging up his coat with his own hands, went into the room, and at the same moment there flashed before his eyes a vision of candles, clerks, pipes, and card tables, together with the confused sounds of conversation rising up on all sides and the noise of moving chairs. He stopped very awkwardly in the middle of the room, looking about and trying to think what to do, but he was observed and received with a shout and they all went at once into the entry and again took a look at his overcoat. Though Akaky Akakyevitch was somewhat embarrassed, yet, being a simple-hearted man, he could not help being pleased at seeing how they all admired his coat. Then of course they all abandoned him and his coat, and turned their attention as usual to the tables set for whist. All this—the noise, the talk, and the crowd of people—was strange and wonderful to Akaky Akakyevitch. He simply did not know how to behave, what to do with his arms and legs and his whole figure; at last he sat down beside the players, looked at the cards, stared first at one and then at another of the faces, and in a little while began to yawn and felt that he was bored— especially as it was long past the time at which he usually went to bed. He tried to take leave of his hosts, but they would not let him go, saying that he absolutely must have a glass of champagne in honor of the new coat. An hour later supper was served, consisting of salad, cold veal, a pasty, pies, and tarts from the confectioner's, and cham-pagne. They made Akaky Akakyevitch drink two glasses, after which he felt that things were much more cheerful, though he could not forget that it was twelve o'clock and that he ought to have been home long ago. That his host might not take it into his head to detain him, he slipped out of the room, hunted in the entry for his greatcoat, which he found, not without regret, lying on the floor, shook it, removed some fluff from it, put it on, and went down the stairs into the street. It was still light in the streets. Some little general shops, those perpetual clubs for house-serfs and all sorts of people, were open; others which were closed showed, however, a long streak of light at every crack of the door, proving that they were not yet deserted, and probably maids and men-servants were still finishing their conversation and discussion, driving their masters to utter perplexity as to their whereabouts. Akaky Akakye-vitch walked along in a cheerful state of mind; he was even on the point of running, goodness knows why, after a lady of some sort who passed by like lightning with every part of her frame in violent motion. He checked himself at once, however, and again walked along very gently, feeling positively surprised himself at the inexplicable impulse that had seized him. Soon the deserted streets, which are not particularly cheerful by day and even less so in the evening, stretched before him. Now they were still more dead and deserted; the light of street lamps was scantier, the oil was evidently running low; then came wooden houses and fences; not a soul anywhere; only the snow gleamed on the streets and the low-pitched slumbering hovels looked black and gloomy with their closed shutters. He approached the spot where the street was intersected by an endless square, which looked like a fearful desert with its houses scarcely visible on the further side.

In the distance, goodness knows where, there was a gleam of light from some sentry-box which seemed to be standing at the end of the world. Akaky Akakyevitch's lightheartedness grew somehow sensibly less at this place. He stepped into the square, not without an involuntary uneasiness, as though his heart had a foreboding of evil. He looked behind him and to both sides—it was as though the sea were all round him. "No, better not look," he thought, and walked on, shutting his eyes, and when he opened them to see whether the end of the square were near, he suddenly saw standing before him, almost under his very nose, some men with moustaches; just what they were like he could not even distinguish. There was a mist before his eyes and a throbbing in his chest. "I say the overcoat is mine!" said one of them in a voice like a clap of thunder, seizing him by the collar. Akaky Akakyevitch was on the point of shouting "Help" when another put a fist the size of a clerk's head against his very lips, saying: "You just shout now." Akaky Akakyevitch felt only that they took the overcoat off, and gave him a kick with their knees, and he fell on his face in the snow and was conscious of nothing more. A few minutes later he came to himself and got on to his feet, but there was no one there. He felt that it was cold on the ground and that he had no overcoat, and began screaming, but it seemed as though his voice could not carry to the end of the square. Overwhelmed with despair and continuing to scream, he ran across the square straight to the sentry-box, beside which stood a sentry leaning on his halberd and, so it seemed, looking with curiosity to see who the devil the man was who was screaming and running towards him from the distance. As Akaky Akakyevitch reached him, he began breathlessly shouting that he was asleep and not looking after his duty not to see that a man was being robbed. The sentry answered that he had seen nothing, that he had only seen him stopped in the middle of the square by two men, and supposed that they were his friends, and that, instead of abusing him for nothing, he had better go the next day to the superintendent and that he would find out who had taken the overcoat. Akaky Akakyevitch ran home in a terrible state: his hair, which was still comparatively abundant on his temples and the back of his head, was completely dishevelled; his sides and chest and his trousers were all covered with snow. When his old landlady heard a fearful knock at the door she jumped hurriedly out of bed and, with only one slipper on, ran to open it, modestly holding her shift across her bosom; but when she opened it she stepped back, seeing what a state Akaky Akakyevitch was in. When he told her what had happened, she clasped her hands in horror and said that he must go straight to the superintendent, that the police constable of the quarter would deceive him, make promises and lead him a dance; that it would be best of all to go to the superintendent, and that she knew him indeed, because Anna the Finnish girl who was once her cook was now in service as a nurse at the superintendent's; and that she often saw him himself when he passed by their house, and that he used to be every Sunday at church too, saying his prayers and

at the same time looking goodhumoredly at every one, and
that therefore by every token he must be a kind-hearted
man. After listening to this advice, Akaky Akakyevitch
made his way very gloomily to his room, and how he spent
that night I leave to the imagination of those who are in
the least able to picture the position of others. Early in
the morning he set off to the police superintendent's, but
was told that he was asleep. He came at ten o'clock, he was
told again that he was asleep; he came at eleven and was
told that the superintendent was not at home; he came at
dinner-time, but the clerks in the ante-room would not
let him in, and insisted on knowing what was the matter
and what business had brought him and exactly what had
happened; so that at last Akaky Akakyevitch for the first
time in his life tried to show the strength of his character
and said curtly that he must see the superintendent himself, that they dare not refuse to admit him, that he had
come from the department on government business, and
that if he made complaint of them they would see. The
clerks dared say nothing to this, and one of them went to
summon the superintendent. The latter received his story
of being robbed of his overcoat in an extremely strange
way. Instead of attending to the main point, he began asking Akaky Akakyevitch questions, why had he been coming home so late? wasn't he going, or hadn't he been, to
some house of ill-fame? so that Akaky Akakyevitch was
overwhelmed with confusion, and went away without
knowing whether or not the proper measures would be
taken in regard to his overcoat. He was absent from the
office all that day (the only time that it had happened in
his life). Next day he appeared with a pale face, wearing
his old "dressing jacket" which had become a still more
pitiful sight. The tidings of the theft of the overcoat—
though there were clerks who did not let even this chance
slip of jeering at Akaky Akakyevitch—touched many of
them. They decided on the spot to get up a subscription
for him, but collected only a very trifling sum, because

the clerks had already spent a good deal on subscribing to the director's portrait and on the purchase of a book, at the suggestion of the head of their department, who was a friend of the author, and so the total realized was very insignificant. One of the clerks, moved by compassion, ventured at any rate to assist Akaky Akakyevitch with good advice, telling him not to go to the district police inspector, because, though it might happen that the latter might be sufficiently zealous of gaining the approval of his superiors to succeed in finding the overcoat, it would remain in the possession of the police unless he presented legal proofs that it belonged to him; he urged that far the best thing would be to appeal to a Person of Consequence; that the Person of Consequence, by writing and getting into communication with the proper authorities, could push the matter through more successfully. There was nothing else for it. Akaky Akakyevitch made up his mind to go to the Person of Consequence. What precisely was the nature of the functions of the Person of Consequence has remained a matter of uncertainty. It must be noted that this Person of Consequence had only lately become a person of consequence, and until recently had been a person of no consequence. Though, indeed, his position even now was not reckoned of consequence in comparison with others of still greater consequence. But there is always to be found a circle of persons to whom a person of little consequence in the eyes of others is a person of consequence. It is true that he did his utmost to increase the consequence of his position in various ways, for instance by insisting that his subordinates should come out on to the stairs to meet him when he arrived at his office; that no one should venture to approach him directly but all proceedings should be by the strictest order of precedence, that a collegiate registration clerk should report the matter to the provincial secretary, and the provincial secretary to the titular councillor or whomsoever it might be, and that business should only reach him by this channel.

Every one in Holy Russia has a craze for imitation, every one apes and mimics his superiors. I have actually been told that a titular councillor who was put in charge of a small separate office, immediately partitioned off a special room for himself, calling it the head office, and set special porters at the door with red collars and gold lace, who took hold of the handle of the door and opened it for every one who went in, though the "head office" was so tiny that it was with difficulty that an ordinary writing table could be put into it. The manners and habits of the Person of Consequence were dignified and majestic, but not complex. The chief foundation of his system was strictness, "strictness, strictness, and—strictness!" he used to say, and at the last word he would look very significantly at the person he was addressing, though, indeed, he had no reason to do so, for the dozen clerks who made up the whole administrative mechanism of his office stood in befitting awe of him; any clerk who saw him in the distance would leave his work and remain standing at attention till his superior had left the room. His conversation with his subordinates was usually marked by severity and almost confined to three phrases: "How dare you? Do you know to whom you are speaking? Do you understand who I am?" He was, however, at heart a good-natured man, pleasant and obliging with his colleagues; but the grade of general had completely turned his head. When he received it, he was perplexed, thrown off his balance, and quite at a loss how to behave. If he chanced to be with his equals, he was still quite a decent man, a very gentlemanly man, in fact, and in many ways even an intelligent man, but as soon as he was in company with men who were even one grade below him, there was simply no doing anything with him: he sat silent and his position excited compassion, the more so as he himself felt that he might have been spending his time to incomparably more advantage. At times there could be seen in his eyes an intense desire to join in some interesting conversation, but he was restrained by the doubt whether it would not be too much on his part, whether it would not be too great a familiarity and lowering of his dignity, and in consequence of these reflections he remained everlastingly in the same mute condition, only uttering from time to time monosyllabic sounds, and in this way he gained the reputation of being a very tiresome man.

So this was the Person of Consequence to whom our friend Akaky Akakyevitch appealed, and he appealed to him at a most unpropitious moment, very unfortunate for himself, though fortunate, indeed, for the Person of Consequence. The latter happened to be in his study, talking in the very best of spirits with an old friend of his childhood who had only just arrived and whom he had not seen for several years. It was at this moment that he was informed that a man called Bashmatchkin was asking to see him. He asked abruptly, "What sort of man is he?" and received the answer, "A government clerk." "Ah! he can wait, I haven't time now," said the Person of Consequence. Here I must observe that this was a complete lie on the part of the Person of Consequence: he had time; his friend and he had long ago said all they had to say to each other and their conversation had begun to be broken by very long pauses during which they merely slapped each other on the knee, saying, "So that's how things are, Ivan Abramovitch!"—"There it is, Stepan Varlamovitch!" but, for all that, he told the clerk to wait in order to show his friend, who had left the service years before and was living at home in the country how long clerks had to wait in his ante-room. At last after they had talked, or rather been silent to their heart's content and had smoked a cigar in very comfortable arm-chairs with sloping backs, he seemed suddenly to recollect, and said to the secretary, who was standing at the door with papers for his signature: "Oh, by the way, there is a clerk waiting, isn't there? tell him he can come in." When he saw Akaky Akakyevitch's meek appearance and old uniform, he turned to him at once and

said: "What do you want?" in a firm and abrupt voice,
which he had purposely practiced in his own room in solitude before the looking-glass for a week before receiving
his present post and the grade of a general. Akaky Akakyevitch, who was overwhelmed with befitting awe beforehand, was somewhat confused and, as far as his tongue
would allow him, explained to the best of his powers, with
even more frequent "ers" than usual, that he had had a
perfectly new overcoat and now he had been robbed of it
in the most inhuman way, and that now he had come to
beg him by his intervention either to correspond with his
honor the head policemaster or anybody else, and find the
overcoat. This mode of proceeding struck the general for
some reason as taking a great liberty. "What next sir," he
went on as abruptly, "don't you know the way to proceed?
To whom are you addressing yourself? Don't you know
how things are done? You ought first to have handed in a
petition to the office; it would have gone to the head clerk
of the room, and to the head clerk of the section, then it
would have been handed to the secretary and the secretary
would have brought it to me. . . ."

"But, your Excellency," said Akaky Akakyevitch, trying
to collect all the small allowance of presence of mind he
possessed and feeling at the same time that he was getting
into a terrible perspiration, "I ventured, your Excellency,
to trouble you because secretaries . . . er . . . are people
you can't depend on. . . ."

"What? what? what?" said the Person of Consequence,
"where did you get hold of that spirit? where did you pick
up such ideas? What insubordination is spreading among
young men against their superiors and betters." The Person of Consequence did not apparently observe that Akaky
Akakyevitch was well over fifty, and therefore if he could
have been called a young man it would only have been in
comparison with a man of seventy. "Do you know to whom
you are speaking? do you understand who I am? do you
understand that, I ask you?" At this point he stamped,

and raised his voice to such a powerful note that Akaky Akakyevitch was not the only one to be terrified. Akaky Akakyevitch was positively petrified; he staggered, trembling all over, and could not stand; if the porters had not run up to support him, he would have flopped upon the floor; he was led out almost unconscious. The Person of Consequence, pleased that the effect had surpassed his expectations and enchanted at the idea that his words could even deprive a man of consciousness, stole a sideway glance at his friend to see how he was taking it, and perceived not without satisfaction that his friend was feeling very uncertain and even beginning to be a little terrified himself.

How he got downstairs, how he went out into the street —of all that Akaky Akakyevitch remembered nothing, he had no feeling in his arms or his legs. In all his life he had never been so severely reprimanded by a general, and this was by one of another department, too. He went out into the snowstorm, that was whistling through the streets, with his mouth open, and as he went he stumbled off the pavement; the wind, as its way is in Petersburg, blew upon him from all points of the compass and from every side street. In an instant it had blown a quinsy into his throat, and when he got home he was not able to utter a word; with a swollen face and throat he went to bed. So violent is sometimes the effect of a suitable reprimand!

Next day he was in a high fever. Thanks to the gracious assistance of the Petersburg climate, the disease made more rapid progress than could have been expected, and when the doctor came, after feeling his pulse he could find nothing to do but prescribe a fomentation, and that simply that the patient might not be left without the benefit of medical assistance; however, two days later he informed him that his end was at hand, after which he turned to his landlady and said: "And you had better lose no time, my good woman, but order him now a deal coffin, for an oak one will be too dear for him." Whether Akaky Akakyevitch

heard these fateful words or not, whether they produced a
shattering effect upon him, and whether he regretted his
pitiful life, no one can tell, for he was all the time in delirium and fever. Apparitions, each stranger than the one
before, were continually haunting him: first, he saw Petrovitch and was ordering him to make a greatcoat trimmed
with some sort of traps for robbers, who were, he fancied,
continually under the bed, and he was calling his landlady
every minute to pull out a thief who had even got under
the quilt; then he kept asking why his old "dressing jacket"
was hanging before him when he had a new overcoat, then
he fancied he was standing before the general listening
to the appropriate reprimand and saying "I am sorry, your
Excellency," then finally he became abusive, uttering the
most awful language, so that his old landlady positively
crossed herself, having never heard anything of the kind
from him before, and the more horrified because these
dreadful words followed immediately upon the phrase
"your Excellency." Later on, his talk was a mere medley
of nonsense, so that it was quite unintelligible; all that
could be seen was that his incoherent words and thoughts
were concerned with nothing but the overcoat. At last
poor Akaky Akakyevitch gave up the ghost. No seal was
put upon his room nor upon his things, because, in the
first place, he had no heirs and, in the second, the property
left was very small, to wit, a bundle of goose-feathers, a
quire of white government paper, three pairs of socks, two
or three buttons that had come off his trousers, and the
"dressing jacket" with which the reader is already familiar.
Who came into all this wealth God only knows, even I
who tell the tale must own that I have not troubled to
enquire. And Petersburg remained without Akaky Akakyevitch, as though, indeed, he had never been in the city. A
creature had vanished and departed whose cause no one
had championed, who was dear to no one, of interest to
no one, who never even attracted the attention of the stu-
dent of natural history, though the latter does not disdain

to fix a common fly upon a pin and look at him under the microscope—a creature who bore patiently the jeers of the office and for no particular reason went to his grave, though even he at the very end of his life was visited by a gleam of brightness in the form of an overcoat that for one instant brought color into his poor life—a creature on whom calamity broke as insufferably as it breaks upon the heads of the mighty ones of this world . . . !

Several days after his death, the porter from the department was sent to his lodgings with instructions that he should go at once to the office, for his chief was asking for him; but the porter was obliged to return without him, explaining that he could not come, and to the enquiry, "Why?" he added, "Well, you see: the fact is he is dead, he was buried three days ago." This was how they learned at the office of the death of Akaky Akakyevitch, and the next day there was sitting in his seat a new clerk who was very much taller and who wrote not in the same upright hand but made his letters more slanting and crooked.

But who could have imagined that this was not all there was to tell about Akaky Akakyevitch, that he was destined for a few days to make a noise in the world after his death, as though to make up for his life having been unnoticed by anyone? But so it happened, and our poor story unexpectedly finishes with a fantastic ending. Rumors were suddenly floating about Petersburg that in the neighborhood of the Kalinkin Bridge and for a little distance beyond, a corpse had taken to appearing at night in the form of a clerk looking for a stolen overcoat, and stripping from the shoulders of all passers-by, regardless of grade and calling, overcoats of all descriptions—trimmed with cat fur, or beaver or wadded, lined with raccoon, fox and bear—made, in fact, of all sorts of skin which men have adapted for the covering of their own. One of the clerks of the department saw the corpse with his own eyes and at once recognized it as Akaky Akakyevitch; but it excited in him such terror, however, that he ran away as fast as his legs could carry him and so could not get a very clear view of him, and only saw him hold up his finger threateningly in the distance.

From all sides complaints were continually coming that backs and shoulders, not of mere titular councillors, but even of upper court councillors, had been exposed to taking chills, owing to being stripped of their greatcoats. Orders were given to the police to catch the corpse regardless of trouble or expense, alive or dead, and to punish him in the cruellest way, as an example to others, and, indeed, they very nearly succeeded in doing so. The sentry of one district police station in Kiryushkin Place snatched a corpse by the collar on the spot of the crime in the very act of attempting to snatch a frieze overcoat from a retired musician, who used in his day to play the flute. Having caught him by the collar, he shouted until he had brought two other comrades, whom he charged to hold him while he felt just a minute in his boot to get out a snuff-box in order to revive his nose which had six times in his life been frost-bitten, but the snuff was probably so strong that not even a dead man could stand it. The sentry had hardly had time to put his finger over his right nostril and draw up some snuff in the left when the corpse sneezed violently right into the eyes of all three. While they were putting their fists up to wipe them, the corpse completely vanished, so that they were not even sure whether he had actually been in their hands. From that time forward, the sentries conceived such a horror of the dead that they were even afraid to seize the living and confined themselves to shouting from the distance: "Hi, you there, be off!" and the dead clerk began to appear even on the other side of the Kalinkin Bridge, rousing no little terror in all timid people.

We have, however, quite deserted the Person of Consequence, who may in reality almost be said to be the cause of the fantastic ending of this perfectly true story. To begin with, my duty requires me to do justice to the Person of Consequence by recording that soon after poor Akaky Akakyevitch had gone away crushed to powder, he felt something not unlike regret. Sympathy was a feeling not unknown to him; his heart was open to many kindly impulses, although his exalted grade very often prevented them from being shown. As soon as his friend had gone out of his study, he even began brooding over poor Akaky Akakyevitch, and from that time forward, he was almost every day haunted by the image of the poor clerk who had succumbed so completely to the befitting reprimand. The thought of the man so worried him that a week later he actually decided to send a clerk to find out how he was and whether he really could help him in any way. And when they brought him word that Akaky Akakyevitch had died suddenly in delirium and fever, it made a great impression on him, his conscience reproached him and he was depressed all day. Anxious to distract his mind and to forget the unpleasant impression, he went to spend the evening with one of his friends, where he found a genteel company and, what was best of all, almost everyone was of the same grade so that he was able to be quite free from restraint. This had a wonderful effect on his spirits, he expanded, became affable and genial—in short, spent a very agreeable evening. At supper he drank a couple of glasses of champagne—a proceeding which we all know has a happy effect in inducing good humor. The champagne made him inclined to do something unusual, and he decided not to go home yet but to visit a lady of his acquaintance, one Karolina Ivanovna—a lady apparently of German extraction, for whom he entertained extremely friendly feelings. It must be noted that the Person of Consequence was a man no longer young, an excellent husband, and the respectable father of a family. He had two sons, one already serving in his office, and a nice-looking daughter of sixteen with a rather turned-up, pretty little nose, who used to come every morning to kiss his hand, saying: *"Bon jour, Papa."* His wife, who was still bloom-

ing and decidedly good-looking, indeed, used first to give
him her hand to kiss and then would kiss his hand, turning it the other side upwards. But though the Person of
Consequence was perfectly satisfied with the kind ameni-
ties of his domestic life, he thought it proper to have a
lady friend in another quarter of the town. This lady
friend was not a bit better looking nor younger than his
wife, but these mysterious facts exist in the world and it
is not our business to criticize them. And so the Person of
Consequence went downstairs, got into his sledge, and
said to his coachman, "To Karolina Ivanovna," while
luxuriously wrapped in his warm fur coat he remained
in that agreeable frame of mind sweeter to a Russian than
anything that could be invented, that is, when one thinks
of nothing while thoughts come into the mind of themselves, one pleasanter than the other, without the labor
of following them or looking for them. Full of satisfaction,
he recalled all the amusing moments of the evening he
had spent, all the phrases that had set the little circle
laughing; many of them he repeated in an undertone and
found them as amusing as before, and so, very naturally,
laughed very heartily at them again. From time to time,
however, he was disturbed by a gust of wind which, blowing suddenly, God knows whence and wherefore, cut him
in the face, pelting him with flakes of snow, puffing out
his coat-collar like a sack, or suddenly flinging it with unnatural force over his head and giving him endless trouble to extricate himself from it. All at once, the Person of
Consequence felt that some one had clutched him very
tightly by the collar. Turning round he saw a short man
in a shabby old uniform, and not without horror recognized him as Akaky Akakyevitch. The clerk's face was
white as snow and looked like that of a corpse, but the
horror of the Person of Consequence was beyond all
bounds when he saw the mouth of the corpse distorted
into speech and, breathing upon him the chill of the
grave, it uttered the following words: "Ah, so here you

are at last! At last I've ... er ... caught you by the collar.
It's your overcoat I want, you refused to help me and
abused me into the bargain! So now give me yours!" The
poor Person of Consequence very nearly died. Resolute
and determined as he was in his office and before subordinates in general, and though any one looking at his
manly air and figure would have said: "Oh, what a man
of character!" yet in this plight he felt, like very many
persons of athletic appearance, such terror that not without reason he began to be afraid he would have some sort
of fit. He actually flung his overcoat off his shoulders as
fast as he could and shouted to his coachman in a voice
unlike his own: "Drive home and make haste!" The coachman, hearing the tone which he had only heard in critical
moments and then accompanied by something even more
rousing, hunched his shoulders up to his ears in case of
worse following, swung his whip and flew on like an arrow.
In a little over six minutes the Person of Consequence
was at the entrance of his own house. Pale, panic-stricken,
and without his overcoat, he arrived home instead of at
Karolina Ivanovna's, dragged himself to his own room
and spent the night in great perturbation, so that next
morning his daughter said to him at breakfast, "You look
quite pale today, Papa": but her papa remained mute
and said not a word to anyone of what had happened to
him, where he had been, and where he had been going.
The incident made a great impression upon him. Indeed,
it happened far more rarely that he said to his subordinates, "How dare you? do you understand who I am?" and
he never uttered those words at all until he had first heard
all the rights of the case.

What was even more remarkable is that from that time
the apparition of the dead clerk ceased entirely: apparently the general's overcoat had fitted him perfectly, anyway
nothing more was heard of overcoats being snatched from
anyone. Many restless and anxious people refused, however, to be pacified, and still maintained that in remote

parts of the town the ghost of the dead clerk went on appearing. One sentry in Kolomna, for instance, saw with his own eyes a ghost appear from behind a house; but, being by natural constitution somewhat feeble—so much so that on one occasion an ordinary, well-grown pig, making a sudden dash out of some building, knocked him off his feet to the vast entertainment of the cabmen standing round, from whom he exacted two kopecks each for snuff for such rudeness—he did not dare to stop it, and so followed it in the dark until the ghost suddenly looked round and, stopping, asked him: "What do you want?" displaying a fist such as you never see among the living. The sentry said: "Nothing," and turned back on the spot. This ghost, however, was considerably taller and adorned with immense moustaches, and, directing its steps apparently towards Obuhov Bridge, vanished into the darkness of the night.

(Translated by Constance Garnett)

THE PILGRIM HAWK

· ·

Glenway Wescott

Glenway Wescott

. . . .

Glenway Wescott was born in Wisconsin in 1901 and, like so many mid-westerners, like so many Americans, like so many writers of his and the following generation, bid a final good-bye to his home, in his case in 1928, with the publication of *Good-Bye, Wisconsin*, one year after his fine novel *The Grandmothers* won the Harper Prize. Wescott spent a decade or so in France and was associated with many "little magazines," particularly *The Dial*; in this country he is Vice-President of the National Institute of Arts and Letters. He has published but two novels since *Good-Bye, Wisconsin*: they are *Apartment in Athens*, a popular novel of the resistance in Greece; and *The Pilgrim Hawk*. Highly praised as a "stylist," Wescott has much more than impeccable style to offer. *The Pilgrim Hawk* is a masterful fusion of reality and symbol, knowledge of human beings, and sensitive story-telling.

THE PILGRIM HAWK

THE CULLENS were Irish; but it was in France that I met them and was able to form an impression of their love and their trouble. They were on their way to a property they had rented in Hungary; and one afternoon they came to Chancellet to see my great friend Alexandra Henry. That was in May of 1928 or 1929, before we all returned to America, and she met my brother and married him.

Needless to say, the twenties were very different from the thirties, and now the forties have begun. In the twenties it was not unusual to meet foreigners in some country as foreign to them as to you, your peregrination just crossing theirs; and you did your best to know them in an afternoon or so; and perhaps you called that little lightning knowledge, friendship. There was a kind of idealistic or optimistic curiosity in the air. And vagaries of character, and the various war and peace that goes on in the psyche, seemed of the greatest interest and even importance.

Chancellet must be a painful place in the forties, although one of the least changed in France, I suppose, because it is unimportant. As I remember, there was a school of what is now romantically called celestial navigation, with a modest flying field and a few hangars, two or three kilometers away, at Pelors; but if that is in use now the foreigners must have it. In our day, day in and day out, the old Duchesse de Challot and her poor relations and friends in tight coats on windbroken mounts used to hunt in the forest of Pelors. We could hear their hunting horns which sounded like a picnic of boy sopranos, lost. Meanwhile perhaps there have been anti-aircraft guns for the

defense of Paris embedded all amid the earths of foxes:
angry radio stammering in the well-kept branches. Now
at least the foxes and the thrushes can come back. The old
ex-cabinet-minister whose château and little park adjoined
Alex's garden is dead.

Her house was just a section of the village street: two
small dwellings and a large horse-stable combined and
rebuilt and expensively furnished in the plain modern
style. She or her architect made a mistake in the planning
of the ground floor. The dining room and the chief guest-
room were on the street, which is also the highway to
Orléans and the tourist country of the Loire; so that the
reckless French traffic practically brushed the walls, and
heavy trucks alarmed one all night. Not only Alex's bedroom but the kitchen and pantry opened into the spacious
and quiet garden. This delighted the new servants whom
Alex had brought up from Morocco, a romantic pair
named Jean and Eva. They promptly took a far corner of
it under some plane trees for their own use; and all spring
they passed every spare moment there, quarreling and occasionally weeping during the day, but like clockwork
making peace and sealing it with kisses in the twilight or
moonlight. . . . I mention this odd location of the servants'
quarters because, that afternoon of the Cullens' visit, I
went to speak to Jean and happened to look out the kitch-
en window and saw Cullen in the garden, futilely giving
way to his awful jealousy, emancipated from love for a
few minutes.

There had been no mention of their coming, or perhaps
I had forgotten it. I heard the doorbell ring, then ring
again. Jean and Eva must have been outdoors or napping.
Alex had put through a telephone call to London upon
some little annoying matter of business, and wished not
to be disturbed. So I went to the door; and there was the
long dark Daimler entirely occupying the cobbled space
between the house and the highway, and there stood the
Irishman about to ring a third time. "Oh, how d'ya do, is

this Miss Henry's house, my name's Cullen," he said; and turned to help Mrs. Cullen out of the car, which was a delicate operation, for she bore a full-grown hooded falcon on her wrist. A dapper young chauffeur also helped. She was dressed with extreme elegance and she wore the highest heels I ever saw, on which, with one solicitous male at each elbow, she stumbled across the ancient cobblestones, the bird swaying a little and hunching its wings to steady itself.

I told them my name, and they repeated it after me and shook hands with a somewhat grand and vague affability. "I brought my hawk," Mrs. Cullen unnecessarily announced. "She's new. I thought Alex wouldn't mind. And I hope you too," she added and paused a moment, with bright eyes to flatter me just in case I felt entitled to authority of some sort in Alex's house, "I hope you won't mind." She had no way of knowing who or what I was: casual caller or one of Alex's kinsmen or perhaps a sweetheart.

Her eyes were a crystal blue, unmistakably Irish; and she was unmistakable in other ways too, in spite of her brisk London voice and fine French dress. Her make-up was better than you would have expected of a lady falconer; still you could see that her skin was naturally downy and her snub nose tended to be pink. There was also a crookedness, particularly in the alignment of her nostrils and her voluble little lips. How rare pulchritude is among the Irish, I said to myself; therefore what a trouble is made when it does appear: Emer and Deirdre, Mrs. O'Shea and Mrs. McBride. Then my glance fell upon Mrs. Cullen's snowy dimpled fingers, with a considerable diamond on one, a star sapphire on another. Between her sleeve and the rough gauntlet to which the falcon clung, her wrist showed like a bit of Easter lily; and her ankle was a match for it, perfectly straight in a mere glimmer of stocking. No doubt these fine points were enough to entitle her to a certain enchantment and disturbance of the opposite sex:

her husband for one.

Meanwhile Jean had come running in a fine embarrassment, buttoning his white jacket; and I sent him to inform
his mistress of the arrival of her guests and to guide their
chauffeur to the garage, while I tried to usher them into
the living room. But Mrs. Cullen went on explaining the
hawk. "Her name's Lucy. Don't you think she's sweet?
She's Scottish; I've only had her five or six weeks. A gamekeeper near Inverness trapped her, but she's all right, only
one toe bent in the trap. D'you, see, this toe?" She paused
on the threshold and held up the gloved hand and wrist on
which Lucy perched, and I saw: gripping the rugged and
stained leather, one sharp talon that did not grip straight.
The stain on the leather was dried blood.

"I call her Lucy because my old father used to make me
read Scott to him in the winter whenever the weather got
too beastly to hunt. I thought Alex would like to see her."

"We had to bring her anyway," her husband loudly
chimed in. "The most awful things happen if we leave her
in the hotel. She frightens the chambermaids, and they
scream and weep. I have to give immense tips."

He was a large man, not really fat but with bulk and
softness irregularly here and there, not so much in the
middle as up and down his back, all around his head, in
his hands. His British complexion suggested eating and
drinking rather than hunting and shooting; certainly
nothing about him suggested hawking. His hazel eyes were
a little bloodshot, wavering golden now and then; and he
had a way of opening and shutting his lips, like an unsym-
pathetic pout, or a dispirited kiss, under the tufts of his
mustache.

We were about to sit down in the living room when they
both noticed it, and evidently felt obliged to comment.
"What a splendid room, splendid," they said; "most unusual and modern and comfortable." It was not splendid,
but it was very large: the entire former stable with the
hayloft removed so that the roof constituted the ceiling,

with old chestnut rafters gothically pointing up twenty-
five or thirty feet; the woodwork darkly waxed and the
walls painted white. It reminded me of a village church.
At regular intervals all around hung certain modern pictures with only blunt rudimentary drawing and overflowing color, like stained glass. But on as fine a day as this,
modern art was dimmed and dwarfed by the view of the
garden and the park beyond it, Alex's architect having removed almost a third of the wall on that side and put in
two great panes of plate glass.

Mrs. Cullen tripped over to this great window and
courteously exclaimed once more: "Splendid garden. What
luck to have a pond!" It was what the French call an
English garden; no formal flower beds—a few blossoms
amid the grass, paths along the water, and shrubs flourishing, in the muffled brilliance of late May. The characteristic Seine-et-Oise sky, foamy cloud and weak blue, lay
at our feet also, daubed in a soft copy on the surface of the
pond. In the background every tree was draped in a slightly different shade of the same ecstatic color.

But as Mrs. Cullen stood facing all this, I had an impression of indifference and mere courtesy; her look did not
take in much. A little narrow frown, an efficient survey,
only to discover if there was anything in it for her personally; and there was not. In a moment the light eyelashes
began to flutter again, and the blue pupils loosened, merely sparkling. Her prolonged and expressive looks were all
for her husband or her hawk.

Now, what seeing the garden chiefly reminded her of,
was that the hawk could not see: its entire head except
the beak encased in its plumed Dutch hood. "Poor Lucy,
blind as a bat," she murmured; and very deftly, taking one
drawstring in her teeth and the other between thumb and
forefinger of her right hand, she unhooded it. It also
frowned, and stared circularly at the room and blinked at
the window. Then it opened out and rearranged the whit-
ish and bluish feathers around its throat; combed its head

between its tethered legs; smoothed its cheek against its powerful shoulder.

Mrs. Cullen paced up and down, evidently trying to decide which armchair would suit her and Lucy best. Then Alex came in from her long-distance business, with apologies for not welcoming them at once. They replied with another round of compliments upon the house and garden, and there was a new introduction of the falcon. "Lucy, for Lucy Ashton, Lucy of Lammermoor," Mrs. Cullen explained. "Don't you remember her song? *Easy live and quiet die, Vacant hand and heart and eye.*"

To my amusement Cullen hummed a few notes of the Mad Scene from "Lucia" in a manly Irish treble. His wife hushed him by murmuring his name, which was Larry; and went on informing Alex that they were at the Plaza-Honoré, busy shopping in Paris, eager to leave for Hungary via Strasbourg on the morrow. I was impatient for them to cease this small talk and be seated, because I wanted to sit down and admire the falcon comfortably, and to ask certain questions. At last Mrs. Cullen requested a straight chair, which I brought from the dining room.

I was much impressed by Alex's enthusiasm during this first part of the Cullens' visit. It reminded me that she must be lonely here in France with only myself and my cousin and a few other friends rather like us. She had spent a number of years in Scotland with her father, and in Morocco, and journeying around the Orient; and in London also the acquaintances of her girlhood had been outdoor people like these two, self-centered but without any introspection, strenuous but emotionally idle. It was a type of humanity that she no longer quite respected or trusted, but evidently still enjoyed.

Their enthusiasm about themselves and all that exactly appertained to them, always overflowing, coolly playing and bubbling over in mild agitation like a fountain, held your attention and mirrored itself in your mind; little by little you began to bubble with it. One of Alex's obvious

characteristics was lack of curiosity; and I think that was
chiefly fear of arousing or authorizing others' inquiry
about herself. Perhaps selfishness reassured her and made
her less shy. In any case, that afternoon she eagerly asked
questions, including some that I had in mind; and Mrs.
Cullen was charmed to answer; and Cullen was charmed
to listen and give back his approximate echoes. Thus an
odd kind of compatibility was established, in which I too
gradually let myself be included, somewhat to my surprise.

For one thing, the bird charmed me so that nothing else
mattered much. And it served as an embodiment or em-
blem for me of all the truly interesting subjects of conversation that these very sociable, traveling, sporting people
leave out as a rule: illness, poverty, sex, religion, art.
Whenever I began to be bored, a solemn glance of its
maniacal eyes helped me to stop listening and to think
concentratedly of myself instead, or for myself.

Furthermore the Cullens began to puzzle me, to charm
me in that sense. Whether or not I finally arrive at a proper
understanding of people, I often begin in the way of a
vexed, intense superficiality. And indeed they were mere
male and female of that species of well-to-do British which
haunts the entire world with excess of energy and sedate
manner. They were self-absorbed, coldly gregarious, mere
passers of time. But nothing about them was authentically
sedate or even peaceful. There Cullen plumply sat in
Alex's softest armchair, his legs more widely spread or
loosely crossed than you would expect of a conventional
gentleman; licking his lips under his fringy mustache;
evidently thinking of his dinner; interrupting his wife's
conversation at regular intervals as if that were his life
work. Yet he seemed to be constantly fighting against some
strange feeling, and to be somehow outwitted by it. Whenever he spoke, his wife smiled or at least tilted her head
toward him. This, I felt, was chiefly good breeding on her
part; many of his remarks, and especially his tone of voice,
seemed unpleasant. But between remarks, in her glances

at him, there was affection as bright as tears. And during
the loving fuss she made over the great bird on her arm,
she kept shifting her eyes in his direction, imploring him
to try to like it too. It might have been a baby, and he a
lover; or was it the other way around?

Alex expressed surprise that they should willingly leave
Ireland at this lovely time of year. Mrs. Cullen answered
that, in season or out, there was nothing much to do in
Ireland except hunt. "And our terrible sons pinch our
hunters when they come home. We can't afford to keep
enough for them. I can't bear a horse that others have
been riding."

She also alluded mildly to the diminishment of the old
quiet kind of fortune like theirs. The banshee in the
draughty corridor or the weedy hedge crying not the deaths
of relatives, but increase of taxes, decrease of rents and
investments . . . Indeed they still appeared rich, in hand-
woven silk with diamonds, in tweed as soft as silk, stopping
at the Plaza-Honoré, en route to Budapest in a Daimler.
But all that in fact is cheaper than an old country house
full of guests, and the requisite stable and kennel and
larder and cellar, and servants enough. Having closed
Cullen Hall, Mrs. Cullen pointed out, they were in a position to accept invitations half the year; and the continent
was cheap.

Evidently her telling us this vexed Cullen. He warmly
informed us that one of his neighbors, a drunken idiot
anyway, had sold everything that the entail permitted,
and two of his cousins were obliged to rent; and so it went
all over the British Isles. Their own circumstances were
neither discreditable nor hopeless. There were still certain
inheritances due them, on his side, not Mrs. Cullen's. His
sons might be considered grown men, except by their
mother; but they were still engaged in that great postpone-
ment, education, which is expensive. His brother and
sister were happy to have them during their long vaca-
tions; but as a rule they preferred to loiter at Cullen Hall

with two or three servants who were too old to dismiss
anyway; and they hunted with the neighbors. It is easy
for youngsters to get on with new people, even such as the
latest in their county, a manufacturing peer named Bild,
a Jew; not at all easy for him.

Mrs. Cullen said a word in defense of Lord Bild. Thank
heaven it was he who had bought the estate adjoining
Cullen Hall, on their youngsters' account especially. Although of common Germanic origin he was very strict
about manners and sportsmanship and keeping fit; more
so than they were. Neighborly influence is like education;
the best teachers belong to the races and classes which
have been learning themselves just lately.

Now Cullen had risen and was standing at his wife's
elbow, shaking his finger at the falcon teasingly. I thought
that the bird's great eyes showed only a slight natural be-
wilderment; whereas a slow sneer came over his face and
he turned pale. It was the first revelation I had of the interesting fact that he hated Lucy. He would willingly have
sacrificed a finger tip in order to have an excuse to retal-
iate, I thought; and I imagined him picking up a chair or a
coffee table and going at her with smashing blows. What
a difference there is between animals and humans! Lucy
no doubt would be disgustingly fierce when her time came;
but meanwhile sat pleasantly and idly, in abeyance.
Whereas humanity is histrionic, and must prepare and
practice every stroke of passion; so half our life is a vague
and stormy make-believe.

Mrs. Cullen merely looked up at her husband and said
in a velvety tone, "The trouble with Ireland, from my
point of view, is that they don't like our having a falcon.
Naturally Lord Bild disapproves; but I don't mind him.
He's so unsure of himself; he's a Jew furthermore; you
can scarcely expect him to live and let live. But our other
neighbors and the family are almost as tiresome."

Cullen thrust the teasing hand in his pocket and returned to his armchair. Her eyes sparkled fast, perhaps

with that form of contrition which pretends to be joking. Or perhaps it pleased her to break off the subject of their Irish circumstance and worldly situation and to resume the dear theme of hawk, which meant all the world to her.

The summer before, she told us, an old Hungarian had sold her a trained tiercel. "I took him with me last winter when we stayed with some pleasant Americans in Scotland. There's a bad ailment called croaks, and he caught that and died. They had installed their American heating, which I think makes an old house damp; don't you? Then their gamekeeper trapped Lucy and gave her to me. Wasn't that lucky? I've always wanted a real falcon, a haggard, to man and train myself."

In strict terminology of the sport, she explained, only a female is called a falcon; and a haggard is one that has already hunted on her own account, that is, at least a year old when caught.

Except for that one deformed bit of one foot, Lucy was a perfect example of her species, *Falco peregrinus*, pilgrim hawk. Her body was as long as her mistress's arm; the wing feathers in repose a little too long, slung across her back like a folded tent. Her back was an indefinable hue of iron; only a slight patina of the ruddiness of youth still shone on it. Her luxurious breast was white, with little tabs or tassels of chestnut. Out of tasseled pantaloons her legs came down straight to the perch with no apparent flesh on them, enameled a greenish yellow.

But her chief beauty was that of expression. It was like a little flame; it caught and compelled your attention like that, although it did not flicker and there was nothing bright about it nor any warmth in it. It is a look that men sometimes have; men of great energy, whose appetite or vocation has kept them absorbed every instant all their lives. They may be good men but they are often mistaken for evil men, and vice versa. In Lucy's case it appeared chiefly in her eyes, not black but funereally brown, and extravagantly large, set deep in her flattened head.

On each side of the upper beak there was a little tooth or tusk. Mrs. Cullen explained that the able bird in the prime of life uses this to snap the spinal cord of its quarry, which is the most merciful death in nature. It reminded me of the hooked gloves which our farmers wear to husk corn; and so in fact, I thought, it must work: the falcon in the sky like a large angelic hand, stripping the meat of pigeon or partridge out of its feathers, the soul out of its throat.

I think Mrs. Cullen was the most talkative woman I ever met; and it was hawk, hawk, all afternoon. A good many inhabitants of the British Isles are hell-bent all their lives upon killing some wild animal somehow, and naturally are keen about the domestic animals which assist them. Others, who know all about human nature, nevertheless prefer to converse about animals, perhaps because it is the better part of conversational valor. Mrs. Cullen's enthusiasm was nothing like that, and it probably would have annoyed or alarmed the majority of her compatriots. As it seemed to me after listening a while, she felt welling up in her mind some peculiar imagination, or some trouble impossible to ignore, which she tried to relieve by talking, with a kind of continuous double meaning. I think she would never have admitted the duplicity, and perhaps could not have expressed herself in plain terms. People as a rule do mean much more than they understand.

She informed us, for example, that in a state of nature hawks rarely die of disease; they starve to death. Their eyesight fails; some of their flight feathers break off or fall out; and their talons get dull or broken. They cease to be able to judge what quarry is worth flying at; or their flight slows up so that even the likely quarry gets away. Or, because they have lost weight, the victim is not stunned by their swooping down on it. Or when they have clutched it, they cannot hang on long enough to kill. Day after day they make fools of themselves. Then they have to depend upon very young birds or sick birds, or little animals on the ground, which are the hardest of all to see; and in any case there are not enough of these easy conquests to keep them in flesh. The hungrier they get, the more wearily and weakly they hunt. And the weaker they get, the more often they go hungry, in a miserable confusion of cause and effect. Finally what appears to be shame and morbid discouragement overcomes them. They simply sit on the rocks or in a tree somewhere waiting to die, as you might say philosophically, letting themselves die.

"I met a man on the staff of our great madhouse in Dublin last year," Mrs. Cullen added. "I was curious to see what it was like; so he took me with him one afternoon on a tour of inspection. Some of the mad people reminded me of hawks, exactly." The lethargically mad, sitting with their hands in their laps, imaginarily exhausted, unable to speak above a whisper, with burning but unfocusable eyes, unable to concentrate. . . .

Cullen cleared his throat boisterously, perhaps to protest against the curiosity of women or against this folly of reading meaning into the ways of mere birds.

Falconers believe that hunger must be worse for falcons than for other birds and animals, Mrs. Cullen said. It maddens them, with a soreness in every feather; an unrelievable itching in their awful feet; a bloody lump in their throats, with the light plumage wrapped loose around like a bandage. This painful greed, sick single-mindedness, makes it possible to tame them and to perfect the extraordinary technique of falconry, which is more than any other bird can learn. You hear it in their cry—*aik, aik*—as Mrs. Cullen then imitated it for us, ache, ache—a small flat scream with a bubbling or gargling undertone, as if their mouths were full of scalding water. "I suppose human beings never feel anything like it."

"But Madeleine, Madeleine, we're never hungry," her husband protested with a chuckle in which there was great satisfaction. "How can we tell?"

She begged him not to be silly. She had known people

who had starved, Irish republicans hiding from the Black and Tans, Germans in 1922, and had inquired of them; and they had described it as rather a soft cool drowsy feeling.

I wondered about this. Although I had been a poor boy, on a Wisconsin farm and in a slum in Chicago and in Germany in 1922, I could not recollect any exact sensation of hunger, that is to say, hunger of the stomach. And I thought—as the relatively well-fed do think—of the other human hungers, mental and sentimental and so on. For example, my own undertaking in early manhood to be a literary artist. No one warned me that I really did not have talent enough. Therefore my hope of becoming a very good artist turned bitter, hot and nerve-racking; and it would get worse as I grew older. The unsuccessful artist also ends in an apathy, too proud and vexed to fly apart, waiting upon withheld inspiration, bored to death. . . . Naturally I did not speak of this to Alex and the Cullens. It seemed rude and somehow abnormal even to be thinking of it, while they sat exchanging information about real life, really starving nations and greedy species of bird.

Whereupon our present bird mantled, that is, stood a moment on one leg, shook the other leg and wing downward, and spread that half of her plumage in a long fan, gazing at me, blinking or winking at me. But because my writing had gone badly all spring I could not bear to give her more than a passing thought with reference to that. I began to think of her as an image of amorous desire instead. That is the great relief of weariness of work in any case; the natural consolation for its not going well. Or perhaps the Cullens' feeling about each other suggested it to me. No doubt art is too exceptional to be worth talking about; but sex is not. At least in good countries such as France and the United States during prosperous periods like the twenties, it must be the keenest of all appetites for a majority of men most of their lives.

And highly sexed men, unless they give in and get mar-

ried and stay married, more or less starve to death. I myself
was still young then and I had been lucky in love. But
little early quarrels and failures warn one; and in the con-
fidences of friends and in gossip about other men, one
discovers the vague beastly shape of what to expect. Life
goes on and on after one's luck has run out. Youthfulness
persists, alas, long after one has ceased to be young. Love-
life goes on indefinitely, with less and less likelihood of
being loved, less and less ability to love, and the stomach-
ache of love still as sharp as ever. The old bachelor is like
an old hawk.

Civilized human beings have learned how to avoid lit-
eral starvation and the fear of death and real enslavement;
so at least it seemed in the twenties. They have this kind
of thing instead: fear of old age, loss of charm, lack of love.
Therefore I caught myself gazing at my young unmarried
Alex anxiously, sentimentally, and at her Irish guests with
idle envy. But the Irish wife's uneasiness and the husband's captivated but uncomfortable look reminded me
that I was making a false distinction. There is not as much
sweet safety in marriage as one hopes. Hunger and its
twin, disgust, are in it too; need and greed; and passage
of time, the punishment. Of course true love and lust are
not the same, neither are they inseparable, nor indistinguishable. Only they reflect and imitate and elucidate each
other.

Looking back upon that afternoon's talk and thought,
I am inclined to hold Mrs. Cullen responsible for this
daydreaming of mine, personal worry and exhilaration,
which made me inattentive to what she said now and then.
In a woman as energetic and attractive as that, the hint of
hidden emotion and the sense of double meaning naturally
are exciting; and the excitement leads in one's own private
direction. But as it were in a mirror, looking at myself, I
could see something of her character and plight before the
circumstances of the afternoon betrayed her. I think that
was what she instinctively wanted.

Meanwhile she had gone on answering Alex's questions: something about the craftsmen who outfit falcons, generation after generation of avian haberdashers especially in India, and which bell resounds the clearest through the grass and bushes and breezes, and what hood is least likely to ulcerate the waxen lids and lips; and something about an ancient Persian text with a thrice-hyphenated title which is still the best handbook of falconry. I wanted to know all this, yet I failed to pay attention.

Then Lucy bated, that is, threw herself headlong off the fist. The leather jesses around her legs and the leash looped through Mrs. Cullen's fingers held her ignominiously, upside down. It was a painful sight, like an epileptic fit or an insane fit. There was no possibility of the thongs breaking; I half-expected her lean bright legs to snap instead. I expected her to scream, aik! But the only sound was the jingling of her bell and the convulsion of her plumage, air panting through her plumage. The tail feathers and the flight feathers, shooting out rigidly, threshed against herself and against her mistress from head to foot. Mrs. Cullen, not the least disconcerted, raised her left arm straight up over her head, and stood up and stood quite still, only turning her face away from the flapping and whipping. Her equanimity impressed me as much as her strength.

In a minute Lucy gave up little by little. It was extraordinary: you could see her self-control returning, recurring in one feather after another. Then she hung peacefully like a mere turkey or goose hooked up in a butchershop; only for an instant. The long wings began again, but in a different exertion: hugging the air, bracing against the air, until her talons got a grip on the gauntlet and she succeeded in pulling herself up again where she belonged. There she stared or glared at us, blinking the rush of blood back out of her embarrassed eyes and pulling her plumage together.

With a sigh and a half-smile Mrs. Cullen brought her burdened and shaken arm down, and seated herself again in the straight chair. Some such hopeless attempt to escape, crazy fit of freedom, comes over all domesticated falcons at fairly regular intervals, she explained, especially in their first year or two; all their lives if they have not been well manned. "They never get over being wild. It's like malaria or that other intermittent fever, the one you have to be so careful about in the Orient."

Lucy happened to be an unusually frank, active bird, so that you could often tell when her trouble was to be expected; by a soft repeated tinkle of her bells or a steady pull at one of her jesses. The leather might of course be loose or worn out. "And instead it pinches her, which makes her angry, and everything seems hopeless," Mrs. Cullen concluded. "She can't help it, can't bear it. It's like committing suicide."

"Give me liberty or give me death, ha, ha," cried Cullen, seeming to expect special applause from us because we were Americans, or perhaps because Alex's name was Henry like the American who first expressed that sentiment. His wife gave him that look of hers which was the opposite of applause; and he took it as usual. His hazel eyes stood out like jewels, the tip of his tongue brightened his lips.

Meanwhile she was slowly caressing Lucy's lower plumage and tired feet. She might have been a trained nurse and Lucy her patient, after a bout of illness or craziness. Or she might have been in love and Lucy her beloved, pleasure absent-mindedly ebbing . . . And every word she uttered added a little to the confused significance. "Sometimes I can prevent her independent fits. The way a governess gets to know a child, and can see its tantrums beginning and distract it somehow. . . . Being stroked like this often does the trick. At first I used a dried pigeon's wing as you're supposed to, but this suits Lucy as well."

Idly she went on with it: two dimpled fingers with long tinted nails and heavy rings just brushing the spent feathers. "Or if I notice it in time, I lift her over my head for a moment. She likes to perch as high as possible, so she can look down upon everything around her. I think it must frighten her to see things higher than she is. We're like that sometimes ourselves, aren't we?" she added, smiling gently.

Time after time her transitions like this—from hawk to human, objective to subjective—startled me. To be sure, any woman greatly in love must know how a flattery in time saves trouble, how the illusion of superiority counteracts the illusion of inferiority, as well as any governess. But it had not occurred to me that her love for Cullen was great in that sense: cunning, instructive, curative.

Falcons, she informed us, do not breed in captivity. Various attempts have been made to induce them to, but with no success. Thus, the entire sport has to start again from scratch for each falconer, whenever he trains a new playmate. Little by little the perfectly wild creature surrenders, individually, in the awful difficulty of hunger. But surrender is all, domestication is all; they never feel at home. You can carry male and female side by side in the same cage year in and year out; nothing happens. They will cease to fight but they stay solitary. Scorn of each other for giving in, or self-scorn, seems to break their hearts. They never build a nest or lay an egg. Not one chick or eyas is ever reared in bondage. There is no real acceptance or inheritance of the state of surrender.

Mrs. Cullen mentioned, as a kind of exception, the make-hawks: old good-natured birds which some professionals use in the training of the young wild ones. But even their influence must be in the way of a rationalization of necessary evil, inculcation of vice, making the best of a bad bargain. For they too are born in the vacant rocks or uncomfortable trees; and they too keep sterile.

"Like schoolmasters," crowed Cullen. That appealed to my sense of humor. But Cullen's smile was a leer if I ever saw one, and evidently embarrassed his wife and Alex; so I kept from smiling.

Mrs. Cullen then quoted Buffon's famous sentence

about falcons: *"L'individu seul est esclave; l'espèce est libre."* Buffon had been her father's second-best author, after Scott. Her French accent was incorrect but very pretty. Only the individual hawk is a slave; the species is free. . . .

Then Alex spoke up, in what was a loud voice for her: "Oh, dear, it is the opposite of human beings. We are slaves in the mass, aren't we? Only one man can hope to free himself; one at a time, then another, and another."

"Oh, I dare say," Mrs. Cullen assented. "Yes, perhaps." But she smiled patronizingly. I think she was congratulating herself upon knowing a freer and stronger type of humanity than our pampered, subtle, self-questioning American type; and perhaps she did: Irish republicans, wild Hungarians with hawks, Germans during their defeat.

"But it is true, isn't it?" Alex insisted. "The man who really loves freedom is the exception."

"Oh, quite. How right you are," our lady falconer dubiously murmured.

But her husband disagreed. "No, Alex! What a disgusting idea! Love of liberty is the deepest instinct we have—if you will excuse my saying so."

We silently considered this for a moment; the three of us, it seemed, regretfully. Alex wanted freedom more than anything; and if others as a rule did not, she might have a lonely life. In any case it would take a better man than Cullen to dispel her young misanthropy. I myself regretted never having been able to decide what to think: how much liberty is a true human motive, and how much is wasteful and foolish? And for the first time that afternoon Mrs. Cullen gazed at her husband sadly, that is, weakly. She agreed with him, I felt sure. But there are circumstances in which it may be obvious that at least one human being requires freedom; and you bitterly regret that it is so: because you need to keep that one captive.

"Why, hang it all," Cullen still sputtered, "why, independence is the only thing that is human about hawks. Don't you agree, Madeleine?"

She slightly turned her back to him and contemplated Alex and me rather unkindly. It was the careful absence of expression, absence of frown, that you see on a clever lecturer's face when the irrelevant questioning or heckling begins. There was also a sadness about it which, if I read it aright, I have often felt myself. She did not want us to take her hawk, her dear subject-matter, her hobby and symbol—whatever it meant to her—and turn it this way and that to mean what we liked. It was hers and we were spoiling it. Around her eyes and mouth there were lines of that caricatural weariness which is peculiar to those who talk too much.

Indeed our sociability as a whole had gone off; something a little sour and dark had developed in it. We had been sitting there too long. Alex, I fancied, was counting the minutes until they departed. But suddenly she grew hospitable. "You'll stay to dinner, Madeleine, won't you? Please, Larry, do. I can promise you a good dinner," she added with an indulgent smile.

I wondered whether she had mentioned this invitation to Jean and Eva, and whether the short notice would exasperate or inspire them. Mrs. Cullen also thought of that. "Servants are devils, don't you know. Mine used to behave madly, when extra people turned up at Cullen Hall."

Poor Alex was accustomed to the madness of servants; but, as she explained, this new couple did not mind surprises. She had found them in Tangier, where the secretary of the pig-sticking club had engaged them to cook in camp for several tentfuls of unmarried members. With only primitive utensils, a few iron kettles and a spit over an outdoor fire, and unpredictable guests at all hours, it evidently was child's play for them, and a welcome opportunity to show off. One afternoon a French general and a party of eight had motored out from the town, and some thoughtless fellow had asked them to stay. Jean had taken a boar killed that morning, and by slicing it thin, rubbing it with certain herbs which grew there underfoot amid the tents, and marinating it in four bottles of brandy, rendered it quite edible by nightfall. Alex was inclined to think of her entire lifetime as an emergency of that sort. So she had hired the proud pair and secured passports for them and embarked them for France and Chancellet. And this, she told Mrs. Cullen, was what she had hired them for.

"If we do stay," Mrs. Cullen said, "my bird will have to be fed, toward six o'clock." Alex in any case intended to suggest to Jean a dish of pigeons baked with white currants. He would procure them from a neighbor who had an immense old dovecot; and one could be brought back alive for Lucy. The reminiscence of the brandied wild pig, the prospect of *pigeons aux groseilles,* charmed Cullen; you could see the gourmandise shining on his rosy lips.

Alex went to the kitchen, and by her comfortable air when she came back I judged that Jean was well disposed. Then she suggested our taking a walk until dinner-time, which also charmed Cullen, though his appetite did not need whetting. "By Jove," he said, "I do look forward to those squabs."

They were disappointed to learn that the park was not Alex's property. It belonged to the nation, along with the little château de Chancellet in the midst of it. Bidou, the illustrious aged ex-minister, was permitted to live there. But he kept the gates open in the daytime, and the entire village strolled in and out. Meeting all classes when he took his daily exercise perhaps made him think proudly how democratic a statesman he had been all his life. He gave everyone a *bon jour.* He especially liked meeting Alex because she was an American and he vaguely remembered having advocated the payment of the war debts.

"Oh, aren't politicians a bore?" Cullen exclaimed with an odd proud laugh. "Worse than poets."

"Larry, please," his wife said in haste, "please let's not

talk about that." I wondered what that meant.

Alex unlocked the little gate on the far side of the pond, and we strolled along an *allée* of ancient beeches. She warned us that if Bidou should appear in the distance, she would have to turn back. He had a way of inviting her to dine, and Mme. Bidou had asked her not to accept on account of the failing of his health, the folly of his old manhood.

We all felt happier now that we were outdoors. It was beautiful in the park. The trees had been so lovingly tended ever since a pupil of Lenôtre's set them out, that each had developed its maximum character. The way they stood in informal groups, or in line, or alone at a little distance, seemed not only to conform to the art of parks but to express their feelings about each other: idiosyncrasies of affection or obedience, pride or pain. And unlike human characters in such an assembly, they promised or threatened nothing more; no episodes or developments.

Cullen walked up ahead with Alex. Now in the open air he not only laughed but shouted; so that I could hear him telling her a yarn about an old English politician who had attached himself to a young married woman. And one day he and the husband had gone out alone together on the moor for a bit of rough shooting; and he had shot the husband by accident, so to speak. Then he had married her. But he had worried about it all the rest of his life, which was not long; and he had impoverished her in his will. It was ancient gossip: I had heard it before; and at the time I did not see any oddity in Cullen's telling it, except that it seemed funny to him and not to me. When love is diabolic, I thought, a triangle is the simplest form it can take; and a convenient form, if it cannot be endured. The lovers to be pitied perhaps are those who have no one to hate—what they long to kill, and what the killing would be for, incorporated in one and the same person, the one they love—whose rough shooting therefore can take place only in imagination, and never ends.

Presently we came to a crossroads; and there we did see
the short silhouette of old Bidou headed in our direction:
his peculiar march or trudge, and the shrugging of his
shoulders inside a great cape. All his life he had gone
booted like a common soldier and blackly wrapped up,
which had been a boon to caricaturists and a kind of elec-
toral trade mark; which now made it easy to avoid him.
Mrs. Cullen asked if they might go on ahead and have a
look at the famous old fellow.

Alex and I turned back alone toward her house, by a
short cut through a dense plantation of young trees, with
vernal branches of old trees rounded overhead. It was
like walking inside a great recumbent telescope, pointed
at the château half a kilometer away. In the nineteenth
century, under the personal supervision of Viollet-le-Duc
and his friend the author of *Carmen*, Chancellet had been
entirely and fussily restored. In the round bit of sunshine
afar off, the lens of our telescope, it looked too good to be
true, amid the patchy flower beds and the moat, where a
few ducks were splashing and lovemaking.

I was in as foolish a good humor as Cullen; everything
seemed mysterious and sentimental. The rounded frame
of branches in which we strolled, looking ahead into pink-
ish sunlight; the tidy little architecture enframed, with
its associations literary as well as historical; the dying, absent-minded, erotic statesman exercising daily in an immutable circle around it; our odd guests walking to meet
him, woman with hawk and greedy man, whose eyes turned
golden when he looked at her, whose spit ran at the mere
mention of his dinner—all were gathered around me, I
vainly fancied, to make one great vague thing very simple
and clear to me. What more could I ask? But it is always
foolish to expect simplicity. All one can do is to substitute
little facts for great speculations, little performances for
immense desire, and call this, simplification.

The return by ourselves gave me a chance to question
Alex about the Cullens. They had come to Tangier two

or three years before for the pig-sticking. Madeleine rode ideally, but the rule of the club forbade women to carry a spear. Cullen had shown a definite lack of enthusiasm and indeed a lack of talent; however, he had gone out every day and not done badly. When one of the vile brave beasts appeared in the distance—flickering along the shrub, suddenly fleeing out across open ground like the shadow of a flying bird—the Irish woman would gallop out with the very first riders; her husband following hard, looking as if he might fall any minute but not falling. At the last minute, when the spears began to point down along the shoulders of the horses, she would rein up short or turn aside. Suddenly she would not be there any longer, and Cullen still would be. Her ambition for him and his poor horsemanship—so it appeared to the others—betrayed him into prowess. Alex heard a club member say that once or twice at the kill his audacity and ferocity had been rather too much of a good thing; shocking. One morning his horse stepped into a hole and threw him right down beside the boar, a big wicked one already wounded; and he behaved with great sense and courage, and kept his horse away from its tushes, although he was not quite sober. His not being quite sober was the trouble in general.

One afternoon Mrs. Cullen had said as much to Alex. "Poor Larry, when we're in Ireland or in London with nothing to do, is inclined to overeat, and furthermore to drink far too much." Alex must have been impressed by this confession, for she quoted some of it word for word. "Most things are a beastly bore for him, you know; that's his real weakness. But you can't say anything to a grown man about drinking, after all, can you? It's such a horrid little unimportant thing. They're proud, and they resent having to think of it. I had an aunt who talked about it, and it made my uncle worse." As discreetly as she could therefore, she told Alex, she tried to keep him distracted; busy doing things, in good company which inspired him to do well; abroad, and outdoors as much as possible. He often complained that it was no way to live; but it had kept him fit and good-natured.

She was younger than he, Alex pointed out; and she had money of her own; and she was a clever, unconventional, and rather self-indulgent woman. Yet she devoted herself entirely to him, every instant, year in and year out. He on the other hand was not perfectly faithful, in spite of his devotion to her. When they were in Tangier a pretty young American named Baroness Levene came across from Malaga, and flirted with Cullen; and he obviously responded to it. One of the Tangier residents asked them all to dine, and while the men stayed in the dining room, Madeleine had been very rude to the little interloper. A day or two later she spoke of it apologetically. It was disgraceful of her, she assured Alex, to mind her husband's virile frivolity. She never doubted for an instant that he loved her, and no other woman. His response to the others was all make-believe or in fun. She alluded again to his deadly tedium; his need of some novelty to pass the time somehow, every day of his life, every hour; and his other weaknesses in direct consequence. A little philandering, like eating and drinking, gave him something to think about.

Whereas marriage was infinitely simple for her, she said; she never needed the attention of other men. She supposed this to be so settled and so apparent in her character that it bored men and they let her alone. Alex had observed a number of acceptable men not letting her alone in the least; rather smitten. Yet there seemed to be no affectation or insincerity in Mrs. Cullen's account of herself. Women who have been spoiled by the many, tormented by one, often have an air of innocence.

Alex had seen a great deal of them the following winter in London; and there they were engaged in a very odd sport indeed: underground activity of Irish rebellion. Cullen was perfectly and anciently Irish, and one of his brothers had been a friend of Casement's. Whereas Madeleine was not a Catholic; and she had Ulster blood and English blood; and as a child she had lived in Canada. Yet she was the rebel, or she ardently played the part of one; Larry followed. Alex heard him speak very angrily of the British, disgustedly of de Valera. But he loved joining in others' opinion, no matter what, and embellishing his repetition of it, as best he could—how could one tell what he thought? Perhaps it was hard for him to tell himself.

All that winter they were at home informally almost every evening to the oddest patriots. At first glance it looked like a literary salon. The ringleader was the poet McVoy: a young man of great conversation, with a half-rapacious, half-religious face. Alex also met a man who had done a little bombing, another with a bit of his cheek shot away, and certain bereaved and cruel women, and a bizarre priest. Their political opinion was all tinged with piety, even puritanism. They would have been ashamed to eat or drink or be merry in any way, with so much to be done for Eire. Cullen yielded to the general austerity. Furthermore, he told Alex, they could not afford to live well that winter, because of their contributions to the cause. Alex had never seen him in better form, lean and youthful and if not exactly cheerful, amiable. Rebellion evidently served as an excellent exercise and diet. There was also amorous anxiety: he thought McVoy in love with Madeleine. Alex indeed thought so too. But all Madeleine appeared to want of the poet was to keep on his political high horse, in his fascinating conspiratorial vein, for Larry's amusement. Rioting and sabotage and perhaps even assassination—as it were sticking of the Ulster pig, mort of the English stag—with poor Larry in the thick of it, because it would be good for him. . . . Suddenly all that ceased, Alex never heard why. They sublet their house and spent the summer in Vienna and Budapest. That was the summer Mrs. Cullen bought her first hawk, the tiercel that died of the croaks.

This little information Alex gave me as we sauntered slowly through the ex-minister's park. Now we were back near our gate, under the great beeches. Alex had been a little anxious lest the Cullens get lost. But there in the broken light, pallid shade, there they came at a brisk pace, engaged in a vivacious discussion of some sort, which they ceased as soon as they saw us. "He's a dear, your old politician," Mrs. Cullen said. "He spoke to us, and then what do you suppose he did? He did bird imitations for Lucy; I mean to say, he whistled at her."

Evidently Cullen preferred French politicians to Irish. "A good old boy! He did a nightingale and a lark and some bird I didn't know. He told us what it was, but it was French. Quite good."

"And Larry, wasn't he cheerful and civil? Perhaps he thought that if he kept whistling long enough, Lucy would answer. Wasn't it funny?"

I thought it touching as well as funny: that old man had been whistling to his compatriots like that for half a century, and as a rule a majority had answered; but, alas, nothing much had come of it, for France.

Now Mrs. Cullen was ready to feed Lucy. But her chauffeur and Jean who had gone to the neighbor's dovecot, had not returned. Foolish Eva felt sure they were in a ditch somewhere, or quarreling, or lost. So we sat down again; and I like a fool inquired what they thought of French and English and German politics. Cullen was out of breath but he sniffed wonderfully and cleared his throat, preliminary to an opinion. "Please, Larry, no politics," his wife requested, smiling at me to make it less impolite.

She was fondling Lucy, gazing at her eye to eye, slowly shaking her head at her; and the wicked beak moved in exact obedience to the tip of her nose as if it were magnetized. "Lucy's hungry," she said solemnly.

"Feel her breast." She took my hand and held it against the tasseled plumage; and indeed there was a humming and stiffening in it, like a little voltage of electricity. Her eyes were moist and explosive; and the instant her mistress's eyes released them, down they went to the gauntlet, as if expecting a feathery form in agony to materialize out of the leather.

"Feel her feet," Mrs. Cullen added; and I did, while she explained that birds always have a higher temperature than animals. Fever heat; and yet they were slick and dry like a serpent. I could feel what they wanted to do, what they wanted to have, swelling in them and ticking the dull minutes meanwhile with little throbs. My pleasure in touching them was half embarrassment; and it set my mind running back to the thought I had left off an hour ago; that this hawk's hunger was like amorous appetite. I call it thought—and it is thought now, as I remember and try to tell it—but at the time it was only a vague flashing daydream. It all came together like one large composite phrase: old bachelor hungry bird, aging-hungry-man-bird, and how I hate desire, how I need pleasure, how I adore love, how difficult middle age must be!

Then, I lamented to myself, if your judgment is poor you fall in love with those who could not possibly love you. If romance of the past has done you any harm, you will not be able to hold on to love when you do attain it; your grasp of it will be out of alignment. Or pity or self-pity may have blunted your hand so that it makes no mark. Back you fly to your perch, ashamed as well as frustrated. Life is almost all perch. There is no nest; and no one is with you, on exactly the same rock or out on the same limb. The circumstances of passion are all too petty to be companionable. So there you sit, and you try to sit still, and doze and dream to save trouble. It is the kind of thing you have to keep quiet about for others' sake, politeness's sake: itching palm and ugly tongue and unsighted eye and empty flatulent physiology as a whole; and your cry of desire, ache, ache, ringing in your own ears. No one else hears it; and you get so tired of it yourself that you can't wait to grow old. . . .

Thus in an instant I foolishly imagined myself growing old; and meanwhile Mrs. Cullen had not ceased speaking with that single-minded vivacity of hers, but a little somber. "Since we caught Lucy," she said, "she's never had a mouthful to eat except out of my hand, and I've always worn the same glove. Think what it must mean to her!"

It was an impressive unpleasant object, that glove, stiffened and discolored by a hundred little sanguinary banquets. It resembled things you see in cases in anthropological museums; fetishes of awful religion, sacrificial utensils, witch-doctors' kits. And the feet with crescent toenails trod it so passionately that you wondered how the wrist inside endured it.

"You know, she's not really attached to me personally," Mrs. Cullen said. "If I gave you the glove she'd be yours instead of mine. It's as simple as that, I think. It's what's called behaviorism, isn't it? Would you like to try it? Try taking her a moment."

She turned around and held Lucy some five or six inches below the chair-back, and after a moment's hesitation Lucy hopped up there. Mrs. Cullen's hand was large and mine is not; so that I was able to squeeze into the gauntlet. It surprised me to see that she wore another large diamond on that hand, which under the pressure of the leather had bruised her finger a little. . . Then I held my wrist five or six inches above the chair-back; and Lucy, with her belief in food-stained leather added to her belief in the highest possible perch, hopped again.

"That's what they call an inferiority complex, don't they?" Cullen proudly demanded, not to be outdone by his wife's use of that other catchword. "Madeleine can't understand one thing about psychology."

"Very well, Larry. I tell you she's hungry," his wife answered. And by the tone of her voice you would have thought her the hungry one.

I drew a deep breath, in which I got the hawk odor, slightly bloody, slightly peppery. I had noticed it before, but without distinguishing it from Mrs. Cullen's French scent. The body, well balanced on its hot feet, weighed less than I had supposed. At the least move her talons pricked the leather and pulled it a bit—as fashionable women's fingernails do on certain fabrics—though evidently she held them as loose and harmless as she could. Only her grip as a whole was hard, like a pair of tight, heated iron bracelets.

Alex offered her congratulations upon Lucy's evident peace of mind with me; I would make a good falconer. That reminded me of my father and his magic with animals which filled me with envy and antipathy when I was a boy. He could force a crazy colt to its knees, or castrate a young boar, or chloroform a desperate trapped owl; and their wretched muscles relaxed and surrendered, their eyes blinked in perfect gentleness in alignment with his eyes. His eyes, or perhaps it was his hands, seemed able to promise them something. Half my life, I said to myself, has been discovering that my character is not the antithesis or the contradiction of his; here was a new kinship. Perhaps I could cope with horse or hog or doomed bird too, if I had to; perhaps even with a wild antipathetic son, disinclined to live—who knows? This was a gratifying thought but not altogether happy: vast vague potentiality of things I did not wish to do in any case.

I happen to be a trifle long-sighted; and now Lucy was so close that I could not quite see her in focus; and I have always had a fear of going blind. One good flutter, one simple thrust, and she could have slit an eyelid or ruptured an eyeball in an instant. She did not shuffle much on the borrowed gauntlet. But the vague dilated dark of her eye, the naked ring around it, the inner eyelids opening and closing as instantly as bubbles, seemed worse than restlessness. I was ashamed to tell her mistress that I was afraid. No doubt the chances of her actually hurting me were negligible. Mrs. Cullen's half-supercilious glance at us was reassuring. Still, I felt rather as if I had a great thought of death concentrated and embodied and perched on me. Whatever had possessed me, I wondered, to think of this Lucy—bloodthirsty brute with a face like a gouge, feet like two sets of dirty scalpels—as significant of love? Perhaps those two things, imaginary death and hopeless desire, always lie close together in one's mind, foolishly interchangeable.

Mrs. Cullen meanwhile, with vacated wrist, seemed the most restless woman in the world. She kept crossing and uncrossing her perfect stilted feet; leaning this way and that in the soft armchair; clasping and unclasping her jeweled fingers. It suggested one more explanation of her attachment to Lucy; falconry made her sit still. Perhaps too she was slightly jealous of my successful deputyship. "The real reason Lucy likes you so much," she murmured, "is that it's getting on toward mealtime. She fancies you may have a little steak or half a pigeon in your pocket. You look promising to her. What do you suppose has become of your cook? I do hope he and Ricketts haven't gone off to get drunk together."

She rose and tripped across to the great window. She tripped back and paused beside us and teased Lucy as Cullen had done, but in the opposite spirit. The star sapphire slid a little from one teasing finger to the next, which Lucy observed with interest. It looked like an unsocketed eye, I thought.

"Oh, Alex," Mrs. Cullen said, "you're so intelligent. I'm afraid you think me very sentimental. I'm not really. I do not want a falcon to be attached to me personally. When animals get that sort of feeling, it's too awful. Knowing the sound of your voice, liking the way you smell, wanting to be touched, all that. I hate it. It's such a parody of us, it's worse than we are. A bird like Lucy is so simple and straight. You make a promise and she expects you to keep it, that's all. She knows what she wants, and who gives it to her, and that's that."

Cullen grunted, and assured us that his wife didn't mean

a word of this cynical stuff. But he did agree about one thing: "Birds are selfish as the devil. That's why I can't care for them. I'd rather have a dog, I tell you."

"Do you hear, Lucy? He'd rather have a dog." She said this in the way of wicked affectation, perhaps toying with the idea of being hated by him for it.

Then she turned briskly to me: "I'll take her back now, Mr. Tower, if you please. I think she'll bate in a minute."

Once more we exchanged the glove. Once more Lucy considered, on the rough leather, the stain of yesterdays' meals and the hope of today's and tomorrow's, and leaped up with alacrity. Her mistress carefully fondled her to prevent her bating, but she bated nevertheless.

After that, Mrs. Cullen heaved a greater sigh than before, not because it had been a harder struggle, but because her own light but significant remarks had hurt her at last, I fancied. And now she added that, simple though hawks all were, you could never really trust one. "Oh, I shall have to be so careful, never to fly Lucy at things she cannot catch and kill. The least failure makes her hopeless. My man in Hungary says that if she misses her quarry twice, I must call it a day and keep her hooded; otherwise it's risky. Because if she should miss a third time she might leave me; fly off and never return. They're all alike: the haggard you've hunted with for years; even the eyas you have taken from the nest and babied all its life. . . ."

"Damned ungrateful, I say," Cullen jeered.

"No, Larry. Lucy gives up her freedom and stays with me because it's a better life, more food and more fun. If it doesn't work, after all, what's the use? If my falconry isn't good enough. . . ."

Cullen giggled. I didn't. For it is the way religious faith goes, in the sense of God's failure; and it is the way true love ends: missing the third time. That much of life I already knew; I had missed twice. I glanced at Alex, wondering if the mysterious turn this small talk was taking troubled her too. But her face had its pretty well-bred passivity; I could not tell. The light in the Irish woman's eyes was fantastic, focused like glass on her great weak husband, then on me for just a moment with something like embarrassing affection. She and I understood each other.

She seemed to me a very passionate woman, but it was a kind of plural passion, all confused or crossed: work and play and sense of beauty, the maternal and the conjugal and the misanthropic, mixed. Perhaps that is a peculiarity of childless women. Female character has a great many secondary traits and minor talents; the wear and tear of motherhood may weaken them or stamp them out. It is anarchy if they all flourish.

"Tower," she said, "you would make a good falconer. Why don't you take it up, in the States? And you too, Alex. Everyone should have some hobby, some pet, I think. And all the other pets really are too awful.

"Ugh, how I despise dogs!" she then exclaimed in a dull disgusted tone of voice. "Do you know what dogs remind me of? It's not a nice thing to say but I do mean it. Prostitutes; all things to all men, and all that. And all shapes and sizes, from adapting themselves to everything and everybody for centuries, with no integrity. Men love them for that; it's flattering.

"Falcons have never changed. Forty centuries of falconry, think of it! And still wild; every feather as it was, and the same everywhere. I tell you, there's nothing like it in nature. Cats have more character than dogs, if they only weren't so damned amorous. Kittens to be drowned every few months, isn't it awful!"

My well-bred Alex in spite of herself made a little shocked face. It startled me too, because just then like a fool I had been thinking of Mrs. Cullen as a childless woman. What about those wild Irish sons of hers, shifting for themselves at Cullen Hall, riding and spoiling her favorite hunters, hunting with Lord Bild? I said a kind of prayer for them. That is, I hoped that they really were wild. Cullen had spoken of them as practically mature men; but perhaps he himself was not mature enough to judge of it. I hoped that they did not love their mother much. If they were at all backward or sensitive it was good of her, wise of her, to keep out of Ireland.

At this point wild Lucy flung up her wings and let her mute drop to the floor. Mrs. Cullen cheerfully apologized, and also proudly called our attention to its whiteness. It meant that Lucy was in excellent health. A healthy falcon's mute is the cleanest wastage in nature, and by no stretch of imagination could Alex or I have been offended by it. Cullen offendedly stirred his great body about in the great soft armchair; his face got redder; his light eyes protruded. But they protruded at us rather than it. Perhaps he feared, or perhaps hoped, that we would somehow express disapprobation or disgust. Alex rang for Eva, and of course that simple creature did not mind; it rather amused her. She fetched a towel and some wax, and knelt beautifully, and gave the parquet a very good restoration.

During which, Jean came rushing in, sweaty and pleased with himself. When he saw his dear beauty there on her knees he made a gleeful sound and gave her a tap as he passed, which made her blush. He and Ricketts in the Daimler had had a blowout on the back road. But dinner would not be much delayed; for while Ricketts had changed the tire, he had seated himself by the roadside and dressed the pigeons with his jackknife.

Mrs. Cullen asked him how large Lucy's pigeon was; and he sent Eva after it: a rumpled thing in a basket with warm damned eyes. She instructed them to wring its neck and chop it in half and bring it back, with its feathers and half the giblets. Meanwhile she asked me to move the straight chair into a dusky corner under the staircase. Though the least shy hawk in the world, Lucy would not feed properly outdoors or with a light in her eyes. Next Mrs. Cullen requested a number of towels to protect her dress, and Eva brought a worn-out tablecloth; and Alex helped tie this under her chin like a bib and spread it out over her lap. She sat with her pretty legs far apart, no longer a fashionable woman but rather like a gypsy or a priestess; or as if this were to be some surgical operation or painful travail.

Whereupon Jean returned with the portion of pigeon. He let two or three drops of blood and a bit of gizzard fall on the waxed floor; and again Eva cheerfully mopped up. Mrs. Cullen took the half-bird in the hand on which Lucy perched, pinching it between gloved forefinger and thumb, at Lucy's feet; turning it temptingly. At first Lucy stared at Alex and me so insolently that we drew a few steps away from the staircase. Jean and Eva also wanted to watch, but Alex reminded them that we too were hungry.

I had been hearing so much and thinking so romantically of hawk-hunger, that I expected a lunge and a grab, like a wolf or a cat; it was not so at all. It took two or three minutes for Lucy's appetite to develop, to accumulate. In a state of nature, no doubt it depends upon the fun of pursuit, voluptuous air in her wings, and the hovering and teasing; and there would not be any real spasm of Lucy's love of food until the instant she felt food in her beak. Now there had to be time for some equivalent of all that to take place in her narrow mind; time at least to regret it. The tedium of this conjugal kind of repast had to be overcome somehow, so she doubted and deliberated and imagined.

"Damn your pride, Lucy," Mrs. Cullen muttered; then murmured to us in her schoolgirl French, because Lucy did not understand French, *"l'appétit vient en mangeant."* Upon which I reminded myself that on the whole, throughout life as a whole, the appetites which do not arise until we have resolved to eat, which we cannot comprehend until we have eaten, are the noblest—marital, aesthetic, religious. . . .

At last Lucy's curly breast did throb; a few feathers bristled up; her wings stood out a few inches; her greenish fists clenched on the glove; then her whole body began to point down beak first like a water-diviner's stick. She set her feet a little farther apart on her mistress's wrist. Then she stooped straight between them and thrust into the piece of pigeon. Mrs. Cullen held it tight. Lucy braced her legs and pulled and straightened back up with a morsel, which after a moment she shifted away into her throat and with a sinuous motion or a toss, swallowed.

Until the end, until there was no more pigeon, Mrs. Cullen had to encourage her to keep her mind on what she was doing. "The important thing," she said, "is to get her to take feathers enough. Her digestion depends a good deal on that."

When Lucy paused and raised her weird face between mouthfuls, it seemed spiritual rather than sensual; a bigoted face. There was no histrionic angry temper, no showing off. Thoroughly and slowly it went on to the end, with meditation upon every feather, every crumb of meat, every sip of blood—sacramental. Once or twice, because she did not like the way some wisp of plumage or tiny tendon felt —or because she liked it extremely—she shook her head hard; and a spot of blood appeared on Mrs. Cullen's bib, a feather drifted to the floor. Perhaps you could not have watched it if you were squeamish; neither Alex nor I were. But after the fourth or fifth beakful Lucy had a bad moment, modesty or imaginary repletion, and Mrs. Cullen asked us to move still farther away; and we were glad to go. We sat down beside Cullen in front of the big window.

It interested me to observe, or to guess at, his feeling about this. When his wife first called for Lucy's banquet he had pulled a long face. I think that may have been only fond anxiety, lest in her serving of it she appear to Alex and me coarse, or comical. He kept his eyes averted, but it was not disgust, surely, for it put him in mind of his own eating. He talked to us of that with enthusiasm and in great detail. In Paris the past week someone had sent them away out on the Avenue Jean Jaurès for a steak: year after year they always telephoned a certain small unsuccessful

restaurant to prepare a supreme *cassoulet* which took two
days; and so forth. Which brought him finally to the present, the great casserole of pigeons which Jean was pre-
paring. At that point, I think, Alex regarded him almost
with detestation.

The half-pigeon out of the way, Mrs. Cullen decided to
put Lucy outdoors to weather, as it is called. We followed
her into the garden where she selected the back of a rustic
bench as a suitable perch. But there had been signs of
more than usual nervousness during the feeding: it seemed
best to leave her hooded. Because of the unaccustomed
warmth of the afternoon, after Scotland, Mrs. Cullen said,
she had a slight headache; and she retired with Alex to
the bedroom for some aspirin and a moment's repose.

Then I offered Cullen a cocktail. He rose with enthusiasm and followed me to what I called the choir loft, that
is, the balcony, where Alex's decorator had seen fit to in-
stall a bar, in the fashion of the twenties: all chromium
and copper with a fine hierarchy of glasses and remarkable
liquors in odd bottles. My Irishman had never seen the
like of it. There was a magnum of prewar vodka; and I
suggested a kind of modified Alexander with that in it instead of gin. Missing a syllable, he thought it charming of
me, and so American, to serve a drink named after our
hostess. I tried to set him right on that point but he was
too charmed to care. The drink itself also suited him and
for a while he concentrated on it, without a word.

The ladies did not return, so presently I mixed a second
shakerful; and Alex's silver shaker was large. It was indiscreet, perhaps a little perverse, and in a way characteristic of me. As a rule I dislike being with people who have had
too much to drink. It often brings on in me a kind of
misanthropic fit; pity verging upon repugnance, and a
mean sense of humor which they sometimes notice. But
just because I am aware of the old-maidishness and even
injustice of this, whenever the hospitality of the bottle is
up to me I am inclined to overdo it.

Cullen in fact had been a little tight all afternoon, and I had not realized it. Now as he got tighter I saw that it was the same thing. They had arrived at Chancellet about two-thirty; so probably it had happened at luncheon, perhaps at breakfast. That explained his wife's anxious and resentful air, and her rude motherly snubs to keep him in order. He must have been in misery the last few hours, while we failed to offer him anything: thoughtlessness on my part, perhaps prudence or dislike on Alex's. She of course knew him well and must have noticed.

Perhaps the unnoticeable sort of heavy daytime drinker has the worst trouble; certainly they are more troublesome to others than they think. And others—sobersides like myself—are often more unjust to them than to their reeling, roaring, festive confreres. Half the time they themselves are only half aware of any incapacity or lack of charm. Or perhaps they know, and they think that you do not, and you do, and of course it is not manners to tell them so. They make an effort, often a heroic effort; and you feel that you have to respect and applaud that, whether or not it is fun for you.

But the worst injustice must be when you scarcely know them, and you judge them without reference to their habit, as in my case with Cullen that afternoon. He had simply seemed to me mediocre; old for his age, and weak for his size, dull, vain, and rather cross. No one had warned me that I was not seeing him at his best. It was his character, for all I knew, the nature of the creature; take it or leave it. That is to say, I had left it. So now I felt a slight embarrassment and grudging contrition.

Perhaps at other times, I reminded myself, his character was ideal; his mind vigorous; his great physique fresh and energetic. That would explain the love his wife bore him. Suppose you have learned to like or to love such a man when he was sober; and you happen to dislike him when he is not; and he doesn't know the difference or can't help it. The temptation to interfere, the fond hope of reforma-

tion, must be very great. Thus I began to think indulgent-
ly of Mrs. Cullen's selfish nervousness and sharp tongue.
Although, if what I had seen that afternoon was the worst
of it, certainly she exaggerated and overemphasized the
plight she was in with him. An ordinary boring conceited
uneasy childish man! Yet out of his petty instability she
seemed to expect something odious or dangerous to develop any minute—as if she felt the ground underfoot
move a bit, like a landslide starting, and caught glimpses
of little creeping sickening things close to the surface,
coming up! Love itself is an exaggeration, and very likely
to lead to others.

After the first pouring of the second round, suddenly
Cullen began a long complaint of the merry chase she led
him year in and year out: her Mediterranean cruises, her
falcons, her Irish republicans. No home to speak of, no
creature comforts; nothing like the good time Alex and I
had here in Chancellet, this pretty bar for example. Nothing but wild men, wild birds, and two silly maids to mop
up after the birds instead of a good cook: hotel food all
the year round, never a leg of boar soaked in brandy nor
squab with currants.

At first, I think his outburst embarrassed him as well as
me. For he explained that if I were an Englishman he
would not be talking to me in this way; nor, for that matter, if he were an Englishman! But the Irish are like Americans in this respect. He had been in the States three or
four years when he was a young fellow; therefore he felt
the likeness. "The English never talk freely, as we're talking now. They're sly; they simply rule, and have their own
way about everything. Britannia rules the waves and so on.
You know, Tower, my wife's English. . . ."

These little distinctions of nationality were what reminded him of their winter in London with the Irish republicans. He not only disliked that type of Irish; their
political principle seemed suspect to him. "They're not
really republicans, that's just talk. They're anarchists. It

was beastly for me. I'm a fool, I'd do anything in the world for my wife, and she does whatever strikes her fancy. She kept asking those patriots to the house. It cost me a pretty penny too, I can tell you. I had to pay for a lot of pamphlets, I had to support two widows, I had to hire halls for their meetings. Then, if you please, some of 'em said they needed some guns and bombs. Can you believe it? Only I don't think they got any bombs. Nothing happened. It would serve the English right if they did blow things up, you know. I suppose my wife's little friends just pocketed the money; or they bought a poor make of bomb that wouldn't do. Nothing happened."

He also complained that they were comic little characters, not gentlemen. And all their women appeared half-crazed with loving them, weeping in the corridor, losing their tempers with each other; some of them occult, some religious, and all of course talking Ireland, Ireland. Not a class of women that a man of a sensual nature would look twice at, not if he had any self-respect; nothing soft or sweet or tidy about them. "But I must say I enjoyed it for a while," he admitted, "seeing how that class of people get on and hearing their stories. I could always shut them up when I felt like it, or chuck them all altogether, you understand, because I had the money."

Of course I had begun to feel my misanthropy; but still his monologue amused me, especially the vulgar touches like this last. No doubt he was a quite good county aristocrat of that modest rank which as a rule is less mixed than any other. But not even aristocracy can be expected to give good examples of itself all the time. It seems rather to secrete commonness little by little, and to keep it in reserve, along with those odds and ends of mere human nature which aristocratic manners are intended to hide. And every generation or two it purges itself, in the form of some odd son or daughter, perfect little shopkeeper or predestined courtesan, upon whom manners wear thin.

Cullen silently ruminated two or three minutes; and

when he began again it was in the middle of a new bit of
subject matter. Probably it seemed to him that he had told
me something which he had been saying to himself, something about his wife. "Make no mistake, Tower, I respect
my wife." And he went on to assure me, or to warn me,
that anyone who doubted it or slighted her in the least
was quite likely to be knocked down by him; in fact he had
done it once. She was like a swan in his opinion; pure as
snow, with never a harmful thought all her life. "Only
she's thoughtless," he added. "She never thinks of anything except what she happens to want. She's spoiled.
When I met her she was the prettiest girl in Dublin. Lovely breasts for one thing. And ankles; you saw her ankles!
Her family wasn't well off either. I took her without a
penny; and I've spoiled her."

Aristocracy had nothing to do with it. It was my own
fault; the vodka and cream had done it. Alcohol is the
great leveler. Given a stiff drink, the true descendant of
princes boasts of it as if it were not true, the multimillion-
aire feels poor, and Tristan talks to you about Isolde like
a pimp, I said to myself. My malice was beginning to keep
pace with my companion's folly.

"I spoiled her myself," he continued. "That's why she's
so restless. Damn it, Tower, for years now she's kept me
on the go like a gypsy. We've done everything." He held
up one large moist freckled hand and counted on its un-
steady fingers the things they had done: salmon fishing
and photography and pig-sticking and now hawking. They
had also been everywhere, and he counted places too, with
a boastful as well as pathetic intonation: Norway and
America and Java and Morocco and Africa—to say nothing
of that winter when she had insisted on Irish rebellion,
the most expensive thing on earth.

"I've let her have all my money," he said proudly. "She
isn't as pretty as she was; but you know, I let her go to
London for all her dresses, or Paris; and she has two maids.
Before I married her I had a man to look after me; I gave

him up. Now we need this chauffeur, Ricketts, because
we're always on the go. I have to keep an eye on him too,
because he has an eye for a pretty woman. Funny thing,
one day when we were shooting in Scotland with those
Americans, I thought Ricketts was insolent about Mrs.
Cullen, and I'd have killed him. But she said I imagined
it."

All alcoholism in a nutshell, I foolishly mused. And
while he, poor man, counted his sports and his travels on
his fingers, I meanly ticked off the drunkard's faults and
pitfalls of drink as it were on my fingers—indiscretion and
boastfulness and snobbism; and sentimentality so nervous
that it may switch any minute to the exact opposite; and
the sexual note and the sadistic note, undesirable desire,
improbable murder. All of it of course a bit unreal and
unrealizable in fact. . . .

What exaggeration I had drifted into! Cullen really was
not in very bad shape; I have spent afternoons with a hundred drunker men. The point is that I exaggerated at the
time, item by item as he talked along; and I think he
sensed it and played up to it: a fatalist and a play-actor.
The presence of my fastidious Alex and his over-wrought
wife downstairs—my wishing they would hurry up and
join us, and my dreading it at the same time—made his
loose talk more exciting than it would have been in ordinary circumstances. I had been too happy all afternoon,
thinking meanwhile of unhappiness; which is a heady
combination. Sometimes I am as sensitive as a woman to
others' temper or temperament; and it is a kind of sensi-
tivity which may turn, almost by chance, for them or
against them. Perhaps at the end of our tête-à-tête I was
not much soberer than my companion.

I began to wonder whether, after all, he was not going
to tell me the little tale of anxiety or jealousy that winter
in London which Alex had half told me in the park. And
then he did.

"That winter in London one of our patriots," he began,

"had the insolence to fall in love with my wife. A brute of a young fellow named McVoy who was a poet. It got very sticky then. I made up my mind to show them the door, the lot of them. But the more I worried about it, the easier it was for my wife to get around me and have her own way. I didn't want to be unjust to her; and if I'd made a scene before I knew what was up, you see, I might never have known. Terrible, the power a woman has over a man of my nature. You see that side of it, don't you?"

He told it tranquilly enough, though with some breathing between words. He reached out and grasped the cocktail shaker; and having helped himself, kept a tight hold on it. Once or twice he slipped off the tall stool and took steps up and down, carrying the shaker with him instead of his glass, to gesture with; coming back to drink and refill. I had not poured any of this second shakerful for myself; it was almost empty. The whites of his eyes grew more and more untidy, the hazel pupils a harder color; sense of humor and self-knowledge dying down in them. The strong though puffy fingers fixed on the large silver vessel, melting the frostiness off it in patches. I thought of wresting it away from him; emptying it slyly down the little chromium sink; perhaps pretending to be getting drunk myself, and jollying and bullying him along downstairs. . . . Naturally I did nothing; I looked and listened; I nodded. I wiped the copper top of the bar more than it needed, like a bartender. Probably even bartenders feel a little ignominious curiosity amid their professional boredom.

"One fine day there had to be an end of it, McVoy and all that. Especially one night. The police misunderstood something about him, and were waiting for him at his lodgings; so we had to put him up for the night. I couldn't sleep a wink. I kept hearing him sneaking around in the dark after my wife, I thought. All imagination; I've too much imagination anyway. My wife and I shared a bedroom; we always do; and he'd never have had the courage to come in there.

"Then I had a disgusting dream. I woke up standing beside my wife's bed. There was a moon, and I could see her, and she was sleeping. But I couldn't sleep. So about three o'clock I got up and took a knife from the butler's pantry. I thought I'd tackle McVoy with it. But my wife woke up and came and followed me, across the hall. When she saw the knife naturally it frightened her terribly. And the funny thing was, she frightened me too: there on the landing in her white nightgown. She made me give her the knife and go back to our bedroom. The wonder is we didn't wake McVoy. If we had, there'd have been an awful fuss, I expect. But he slept through it all. Or perhaps he was listening and hiding, scared, under his bed.

"After that I think my wife saw my point of view about it, and was sorry for me. She wept, and it wasn't like her to weep. In a way I was sorry for her too. Think of it, Tower! Think of a common little fellow like that coming to your house, whinnying like a horse around a respectable married woman. He'd have had only himself to blame if I had knifed him. After that Mrs. Cullen sent them all packing, believe me. All the rebels."

He picked up the shaker and shook it hopefully. Now there was only the clunk of small ice in diluted cream, to which I was deaf: a poor host at last, now that it was too late. My feeling about it all really was an absurd mixture. I felt a certain compassion; all the world loves a lover, and especially I do. I also longed to laugh aloud and to tease him. I also itched to tell him the miserable truth about himself, and rather vengefully than for the good it might do. There are a number of circumstances in which the truth does no good; and oh, this was one. I began to feel a mixture of sadness with my malice; a fellow feeling in spite of myself.

Drunkenness does superimpose a certain peculiarity and opaqueness of its own—monotonous complexion, odd aroma, pitch of voice, and nervous twitch—on the rest of a man's humanity; over the personality that you have known sober. But worse still is the transparency and the revelation, as it were sudden little windows uncurtained, or little holes cut, into common recesses of character. It is an anatomy lesson: behold the ducts and sinuses and bladders of the soul, common to every soul ever born! Drunken tricks are nothing but basic human traits. Ordinary frame of mind is never altogether unlike this babble of morbid Irishman. I felt the sickish embarrassment of being mere human clay myself. It seems to me that only art has the right to make one feel that. I am inclined to detest anyone who makes me feel it, as you might say, socially.

"God, Tower, it's tragic," my man sighed. "There's always something. Now I have to keep an eye on our damned Ricketts." He kept it on me for a while then, flashing it or rolling it; sometimes as simply as Othello, sometimes with the imagination and abstraction of a eunuch.

"You know, Tower, it's very interesting. My wife and I are the ideal married couple, so to speak. It's real love. She wouldn't look at another man. I'm as good a man as ever in spite of my age; it runs in the family; and I understand women. Oh, it's not all roses; it never was all roses. There were times when I thought I'd leave her, after some of the mistreatment she's given me. At least I could pretend to, and she might learn to treat me better. All it would need to summon her back would be a wink and a beckoning. She'd do it; she'd stoop her proud neck, I tell you; she'd come on her hands and knees. But I'd never humiliate her, Tower; I never have. To me she's still the proud ignorant girl as I married her; the prettiest in all Dublin.

"The worst mistreatment I've had to bear, you know, is this hawk. There are things only a common fellow could bear peaceably, and a hawk is one of 'em. Funny about hawks, you know, they can't learn to control themselves. They make their messes when they feel the need. Oh, well, you saw it with your own eyes; I sympathized with you.

It happens in the hotel, the maids mop up after it, and I can't tell you how ashamed I am. I can't look the man at the desk in the face; he might make a joke of it. Madeleine has to tell him what we want; I won't go near him. . . . Funny about women, isn't it? They haven't the same natural shame about things that men have. Let's face it: that's why the church has to keep them in their place, they can't help it. I suppose if they had finer feelings, we men would get left out in the cold, wouldn't we? They'd have none of our kisses. So there you are.

"My wife's a fine trainer of hawks; her crooked old Hungarian admits it himself. But that is one way she can't subdue 'em; it's their nature. She can't teach me much either. She's got to get rid of that hawk, pretty quick; I won't stand for it. You see, I love her, Tower; that's the trouble. Suppose I want to put my arm around her, and she has that hawk on her arm. Can I? No, Larry, no, dear, you'll break a feather, a very important flight feather! Day after day now on the way to Hungary I'll have to sit there pushed over in the corner of the back seat out of Lucy's way; and I tell you, it makes me sick.

"She's been keeping it in our bedroom, because it doesn't like the bathroom. She's sorry for it. I lie awake all night hearing it stir on the perch, and I never forget it for a minute. When I'm beginning to fall asleep I think it's coming to attack me with its nasty beak. You can't imagine what it means to me. I dream of it. I dream sometimes it's an obscene thing; and that wakes me and I reach my arm over to my wife's bed; but she's asleep and takes no notice of me. I tell you, it's not healthy. I dream sometimes it's death. You know, I had an old uncle who saw ghosts, in a big house we had in Galway. I inherited that kind of feeling, you see, and Lucy brings it on. I'll tell you another dream. When I was a boy my old nurse taught me to weave osier baskets; and the other night I dreamed Lucy was a basket. Her feathers weren't right for it because they were sticky, but I wove her; and I gave her to my wife. But this is the end! No more Lucy!"

That was a lovely moment, to my way of thinking. My animosity toward this fool husband suddenly wafted away. It is a manner of self-revelation that I especially delight in: by means of loose imagery, and dreams, and careless connection of odd bits of memory as they come. Even as he spoke I hoped that I should be able to remember every word.

For alcohol is a god, as the Greeks decided when it was first introduced from the East, although a god of vengeance. The drinker becomes the drunkard. Everyone is to blame. The soberest man or woman in the world at some time or another has helped the sad process along in some poor dear drinker's case. For example, I think someone must have looked at Cullen in his youth when drunkenness became him, and so loved or admired him in it that he began to regard that as the secret of love and admiration. There are men who master the trick of drink, and practically never take a drop without being made admirable by it. I have known one or two; they were extraordinary men in other ways as well.

But even for the average man, even in the poorest boozefight—between the vanity of the beginning and the sickness at last—there is a fine moment. It is the mark of its oriental origin and the proof of the Greek belief in it. The fumes seem suddenly mixed with more light and air than usual, and it is the right mixture. The silly self-consciousness clears up; the chip falls from the shoulder. Your friend is drinking, and you are not, or not much; so naturally there is an undercurrent of quarrel between you; now suddenly it ceases, peaceful. His tipsy mind is as it were sitting quiet, like an oracle on a tripod, under the influence not of alcohol simply, but of himself, his very nature, his fatality, his childhood. Whatever has been kept secret, damped in ashes, smothered and contemptible, begins to come out; and for the average man there is no harm in it. The murderous man may murder then, the madman talk nonsense; who cares? For most of us the ashes are bad, the secrecy mistaken, the contempt and self-contempt contemptible—and the raking of the ashes is good. For a moment, drunk as a lord, instead of coarseness and looseness you have the intuition of a child or an old woman. . . .

Of course it does not last long. Ordinarily when it has occurred, befuddlement and some bodily incompetence are in the offing. Too much delight in it may cause one to keep the worst company in the world all one's life. But certainly it is one of the main things in human nature, worth experiencing and worth watching. Cullen did not quite reach it that afternoon, on vodka and cream in Alex's silly de luxe bar. But I thought he was about to, when we were interrupted. As I really did not like him anyway I did not care much.

It was Alex who interrupted us, coming into the big room under the balcony and calling to me. She wanted me to visit Jean and Eva in the kitchen, and encourage them about the impromptu dinner and hurry them up. She had been hearing strange tones of voice out there; and she was afraid that if she went herself, Jean might make speeches and Eva might weep.

It was a large, unmistakably French kitchen: the stove in a deep niche of brick; dim walls and array of copper; the open doorway and windows full of little landscape with afternoon sunlight slanting across it. The Cullens' chauffeur was there with our two servants, and somehow it seemed to me dramatic as well as picturesque. Jean was the classic manservant, a type that you find more or less the same all around the Mediterranean: doubtless very good-looking and amorous as a boy; forty now and the worse for wear, with a bald spot and dark jowls and several teeth missing; a man broken to harness but still apt to show off his emotions, and still amorous. He had acquired Eva in Morocco; and she certainly had Moorish blood though she called herself Italian. She was half his age and lovely, although of an increasing billowy fatness; pale in the way that seems sallow at times, silvery at other times. Ricketts was a fine Cockney, bright-eyed and sharp-nosed. He sat at the table in the middle of the room in a spoiled young male attitude, with a bottle of wine half empty and half a plate of Eva's little Moorish cakes.

Dinner was flourishing; that I could tell by the smell of it. Along with which I breathed the early summer wafting in: a tart exhalation of the sod, a scent of some shrub that was like a dark candy. In spite of the open door, the stove going full tilt for the squabs and the strawberry tart made the room hot, which brought out the men's untidy healthy body odor. Eva had one of those cheap North African perfumes in a little cake like a rubber eraser, and had put that on to excess, which, alas, I fancied, was for the young Englishman's benefit. And the mood of the room, the morality or psychology of the three together, was as confusing as this fragrant air in it. Eva stood and stared at Ricketts. Her great eyes were a little reddened; probably she had been weeping; at the moment she was smiling vaguely. Ricketts poured the sour red wine down his throat half a glass at a time; and between throatfuls looked up at her with a becoming brightness. Jean pretended to be busy beside the stove with his back to them. But he agitated the pots and pans, and flashed glances over his shoulder, and replied to my questions about the tart and the cheese with a little more obscurity and more assurance than I liked.

Then I happened to look outdoors. It pleased me to be able to see, in a little interval between two shrubs, the dreamy hawk hunched up on the rustic bench. And then, to my amazement, I saw Cullen on the left coming across the lawn. Very slowly, with a kind of noticeable alcoholic endeavor not to be noticed; on tiptoe, and as if the grass were a loud and slippery surface like a ballroom floor. . . . Instantly I sensed that it was abnormal and scandalous. But I could not run out to see what he was up to, without making a little scandal myself. Jean and Eva and Ricketts would follow or at least watch. So there I stood, acting absent-minded, murmuring about the Camembert and the iced hock.

Cullen vanished for a moment behind one of those two shrubs near Lucy's perch. When he reappeared he was crouching, and hitching along on the balls of his feet, and steadying himself with one hand, closer and closer to her. The grotesque furtive approach indicated for one thing that he had no rational plan, no serious intention. For Lucy was hooded as well as leashed; she could not see him. He kept stretching out one hand, very tense; but he could scarcely have reached her from that quadruped position. I began to think it funny. But from the bedroom window Alex and Mrs. Cullen could have seen him as well as I: that was a pity. . . .

Perhaps it occurred to him. He scrambled to his feet, and somewhat assumed an attitude of knowing what he was about, and leaned over the bench with his back to me. Perhaps he was undoing the knot or knots of the leash. Evidently he was not alarming Lucy much; she opened her wings a few inches, as if expecting to be picked up. But he drew back, and to my dismay, my disgust, thrust his hand in his pocket and brought out a large pocketknife and opened it. Murder at last, I thought. It was Lucy's turn; no more Lucy!

Before I even got started to run out and stop him, he simply pushed her hard off the back of the bench, recoiling away from her at the same time. It was obvious how afraid of her he was. With a large indignant flutter she landed on the grass. He had cut the leash; he had not cut her throat. Also he had unhooded her. On the grass for a moment she took a rapid confused look in every direction. Then with a great lift of her legs and two or three strokes of her wings, she climbed up on top of the air, and above the lawn, and across the pond. It was lovely. Her searching looks still, this way and that—to discover why she had been loosed, what quarry there was for her—made her appear to be shaking her head, saying no, no.

I lost sight of her when she passed behind a tree; again, when she rose beyond the scope of the kitchen window. Down she came then, with neck and wing and tail and legs all out—in the shape of a sixpointed star, big and dim, collapsing. She rested her weight on the air again for an instant, and alighted on a post in the far corner of the garden. It was one of two posts from which Eva hung Alex's lingerie to dry early in the morning. The gesture of alighting was lovely: her rigid hands clutching the top of the post like a living victim. It might have been a little angel seizing a tall man by the hair. Then there she sat, still wondering what in the world—what, in terms of a hawk's simple murderous instinct—this liberation meant.

Meanwhile, of course Cullen too had gazed up at her, gazed across the pond at her. Now like a ninny he waved good-bye, good-bye. Then he turned and ambled back through the bushes. Jean and Eva and Ricketts, in their matrimonial or adulterous absorption, had not seen a thing. I was thankful for that; I also felt a childish optimism because of it. I waited a bit, to give Cullen time to get settled in the living room. Then I dashed out of the kitchen, and knocked at Alex's bedroom door, and shouted through it to Mrs. Cullen. I simply said that Lucy was no longer on her perch. Then I hastened away to see what state of mind Cullen was in. There he sat in the living room, one leg over the arm of his easy chair, stoutly puffing; sorrowful and also smug, I thought, and somewhat sobered by his exploit; that at least was a blessing.

"The hawk has got loose. It's not on the bench. I've called Mrs. Cullen. She's coming to look for it. It must have untied the leash itself." I said this as emphatically as I could, to suggest to him the line he should take.

"But what about the hood?" he asked in an infuriating little tone. "I cut the leash myself, damn it all."

Whereupon I groaned or I cursed; I can't remember which. I didn't want him to confess; I should have spoken to him before I called his wife; now it was too late. She came rushing from the bedroom; and it was as if the news had instantly disheveled her from head to foot. She shuffled, her fine shoes half unlaced. Her perfect dress hung or clung around her one-sidedly. She was pulling on the blood-stained gauntlet; and as she crossed the room she impatiently ran her other hand up through her hair, which fell down on that side over her cheek. She did not close her mouth between her voluble exclamations. "Damn, damn. Oh, I am so unhappy. I must get her back, I can't bear to lose her."

At the sight of her, Cullen pulled himself up out of the easy chair and stood at a kind of attention: but badly, not a bit brave. She must have seen him; she took no notice. I had a sense of her knowing what had happened, who had done it. She looked like the type of old Irishwoman who has second sight: countrified, frumpy, and frightened. And in spite of her outcries and panicky movements, it seemed to me that she had an air of experience and familiarity; familiarity with fright.

"Oh, Mr. Tower, can you get me the other half of that pigeon?" she begged. "The pigeon I fed her. She hasn't, I hope she hasn't, gone far away."

Upon which her husband behind us chimed in as usual, worse than usual: "Madeleine, Madeleine, surely they've cooked it. That's the dinner, you know, pigeons with white currants."

She took notice of that. She swung around and answered in a devilish voice, "Of course they have not cooked it." For one second I thought she might strike him; perhaps he did too. He wrinkled his nose and flung up his hands.

I started toward the kitchen and she followed, explaining, "I'll never catch her without a lure. Thank heaven it was a small pigeon, she'll still be hungry." She gave me a perhaps affectionate pat on the shoulder which amounted to a push.

Then she ran back to the window and there gave a wonderful small shriek. It should have been hawklike, I said to myself; what it really made me think of was a valkyrie, a very small valkyrie. For in spite of my admiration of Lucy and sympathy for the other two, I was enjoying all this.

I met Alex at the kitchen door, and she had the half-pigeon. Mrs. Cullen called to us, "What in God's name did I do with my bag? My extra leash is in it. She must have broken hers."

Alex ran for the bag, handing me the pigeon. I dropped it, and it smudged the parquet. Jean and Eva were there beside me, but they were too thrilled to do any mopping now. Then Mrs. Cullen lost one shoe and stumbled into an armchair; and her husband knelt and tried to put it back on, fumbling around her silky ankle with those freckled fingers which could so easily have snapped it in two like a twig—until she lost patience and kicked the other shoe off, over his shoulder, and rose to go in her stocking-feet.

"Stay here, all of you," she ordered. "Please, please, let me go alone." She paused a moment on the threshold staring across the pond at heedless Lucy. She held her gloved fingers up to her mouth as you do when you blow a kiss. Then she swung around toward us, demanding, with a kind of loud lump in her throat, "Where in God's name is her hood? How wicked! Who did it? One of you, how wicked!"

It was poor Eva who answered, with her primitive sensibility, primitive expectation of blame: "Oh, Madame, Madame, Jean and I never left the kitchen," and began to cry.

Alex told her to hush, which she did, more or less. As I watched our angry birdcatcher, I still kept one eye on these other watchers, so assorted and attractive, there inside the house in a row close to the plate-glass window in the last murky sunshine. I thought that Alex glanced oddly back at me; perhaps my eyewitnessing and slight complicity had given me an odd expression. Certainly she

hated their disorder: obscure common blundering around
her house, and general self-betrayal, with the servants gog-
gle-eyed. On the other hand catching a great runaway bird
was the sort of problem she loved. Her mild brown eyes
lit up, and she breathed like a happy child. Ricketts came
tip-toeing in and stood behind us as close to Eva as he
dared. Whereupon Jean began whispering to her in Italian, *prestissimo,* until Alex hushed him too. Eva dabbed
her eyes with the corner of the towel, another corner of
which had pigeon's blood on it. As for Cullen, his face
was quite mottled with his mixed emotions; heaven knows
what they were.

As Mrs. Cullen left us, across the lawn, along the left
side of the pond, I was struck by the change this emergency had made in her appearance and carriage. Perhaps
it was chiefly her going in stocking-feet. When she first
descended from the Daimler, how delicately she had stumbled on the cobblestones; then foolishly tripped back and
forth on the waxed parquet, and weakly strolled in the
park! That French or Italian footwear of hers with three-
inch heels not only incapacitated her but flattered her,
and disguised her. Now her breasts seemed lower on her
torso, out of the way of her nervous arms. Her hips were
wide and her back powerful, with that curve from the
shoulder blades to the head which you see in the nudes
of Ingres. She walked with her legs well apart, one padding
footfall after another, as impossible to trip up as a cat.

Suddenly she must have remembered that she had
brought an extra leash but no extra hood. She hurried
back along the water and across to the rustic bench, where
she picked up the one Cullen had removed and let fall;
then set out again, by the right bank, more slow and cat-
like as she approached her quarry. What followed took
only a few moments. We heard the falconer's cry: *hai, hai,*
a desolate sound, which probably has not varied much in
the three or four thousand years of falconry, for it is based
on eternal acoustics, agreeable to the changeless ears of

hawks. I loved to hear it. Lucy's head stirred swiftly
around in response to it. I wanted her to cry back, *aik*,
which she did not. They were too far away for us to see
much. We saw the swing of Mrs. Cullen's arm as she tossed
the piece of the pigeon over the hedge, toward the foot of
the post; and after a breathless instant, we saw Lucy's
descent upon it, down in one smooth rush, like a large,
dusky, finished flower off its stem. Instantly the birdcatcher bent over, lurked along the hedge, and squattingly
slipped around behind it. Then we had to wait, wait—until she briskly stood up and started back toward us with
Lucy hooded on her wrist, where she belonged. Before
hooding her, I suppose, she let her have a few good beak-
fuls of the unscheduled pigeon so that even this mishap
or misdemeanor should be a lesson to her, as it was to us
all in a sense.

Inside the house, before the great window, we were
smiling from ear to ear, and murmuring or exclaiming
each in his or her way. Only Cullen was deathly still, not
even puffing. I moved far enough away from him to see
his face, and found there, added to the bibulous pink, a
pale light of wild relief, reprieve, even rapture, as if that
horrid bird on his wife's arm returning to haunt him
again had been his heart's desire. It was too much of a
good thing; he was sober perhaps, but tormentedly sentimental; I should not have trusted him an instant.

Mrs. Cullen came down the left side of the pond, the
long way. The sun, muffled all afternoon, was setting
brightly. Some of its beams turned back up from the
water, broken into a sparkle, through which we could not
see her well. There were vague irises and something else
up to her ankles; and branches of lilac occasionally hung
between us and her. Her face looked to me calm, careless.
Her hair still absurdly fell down one cheek; now and then
she blew it out of her eyes. Dress disarranged and petticoat
showing and stocking-feet and all, she walked back proudly, taking her time; a springy walk that reminded me of

Isadora Duncan.

The five of us happy onlookers trooped out on the lawn to meet her. "Isn't it wonderful?" she rejoiced. "You see, she's perfectly manned. She understands. Otherwise I could never have caught her. I'll be hunting with her in no time. Larry, go and find the other leash; which I left on the bench." And she decidedly emphasized the I. She too wished him not to admit what he had done.

He went meekly for the leash. The servants returned to the kitchen. Mrs. Cullen asked permission to retire and put herself to rights, declining Alex's offer of company and assistance. "No more weathering for you, my haggard Lucy," I heard her mutter as she left us.

I had not dared hope that Lucy—haggard that she was, with only two months of the least comfortable phase of captivity to look back upon, and none of the pleasure of the chase so far, and one toe still sore from the trap— would allow herself to be caught. That had made the little spectacle of her capture or surrender the more exciting for me. On the other hand I had not wanted her to escape. I had not pictured her setting out lonelily over Normandy toward Scotland, or whatever resort in the summer she might instinctively choose. Given my sentimental imagination, it was an odd lapse. And it made me aware of my really not wanting Larry Cullen to escape from Mrs. Cullen either, or vice versa. Perhaps I do not believe in liberty, or I regard it as only episodic in life; a circumstance that one must be able to bear and profit by when it occurs; a kind of necessary evil. When love itself is at stake, love of liberty as a rule is only fear of captivity.

Alex thought a drink would help at this juncture, and started to the balcony; but with one glance in Cullen's direction and another in mine, she returned and sat down. Cullen slumped in his armchair, gazing at apparently nothing, in that calm which is only the entire expenditure of energy; the coming down of a dull curtain upon the drama in head or heart. But probably it was only

entr'acte. There was something turgid if not turbulent
throughout his aging bulky frame; his jaws stirred a bit
in his double chin; his bloodshot eyes kept lighting up.

Then we heard a persistent ringing of the bell in Alex's
room, and Alex went anxiously to see what it meant, and
came back and informed us that Mrs. Cullen had decided
to return to town at once, before dinner. She had a brother
in Paris, and she had telephoned him; something had
gone wrong in Paris, and he needed her. I did not believe
a word of this, and Alex's expression confirmed my disbelief. Evidently it did not surprise Cullen. He sighed
hard, which perhaps referred to *pigeons aux groseilles;*
but he said nothing even about that.

Alex left it to me to inform Jean and Eva of the super-
fluity of their dinner. I could scarcely tell how Eva took
it, not well in any case: she gaped at me and fled to her
bedroom. Jean on the other hand chose to be superior and
calm. Something always went wrong, he observed, when
the English upper classes came to see poor Mademoiselle,
in their automobiles as big as busses driven by idiotic
little boys. In his opinion also the boy Ricketts had something to do with the escape of Madame Cullen's eagle. At
that moment the idiot was paying a visit to the *bistrot* or
bar at the corner. I let Jean go after him. The announcement of the Cullens' change of plan might somewhat relieve his evident personal desire to put him out of the
house.

Meanwhile with a certain simplicity our unhappy guests
gathered up their belongings here and there: severed leash
and mislaid lipstick and cigarette case with a diamond
button. As we waited in the hallway for the Daimler to be
brought around Mrs. Cullen quietly asked, "Dear Alex,
you don't need a new chauffeur, do you?"

As it happened Alex did need one. "What luck! I wish
you'd take Ricketts," Mrs. Cullen quietly continued. "I'll
be giving him notice when we get to Budapest. And I know
he hates Ireland, and he speaks quite decent French. He's

very good, very fast, and a mechanic and all that." And she recommended him in other particulars as well, including semi-genteel birth.

Cullen beside me was shuffling and loudly hemming, and at last could not hold his peace. "But Madeleine, really, my dear woman, you're fantastic. We've never had anybody as good as Ricketts. What in the world!"

Slightly embarrassed, Alex said that indeed they might have difficulty in finding a chauffeur in Hungary in summer; it should not be decided in haste on her account. Perhaps she sensed what was coming; I did.

"Oh, I shall easily find another," Mrs. Cullen said, "or I can do without. You see, Ricketts doesn't like Lucy. He laughs at me up his sleeve. I doubtless am an old fool, but I cannot have people around me who think so." She said this in a great sad false way; and it was unmistakably intended for her husband.

Again I could not see his banal but significant face when I wished, to read the emotion in it; we stood shoulder to shoulder facing our dear women. There was still some of that fine pre-bolshevik distillation on his somewhat accelerated and audible breath; but its troublesome effects must have passed. We all kept silent for a moment.

Mrs. Cullen was quite willing to look either of us in the eye; but her sparkle was all extinguished. It would have seemed healthier, more rational, if her eyes had looked angry; they looked nothing at all, nullified. Lucy was hooded now; under her mistress's chin the frivolous topknot on the stitched leather nodded very slightly; and Mrs. Cullen's crooked Irish face as a whole was not much more expressive than that. Her serenity, her stoical wit, her obscurity, were a sort of mental or moral craftsmanship; ornamentation. Inside all that, I suspected, her spirit was as bland as Lucy's. The point of not allowing a hawk to see is to keep it from being frightened; and I hoped that Mrs. Cullen's grand, mean manner served that purpose as well. I was afraid it did not.

Along the cobblestones under the plane trees I heard
the Daimler come purring, not a moment too soon. By
that time I also felt—as it seemed, aching in my bones and
running in my veins and tempering my nerves—something
like the mixture of hot and cold, good and bad, which
troubled the difficult hearts of this odd couple.

Unrequited passion; romance put asunder by circumstances or mistakes; sexually pretending to be love—all
that is a matter of little consequence, a mere voluntary
temporary uneasiness, compared with the long course of
true love, especially marriage. In marriage, insult arises
again and again and again; and pain has to be not only
endured, but consented to; and the amount of forgiveness
that it necessitates is incredible and exhausting. When
love has given satisfaction, then you discover how large a
part of the rest of life is only payment for it, installment
after installment . . . That was the one definite lesson
which these petty scenes of the Cullens illustrated. Early
in life I had learned it for myself well enough. It was on
Alex's account that I minded. To see the cost of love before one has felt what it is worth, is a pity; one may never
have the courage to begin.

There stood the Daimler; and Cullen and I helped
Mrs. Cullen and Lucy up into it, while Ricketts, cap in
hand, held the door. I observed that in fact Ricketts was
laughing, in a silent subaltern way; but surely it was not
at his mistress or her bird. Thin lips very red, rough eyelashes very shadowy: the effect of a Moorish-Italian kiss
behind the kitchen door, I fancied. Or perhaps—for Cock-
neys are a malicious breed—the mere discomfiture of Jean
amused him. He glanced over my shoulder, then up at a
likely window, and so did I; but I did not discover the
Mediterranean couple peeping out anywhere.

Neither the Cullens nor Alex and I had the heart for
much repetition of farewell. Cullen had tears in his eyes.
We turned back to the house and shut the door before
Ricketts could get the long car out onto the highway,

amid cars coming toward him from Paris.

There had been just time for us to reach the living room and sit down and light cigarettes, when we heard a fearful grinding of brakes; then several cars honking as in panic; and a Frenchman shouting the usual insults. A moment after, a car drove in under our plane trees. I got up and looked out a small window on that side: it was the Daimler.

Alex and I hastened back through the hall to see what had happened. There we heard Mrs. Cullen's voice, very loud and exclamatory but incomprehensible; and she was pushing the doorbell, rattling the doorknob, and calling, "Alex, Alex!" As I opened the door she stepped back, turning away from us, gesticulating and exclaiming, "No, Ricketts, stay where you are. Larry, please! Now wait for me, Ricketts. Oh, dear, you fool, you fool!"

She stumbled on the cobblestones; Lucy was having a hard time. Then she returned to us and grasped Alex's arm and motioned us back inside the house. "Don't get out of the car, Larry, I'll attend to it," she cried, over her shoulder.

"Alex, dear, I'm sorry, I've forgotten something. Poor damned fool," she repeated. By the heart-broken tone of her voice I judged that the fool was not Ricketts.

That young man was not laughing now, nor smacking his lips upon any recollection of pleasure or rivalry. His lips were white; he was badly frightened. The Daimler stood at a very odd angle between two trees; he must have made a U-turn on the highway. A little further along on the verge of a ditch stood an old Renault, with which, I supposed, they had narrowly escaped a collision. Its French driver stood beside it, still vehemently expressing himself, shaking his fist. But, oddly, neither the Cullens nor Ricketts even glanced in that Frenchman's direction. Something else must have happened; just before, just after, or at the same time. Inside the Daimler, Cullen had his great hand pressed over his mouth as if he were gnawing it, and

he too was pale: the worst pallor in the world, like cooked
veal. During the little drama of recapturing Lucy he had
ceased to be drunk, I thought. But now I was afraid that
he was going to be sick.

Alex and I followed Mrs. Cullen inside the house. She
too was in a worse emotion and looked worse than before.
Not only a portion of her lovely hair but her hat as well
this time, hung over one ear. There were beads of sweat
on her brow and her upper lip. "Oh, Alex, do forgive us,"
she kept saying, "I'm so ashamed, so ashamed;" and hurried past us into the living room.

Shame, I must say, was one thing which all this did not
suggest. Across that great expanse of waxed parquet toward the garden door she sped ahead of us—her pretty feet
on her too high heels wide apart, lest she skid and fall
headlong—saying to Alex over her shoulder, "Excuse me.
Please, dear. Don't mind me. Let me go into the garden
alone a minute."

On her wrist of course Lucy still perched, that is, rode,
with some difficulty: her green-gold feet also wide apart,
ducking or dipping to keep her balance, with characteristic
indignation of her shoulders and that nervous puffing of
breast-feathers which, as Mrs. Cullen had informed us, is
a good sign in a hunting hawk. Hawks are not really tree-
birds; and if in a state of nature Lucy had ever found
herself on a perch as agitated as this female arm, blown by
any such passionate wind as this, whatever this was—she
would have left it instantly and sought out a rock. It was
absurd. Even her little blind headgear with parrot feathers seemed to me absurd; it matched the French hat which
her mistress was wearing at so Irish an angle, except that
it was provided with secure drawstrings. In spite of my be-
wilderment and alarm, I began to laugh. It struck me as a
completion of the cycle of the afternoon, an end of the
sequence of meanings I had been reading into everything,
especially Lucy. The all-embracing symbolic bird; primitive image with iron wings and rusty tassels and enameled

feet; airy murderess like an angel; young predatory sanguinary de luxe hen—now she was funny; she had not
seemed funny before. Perhaps all pets, all domesticated
animals, no matter how ancient or beautiful or strange,
show a comic aspect sooner or later; a part of the shame
of our humanity that we gradually convey to them.

Just then I saw what Mrs. Cullen had in her right hand,
half concealed against her breast and behind Lucy's wing:
a large revolver. Alex must have seen it before I did. She
was clinging to my elbow and whispering, "Stay back.
Don't laugh, don't follow her."

I am not a judge of firearms, but this was a grim important object, glimmering, apparently brand-new and
in working order. "Shall I try to take it away from her?"
I asked Alex in a whisper.

"Heavens, no. She'll be all right. Don't worry her."
Women, even some young girls, have this ability to guess
at degrees of trouble; this equanimity of a trained nurse.
And, with or without much affection, they sometimes suddenly know each other as if they were twins.

There was more to it than that. Looking back on that
moment I have wondered just how her friend's passion
appeared to Alex. How could she tell, as the disheveled
creature fled ahead of us into the garden, that she was not
going to kill herself? Then it occurred to me that in my
friend's character and way of life in those days there was
a certain passivity; at least abstention from other's lives.
Whatever she did not understand about them might, she
felt, be more awful than anything she could imagine. If
others said that things were unbearable, she could well
believe it. If the Irishwoman's life had reached that point,
the point of suicide, I think she might not have cared to
interfere or prevent it.

Outside on the terrace Mrs. Cullen stopped; and grasping the gun by the barrel, brought it back over her shoulder and hurled it high above the shrubs, far across the
lawn, so that it splashed into the pond.

This important gesture was too much for Lucy. Off the
dear wrist she went, hung in a paroxysm once more. But
this time it was not bating, not mystical dread or symbol-
ical love of liberty; it was just ordinary loss of balance.
Symbol or no symbol, I said to myself, if I were busy getting rid of a suicidal or murderous weapon I should hate
to have a heavy hysterical bird tied to me, yanking my
wrist, flapping in my face. Mrs. Cullen, the good sportswoman, did not mind. Perhaps because of her own hysteria
—the real meaning of this episode pulling at her heart-
strings and beating upon her intellect—she merely did the
thing to do, as usual. Up went her embattled left arm over
her head; stock-still she stood, until terrible Lucy grew
tired, and recovered her self-control, and resumed her
domestication.

From our viewpoint, behind her, seeing her through
the sunset-streaked window, against the background of the
old park and the shrubs and the gray pond with ripples
unclosing away from the place where the gun had gone
down, Mrs. Cullen was beautiful. Throughout her somewhat bulky body—motherly torso and panting breasts and
round neck—there was wonderful strength; and between
her absurd high heels and her fist in the rough glove, there
was exact perpendicularity: the yard-wind wings now settling back on top. And the fact that she looked a bit ridiculous, disheveled and second-rate and past her prime,
made it all the finer, I thought, as she turned and came
slowly back indoors.

There were tears in her eyes, but she chuckled, or pretended to, or tried to. "Darling Alex," she said hoarsely,
"did you ever have guests who behaved so madly? Don't,
please, don't ever ask me what this was all about."

Then in her way, in a series of little dull, prosaic, but
shameless statements, she told us what it was about. "You
see, dear, why we can't live in Ireland. It's such a bad
example for my silly sons."

My presence did not make her shy. For a moment that

flattered me; upon second thought it seemed to me to have the opposite implication. Quite early in the afternoon, I suppose, she had perceived that Alex was not in love with me; therefore, in her view of life, I did not count, I was a supernumerary. What harm could I do with her secrets? Women are fantastic.

Holding her left arm and Lucy well out of the way, she threw her right arm somewhat around Alex and kissed her. "Dear, dear friend," she murmured. "You're so clever, you'll marry well when the time comes. Thank you so much for your patience with us." Alex shrank a little as she always did from female affection, but the odd compliment seemed to please her.

"Larry's been threatening to leave me for weeks," Mrs. Cullen added. "Oh, I'm so afraid he will one day. I don't know what would become of him by himself, the fool, the old darling."

Poor Larry, I sighed; poor supernumerary me! Women are no respecters of men. I also felt a little indignation on Lucy's account. Trapped out of the real wind and rock, and perverted rather than domesticated, kept blind and childish, at the mercy of every human absurdity, vodka and automobiles, guns and kisses: poor Lucy! She no doubt personified for Mrs. Cullen the deep problems of life; certainly. Mrs. Cullen now devoted a large part of her life to her. Yet again and again, splendid *falco's* position in fact, her proprietress's handling of her, was in the way of a handkerchief or a muff or a hat. Absorbed in her narration of what had just occurred on the highway in the Daimler, Mrs. Cullen forgot about her and gestured a little with her left hand as well as her right. Lucy had to embrace the air desperately to stabilize herself; her plumage all thickened up and homely, sick-looking. It afforded me an instant's characteristic grim amusement to think how often the great issues which I had taken this bird to augur, come down in fact to undignified appearance, petty neurasthenic anecdote; bring one in fact at last to a poor domestication like Lucy's. It also reminded me of the absurd position of the artist in the midst of the disorders of those who honor and support him, but who can scarcely be expected to keep quiet around him for art's sake.

"I don't even know which of us Larry thought of shooting," Mrs. Cullen said. "Wife or chauffeur or haggard. I dare say I never shall know, unless some day he does it. The minute you closed your door, he began saying things at the top of his voice about Lucy and Ricketts. It upset Ricketts, and there was a car coming toward us, and for a moment I really thought we would crash. I told Ricketts to stop at the side of the road, and instead he turned back here, with two other cars speeding around the corner. That was what made the little Frenchman in the Renault angry. In the midst of which poor Larry began to threaten us with the revolver. It was in the side pocket of the car. I can't imagine when he put it there, or where he got it. You know, I think the Frenchman saw it. Lucky for us he didn't call the police."

She began to have an almost cheerful expression. If you have been lonelily excited a long while, expecting the worst to happen, with no validation for your fear in fact, no excuse that others would understand—perhaps the trouble in question must always come as a slight relief. At least you know then that you have not morbidly made it all up out of whole cloth.

"I'll tell you an odd thing about myself," she said, with her vaguest smile. "I happen to be a very good shot; and d'you know, all the while I was trying to take that beastly gun away from Larry—with Ricketts driving like a fool, and poor Lucy on my arm so awfully in the way—I kept calculating every instant just where the bullet would go if he pulled the trigger. The trajectory and all that. I suppose I'm a born sportswoman; how childish it is! At the last moment I simply can't take things quite seriously. I suppose that's what made me good at lions in Kenya years ago."

She frowned and sighed then, as if ashamed of her coldness or lightheartedness. "Now Ricketts of course is quite out of patience with Larry. I suppose I shall have to give him notice; what a pity! If Larry wasn't quiet after I got out of the car, I expect Ricketts knocked him out. He did once before. There's nothing I can do; Larry is as strong as an ox. But I'd have gone mad, I'd have killed Ricketts—if I had waited to see what happened. Ricketts is so damned English; the instant he clenches his fist he makes a smug face, like a governess. But I say it's time to go back now; I've been cowardly long enough; perhaps at this point I can be of some comfort to my man."

She intended to give Alex another kiss, but Alex avoided it. "Oh, Alex, I do," she lamented, "do love that great fool desperately. Whatever shall I do with him? Oh, well, we'll see. Do you think I must get rid of Lucy? It was astonishing, you know, how well Larry hawked, last summer in Hungary. I thought he'd enjoy it so."

Then she laughed, and all afternoon I think she had not laughed; rather a bad sound, two loud liquid feverish notes. "Ho, ho, perhaps this may have done him good. He has bated, don't you know."

So she took her second departure. "Good-bye, Mr. Tower. Good-bye, Alex, dear child. I shall miss you. Larry will be ashamed to see you after all this, I'm afraid. Don't come out to the car; it would embarrass them." She slipped across the hall and out the door, opening it only a little and immediately slamming it.

"Well!" exclaimed Alex, as we returned to the living room, and her delivery of that syllable made me laugh: ooo-ell; the soft bark of a very small dog.

After so much disorder we thought it would be indiscreet to seem impatient for our dinner. We wandered into the garden, sighing, tired. "I hope Jean and Eva did not see this last bit of melodrama," Alex said. "It's not the kind of idea I should like him to get into his head and develop. He's no Cullen; he's an imitative Italian, and he might not muff it."

"That great comfortable greedy easy old boy," I mumbled, meaning Cullen. "Did you dream he had murder in him? Vodka or no vodka."

"But it was suicide surely, not murder," said Alex. "Madeleine Cullen has no imagination."

"I wonder. It overlaps in any case. People do kill themselves just because they want to murder someone," I replied in my quibbling way. "Someone they love."

Alex made a little face, expressive of skepticism of everything and practically universal disapproval. "You know, he wasn't really very drunk."

"Two shakerfuls of prewar vodka," I reminded her.

"No matter. That's not much for those immense Irishmen. I've seen him drunk and it wasn't anything like this. Or perhaps he pretended to be drunk for your benefit; and to have an excuse for what was happening anyway, what was bound to happen. You're such a sober creature, my dear; you naturally overestimate other people's intoxication."

Her saying that made me suddenly unhappy. I thought of the wicked way I had watched him as he drank, the grandiose theories of drunkenness I had spun for myself meanwhile; and I blushed. Half the time, I am afraid, my opinion of people is just guessing; cartooning. Again and again I give way to a kind of inexact and vengeful lyricism; I cannot tell what right I have to be avenged, and I am ashamed of it. Sometimes I entirely doubt my judgment in moral matters; and so long as I propose to be a storyteller, that is the whisper of the devil for me.

But my dear Alex then sensed, as a good young woman should, my doubt and weak self-criticism; and she smiled. "You must tell me what he said to you, before you forget it. I gathered from your expression that he'd been weeping on your shoulder."

Then Eva, with even less etiquette than usual, came out of the kitchen waving a napkin, huskily imploring us to hurry in to dinner, half-spoiled in any case, she thought. As if to point the moral of the changes of the day from a cook's angle, Jean sent in to us eight pigeons, a veritable sheaf of asparagus, and two good-sized tarts. It was perfect; and melodrama all afternoon evidently gave us appetite. Eva shed a sequence of tears as she served, mutely and prettily, with a wan smile whenever I looked at her, like a seventeenth-century Magdalen. Jean brought the tart himself and thanked us for our overeating, as if it had been a special effort to console him.

After he had served our coffee in the living room, I told Alex what I had seen from the kitchen window. I was surprised to learn that she too had seen it, from her bedroom window, while Mrs. Cullen lay stretched on the bed with her eyes shut. But she had missed the jackknife. Then I tried to remember and report to her Cullen's confession to me, man to man over our vodka, which entertained her, although I think it shocked her.

Then she went to write a note and send a telegram, and she did not return for three-quarters of an hour. I sat there by myself, not even trying to read. I was still excited; and I fell into a form of fatigued stupidity which, while it lasts, often seems to me an important intellectual effort. It was an effort to compress the excessive details of the afternoon into an abstraction or two, a formula of a moral; in order to store that away in my head for future use, and yet leave room for something new, for the next thing. Morally speaking, those Cullens had crowded me out of myself. I also hoped to distinguish a little more clearly between what the Cullens meant to me and certain fine points of my own meaning to myself which had fascinated me in the midst of their afternoon's performance. Of course it was not possible.

I have learned—but again and again I forget—that abstraction is a bad thing, innumerable and infinitesimal and tiresome; worse than any amount of petty fact. The emotion that comes blurring my retrospect is warmer and

weaker than the excitement of whatever happened, good
or bad. It is like a useless, fruitless vegetation, spreading
and twining and fading and corrupting; even the ego dis-
appears under it. . . . Therefore I scarcely noticed how
long my dear friend stayed away in her bedroom; and
therefore I was glad when she came back. For me, putting
a stop to so-called thought is one of the functions of friendship.

It was not writing or telegraphing which had kept her;
it was Eva weeping and denouncing Jean, laughing and
worshiping Jean. They had quarreled about Ricketts, and
after that he had gone to the village to get drunk. He
would kill her, he had said, and sooner or later he might
well, Eva thought; certainly he would beat her the minute
he returned. He was the most jealous man alive, in her
opinion, and she worshiped him.

In any case she was much to blame. She had a way of
obviously reveling in the sense of her own beauty whenever
a new man appeared in the kitchen; a look of being at the
mercy of circumstances, or perhaps at the man's mercy.
Neighbor or workman or tradesman would appear; and
casually Eva would come up, and stand close by, with a
sleepy stare, letting her eyes drop sideways in their wide
sockets amid African eyelashes, giving off her sweetness
like a flower bed—while Jean watched her, admiring and
suffering, until his storm broke.

Alex had asked what made her behave so; why she flirted
with men like Ricketts if she loved Jean and wanted to be
at peace with him. Seriously she had explained that, when
she flirted, it gave him a chance to come between her and
the rival, which made her feel his love, and to that of
course she promptly yielded; and her yielding also gave
him assurance that she loved him. "And if you please,
terrible female that she is," said Alex, "she laughed as she
explained it, deep in her fat throat.

"But she would not go on laughing. This time, she
thinks, it has gone too far. He will beat her, and he may

kill her, and *tutti quanti*. Therefore she began to cry
again, and she wanted to tell me their story again, from
the beginning. I pretended to lose my temper and sent
her to bed.

"I shall have to dismiss them, you know, if they go on
like this," Alex added. "The lower classes have a way of
making one ashamed of one's sex."

She always had trouble with servants. The trouble really
was that her kind interest in them, if aroused at all, soon
went too far. Shrinking from them, but pinned down by
them at last, she gave a great deal of the warmth that lay
in her. But between their demands upon her, she fancied
that she had no sympathy for them at all. She often said
that she wished she could be served by machinery.

The door stood open; but amid the breath of the garden,
it seemed to me that I could detect, at least I could strongly remember, Lucy's little body odor of blood and honey.
The talk of Jean and Eva and Ricketts had carried my
imagination again to the Cullen triangle: the virtuous passionate hard-hearted woman, the sad man, and the bird;
and I had a new notion. It was that Mrs. Cullen now loved
Cullen less than she intended; and lived with him, lived
for him, perhaps only to fulfil a dear bootless contract
with herself. In any case she loved Lucy, and I hoped she
would refuse to give her up.

In the garden, over by the kitchen door, we heard a few
notes of mellow laughter. Jean had returned and it had
not gone according to Eva's expectation. Laughter, and a
rustle and scuffle—the make-believe fighting that when all
goes well, relaxes and relieves the true struggle of love—
and footsteps diminishing toward the far corner of the
garden hidden by the plane trees. The moon that night
was not a fine carved shape. It hung under a little loose
cloud; only a piece of pallor, a bit of anti-darkness. The
air was as warm as Tangier but one could not lie outdoors,
I thought, for the grass would be splashed with dew.

"You'll never marry, dear," I said, to tease Alex. "Your

friend Mrs. Cullen thinks you will, but she has no imagination. You'll be afraid to, after this fantastic bad luck."

"What bad luck, if you please?" she inquired, smiling to show that my mockery was welcome.

"Fantastic bad object lessons."

"You're no novelist," she said, to tease me. "I envy the Cullens, didn't you know?" And I concluded from the look on her face that she herself did not quite know whether she meant it.

THE BEAR

William Faulkner

William Faulkner

William Faulkner received the 1949 Nobel Prize for Literature. This award gave public recognition to work that he has produced steadily and with increasing mastery since 1924 when the *Marble Faun* was published. Born in 1897 in New Albany, Mississippi, Faulkner has spent much of his life in Oxford, Mississippi, a town and state he has helped make world-famous. Most of Faulkner's novels are available in Random House editions, in Modern Library and paper-cover reprints.

So much has recently been written explaining and explicating Faulkner's work that it seems pertinent to quote here the simple and exalting speech he made on receiving the Nobel Prize:

"I feel that this award was not made to me as a man, but to my work—a life's work in the agony and sweat of the human spirit, not for glory and least of all for profit, but to create out of the materials of the human spirit something which did not exist before. So this award is only mine in trust. It will not be difficult to find a dedication for the money part of it commensurate with the purpose and significance of its origin. But I would like to do the same with the acclaim too, by using this moment as a pinnacle from which I might be listened to by the young men and women already dedicated to the same anguish and travail, among whom is already that one who will some day stand here where I am standing.

"Our tragedy today is a general and universal physical fear so long sustained by now that we can even bear it. There are no longer problems of the spirit. There is only the question: When will I be blown up? Because of this, the young man or woman writing today has forgotten the problems of the human heart in conflict with itself which alone can make good writing because only that is worth writing about, worth the agony and the sweat.

"He must learn them again. He must teach himself that the basest of all things is to be afraid; and, teaching himself that, forget it forever, leaving no room in his workshop for anything but the old verities and truths of the heart, the old universal truths lacking which any story is ephemeral and doomed—love and honor and pity and pride and compassion and sacrifice. Until he does so, he labors under a curse. He writes not of love but of lust, of defeats in which nobody loses anything of value, of victories without hope and, worst of all, without pity or compassion. His griefs grieve on no universal bones, leaving no scars. He writes not of the heart but of the glands.

"Until he relearns these things, he will write as though he stood among and watched the end of man. I decline to accept the end of man. It is easy enough to say that man is immortal simply because he will endure: that when the last ding-dong of doom has clanged and faded from the last worthless rock hanging tideless in the last red and dying evening, that even then there will still be one more sound: that of his puny inexhaustible voice, still talking. I refuse to accept this. I believe that man will not merely endure: he will prevail. He is immortal, not because he alone among creatures has an inexhaustible voice, but because he has a soul, a spirit capable of compassion and sacrifice and endurance. The poet's, the writer's, duty is to write about these things. It is his privilege to help man endure by lifting his heart, by reminding him of the courage and honor and hope and pride and compassion and pity and sacrifice which have been the glory of his past. The poet's voice need not merely be the record of man, it can be one of the props, the pillars to help him endure and prevail."

10 December 1950

THE BEAR

THERE WAS a man and a dog too this time. Two beasts, counting Old Ben, the bear, and two men, counting Boon Hogganbeck, in whom some of the same blood ran which ran in Sam Fathers, even though Boon's was a plebeian strain of it and only Sam and Old Ben and the mongrel Lion were taintless and incorruptible.

He was sixteen. For six years now he had been a man's hunter. For six years now he had heard the best of all talking. It was of the wilderness, the big woods, bigger and older than any recorded document:—of white man fatuous enough to believe he had bought any fragment of it, of Indian ruthless enough to pretend that any fragment of it had been his to convey; bigger than Major de Spain and the scrap he pretended to, knowing better; older than old Thomas Sutpen of whom Major de Spain had had it and who knew better; older even than old Ikkemotubbe, the Chickasaw chief, of whom old Sutpen had had it and who knew better in his turn. It was of the men, not white nor black nor red but men, hunters, with the will and hardihood to endure and the humility and skill to survive, and the dogs and the bear and deer juxtaposed and reliefed against it, ordered and compelled by and within the wilderness in the ancient and unremitting contest according to the ancient and immitigable rules which voided all regrets and brooked no quarter;—the best game of all, the best of all breathing and forever the best of all listening,. the voices quiet and weighty and deliberate for retrospection and recollection and exactitude among the concrete trophies—the racked guns and the heads and skins—in the libraries of town houses or the offices of plantation houses or (and best of all) in the camps themselves where the

intact and still-warm meat yet hung, the men who had
slain it sitting before the burning logs on hearths when
there were houses and hearths or about the smoky blazing
of piled wood in front of stretched tarpaulins when there
were not. There was always a bottle present, so that it
would seem to him that those fine fierce instants of heart
and brain and courage and wiliness and speed were concentrated and distilled into that brown liquor which not
women, not boys and children, but only hunters drank,
drinking not of the blood they spilled but some condensa-
tion of the wild immortal spirit, drinking it moderately,
humbly even, not with the pagan's base and baseless hope
of acquiring thereby the virtues of cunning and strength
and speed but in salute to them. Thus it seemed to him
on this December morning not only natural but actually
fitting that this should have begun with whisky.

He realised later that it had begun long before that. It
had already begun on that day when he first wrote his age
in two ciphers and his cousin McCaslin brought him for
the first time to the camp, the big woods, to earn for himself from the wilderness the name and state of hunter provided he in his turn were humble and enduring enough.
He had already inherited then, without ever having seen
it, the big old bear with one trap-ruined foot that in an
area almost a hundred miles square had earned for himself
a name, a definite designation like a living man:—the long
legend of corncribs broken down and rifled, of shoats and
grown pigs and even calves carried bodily into the woods
and devoured and traps and deadfalls overthrown and
dogs mangled and slain and shotgun and even rifle shots
delivered at point-blank range yet with no more effect
than so many peas blown through a tube by a child—a corridor of wreckage and destruction beginning back before
the boy was born, through which sped, not fast but rather
with the ruthless and irresistible deliberation of a locomotive, the shaggy tremendous shape. It ran in his knowledge
before he ever saw it. It loomed and towered in his dreams

before he even saw the unaxed woods where it left its crooked print, shaggy, tremendous, red-eyed, not malevolent but just big, too big for the dogs which tried to bay it, for the horses which tried to ride it down, for the men and the bullets they fired into it; too big for the very country which was its constricting scope. It was as if the boy had already divined what his senses and intellect had not encompassed yet: that doomed wilderness whose edges were being constantly and punily gnawed at by men with plows and axes who feared it because it was wilderness, men myriad and nameless even to one another in the land where the old bear had earned a name, and through which ran not even a mortal beast but an anachronism indomitable and invincible out of an old dead time, a phantom, epitome and apotheosis of the old wild life which the little puny humans swarmed and hacked at in a fury of abhorrence and fear like pygmies about the ankles of a drowsing elephant;—the old bear, solitary, indomitable, and alone; widowered childless and absolved of mortality—old Priam reft of his old wife and outlived all his sons.

Still a child, with three years then two years then one year yet before he too could make one of them, each November he would watch the wagon containing the dogs and the bedding and food and guns and his cousin McCaslin and Tennie's Jim and Sam Fathers too until Sam moved to the camp to live, depart for the Big Bottom, the big woods. To him, they were going not to hunt bear and deer but to keep yearly rendezvous with the bear which they did not even intend to kill. Two weeks later they would return, with no trophy, no skin. He had not expected it. He had not even feared that it might be in the wagon this time with the other skins and heads. He did not even tell himself that in three years or two years or one year more he would be present and that it might even be his gun. He believed that only after he had served his apprenticeship in the woods which would prove him worthy to be a hunter, would he even be permitted to dis-

tinguish the crooked print, and that even then for two
November weeks he would merely make another minor
one, along with his cousin and Major de Spain and General Compson and Walter Ewell and Boon and the dogs
which feared to bay it and the shotguns and rifles which
failed even to bleed it, in the yearly pageant-rite of the old
bear's furious immortality.

His day came at last. In the surrey with his cousin and
Major de Spain and General Compson he saw the wilderness through a slow drizzle of November rain just above
the ice point as it seemed to him later he always saw it or
at least always remembered it—the tall and endless wall
of dense November woods under the dissolving afternoon
and the year's death, sombre, impenetrable (he could not
even discern yet how, at what point they could possibly
hope to enter it even though he knew that Sam Fathers
was waiting there with the wagon), the surrey moving
through the skeleton stalks of cotton and corn in the last
of open country, the last trace of man's puny gnawing at
the immemorial flank, until, dwarfed by that perspective
into an almost ridiculous diminishment, the surrey itself
seemed to have ceased to move (this too to be completed
later, years later, after he had grown to a man and had
seen the sea) as a solitary small boat hangs in lonely immobility, merely tossing up and down, in the infinite waste
of the ocean while the water and then the apparently impenetrable land which it nears without appreciable progress, swings slowly and opens the widening inlet which is
the anchorage. He entered it. Sam was waiting, wrapped
in a quilt on the wagon seat behind the patient and steaming mules. He entered his novitiate to the true wilderness
with Sam beside him as he had begun his apprenticeship
in miniature to manhood after the rabbits and such with
Sam beside him, the two of them wrapped in the damp,
warm Negro-rank quilt while the wilderness closed behind
his entrance as it had opened momentarily to accept him,
opening before his advancement as it closed behind his

progress, no fixed path the wagon followed but a channel nonexistent ten yards ahead of it and ceasing to exist ten yards after it had passed, the wagon progressing not by its own volition but by attrition of their intact yet fluid circumambience, drowsing, earless, almost lightless.

It seemed to him that at the age of ten he was witnessing his own birth. It was not even strange to him. He had experienced it all before, and not merely in dreams. He saw the camp—a paintless six-room bungalow set on piles above the spring high-water—and he knew already how it was going to look. He helped in the rapid orderly disorder of their establishment in it and even his motions were familiar to him, foreknown. Then for two weeks he ate the coarse, rapid food—the shapeless sour bread, the wild strange meat, venison and bear and turkey and coon which he had never tasted before—which men ate, cooked by men who were hunters first and cooks afterward; he slept in harsh sheetless blankets as hunters slept. Each morning the gray of dawn found him and Sam Fathers on the stand, the crossing, which had been allotted him. It was the poorest one, the most barren. He had expected that; he had not dared yet to hope even to himself that he would even hear the running dogs this first time. But he did hear them. It was on the third morning—a murmur, sourceless, almost indistinguishable, yet he knew what it was although he had never before heard that many dogs running at once, the murmur swelling into separate and distinct voices until he could call the five dogs which his cousin owned from among the others. "Now," Sam said, "slant your gun up a little and draw back the hammers and then stand still."

But it was not for him, not yet. The humility was there; he had learned that. And he could learn the patience. He was only ten, only one week. The instant had passed. It seemed to him that he could actually see the deer, the buck, smoke-colored, elongated with speed, vanished, the woods, the gray solitude still ringing even when the voices of the dogs had died away; from far away across the sombre woods and the gray half-liquid morning there came two shots. "Now let your hammers down," Sam said.

He did so. "You knew it too," he said.

"Yes," Sam said. "I want you to learn how to do when you didn't shoot. It's after the chance for the bear or the deer has done already come and gone that men and dogs get killed."

"Anyway, it wasn't him," the boy said. "It wasn't even a bear. It was just a deer."

"Yes," Sam said, "it was just a deer."

Then one morning, it was in the second week, he heard the dogs again. This time before Sam even spoke he readied the too-long, too-heavy, man-size gun as Sam had taught him, even though this time he knew the dogs and the deer were coming less close than ever, hardly within hearing even. They didn't sound like any running dogs he had ever heard before even. Then he found that Sam, who had taught him first of all to cock the gun and take position where he could see best in all directions and then never to move again, had himself moved up beside him. "There," he said. "Listen." The boy listened, to no ringing chorus strong and fast on a free scent but a moiling yapping an octave too high and with something more than indecision and even abjectness in it which he could not yet recognise, reluctant, not even moving very fast, taking a long time to pass out of hearing, leaving even then in the air that echo of thin and almost human hysteria, abject, almost humanly grieving, with this time nothing ahead of it, no sense of a fleeing unseen smoke-colored shape. He could hear Sam breathing at his shoulder. He saw the arched curve of the old man's inhaling nostrils.

"It's Old Ben!" he cried, whispering.

Sam didn't move save for the slow gradual turning of his head as the voices faded on and the faint steady rapid arch and collapse of his nostrils. "Hah," he said. "Not even running. Walking."

"But up here!" the boy cried. "Way up here!"

"He do it every year," Sam said. "Once. Ash and Boon say he comes up here to run the other little bears away. Tell them to get to hell out of here and stay out until the hunters are gone. Maybe." The boy no longer heard anything at all, yet still Sam's head continued to turn gradually and steadily until the back of it was toward him. Then it turned back and looked down at him—the same face, grave, familiar, expressionless until it smiled, the same old man's eyes from which as he watched there faded slowly a quality darkly and fiercely lambent, passionate and proud. "He dont care no more for bears than he does for dogs or men neither. He come to see who's here, who's new in camp this year, whether he can shoot or not, can stay or not. Whether we got the dog yet that can bay and hold him until a man gets there with a gun. Because he's the head bear. He's the man." It faded, was gone; again they were the eyes as he had known them all his life. "He'll let them follow him to the river. Then he'll send them home. We might as well go too; see how they look when they get back to camp."

The dogs were there first, ten of them huddled back under the kitchen, himself and Sam squatting to peer back into the obscurity where they crouched, quiet, the eyes rolling and luminous, vanishing, and no sound, only that effluvium which the boy could not quite place yet, of something more than dog, stronger than dog and not just animal, just beast even. Because there had been nothing in front of the abject and painful yapping except the solitude, the wilderness, so that when the eleventh hound got back about midafternoon and he and Tennie's Jim held the passive and still trembling bitch while Sam daubed her tattered ear and raked shoulder with turpentine and axle-grease, it was still no living creature but only the wilderness which, leaning for a moment, had patted lightly once her temerity. "Just like a man," Sam said. "Just like folks. Put off as long as she could having to be brave, knowing all the time that sooner or later she would have to be brave once so she could keep on calling herself a dog, and knowing beforehand what was going to happen when she done it."

He did not know just when Sam left. He only knew that he was gone. For the next three mornings he rose and ate breakfast and Sam was not waiting for him. He went to his stand alone; he found it without help now and stood on it as Sam had taught him. On the third morning he heard the dogs again, running strong and free on a true scent again, and he readied the gun as he had learned to do and heard the hunt sweep past on since he was not ready yet, had not deserved other yet in just one short period of two weeks as compared to all the long life which he had already dedicated to the wilderness with patience and humility; he heard the shot again, one shot, the single clapping report of Walter Ewell's rifle. By now he could not only find his stand and then return to camp without guidance, by using the compass his cousin had given him he reached Walter waiting beside the buck and the moiling of dogs over the cast entrails before any of the others except Major de Spain and Tennie's Jim on the horses, even before Uncle Ash arrived with the one-eyed wagon-mule which did not mind the smell of blood or even, so they said, of bear.

It was not Uncle Ash on the mule. It was Sam, returned. And Sam was waiting when he finished his dinner and, himself on the one-eyed mule and Sam on the other one of the wagon team, they rode for more than three hours through the rapid shortening sunless afternoon, following no path, no trail even that he could discern, into a section of country he had never seen before. Then he understood why Sam had made him ride the one-eyed mule which would not spook at the smell of blood, of wild animals. The other one, the sound one, stopped short and tried to whirl and bolt even as Sam got down, jerking and wrenching at the rein while Sam held it, coaxing it forward with his voice since he did not dare risk hitching it, drawing it forward while the boy dismounted from the marred one which would stand. Then, standing beside Sam in the thick great gloom of ancient woods and the winter's dying afternoon, he looked quietly down at the rotted log scored and gutted with claw-marks and, in the wet earth beside it, the print of the enormous warped two-toed foot. Now he knew what he had heard in the hounds' voices in the woods that morning and what he had smelled when he peered under the kitchen where they huddled. It was in him too, a little different because they were brute beasts and he was not, but only a little different—an eagerness, passive; an abjectness, a sense of his own fragility and impotence against the timeless woods, yet without doubt or dread; a flavor like brass in the sudden run of saliva in his mouth, a hard sharp constriction either in his brain or his stomach, he could not tell which and it did not matter; he knew only that for the first time he realised that the bear which had run in his listening and loomed in his dreams since before he could remember and which therefore must have existed in the listening and the dreams of his cousin and Major de Spain and even old General Compson before they began to remember in their turn, was a mortal animal and that they had departed for the camp each November with no actual intention of slaying it, not because it could not be slain but because so far they had no actual hope of being able to. "It will be tomorrow," he said.

"You mean we will try tomorrow," Sam said. "We aint got the dog yet."

"We've got eleven," he said. "They ran him Monday."

"And you heard them," Sam said. "Saw them too. We aint got the dog yet. It wont take but one. But he aint there. Maybe he aint nowhere. The only other way will be for him to run by accident over somebody that had a gun and knowed how to shoot it."

"That wouldn't be me," the boy said. "It would be Walter or Major or—"

"It might," Sam said. "You watch close tomorrow. Be-

cause he's smart. That's how come he has lived this long.
If he gets hemmed up and has got to pick out somebody
to run over, he will pick out you."

"How?" he said. "How will he know. . . ." He ceased.
"You mean he already knows me, that I aint never been
to the big bottom before, aint had time to find out yet
whether I . . ." He ceased again, staring at Sam; he said
humbly, not even amazed: "It was me he was watching. I
dont reckon he did need to come but once."

"You watch tomorrow," Sam said. "I reckon we better
start back. It'll be long after dark now before we get to
camp."

The next morning they started three hours earlier than
they had ever done. Even Uncle Ash went, the cook, who
called himself by profession a camp cook and who did
little else save cook for Major de Spain's hunting and
camping parties, yet who had been marked by the wilderness from simple juxtaposition to it until he responded as
they all did, even the boy who until two weeks ago had
never even seen the wilderness, to a hound's ripped ear
and shoulder and the print of a crooked foot in a patch of
wet earth. They rode. It was too far to walk: the boy and
Sam and Uncle Ash in the wagon with the dogs, his cousin
and Major de Spain and General Compson and Boon and
Walter and Tennie's Jim riding double on the horses;
again the first gray light found him, as on that first morning two weeks ago, on the stand where Sam had placed and
left him. With the gun which was too big for him, the
breech-loader which did not even belong to him but to
Major de Spain and which he had fired only once, at a
stump on the first day to learn the recoil and how to reload
it with the paper shells, he stood against a big gum tree
beside a little bayou whose black still water crept without
motion out of a cane-brake, across a small clearing and
into the cane again, where, invisible, a bird, the big woodpecker called Lord-to-God by Negroes, clattered at a dead
trunk. It was a stand like any other stand, dissimilar only

in incidentals to the one where he had stood each morning for two weeks; a territory new to him yet no less familiar than that other one which after two weeks he had come to believe he knew a little—the same solitude, the same loneliness through which frail and timorous man had merely passed without altering it, leaving no mark nor scar, which looked exactly as it must have looked when the first ancestor of Sam Fathers' Chickasaw predecessors crept into it and looked about him, club or stone axe or bone arrow drawn and ready, different only because, squatting at the edge of the kitchen, he had smelled the dogs huddled and cringing beneath it and saw the raked ear and side of the bitch that, as Sam had said, had to be brave once in order to keep on calling herself a dog, and saw yesterday in the earth beside the gutted log, the print of the living foot. He heard no dogs at all. He never did certainly hear them. He only heard the drumming of the woodpecker stop short off, and knew that the bear was looking at him. He never saw it. He did not know whether it was facing him from the cane or behind him. He did not move, holding the useless gun which he knew now he would never fire at it, now or ever, tasting in his saliva that taint of brass which he had smelled in the huddled dogs when he peered under the kitchen.

Then it was gone. As abruptly as it had stopped, the woodpecker's dry hammering set up again, and after a while he believed he even heard the dogs—a murmur, scarce a sound even, which he had probably been hearing for a time, perhaps a minute or two, before he remarked it, drifting into hearing and then out again, dying away. They came nowhere near him. If it was dogs he heard, he could not have sworn to it; if it was a bear they ran, it was another bear. It was Sam himself who emerged from the cane and crossed the bayou, the injured bitch following at heel as a bird dog is taught to walk. She came and crouched against his leg, trembling. "I didn't see him," he said. "I didn't, Sam."

"I know it," Sam said. "He done the looking. You didn't
hear him neither, did you?"

"No," the boy said. "I—"

"He's smart," Sam said. "Too smart." Again the boy saw
in his eyes that quality of dark and brooding lambence as
Sam looked down at the bitch trembling faintly and steadily against the boy's leg. From her raked shoulder a few
drops of fresh blood clung like bright berries. "Too big.
We aint got the dog yet. But maybe some day."

Because there would be a next time, after and after. He
was only ten. It seemed to him that he could see them, the
two of them, shadowy in the limbo from which time
emerged and became time: the old bear absolved of mortality and himself who shared a little of it. Because he
recognised now what he had smelled in the huddled dogs
and tasted in his own saliva, recognised fear as a boy, a
youth, recognises the existence of love and passion and
experience which is his heritage but not yet his patrimony,
from entering by chance the presence or perhaps even
merely the bedroom of a woman who has loved and been
loved by many men. *So I will have to see him,* he thought,
without dread or even hope. *I will have to look at him.* So
it was in June of the next summer. They were at the camp
again, celebrating Major de Spain's and General Compson's birthdays. Although the one had been born in September and the other in the depth of winter and almost
thirty years earlier, each June the two of them and McCaslin and Boon and Walter Ewell (and the boy too from
now on) spent two weeks at the camp, fishing and shooting
squirrels and turkey and running coons and wildcats with
the dogs at night. That is, Boon and the Negroes (and the
boy too now) fished and shot squirrels and ran the coons
and cats, because the proven hunters, not only Major de
Spain and old General Compson (who spent those two
weeks sitting in a rocking chair before a tremendous iron
pot of Brunswick stew, stirring and tasting, with Uncle
Ash to quarrel with about how he was making it and

Tennie's Jim to pour whisky into the tin dipper from which he drank it) but even McCaslin and Walter Ewell who were still young enough, scorned such other than shooting the wild gobblers with pistols for wagers or to test their marksmanship.

That is, his cousin McCaslin and the others thought he was hunting squirrels. Until the third evening he believed that Sam Fathers thought so too. Each morning he would leave the camp right after breakfast. He had his own gun now, a new breech-loader, a Christmas gift; he would own and shoot it for almost seventy years, through two new pairs of barrels and locks and one new stock, until all that remained of the original gun was the silver-inlaid trigger-guard with his and McCaslin's engraved names and the date in 1878. He found the tree beside the little bayou where he had stood that morning. Using the compass he ranged from that point; he was teaching himself to be better than a fair woodsman without even knowing he was doing it. On the third day he even found the gutted log where he had first seen the print. It was almost completely crumbled now, healing with unbelievable speed, a passionate and almost visible relinquishment, back into the earth from which the tree had grown. He ranged the summer woods now, green with gloom, if anything actually dimmer than they had been in November's gray dissolution, where even at noon the sun fell only in windless dappling upon the earth which never completely dried and which crawled with snakes—moccasins and watersnakes and rattlers, themselves the color of the dappled gloom so that he would not always see them until they moved; returning to camp later and later and later, first day, second day, passing in the twilight of the third evening the little log pen enclosing the log barn where Sam was putting up the stock for the night. "You aint looked right yet," Sam said.

He stopped. For a moment he didn't answer. Then he said peacefully, in a peaceful rushing burst, as when a boy's

miniature dam in a little brook gives way: "All right. Yes.
But how? I went to the bayou. I even found that log
again. I—"

"I reckon that was all right. Likely he's been watching
you. You never saw his foot?"

"I . . ." the boy said. "I didn't . . . I never thought . . ."

"It's the gun," Sam said. He stood beside the fence, motionless, the old man, son of a Negro slave and a Chickasaw
chief, in the battered and faded overalls and the frayed
five-cent straw hat which had been the badge of the Negro's slavery and was now the regalia of his freedom. The
camp—the clearing, the house, the barn and its tiny lot with
which Major de Spain in his turn had scratched punily
and evanescently at the wilderness—faded in the dusk,
back into the immemorial darkness of the woods. *The gun,*
the boy thought. *The gun.* "You will have to choose," Sam
said.

He left the next morning before light, without breakfast, long before Uncle Ash would wake in his quilts on
the kitchen floor and start the fire. He had only the compass and a stick for the snakes. He could go almost a mile
before he would need to see the compass. He sat on a log,
the invisible compass in his hand, while the secret night-
sounds which had ceased at his movements, scurried again
and then fell still for good and the owls ceased and gave
over to the waking day birds and there was light in the
gray wet woods and he could see the compass. He went
fast yet still quietly, becoming steadily better and better
as a woodsman without yet having time to realise it; he
jumped a doe and a fawn, walked them out of the bed,
close enough to see them—the crash of undergrowth, the
white scut, the fawn scudding along behind her, faster
than he had known it could have run. He was hunting
right, upwind, as Sam had taught him, but that didn't
matter now. He had left the gun; by his own will and relinquishment he had accepted not a gambit, not a choice,
but a condition in which not only the bear's heretofore

inviolable anonymity but all the ancient rules and balances of hunter and hunted had been abrogated. He would not even be afraid, not even in the moment when the fear would take him completely: blood, skin, bowels, bones, memory from the long time before it even became his memory—all save that thin clear quenchless lucidity which alone differed him from this bear and from all the other bears and bucks he would follow during almost seventy years, to which Sam had said: "Be scared. You cant help that. But dont be afraid. Aint nothing in the woods going to hurt you if you dont corner it or it dont smell that you are afraid. A bear or a deer has got to be scared of a coward the same as a brave man has got to be."

By noon he was far beyond the crossing on the little bayou, farther into the new and alien country than he had ever been, traveling now not only by the compass but by the old, heavy, biscuit-thick silver watch which had been his father's. He had left the camp nine hours ago; nine hours from now, dark would already have been an hour old. He stopped, for the first time since he had risen from the log when he could see the compass face at last, and looked about, mopping his sweating face on his sleeve. He had already relinquished, of his will, because of his need, in humility and peace and without regret, yet apparently that had not been enough, the leaving of the gun was not enough. He stood for a moment—a child, alien and lost in the green and soaring gloom of the markless wilderness. Then he relinquished completely to it. It was the watch and the compass. He was still tainted. He removed the linked chain of the one and the looped thong of the other from his overalls and hung them on a bush and leaned the stick beside them and entered it.

When he realised he was lost, he did as Sam had coached and drilled him: made a cast to cross his backtrack. He had not been going very fast for the last two or three hours, and he had gone even less fast since he left the compass and watch on the bush. So he went slower still now, since

the tree could not be very far; in fact, he found it before
he really expected to and turned and went to it. But there
was no bush beneath it, no compass nor watch, so he did
next as Sam had coached and drilled him: made this next
circle in the opposite direction and much larger, so that
the pattern of the two of them would bisect his track
somewhere, but crossing no trace nor mark anywhere of
his feet or any feet, and now he was going faster though
still not panicked, his heart beating a little more rapidly
but strong and steady enough, and this time it was not
even the tree because there was a down log beside it which
he had never seen before and beyond the log a little swamp,
a seepage of moisture somewhere between earth and water,
and he did what Sam had coached and drilled him as the
next and the last, seeing as he sat down on the log the
crooked print, the warped indentation in the wet ground
which while he looked at it continued to fill with water
until it was level full and the water began to overflow and
the sides of the print began to dissolve away. Even as he
looked up he saw the next one, and, moving, the one beyond it; moving, not hurrying, running, but merely keeping pace with them as they appeared before him as though
they were being shaped out of thin air just one constant
pace short of where he would lose them forever and be
lost forever himself, tireless, eager, without doubt or
dread, panting a little above the strong rapid little hammer of his heart, emerging suddenly into a little glade and
the wilderness coalesced. It rushed, soundless, and solidi-
fied—the tree, the bush, the compass and the watch glinting
where a ray of sunlight touched them. Then he saw the
bear. It did not emerge, appear: it was just there, immobile,
fixed in the green and windless noon's hot dappling, not
as big as he had dreamed it but as big as he had expected,
bigger, dimensionless against the dappled obscurity, looking at him. Then it moved. It crossed the glade without
haste, walking for an instant into the sun's full glare and
out of it, and stopped again and looked back at him across

one shoulder. Then it was gone. It didn't walk into the woods. It faded, sank back into the wilderness without motion as he had watched a fish, a huge old bass, sink back into the dark depths of its pool and vanish without even any movement of its fins.

—2—

So he should have hated and feared Lion. He was thirteen then. He had killed his buck and Sam Fathers had marked his face with the hot blood, and in the next November he killed a bear. But before that accolade he had become as competent in the woods as many grown men with the same experience. By now he was a better woodsman than most grown men with more. There was no territory within twenty-five miles of the camp that he did not know—bayou, ridge, landmark trees and path; he could have led anyone direct to any spot in it and brought him back. He knew game trails that even Sam Fathers had never seen; in the third fall he found a buck's bedding-place by himself and unbeknown to his cousin he borrowed Walter Ewell's rifle and lay in wait for the buck at dawn and killed it when it walked back to the bed as Sam had told him how the old Chickasaw fathers did.

By now he knew the old bear's footprint better than he did his own, and not only the crooked one. He could see any one of the three sound prints and distinguish it at once from any other, and not only because of its size. There were other bears within that fifty miles which left tracks almost as large, or at least so near that the one would have appeared larger only by juxtaposition. It was more than that. If Sam Fathers had been his mentor and the backyard rabbits and squirrels his kindergarten, then the wilderness the old bear ran was his college and the old male bear itself, so long unwifed and childless as to have become its own ungendered progenitor, was his alma mater.

He could find the crooked print now whenever he

wished, ten miles or five miles or sometimes closer than
that, to the camp. Twice while on stand during the next
three years he heard the dogs strike its trail and once even
jump it by chance, the voices high, abject, almost human
in their hysteria. Once, still-hunting with Walter Ewell's
rifle, he saw it cross a long corridor of down timber where
a tornado had passed. It rushed through rather than across
the tangle of trunks and branches as a locomotive would,
faster than he had ever believed it could have moved, almost as fast as a deer even because the deer would have
spent most of that distance in the air; he realised then
why it would take a dog not only of abnormal courage but
size and speed too ever to bring it to bay. He had a little
dog at home, a mongrel, of the sort called fyce by Negroes,
a ratter, itself not much bigger than a rat and possessing
that sort of courage which had long since stopped being
bravery and had become foolhardiness. He brought it with
him one June and, timing them as if they were meeting
an appointment with another human being, himself carrying the fyce with a sack over its head and Sam Fathers
with a brace of the hounds on a rope leash, they lay down-
wind of the trail and actually ambushed the bear. They
were so close that it turned at bay although he realised
later this might have been from surprise and amazement
at the shrill and frantic uproar of the fyce. It turned at
bay against the trunk of a big cypress, on its hind feet; it
seemed to the boy that it would never stop rising, taller
and taller, and even the two hounds seemed to have taken
a kind of desperate and despairing courage from the fyce.
Then he realised that the fyce was actually not going to
stop. He flung the gun down and ran. When he overtook
and grasped the shrill, frantically pinwheeling little dog,
it seemed to him that he was directly under the bear. He
could smell it, strong and hot and rank. Sprawling, he
looked up where it loomed and towered over him like a
thunderclap. It was quite familiar, until he remembered:
this was the way he had used to dream about it.

Then it was gone. He didn't see it go. He knelt, holding the frantic fyce with both hands, hearing the abased wailing of the two hounds drawing further and further away, until Sam came up, carrying the gun. He laid it quietly down beside the boy and stood looking down at him. "You've done seed him twice now, with a gun in your hands," he said. "This time you couldn't have missed him."

The boy rose. He still held the fyce. Even in his arms it continued to yap frantically, surging and straining toward the fading sound of the hounds like a collection of live-wire springs. The boy was panting a little. "Neither could you," he said. "You had the gun. Why didn't you shoot him?"

Sam didn't seem to have heard. He put out his hand and touched the little dog in the boy's arms which still yapped and strained even though the two hounds were out of hearing now. "He's done gone," Sam said. "You can slack off and rest now, until next time." He stroked the little dog until it began to grow quiet under his hand. "You's almost the one we wants," he said. "You just aint big enough. We aint got that one yet. He will need to be just a little bigger than smart, and a little braver than either." He withdrew his hand from the fyce's head and stood looking into the woods where the bear and the hounds had vanished. "Somebody is going to, some day."

"I know it," the boy said. "That's why it must be one of us. So it wont be until the last day. When even he dont want it to last any longer."

So he should have hated and feared Lion. It was in the fourth summer, the fourth time he had made one in the celebration of Major de Spain's and General Compson's birthday. In the early spring Major de Spain's mare had foaled a horse colt. One evening when Sam brought the horses and mules up to stable them for the night, the colt was missing and it was all he could do to get the frantic mare into the lot. He had thought at first to let the mare lead him back to where she had become separated from the foal. But she would not do it. She would not even feint toward any particular part of the woods or even in any particular direction. She merely ran, as if she couldn't see, still frantic with terror. She whirled and ran at Sam once, as if to attack him in some ultimate desperation, as if she could not for the moment realise that he was a man and a long-familiar one. He got her into the lot at last. It was too dark by that time to back-track her, to unravel the erratic course she had doubtless pursued.

He came to the house and told Major de Spain. It was an animal, of course, a big one, and the colt was dead now, wherever it was. They all knew that. "It's a panther," General Compson said at once. "The same one. That doe and fawn last March." Sam had sent Major de Spain word of it when Boon Hogganbeck came to the camp on a routine visit to see how the stock had wintered—the doe's throat torn out, and the beast had run down the helpless fawn and killed it too.

"Sam never did say that was a panther," Major de Spain said. Sam said nothing now, standing behind Major de Spain where they sat at supper, inscrutable, as if he were just waiting for them to stop talking so he could go home. He didn't even seem to be looking at anything. "A panther might jump a doe, and he wouldn't have much trouble catching the fawn afterward. But no panther would have jumped that colt with the dam right there with it. It was Old Ben," Major de Spain said. "I'm disappointed in him. He has broken the rules. I didn't think he would have done that. He has killed mine and McCaslin's dogs, but that was all right. We gambled the dogs against him; we gave each other warning. But now he has come into my house and destroyed my property, out of season too. He broke the rules. It was Old Ben, Sam." Still Sam said nothing, standing there until Major de Spain should stop talking. "We'll back-track her tomorrow and see," Major de Spain said.

Sam departed. He would not live in the camp; he had built himself a little hut something like Joe Baker's, only stouter, tighter, on the bayou a quarter-mile away, and a stout log crib where he stored a little corn for the shoat he raised each year. The next morning he was waiting when they waked. He had already found the colt. They did not even wait for breakfast. It was not far, not five hundred yards from the stable—the three-months' colt lying on its side, its throat torn out and the entrails and one ham partly eaten. It lay not as if it had been dropped but as if it had been struck and hurled, and no cat-mark, no claw-mark where a panther would have gripped it while finding its throat. They read the tracks where the frantic mare had circled and at last rushed in with that same ultimate desperation with which she had whirled on Sam Fathers yesterday evening, and the long tracks of dead and terrified running and those of the beast which had not even rushed at her when she advanced but had merely walked three or four paces toward her until she broke, and General Compson said, "Good God, what a wolf!"

Still Sam said nothing. The boy watched him while the men knelt, measuring the tracks. There was something in Sam's face now. It was neither exultation nor joy nor hope. Later, a man, the boy realised what it had been, and that Sam had known all the time what had made the tracks and what had torn the throat out of the doe in the spring and killed the fawn. It had been foreknowledge in Sam's face that morning. *And he was glad,* he told himself. *He was old. He had no children, no people, none of his blood anywhere above earth that he would ever meet again. And even if he were to, he could not have touched it, spoken to it, because for seventy years now he had had to be a Negro. It was almost over now and he was glad.*

They returned to camp and had breakfast and came back with guns and the hounds. Afterward the boy realised that they also should have known then what killed the colt as well as Sam Fathers did. But that was neither the

first nor the last time he had seen men rationalise from
and even act upon their misconceptions. After Boon, standing astride the colt, had whipped the dogs away from it
with his belt, they snuffed at the tracks. One of them, a
young dog hound without judgment yet, bayed once, and
they ran for a few feet on what seemed to be a trail. Then
they stopped, looking back at the men, eager enough, not
baffled, merely questioning, as if they were asking "Now
what?" Then they rushed back to the colt, where Boon,
still astride it, slashed at them with the belt.

"I never knew a trail to get cold that quick," General
Compson said.

"Maybe a single wolf big enough to kill a colt with the
dam right there beside it dont leave scent," Major de
Spain said.

"Maybe it was a hant," Walter Ewell said. He looked at
Tennie's Jim. "Hah, Jim?"

Because the hounds would not run it, Major de Spain
had Sam hunt out and find the tracks a hundred yards
farther on and they put the dogs on it again and again the
young one bayed and not one of them realised then that
the hound was not baying like a dog striking game but
was merely bellowing like a country dog whose yard has
been invaded. General Compson spoke to the boy and
Boon and Tennie's Jim: to the squirrel hunters. "You
boys keep the dogs with you this morning. He's probably
hanging around somewhere, waiting to get his breakfast
off the colt. You might strike him."

But they did not. The boy remembered how Sam stood
watching them as they went into the woods with the
leashed hounds—the Indian face in which he had never
seen anything until it smiled, except that faint arching of
the nostrils on that first morning when the hounds had
found Old Ben. They took the hounds with them on the
next day, though when they reached the place where they
hoped to strike a fresh trail, the carcass of the colt was
gone. Then on the third morning Sam was waiting again,

this time until they had finished breakfast. He said, "Come." He led them to his house, his little hut, to the corn-crib beyond it. He had removed the corn and had made a deadfall of the door, baiting it with the colt's carcass; peering between the logs, they saw an animal almost the color of a gun or pistol barrel, what little time they had to examine its color or shape. It was not crouched nor even standing. It was in motion, in the air, coming toward them—a heavy body crashing with tremendous force against the door so that the thick door jumped and clattered in its frame, the animal, whatever it was, hurling itself against the door again seemingly before it could have touched the floor and got a new purchase to spring from. "Come away," Sam said, "fore he break his neck." Even when they retreated the heavy and measured crashes continued, the stout door jumping and clattering each time, and still no sound from the beast itself—no snarl, no cry.

"What in hell's name is it?" Major de Spain said.

"It's a dog," Sam said, his nostrils arching and collapsing faintly and steadily and that faint, fierce milkiness in his eyes again as on that first morning when the hounds had struck the old bear. "It's the dog."

"*The* dog?" Major de Spain said.

"That's gonter hold Old Ben."

"Dog the devil," Major de Spain said. "I'd rather have Old Ben himself in my pack than that brute. Shoot him."

"No," Sam said.

"You'll never tame him. How do you ever expect to make an animal like that afraid of you?"

"I don't want him tame," Sam said; again the boy watched his nostrils and the fierce milky light in his eyes. "But I almost rather he be tame than scared, of me or any man or any thing. But he wont be neither, of nothing."

"Then what are you going to do with it?"

"You can watch," Sam said.

Each morning through the second week they would go

to Sam's crib. He had removed a few shingles from the
roof and had put a rope on the colt's carcass and had
drawn it out when the trap fell. Each morning they would
watch him lower a pail of water into the crib while the
dog hurled itself tirelessly against the door and dropped
back and leaped again. It never made any sound and there
was nothing frenzied in the act but only a cold and grim
indomitable determination. Toward the end of the week
it stopped jumping at the door. Yet it had not weakened
appreciably and it was not as if it had rationalised the
fact that the door was not going to give. It was as if for that
time it simply disdained to jump any longer. It was not
down. None of them had ever seen it down. It stood, and
they could see it now—part mastiff, something of Airedale
and something of a dozen other strains probably, better
than thirty inches at the shoulders and weighing as they
guessed almost ninety pounds, with cold yellow eyes and
a tremendous chest and over all that strange color like a
blued gun-barrel.

Then the two weeks were up. They prepared to break
camp. The boy begged to remain and his cousin let him.
He moved into the little hut with Sam Fathers. Each morning he watched Sam lower the pail of water into the crib.
By the end of that week the dog was down. It would rise
and half stagger, half crawl to the water and drink and
collapse again. One morning it could not even reach the
water, could not raise its forequarters even from the floor.
Sam took a short stick and prepared to enter the crib.
"Wait," the boy said. "Let me get the gun—"

"No," Sam said. "He cant move now." Nor could it. It
lay on its side while Sam touched it, its head and the
gaunted body, the dog lying motionless, the yellow eyes
open. They were not fierce and there was nothing of petty
malevolence in them, but a cold and almost impersonal
malignance like some natural force. It was not even looking at Sam nor at the boy peering at it between the logs.

Sam began to feed it again. The first time he had to raise

its head so it could lap the broth. That night he left a bowl of broth containing lumps of meat where the dog could reach it. The next morning the bowl was empty and the dog was lying on its belly, its head up, the cold yellow eyes watching the door as Sam entered, no change whatever in the cold yellow eyes and still no sound from it even when it sprang, its aim and co-ordination still bad from weakness so that Sam had time to strike it down with the stick and leap from the crib and slam the door as the dog, still without having had time to get its feet under it to jump again seemingly, hurled itself against the door as if the two weeks of starving had never been.

At noon that day someone came whooping through the woods from the direction of the camp. It was Boon. He came and looked for a while between the logs, at the tremendous dog lying again on its belly, its head up, the yellow eyes blinking sleepily at nothing: the indomitable and unbroken spirit. "What we better do," Boon said, "is to let that son of a bitch go and catch Old Ben and run him on the dog." He turned to the boy his weather-reddened and beetling face. "Get your traps together. Cass says for you to come on home. You been in here fooling with that horse-eating varmint long enough."

Boon had a borrowed mule at the camp; the buggy was waiting at the edge of the bottom. He was at home that night. He told McCaslin about it. "Sam's going to starve him again until he can go in and touch him. Then he will feed him again. Then he will starve him again, if he has to."

"But why?" McCaslin said. "What for? Even Sam will never tame that brute."

"We dont want him tame. We want him like he is. We just want him to find out at last that the only way he can get out of that crib and stay out of it is to do what Sam or somebody tells him to do. He's the dog that's going to stop Old Ben and hold him. We've already named him. His name is Lion."

Then November came at last. They returned to the camp. With General Compson and Major de Spain and his cousin and Walter and Boon he stood in the yard among the guns and bedding and boxes of food and watched Sam Fathers and Lion come up the lane from the lot—the Indian, the old man in battered overalls and rubber boots and a worn sheepskin coat and a hat which had belonged to the boy's father; the tremendous dog pacing gravely beside him. The hounds rushed out to meet them and stopped, except the young one which still had but little of judgment. It ran up to Lion, fawning. Lion didn't snap at it. He didn't even pause. He struck it rolling and yelping for five or six feet with a blow of one paw as a bear would have done and came on into the yard and stood, blinking sleepily at nothing, looking at no one, while Boon said, "Jesus. Jesus.—Will he let me touch him?"

"You can touch him," Sam said. "He dont care. He dont care about nothing or nobody."

The boy watched that too. He watched it for the next two years from that moment when Boon touched Lion's head and then knelt beside him, feeling the bones and muscles, the power. It was as if Lion were a woman—or perhaps Boon was the woman. That was more like it—the big, brave, sleepy-seeming dog which, as Sam Fathers said, cared about no man and no thing; and the violent, insensitive, hard-faced man with his touch of remote Indian blood and the mind almost of a child. He watched Boon take over Lion's feeding from Sam and Uncle Ash both. He would see Boon squatting in the cold rain beside the kitchen while Lion ate. Because Lion neither slept nor ate with the other dogs though none of them knew where he did sleep until in the second November, thinking until then that Lion slept in his kennel beside Sam Fathers' hut, when the boy's cousin McCaslin said something about it to Sam by sheer chance and Sam told him. And that night the boy and Major de Spain and McCaslin with a lamp entered the back room where Boon slept—the little, tight, airless room rank with the smell of Boon's unwashed body and his wet hunting-clothes—where Boon, snoring on his back, choked and waked and Lion raised his head beside him and looked back at them from his cold, slumbrous yellow eyes.

"Damn it, Boon," McCaslin said. "Get that dog out of here. He's got to run Old Ben tomorrow morning. How in hell do you expect him to smell anything fainter than a skunk after breathing you all night?"

"The way I smell aint hurt my nose none that I ever noticed," Boon said.

"It wouldn't matter if it had," Major de Spain said. "We're not depending on you to trail a bear. Put him outside. Put him under the house with the other dogs."

Boon began to get up. "He'll kill the first one that happens to yawn or sneeze in his face or touches him."

"I reckon not," Major de Spain said. "None of them are going to risk yawning in his face or touching him either, even asleep. Put him outside. I want his nose right tomorrow. Old Ben fooled him last year. I dont think he will do it again."

Boon put on his shoes without lacing them; in his long soiled underwear, his hair still tousled from sleep, he and Lion went out. The others returned to the front room and the poker game where McCaslin's and Major de Spain's hands waited for them on the table. After a while McCaslin said, "Do you want me to go back and look again?"

"No," Major de Spain said. "I call," he said to Walter Ewell. He spoke to McCaslin again. "If you do, dont tell me. I am beginning to see the first sign of my increasing age: I dont like to know that my orders have been disobeyed, even when I knew when I gave them that they would be.—A small pair," he said to Walter Ewell.

"How small?" Walter said.

"Very small," Major de Spain said.

And the boy, lying beneath his piled quilts and blankets waiting for sleep, knew likewise that Lion was already back in Boon's bed, for the rest of that night and the next one and during all the nights of the next November and the next one. He thought then: *I wonder what Sam thinks. He could have Lion with him, even if Boon is a white man. He could ask Major or McCaslin either. And more than that. It was Sam's hand that touched Lion first and Lion knows it.* Then he became a man and he knew that too. It had been all right. That was the way it should have been. Sam was the chief, the prince; Boon, the plebeian, was his huntsman. Boon should have nursed the dogs.

On the first morning that Lion led the pack after Old Ben, seven strangers appeared in the camp. They were swampers: gaunt, malaria-ridden men appearing from nowhere, who ran trap-lines for coons or perhaps farmed little patches of cotton and corn along the edge of the bottom, in clothes but little better than Sam Fathers' and nowhere near as good as Tennie's Jim's, with worn shotguns and rifles, already squatting patiently in the cold drizzle in the side yard when day broke. They had a spokesman; afterward Sam Fathers told Major de Spain how all during the past summer and fall they had drifted into the camp singly or in pairs and threes, to look quietly at Lion for a while and then go away: "Mawnin, Major. We heerd you was aimin to put that ere blue dawg on that old two-toed bear this mawnin. We figgered we'd come up and watch, if you dont mind. We wont do no shooting, lessen he runs over us."

"You are welcome," Major de Spain said. "You are welcome to shoot. He's more your bear than ours."

"I reckon that aint no lie. I done fed him enough cawn to have a sheer in him. Not to mention a shoat three years ago."

"I reckon I got a sheer too," another said. "Only it aint in the bear." Major de Spain looked at him. He was chewing tobacco. He spat. "Hit was a heifer calf. Nice un too. Last year. When I finally found her, I reckon she looked about like that colt of yourn looked last June."

"Oh," Major de Spain said. "Be welcome. If you see game in front of my dogs, shoot it."

Nobody shot Old Ben that day. No man saw him. The dogs jumped him within a hundred yards of the glade where the boy had seen him that day in the summer of his eleventh year. The boy was less than a quarter-mile away. He heard the jump but he could distinguish no voice among the dogs that he did not know and therefore would be Lion's, and he thought, believed, that Lion was not among them. Even the fact that they were going much faster than he had ever heard them run behind Old Ben before and that the high thin note of hysteria was missing now from their voices was not enough to disabuse him. He didn't comprehend until that night, when Sam told him that Lion would never cry on a trail. "He gonter growl when he catches Old Ben's throat," Sam said. "But he aint gonter never holler, no more than he ever done when he was jumping at that two-inch door. It's that blue dog in him. What you call it?"

"Airedale," the boy said.

Lion was there; the jump was just too close to the river. When Boon returned with Lion about eleven that night, he swore that Lion had stopped Old Ben once but that the hounds would not go in and Old Ben broke away and took to the river and swam for miles down it and he and Lion went down one bank for about ten miles and crossed and came up the other but it had begun to get dark before they struck any trail where Old Ben had come up out of the water, unless he was still in the water when he passed the ford where they crossed. Then he fell to cursing the hounds and ate the supper Uncle Ash had saved for him and went off to bed and after a while the boy opened the door of the little stale room thunderous with snoring and the great grave dog raised its head from Boon's pillow and blinked at him for a moment and lowered its head again.

When the next November came and the last day, the

day on which it was now becoming traditional to save for
Old Ben, there were more than a dozen strangers waiting.
They were not all swampers this time. Some of them were
townsmen, from other county seats like Jefferson, who had
heard about Lion and Old Ben and had come to watch
the great blue dog keep his yearly rendezvous with the
old two-toed bear. Some of them didn't even have guns
and the hunting-clothes and boots they wore had been on
a store shelf yesterday.

This time Lion jumped Old Ben more than five miles
from the river and bayed and held him and this time the
hounds went in, in a sort of desperate emulation. The
boy heard them; he was that near. He heard Boon whooping; he heard the two shots when General Compson delivered both barrels, one containing five buckshot, the
other a single ball, into the bear from as close as he could
force his almost unmanageable horse. He heard the dogs
when the bear broke free again. He was running now;
panting, stumbling, his lungs bursting, he reached the
place where General Compson had fired and where Old
Ben had killed two of the hounds. He saw the blood from
General Compson's shots, but he could go no further. He
stopped, leaning against a tree for his breathing to ease
and his heart to slow, hearing the sound of the dogs as it
faded on and died away.

In camp that night—they had as guests five of the still
terrified strangers in new hunting coats and boots who
had been lost all day until Sam Fathers went out and got
them—he heard the rest of it: how Lion had stopped and
held the bear again but only the one-eyed mule which did
not mind the smell of wild blood would approach and
Boon was riding the mule and Boon had never been
known to hit anything. He shot at the bear five times with
his pump gun, touching nothing, and Old Ben killed another hound and broke free once more and reached the
river and was gone. Again Boon and Lion hunted as far
down one bank as they dared. Too far; they crossed in the

first of dusk and dark overtook them within a mile. And this time Lion found the broken trail, the blood perhaps, in the darkness where Old Ben had come up out of the water, but Boon had him on a rope, luckily, and he got down from the mule and fought Lion hand-to-hand until he got him back to camp. This time Boon didn't even curse. He stood in the door, muddy, spent, his huge gargoyle's face tragic and still amazed. "I missed him," he said. "I was in twenty-five feet of him and I missed him five times."

"But we have drawn blood," Major de Spain said. "General Compson drew blood. We have never done that before."

"But I missed him," Boon said. "I missed him five times. With Lion looking right at me."

"Never mind," Major de Spain said. "It was a damned fine race. And we drew blood. Next year we'll let General Compson or Walter ride Katie, and we'll get him."

Then McCaslin said, "Where is Lion, Boon?"

"I left him at Sam's," Boon said. He was already turning away. "I aint fit to sleep with him."

So he should have hated and feared Lion. Yet he did not. It seemed to him that there was a fatality in it. It seemed to him that something, he didn't know what, was beginning; had already begun. It was like the last act on a set stage. It was the beginning of the end of something, he didn't know what except that he would not grieve. He would be humble and proud that he had been found worthy to be a part of it too or even just to see it too.

—3—

It was December. It was the coldest December he had ever remembered. They had been in camp four days over two weeks, waiting for the weather to soften so that Lion

and Old Ben could run their yearly race. Then they would
break camp and go home. Because of these unforeseen
additional days which they had had to pass waiting on
the weather, with nothing to do but play poker, the whisky
had given out and he and Boon were being sent to Memphis with a suitcase and a note from Major de Spain to
Mr. Semmes, the distiller, to get more. That is, Major de
Spain and McCaslin were sending Boon to get the whisky
and sending him to see that Boon got back with it or most
of it or at least some of it.

Tennie's Jim waked him at three. He dressed rapidly,
shivering, not so much from the cold because a fresh fire
already boomed and roared on the hearth, but in that dead
winter hour when the blood and the heart are slow and
sleep is incomplete. He crossed the gap between house and
kitchen, the gap of iron earth beneath the brilliant and
rigid night where dawn would not begin for three hours
yet, tasting, tongue palate and to the very bottom of his
lungs the searing dark, and entered the kitchen, the lamp-
lit warmth where the stove glowed, fogging the windows,
and where Boon already sat at the table at breakfast,
hunched over his plate, almost in his plate, his working
jaws blue with stubble and his face innocent of water and
his coarse, horse-mane hair innocent of comb—the quarter
Indian, grandson of a Chickasaw squaw, who on occasion
resented with his hard and furious fists the intimation of
one single drop of alien blood and on others, usually after
whisky, affirmed with the same fists and the same fury that
his father had been the full-blood Chickasaw and even a
chief and that even his mother had been only half white.
He was four inches over six feet; he had the mind of a
child, the heart of a horse, and little hard shoe-button
eyes without depth or meanness or generosity or viciousness or gentleness or anything else, in the ugliest face the
boy had ever seen. It looked like somebody had found a
walnut a little larger than a football and with a machin-
ist's hammer had shaped features into it and then painted

it, mostly red; not Indian red but a fine bright ruddy color which whisky might have had something to do with but which was mostly just happy and violent out-of-doors, the wrinkles in it not the residue of the forty years it had survived but from squinting into the sun or into the gloom of cane-brakes where game had run, baked into it by the camp fires before which he had lain trying to sleep on the cold November or December ground while waiting for daylight so he could rise and hunt again, as though time were merely something he walked through as he did through air, aging him no more than air did. He was brave, faithful, improvident and unreliable; he had neither profession job nor trade and owned one vice and one virtue: whisky, and that absolute and unquestioning fidelity to Major de Spain and the boy's cousin McCaslin. "Sometimes I'd call them both virtues," Major de Spain said once. "Or both vices," McCaslin said.

He ate his breakfast, hearing the dogs under the kitchen, wakened by the smell of frying meat or perhaps by the feet overhead. He heard Lion once, short and peremptory, as the best hunter in any camp has only to speak once to all save the fools, and none other of Major de Spain's and McCaslin's dogs were Lion's equal in size and strength and perhaps even in courage, but they were not fools; Old Ben had killed the last fool among them last year.

Tennie's Jim came in as they finished. The wagon was outside. Ash decided he would drive them over to the log-line where they would flag the outbound log-train and let Tennie's Jim wash the dishes. The boy knew why. It would not be the first time he had listened to old Ash badgering Boon.

It was cold. The wagon wheels banged and clattered on the frozen ground; the sky was fixed and brilliant. He was not shivering, he was shaking, slow and steady and hard, the food he had just eaten still warm and solid inside him while his outside shook slow and steady around it as though his stomach floated loose. "They wont run this morning," he said. "No dog will have any nose today."

"Cep Lion," Ash said. "Lion dont need no nose. All he need is a bear." He had wrapped his feet in towsacks and he had a quilt from his pallet bed on the kitchen floor drawn over his head and wrapped around him until in the thin brilliant starlight he looked like nothing at all that the boy had ever seen before. "He run a bear through a thousand-acre ice-house. Catch him too. Them other dogs dont matter because they aint going to keep up with Lion nohow, long as he got a bear in front of him."

"What's wrong with the other dogs?" Boon said. "What the hell do you know about it anyway? This is the first time you've had your tail out of that kitchen since we got here except to chop a little wood."

"Aint nothing wrong with them," Ash said. "And long as it's left up to them, aint nothing going to be. I just wish I had knowed all my life how to take care of my health good as them hounds knows."

"Well, they aint going to run this morning," Boon said. His voice was harsh and positive. "Major promised they wouldn't until me and Ike get back."

"Weather gonter break today. Gonter soft up. Rain by night." Then Ash laughed, chuckled, somewhere inside the quilt which concealed even his face. "Hum up here, mules!" he said, jerking the reins so that the mules leaped forward and snatched the lurching and banging wagon for several feet before they slowed again into their quick, short-paced, rapid plodding. "Sides, I like to know why Major need to wait on you. It's Lion he aiming to use. I aint never heard tell of you bringing no bear nor no other kind of meat into this camp."

Now Boon's going to curse Ash or maybe even hit him, the boy thought. But Boon never did, never had; the boy knew he never would even though four years ago Boon had shot five times with a borrowed pistol at a Negro on the street in Jefferson, with the same result as when he had shot five times at Old Ben last fall. "By God," Boon said, "he aint going to put Lion or no other dog on nothing until I get back tonight. Because he promised me. Whip up them mules and keep them whipped up. Do you want me to freeze to death?"

They reached the log-line and built a fire. After a while the log-train came up out of the woods under the paling east and Boon flagged it. Then in the warm caboose the boy slept again while Boon and the conductor and brakeman talked about Lion and Old Ben as people later would talk about Sullivan and Kilrain and, later still, about Dempsey and Tunney. Dozing, swaying as the springless caboose lurched and clattered, he would hear them still talking, about the shoats and calves Old Ben had killed and the cribs he had rifled and the traps and deadfalls he had wrecked and the lead he probably carried under his hide—Old Ben, the two-toed bear in a land where bears with trap-ruined feet had been called Two-Toe or Three-Toe or Cripple-Foot for fifty years, only Old Ben was an extra bear (the head bear, General Compson called him) and so had earned a name such as a human man could have worn and not been sorry.

They reached Hoke's at sunup. They emerged from the warm caboose in their hunting clothes, the muddy boots and stained khaki and Boon's blue unshaven jowls. But that was all right. Hoke's was a sawmill and commissary and two stores and a loading-chute on a sidetrack from the main line, and all the men in it wore boots and khaki too. Presently the Memphis train came. Boon bought three packages of popcorn-and-molasses and a bottle of beer from the news butch and the boy went to sleep again to the sound of his chewing.

But in Memphis it was not all right. It was as if the high buildings and the hard pavements, the fine carriages and the horse cars and the men in starched collars and neckties made their boots and khaki look a little rougher and a little muddier and made Boon's beard look worse and more unshaven and his face look more and more like he should never have brought it out of the woods at all or at least out of reach of Major de Spain or McCaslin or someone who knew it and could have said, "Dont be afraid. He wont hurt you." He walked through the station, on the slick floor, his face moving as he worked the popcorn out of his teeth with his tongue, his legs spraddled and stiff in the hips as if he were walking on buttered glass, and that blue stubble on his face like the filings from a new gun-barrel. They passed the first saloon. Even through the closed doors the boy could seem to smell the sawdust and the reek of old drink. Boon began to cough. He coughed for something less than a minute. "Damn this cold," he said. "I'd sure like to know where I got it."

"Back there in the station," the boy said.

Boon had started to cough again. He stopped. He looked at the boy. "What?" he said.

"You never had it when we left camp nor on the train either." Boon looked at him, blinking. Then he stopped blinking. He didn't cough again. He said quietly:

"Lend me a dollar. Come on. You've got it. If you ever had one, you've still got it. I dont mean you are tight with your money because you aint. You just dont never seem to ever think of nothing you want. When I was sixteen a dollar bill melted off of me before I even had time to read the name of the bank that issued it." He said quietly: "Let me have a dollar, Ike."

"You promised Major. You promised McCaslin. Not till we get back to camp."

"All right," Boon said in that quiet and patient voice. "What can I do on just one dollar? You aint going to lend me another."

"You're damn right I aint," the boy said, his voice quiet too, cold with rage which was not at Boon, remembering: Boon snoring in a hard chair in the kitchen so he could watch the clock and wake him and McCaslin and drive them the seventeen miles in to Jefferson to catch the train to Memphis; the wild, never-bridled Texas paint pony which he had persuaded McCaslin to let him buy and which he and Boon had bought at auction for four dollars and seventy-five cents and fetched home wired between two gentle old mares with pieces of barbed wire and which had never even seen shelled corn before and didn't even know what it was unless the grains were bugs maybe and at last (he was ten and Boon had been ten all his life) Boon said the pony was gentled and with a towsack over its head and four Negroes to hold it they backed it into an old two-wheeled cart and hooked up the gear and he and Boon got up and Boon said, "All right, boys. Let him go" and one of the Negroes—it was Tennie's Jim—snatched the towsack off and leaped for his life and they lost the first wheel against a post of the open gate only at that moment Boon caught him by the scruff of the neck and flung him into the roadside ditch so he only saw the rest of it in fragments: the other wheel as it slammed through the side gate and crossed the back yard and leaped up onto the gallery and scraps of the cart here and there along the road and Boon vanishing rapidly on his stomach in the leaping and spurting dust and still holding the reins until they broke too and two days later they finally caught the pony seven miles away still wearing the hames and the headstall of the bridle around its neck like a duchess with two necklaces at one time. He gave Boon the dollar.

"All right," Boon said. "Come on in out of the cold."

"I aint cold," he said.

"You can have some lemonade."

"I dont want any lemonade."

The door closed behind him. The sun was well up now. It was a brilliant day, though Ash had said it would rain before night. Already it was warmer; they could run tomorrow. He felt the old lift of the heart, as pristine as ever, as on the first day; he would never lose it, no matter how old in hunting and pursuit: the best, the best of all breathing, the humility and the pride. He must stop thinking about it. Already it seemed to him that he was running,

back to the station, to the tracks themselves: the first train
going south; he must stop thinking about it. The street
was busy. He watched the big Norman draft horses, the
Percherons; the trim carriages from which the men in the
fine overcoats and the ladies rosy in furs descended and
entered the station. (They were still next door to it but
one.) Twenty years ago his father had ridden into Memphis as a member of Colonel Sartoris' horse in Forrest's
command, up Main street and (the tale told) into the
lobby of the Gayoso Hotel where the Yankee officers sat
in the leather chairs spitting into the tall bright cuspidors
and then out again, scot-free—

The door opened behind him. Boon was wiping his
mouth on the back of his hand. "All right," he said. "Let's
go tend to it and get the hell out of here."

They went and had the suitcase packed. He never knew
where or when Boon got the other bottle. Doubtless Mr.
Semmes gave it to him. When they reached Hoke's again
at sundown, it was empty. They could get a return train
to Hoke's in two hours; they went straight back to the
station as Major de Spain and then McCaslin had told
Boon to do and then ordered him to do and had sent the
boy along to see that he did. Boon took the first drink
from his bottle in the washroom. A man in a uniform cap
came to tell him he couldn't drink there and looked at
Boon's face once and said nothing. The next time he was
pouring into his water glass beneath the edge of a table in
the restaurant when the manager (she was a woman) did
tell him he couldn't drink there and he went back to the
washroom. He had been telling the Negro waiter and all
the other people in the restaurant who couldn't help but
hear him and who had never heard of Lion and didn't
want to, about Lion and Old Ben. Then he happened to
think of the zoo. He had found out that there was another
train to Hoke's at three oclock and so they would spend
the time at the zoo and take the three oclock train until
he came back from the washroom for the third time. Then

they would take the first train back to camp, get Lion and come back to the zoo where, he said, the bears were fed on ice cream and lady fingers and he would match Lion against them all.

So they missed the first train, the one they were supposed to take, but he got Boon onto the three oclock train and they were all right again, with Boon not even going to the washroom now but drinking in the aisle and talking about Lion and the men he buttonholed no more daring to tell Boon he couldn't drink there than the man in the station had dared.

When they reached Hoke's at sundown, Boon was asleep. The boy waked him at last and got him and the suitcase off the train and he even persuaded him to eat some supper at the sawmill commissary. So he was all right when they got in the caboose of the log-train to go back into the woods, with the sun going down red and the sky already overcast and the ground would not freeze tonight. It was the boy who slept now, sitting behind the ruby stove while the springless caboose jumped and clattered and Boon and the brakeman and the conductor talked about Lion and Old Ben because they knew what Boon was talking about because this was home. "Overcast and already thawing," Boon said. "Lion will get him tomorrow."

It would have to be Lion, or somebody. It would not be Boon. He had never hit anything bigger than a squirrel that anybody ever knew, except the Negro woman that day when he was shooting at the Negro man. He was a big Negro and not ten feet away but Boon shot five times with the pistol he had borrowed from Major de Spain's Negro coachman and the Negro he was shooting at outed with a dollar-and-a-half mail-order pistol and would have burned Boon down with it only it never went off, it just went snicksnicksnicksnicksnick five times and Boon still blasting away and he broke a plate-glass window that cost McCaslin forty-five dollars and hit a Negro woman who hap-

pened to be passing in the leg only Major de Spain paid
for that; he and McCaslin cut cards, the plate-glass window
against the Negro woman's leg. And the first day on stand
this year, the first morning in camp, the buck ran right
over Boon; he heard Boon's old pump gun go whow.
whow. whow. whow. whow. and then his voice: "God
damn, here he comes! Head him! Head him!" and when
he got there the buck's tracks and the five exploded shells
were not twenty paces apart.

There were five guests in camp that night, from Jefferson: Mr. Bayard Sartoris and his son and General Compson's son and two others. And the next morning he looked
out the window, into the gray thin drizzle of daybreak
which Ash had predicted, and there they were, standing
and squatting beneath the thin rain, almost two dozen of
them who had fed Old Ben corn and shoats and even
calves for ten years, in their worn hats and hunting coats
and overalls which any town Negro would have thrown
away or burned and only the rubber boots strong and
sound, and the worn and blueless guns and some even
without guns. While they ate breakfast a dozen more arrived, mounted and on foot: loggers from the camp thirteen miles below and sawmill men from Hoke's and the
only gun among them that one which the log-train conductor carried: so that when they went into the woods this
morning Major de Spain led a party almost as strong, ex-
cepting that some of them were not armed, as some he had
led in the last darkening days of '64 and '65. The little
yard would not hold them. They overflowed it, into the
lane where Major de Spain sat his mare while Ash in his
dirty apron thrust the greasy cartridges into his carbine
and passed it up to him and the great grave blue dog stood
at his stirrup not as a dog stands but as a horse stands,
blinking his sleepy topaz eyes at nothing, deaf even to the
yelling of the hounds which Boon and Tennie's Jim held
on leash.

"We'll put General Compson on Katie this morning,"

Major de Spain said. "He drew blood last year; if he'd had a mule then that would have stood, he would have—"

"No," General Compson said. "I'm too old to go helling through the woods on a mule or a horse or anything else any more. Besides, I had my chance last year and missed it. I'm going on a stand this morning. I'm going to let that boy ride Katie."

"No, wait," McCaslin said. "Ike's got the rest of his life to hunt bears in. Let somebody else—"

"No," General Compson said. "I want Ike to ride Katie. He's already a better woodsman than you or me either and in another ten years he'll be as good as Walter."

At first he couldn't believe it, not until Major de Spain spoke to him. Then he was up, on the one-eyed mule which would not spook at wild blood, looking down at the dog motionless at Major de Spain's stirrup, looking in the gray streaming light bigger than a calf, bigger than he knew it actually was—the big head, the chest almost as big as his own, the blue hide beneath which the muscles flinched or quivered to no touch since the heart which drove blood to them loved no man and no thing, standing as a horse stands yet different from a horse which infers only weight and speed while Lion inferred not only courage and all else that went to make up the will and desire to pursue and kill, but endurance, the will and desire to endure beyond all imaginable limits of flesh in order to overtake and slay. Then the dog looked at him. It moved its head and looked at him across the trivial uproar of the hounds, out of the yellow eyes as depthless as Boon's, as free as Boon's of meanness or generosity or gentleness or viciousness. They were just cold and sleepy. Then it blinked, and he knew it was not looking at him and never had been, without even bothering to turn its head away.

That morning he heard the first cry. Lion had already vanished while Sam and Tennie's Jim were putting saddles on the mule and horse which had drawn the wagon and he watched the hounds as they crossed and cast, snuffing and whimpering, until they too disappeared. Then he and Major de Spain and Sam and Tennie's Jim rode after them and heard the first cry out of the wet and thawing woods not two hundred yards ahead, high, with that abject, almost human quality he had come to know, and the other hounds joining in until the gloomed woods rang and clamored. They rode then. It seemed to him that he could actually see the big blue dog boring on, silent, and the bear too: the thick, locomotive-like shape which he had seen that day four years ago crossing the blow-down, crashing on ahead of the dogs faster than he had believed it could have moved, drawing away even from the running mules. He heard a shotgun, once. The woods had opened, they were going fast, the clamor faint and fading on ahead; they passed the man who had fired—a swamper, a pointing arm, a gaunt face, the small black orifice of his yelling studded with rotten teeth.

He heard the changed note in the hounds' uproar and two hundred yards ahead he saw them. The bear had turned. He saw Lion drive in without pausing and saw the bear strike him aside and lunge into the yelling hounds and kill one of them almost in its tracks and whirl and run again. Then they were in a streaming tide of dogs. He heard Major de Spain and Tennie's Jim shouting and the pistol sound of Tennie's Jim's leather thong as he tried to turn them. Then he and Sam Fathers were riding alone. One of the hounds had kept on with Lion though. He recognised its voice. It was the young hound which even a year ago had had no judgment and which, by the lights of the other hounds anyway, still had none. *Maybe that's what courage is,* he thought. "Right," Sam said behind him. "Right. We got to turn him from the river if we can."

Now they were in cane: a brake. He knew the path through it as well as Sam did. They came out of the undergrowth and struck the entrance almost exactly. It would traverse the brake and come out onto a high open ridge above the river. He heard the flat clap of Walter Ewell's rifle, then two more. "No," Sam said. "I can hear the hound. Go on."

They emerged from the narrow roofless tunnel of snapping and hissing cane, still galloping, onto the open ridge below which the thick yellow river, reflectionless in the gray and streaming light, seemed not to move. Now he could hear the hound too. It was not running. The cry was a high frantic yapping and Boon was running along the edge of the bluff, his old gun leaping and jouncing against his back on its sling made of a piece of cotton plowline. He whirled and ran up to them, wild-faced, and flung himself onto the mule behind the boy. "That damn boat!" he cried. "It's on the other side! He went straight across! Lion was too close to him! That little hound too! Lion was so close I couldn't shoot! Go on!" he cried, beating his heels into the mule's flanks. "Go on!"

They plunged down the bank, slipping and sliding in the thawed earth, crashing through the willows and into the water. He felt no shock, no cold, he on one side of the swimming mule, grasping the pommel with one hand and holding his gun above the water with the other, Boon opposite him. Sam was behind them somewhere, and then the river, the water about them, was full of dogs. They swam faster than the mules; they were scrabbling up the bank before the mules touched bottom. Major de Spain was whooping from the bank they had just left and, looking back, he saw Tennie's Jim and the horse as they went into the water.

Now the woods ahead of them and the rain-heavy air were one uproar. It rang and clamored; it echoed and broke against the bank behind them and reformed and clamored and rang until it seemed to the boy that all the hounds which had ever bayed game in this land were yelling down at him. He got his leg over the mule as it came up out of the water. Boon didn't try to mount again. He grasped one stirrup as they went up the bank and crashed through the undergrowth which fringed the bluff

and saw the bear, on its hind feet, its back against a tree
while the bellowing hounds swirled around it and once
more Lion drove in, leaping clear of the ground.

This time the bear didn't strike him down. It caught
the dog in both arms, almost loverlike, and they both
went down. He was off the mule now. He drew back both
hammers of the gun but he could see nothing but moiling
spotted houndbodies until the bear surged up again. Boon
was yelling something, he could not tell what; he could
see Lion still clinging to the bear's throat and he saw the
bear, half erect, strike one of the hounds with one paw
and hurl it five or six feet and then, rising and rising as
though it would never stop, stand erect again and begin
to rake at Lion's belly with its forepaws. Then Boon was
running. The boy saw the gleam of the blade in his hand
and watched him leap among the hounds, hurdling them,
kicking them aside as he ran, and fling himself astride the
bear as he had hurled himself onto the mule, his legs locked
around the bear's belly, his left arm under the bear's throat
where Lion clung, and the glint of the knife as it rose and
fell.

It fell just once. For an instant they almost resembled a
piece of statuary: the clinging dog, the bear, the man
astride its back, working and probing the buried blade.
Then they went down, pulled over backward by Boon's
weight, Boon underneath. It was the bear's back which
reappeared first but at once Boon was astride it again. He
had never released the knife and again the boy saw the
almost infinitesimal movement of his arm and shoulder
as he probed and sought; then the bear surged erect, raising with it the man and the dog too, and turned and still
carrying the man and the dog it took two or three steps
toward the woods on its hind feet as a man would have
walked and crashed down. It didn't collapse, crumple. It
fell all of a piece, as a tree falls, so that all three of them,
man dog and bear, seemed to bounce once.

He and Tennie's Jim ran forward. Boon was kneeling

at the bear's head. His left ear was shredded, his left coat sleeve was completely gone, his right boot had been ripped from knee to instep; the bright blood thinned in the thin rain down his leg and hand and arm and down the side of his face which was no longer wild but was quite calm. Together they prized Lion's jaws from the bear's throat. "Easy, goddamn it," Boon said. "Cant you see his guts are all out of him?" He began to remove his coat. He spoke to Tennie's Jim in that calm voice: "Bring the boat up. It's about a hundred yards down the bank there. I saw it." Tennie's Jim rose and went away. Then, and he could not remember if it had been a call or an exclamation from Tennie's Jim or if he had glanced up by chance, he saw Tennie's Jim stooping and saw Sam Fathers lying motionless on his face in the trampled mud.

The mule had not thrown him. He remembered that Sam was down too even before Boon began to run. There was no mark on him whatever and when he and Boon turned him over, his eyes were open and he said something in that tongue which he and Joe Baker had used to speak together. But he couldn't move. Tennie's Jim brought the skiff up; they could hear him shouting to Major de Spain across the river. Boon wrapped Lion in his hunting coat and carried him down to the skiff and they carried Sam down and returned and hitched the bear to the one-eyed mule's saddle-bow with Tennie's Jim's leash-thong and dragged him down to the skiff and got him into it and left Tennie's Jim to swim the horse and the two mules back across. Major de Spain caught the bow of the skiff as Boon jumped out and past him before it touched the bank. He looked at Old Ben and said quietly: "Well." Then he walked into the water and leaned down and touched Sam and Sam looked up at him and said something in that old tongue he and Joe Baker spoke. "You dont know what happened?" Major de Spain said.

"No, sir," the boy said. "It wasn't the mule. It wasn't anything. He was off the mule when Boon ran in on the

bear. Then we looked up and he was lying on the ground."
Boon was shouting at Tennie's Jim, still in the middle of
the river.

"Come on, goddamn it!" he said. "Bring me that mule!"

"What do you want with a mule?" Major de Spain said.

Boon didn't even look at him. "I'm going to Hoke's to
get the doctor," he said in that calm voice, his face quite
calm beneath the steady thinning of the bright blood.

"You need a doctor yourself," Major de Spain said.
"Tennie's Jim—"

"Damn that," Boon said. He turned on Major de Spain.
His face was still calm, only his voice was a pitch higher.
"Cant you see his goddamn guts are all out of him?"

"Boon!" Major de Spain said. They looked at one another. Boon was a good head taller than Major de Spain;
even the boy was taller now than Major de Spain.

"I've got to get the doctor," Boon said. "His goddamn
guts—"

"All right," Major de Spain said. Tennie's Jim came up
out of the water. The horse and the sound mule had already scented Old Ben; they surged and plunged all the
way up to the top of the bluff, dragging Tennie's Jim with
them, before he could stop them and tie them and come
back. Major de Spain unlooped the leather thong of his
compass from his buttonhole and gave it to Tennie's Jim.
"Go straight to Hoke's," he said. "Bring Doctor Crawford
back with you. Tell him there are two men to be looked
at. Take my mare. Can you find the road from here?"

"Yes, sir," Tennie's Jim said.

"All right," Major de Spain said. "Go on." He turned
to the boy. "Take the mules and the horse and go back
and get the wagon. We'll go on down the river in the boat
to Coon bridge. Meet us there. Can you find it again?"

"Yes, sir," the boy said.

"All right. Get started."

He went back to the wagon. He realised then how far
they had run. It was already afternoon when he put the

mules into the traces and tied the horse's lead-rope to the
tail-gate. He reached Coon bridge at dusk. The skiff was
already there. Before he could see it and almost before
he could see the water he had to leap from the tilting
wagon, still holding the reins, and work around to where
he could grasp the bit and then the ear of the plunging
sound mule and dig his heels and hold it until Boon came
up the bank. The rope of the led horse had already
snapped and it had already disappeared up the road toward camp. They turned the wagon around and took the
mules out and he led the sound mule a hundred yards up
the road and tied it. Boon had already brought Lion up
to the wagon and Sam was sitting up in the skiff now and
when they raised him he tried to walk, up the bank and
to the wagon and he tried to climb into the wagon but
Boon did not wait; he picked Sam up bodily and set him
on the seat. Then they hitched Old Ben to the one-eyed
mule's saddle again and dragged him up the bank and set
two skid-poles into the open tail-gate and got him into
the wagon and he went and got the sound mule and Boon
fought it into the traces, striking it across its hard hollow-
sounding face until it came into position and stood trembling. Then the rain came down, as though it had held
off all day waiting on them.

They returned to camp through it, through the streaming and sightless dark, hearing long before they saw any
light the horn and the spaced shots to guide them. When
they came to Sam's dark little hut he tried to stand up. He
spoke again in the tongue of the old fathers; then he said
clearly: "Let me out. Let me out."

"He hasn't got any fire," Major said. "Go on!" he said
sharply.

But Sam was struggling now, trying to stand up. "Let
me out, master," he said. "Let me go home."

So he stopped the wagon and Boon got down and lifted
Sam out. He did not wait to let Sam try to walk this time.
He carried him into the hut and Major de Spain got light

on a paper spill from the buried embers on the hearth and
lit the lamp and Boon put Sam on his bunk and drew off
his boots and Major de Spain covered him and the boy
was not there, he was holding the mules, the sound one
which was trying again to bolt since when the wagon
stopped Old Ben's scent drifted forward again along the
streaming blackness of air, but Sam's eyes were probably
open again on that profound look which saw further than
them or the hut, further than the death of a bear and the
dying of a dog. Then they went on, toward the long wailing of the horn and the shots which seemed each to linger
intact somewhere in the thick streaming air until the next
spaced report joined and blended with it, to the lighted
house, the bright streaming windows, the quiet faces as
Boon entered, bloody and quite calm, carrying the bun-
dled coat. He laid Lion, blood coat and all, on his stale
sheetless pallet bed which not even Ash, as deft in the
house as a woman, could ever make smooth.

The sawmill doctor from Hoke's was already there. Boon
would not let the doctor touch him until he had seen to
Lion. He wouldn't risk giving Lion chloroform. He put
the entrails back and sewed him up without it while Major
de Spain held his head and Boon his feet. But he never
tried to move. He lay there, the yellow eyes open upon
nothing while the quiet men in the new hunting clothes
and in the old ones crowded into the little airless room
rank with the smell of Boon's body and garments, and
watched. Then the doctor cleaned and disinfected Boon's
face and arm and leg and bandaged them and, the boy in
front with a lantern and the doctor and McCaslin and
Major de Spain and General Compson following, they
went to Sam Fathers' hut. Tennie's Jim had built up the
fire; he squatted before it, dozing. Sam had not moved
since Boon had put him in the bunk and Major de Spain
had covered him with the blankets, yet he opened his eyes
and looked from one to another of the faces and when
McCaslin touched his shoulder and said, "Sam. The doctor

wants to look at you," he even drew his hands out of the
blanket and began to fumble at his shirt buttons until
McCaslin said, "Wait. We'll do it." They undressed him.
He lay there—the copper-brown, almost hairless body, the
old man's body, the old man, the wild man not even one
generation from the woods, childless, kinless, peopleless—
motionless, his eyes open but no longer looking at any of
them, while the doctor examined him and drew the blankets up and put the stethoscope back into his bag and
snapped the bag and only the boy knew that Sam too was
going to die.

"Exhaustion," the doctor said. "Shock maybe. A man
his age swimming rivers in December. He'll be all right.
Just make him stay in bed for a day or two. Will there be
somebody here with him?"

"There will be somebody here," Major de Spain said.

They went back to the house, to the rank little room
where Boon still sat on the pallet bed with Lion's head
under his hand while the men, the ones who had hunted
behind Lion and the ones who had never seen him before
today, came quietly in to look at him and went away. Then
it was dawn and they all went out into the yard to look at
Old Ben, with his eyes open too and his lips snarled back
from his worn teeth and his mutilated foot and the little
hard lumps under his skin which were the old bullets
(there were fifty-two of them, buckshot rifle and ball) and
the single almost invisible slit under his left shoulder
where Boon's blade had finally found his life. Then Ash
began to beat on the bottom of the dishpan with a heavy
spoon to call them to breakfast and it was the first time he
could remember hearing no sound from the dogs under
the kitchen while they were eating. It was as if the old
bear, even dead there in the yard, was a more potent terror
still than they could face without Lion between them.

The rain had stopped during the night. By midmorning
the thin sun appeared, rapidly burning away mist and
cloud, warming the air and the earth; it would be one of

those windless Mississippi December days which are a sort
of Indian summer's Indian summer. They moved Lion
out to the front gallery, into the sun. It was Boon's idea.
"Goddamn it," he said, "he never did want to stay in the
house until I made him. You know that." He took a crow-
bar and loosened the floor boards under his pallet bed so
it could be raised, mattress and all, without disturbing
Lion's position, and they carried him out to the gallery
and put him down facing the woods.

Then he and the doctor and McCaslin and Major de
Spain went to Sam's hut. This time Sam didn't open his
eyes and his breathing was so quiet, so peaceful that they
could hardly see that he breathed. The doctor didn't even
take out his stethoscope nor even touch him. "He's all
right," the doctor said. "He didn't even catch cold. He
just quit."

"Quit?" McCaslin said.

"Yes. Old people do that sometimes. Then they get a
good night's sleep or maybe it's just a drink of whisky, and
they change their minds."

They returned to the house. And then they began to
arrive—the swamp-dwellers, the gaunt men who ran trap-
lines and lived on quinine and coons and river water, the
farmers of little corn- and cotton-patches along the bottom's edge whose fields and cribs and pig-pens the old bear
had rifled, the loggers from the camp and the sawmill men
from Hoke's and the town men from further away than
that, whose hounds the old bear had slain and traps and
deadfalls he had wrecked and whose lead he carried. They
came up mounted and on foot and in wagons, to enter the
yard and look at him and then go on to the front where
Lion lay, filling the little yard and overflowing it until
there were almost a hundred of them squatting and standing in the warm and drowsing sunlight, talking quietly of
hunting, of the game and the dogs which ran it, of hounds
and bear and deer and men of yesterday vanished from the
earth, while from time to time the great blue dog would

open his eyes, not as if he were listening to them but as though to look at the woods for a moment before closing his eyes again, to remember the woods or to see that they were still there. He died at sundown.

Major de Spain broke camp that night. They carried Lion into the woods, or Boon carried him that is, wrapped in a quilt from his bed, just as he had refused to let anyone else touch Lion yesterday until the doctor got there; Boon carrying Lion, and the boy and General Compson and Walter and still almost fifty of them following with lanterns and lighted pine-knots—men from Hoke's and even further, who would have to ride out of the bottom in the dark, and swampers and trappers who would have to walk even, scattering toward the little hidden huts where they lived. And Boon would let nobody else dig the grave either and lay Lion in it and cover him and then General Compson stood at the head of it while the blaze and smoke of the pine-knots streamed away among the winter branches and spoke as he would have spoken over a man. Then they returned to camp. Major de Spain and McCaslin and Ash had rolled and tied all the bedding. The mules were hitched to the wagon and pointed out of the bottom and the wagon was already loaded and the stove in the kitchen was cold and the table was set with scraps of cold food and bread and only the coffee was hot when the boy ran into the kitchen where Major de Spain and McCaslin had already eaten. "What?" he cried. "What? I'm not going."

"Yes," McCaslin said, "we're going out tonight. Major wants to get on back home."

"No!" he said. "I'm going to stay."

"You've got to be back in school Monday. You've already missed a week more than I intended. It will take you from now until Monday to catch up. Sam's all right. You heard Doctor Crawford. I'm going to leave Boon and Tennie's Jim both to stay with him until he feels like getting up."

He was panting. The others had come in. He looked rapidly and almost frantically around at the other faces.

Boon had a fresh bottle. He upended it and started the
cork by striking the bottom of the bottle with the heel of
his hand and drew the cork with his teeth and spat it out
and drank. "You're damn right you're going back to
school," Boon said. "Or I'll burn the tail off of you myself
if Cass dont, whether you are sixteen or sixty. Where in
hell do you expect to get without education? Where would
Cass be? Where in hell would I be if I hadn't never went
to school?"

He looked at McCaslin again. He could feel his breath
coming shorter and shorter and shallower and shallower,
as if there were not enough air in the kitchen for that many
to breathe. "This is just Thursday. I'll come home Sunday
night on one of the horses. I'll come home Sunday, then.
I'll make up the time I lost studying Sunday night. Mc-
Caslin," he said, without even despair.

"No, I tell you," McCaslin said. "Sit down here and eat
your supper. We're going out to—"

"Hold up, Cass," General Compson said. The boy did
not know General Compson had moved until he put his
hand on his shoulder. "What is it, bud?" he said.

"I've got to stay," he said. "I've got to."

"All right," General Compson said. "You can stay. If
missing an extra week of school is going to throw you so
far behind you'll have to sweat to find out what some hired
pedagogue put between the covers of a book, you better
quit altogether.—And you shut up, Cass," he said, though
McCaslin had not spoken. "You've got one foot straddled
into a farm and the other foot straddled into a bank; you
aint even got a good hand-hold where this boy was already
an old man long before you damned Sartorises and Ed-
mondses invented farms and banks to keep yourselves from
having to find out what this boy was born knowing and
fearing too maybe but without being afraid, that could go
ten miles on a compass because he wanted to look at a bear
none of us had ever got near enough to put a bullet in and
looked at the bear and came the ten miles back on the

compass in the dark; maybe by God that's the why and the wherefore of farms and banks.—I reckon you still aint going to tell what it is?"

But still he could not. "I've got to stay," he said.

"All right," General Compson said. "There's plenty of grub left. And you'll come home Sunday, like you promised McCaslin? Not Sunday night: Sunday."

"Yes, sir," he said.

"All right," General Compson said. "Sit down and eat, boys," he said. "Let's get started. It's going to be cold before we get home."

They ate. The wagon was already loaded and ready to depart; all they had to do was to get into it. Boon would drive them out to the road, to the farmer's stable where the surrey had been left. He stood beside the wagon, in silhouette on the sky, turbaned like a Paythan and taller than any there, the bottle tilted. Then he flung the bottle from his lips without even lowering it, spinning and glinting in the faint starlight, empty. "Them that's going," he said, "get in the goddamn wagon. Them that aint, get out of the goddamn way." The others got in. Boon mounted to the seat beside General Compson and the wagon moved, on into the obscurity until the boy could no longer see it, even the moving density of it amid the greater night. But he could still hear it, for a long while: the slow, deliberate banging of the wooden frame as it lurched from rut to rut. And he could hear Boon even when he could no longer hear the wagon. He was singing, harsh, tuneless, loud.

That was Thursday. On Saturday morning Tennie's Jim left on McCaslin's woods-horse which had not been out of the bottom one time now in six years, and late that afternoon rode through the gate on the spent horse and on to the commissary where McCaslin was rationing the tenants and the wage-hands for the coming week, and this time McCaslin forestalled any necessity or risk of having to wait while Major de Spain's surrey was being horsed and harnessed. He took their own, and with Tennie's Jim

already asleep in the back seat he drove in to Jefferson
and waited while Major de Spain changed to boots and
put on his overcoat, and they drove the thirty miles in the
dark of that night and at daybreak on Sunday morning
they swapped to the waiting mare and mule and as the
sun rose they rode out of the jungle and onto the low ridge
where they had buried Lion: the low mound of unan-
nealed earth where Boon's spade-marks still showed and
beyond the grave the platform of freshly cut saplings
bound between four posts and the blanket-wrapped bundle upon the platform and Boon and the boy squatting
between the platform and the grave until Boon, the bandage removed, ripped, from his head so that the long scoriations of Old Ben's claws resembled crusted tar in the sunlight, sprang up and threw down upon them with the old
gun with which he had never been known to hit anything
although McCaslin was already off the mule, kicked both
feet free of the irons and vaulted down before the mule
had stopped, walking toward Boon.

"Stand back," Boon said. "By God, you wont touch him.
Stand back, McCaslin." Still McCaslin came on, fast yet
without haste.

"Cass!" Major de Spain said. Then he said "Boon! You,
Boon!" and he was down too and the boy rose too, quickly,
and still McCaslin came on not fast but steady and walked
up to the grave and reached his hand steadily out, quickly
yet still not fast, and took hold the gun by the middle so
that he and Boon faced one another across Lion's grave,
both holding the gun, Boon's spent indomitable amazed
and frantic face almost a head higher than McCaslin's beneath the black scoriations of beast's claws and then Boon's
chest began to heave as though there were not enough air
in all the woods, in all the wilderness, for all of them, for
him and anyone else, even for him alone.

"Turn it loose, Boon," McCaslin said.

"You damn little spindling—" Boon said. "Dont you
know I can take it away from you? Dont you know I can

tie it around your neck like a damn cravat?"

"Yes," McCaslin said. "Turn it loose, Boon."

"This is the way he wanted it. He told us. He told us exactly how to do it. And by God you aint going to move him. So we did it like he said, and I been sitting here ever since to keep the damn wildcats and varmints away from him and by God—" Then McCaslin had the gun, down-slanted while he pumped the slide, the five shells snicking out of it so fast that the last one was almost out before the first one touched the ground and McCaslin dropped the gun behind him without once having taken his eyes from Boon's.

"Did you kill him, Boon?" he said. Then Boon moved. He turned, he moved like he was still drunk and then for a moment blind too, one hand out as he blundered toward the big tree and seemed to stop walking before he reached the tree so that he plunged, fell toward it, flinging up both hands and catching himself against the tree and turning until his back was against it, backing with the tree's trunk his wild spent scoriated face and the tremendous heave and collapse of his chest, McCaslin following, facing him again, never once having moved his eyes from Boon's eyes. "Did you kill him, Boon?"

"No!" Boon said. "No!"

"Tell the truth," McCaslin said. "I would have done it if he had asked me to." Then the boy moved. He was between them, facing McCaslin; the water felt as if it had burst and sprung not from his eyes alone but from his whole face, like sweat.

"Leave him alone!" he cried. "Goddamn it! Leave him alone!"

—4—

Then he was twenty-one. He could say it, himself and his cousin juxtaposed not against the wilderness but against the tamed land which was to have been his heritage, the land which old Carothers McCaslin his grandfather had bought with white man's money from the wild men whose grandfathers without guns hunted it, and tamed and ordered or believed he had tamed and ordered it for the reason that the human beings he held in bondage and in the power of life and death had removed the forest from it and in their sweat scratched the surface of it to a depth of perhaps fourteen inches in order to grow something out of it which had not been there before and which could be translated back into the money he who believed he had bought it had had to pay to get it and hold it and a reasonable profit too: and for which reason old Carothers McCaslin, knowing better, could raise his children, his descendants and heirs, to believe the land was his to hold and bequeath since the strong and ruthless man has a cynical foreknowledge of his own vanity and pride and strength and a contempt for all his get: just as, knowing better, Major de Spain and his fragment of that wilderness which was bigger and older than any recorded deed: just as, knowing better, old Thomas Sutpen, from whom Major de Spain had had his fragment for money: just as Ikkemotubbe, the Chickasaw chief, from whom Thomas Sutpen had had the fragment for money or rum or whatever it was, knew in his turn that not even a fragment of it had been his to relinquish or sell

not against the wilderness but against the land, not in pursuit and lust but in relinquishment, and in the commissary as it should have been, not the heart perhaps but certainly the solar-plexus of the repudiated and relinquished: the square, galleried, wooden building squatting like a portent above the fields whose laborers it still held in thrall '65 or no and placarded over with advertisements for snuff and cures for chills and salves and potions manufactured and sold by white men to bleach the pigment and straighten the hair of Negroes that they might resemble the very race which for two hundred years had held them in bondage and from which for another hundred years not even a bloody civil war would have set them completely free

himself and his cousin amid the old smells of cheese and salt meat and kerosene and harness, the ranked shelves of tobacco and overalls and bottled medicine and thread and plow-bolts, the barrels and kegs of flour and meal and molasses and nails, the wall pegs dependant with plowlines and plow-collars and hames and trace-chains, and the desk and the shelf above it on which rested the ledgers in which McCaslin recorded the slow outward trickle of food and supplies and equipment which returned each fall as cotton made and ginned and sold (two threads frail as truth and impalpable as equators yet cable-strong to bind for life them who made the cotton to the land their sweat fell on), and the older ledgers clumsy and archaic in size and shape, on the yellowed pages of which were recorded in the faded hand of his father Theophilus and his uncle Amodeus during the two decades before the Civil War, the manumission in title at least of Carothers McCaslin's slaves:

'Relinquish,' McCaslin said. 'Relinquish. You, the direct male descendant of him who saw the opportunity and took it, bought the land, took the land, got the land no matter how, held it to bequeath, no matter how, out of the old grant, the first patent, when it was a wilderness of wild beasts and wilder men, and cleared it, translated it into something to bequeath to his children, worthy of bequeathment for his descendants' ease and security and pride and to perpetuate his name and accomplishments. Not only the male descendant but the only and last descendant in the male line and in the third generation, while I am not only four generations from old Carothers, I derived through a woman and the very McCaslin in my name is mine only by sufferance and courtesy and my grandmother's pride in what that man accomplished whose legacy and monument you think you can repudiate.' and he

'I cant repudiate it. It was never mine to repudiate. It

was never Father's and Uncle Buddy's to bequeath me to
repudiate because it was never Grandfather's to bequeath
them to bequeath me to repudiate because it was never old
Ikkemotubbe's to sell to Grandfather for bequeathment
and repudiation. Because it was never Ikkemotubbe's fathers' fathers' to bequeath Ikkemotubbe to sell to Grandfather or any man because on the instant when Ikkemotubbe discovered, realised, that he could sell it for money,
on that instant it ceased ever to have been his forever, father to father to father, and the man who bought it bought
nothing.'

'Bought nothing?' and he

'Bought nothing. Because He told in the Book how He
created the earth, made it and looked at it and said it was
all right, and then He made man. He made the earth first
and peopled it with dumb creatures, and then He created
man to be His overseer on the earth and to hold suzerainty
over the earth and the animals on it in His name, not to
hold for himself and his descendants inviolable title forever, generation after generation, to the oblongs and
squares of the earth, but to hold the earth mutual and
intact in the communal anonymity of brotherhood, and
all the fee He asked was pity and humility and sufferance
and endurance and the sweat of his face for bread. And I
know what you are going to say,' he said: 'That nevertheless Grandfather—' and McCaslin

'—did own it. And not the first. Not alone and not the
first since, as your Authority states, man was dispossessed
of Eden. Nor yet the second and still not alone, on down
through the tedious and shabby chronicle of His chosen
sprung from Abraham, and of the sons of them who dispossessed Abraham, and of the five hundred years during
which half the known world and all it contained was chattel to one city as this plantation and all the life it contained
was chattel and revokeless thrall to this commissary store
and those ledgers yonder during your grandfather's life,
and the next thousand years while men fought over the

fragments of that collapse until at last even the fragments were exhausted and men snarled over the gnawed bones of the old world's worthless evening until an accidental egg discovered to them a new hemisphere. So let me say it: That nevertheless and notwithstanding old Carothers did own it. Bought it, got it, no matter; kept it, held it, no matter; bequeathed it: else why do you stand here relinquishing and repudiating? Held it, kept it for fifty years until you could repudiate it, while He—this Arbiter, this Architect, this Umpire—condoned—or did He? looked down and saw—or did He? Or at least did nothing: saw, and could not, or did not see; saw, and would not, or perhaps He would not see—perverse, impotent, or blind: which?' and he

'Dispossessed.' and McCaslin

'What?' and he

'Dispossessed. Not impotent: He didn't condone; not blind, because He watched it. And let me say it. Dispossessed of Eden. Dispossessed of Canaan, and those who dispossessed him dispossessed him dispossessed, and the five hundred years of absentee landlords in the Roman bagnios, and the thousand years of wild men from the northern woods who dispossessed them and devoured their ravished substance ravished in turn again and then snarled in what you call the old world's worthless twilight over the old world's gnawed bones, blasphemous in His name until He used a simple egg to discover to them a new world where a nation of people could be founded in humility and pity and sufferance and pride of one to another. And Grandfather did own the land nevertheless and notwithstanding because He permitted it, not impotent and not condoning and not blind because He ordered and watched it. He saw the land already accursed even as Ikkemotubbe and Ikkemotubbe's father old Issetibbeha and old Issetibbeha's fathers too held it, already tainted even before any white man owned it by what Grandfather and his kind, his fathers, had brought into the new land which He had vouchsafed them out of pity and sufferance, on condition of pity and humility and sufferance and endurance, from that old world's corrupt and worthless twilight as though in the sailfuls of the old world's tainted wind which drove the ships—' and McCaslin

'Ah.'

'—and no hope for the land anywhere so long as Ikkemotubbe and Ikkemotubbe's descendants held it in unbroken succession. Maybe He saw that only by voiding the land for a time of Ikkemotubbe's blood and substituting for it another blood, could He accomplish His purpose. Maybe He knew already what that other blood would be, maybe it was more than justice that only the white man's blood was available and capable to raise the white man's curse, more than vengeance when—' and McCaslin

'Ah.'

'—when He used the blood which had brought in the evil to destroy the evil as doctors use fever to burn up fever, poison to slay poison. Maybe He chose Grandfather out of all of them He might have picked. Maybe He knew that Grandfather himself would not serve His purpose because Grandfather was born too soon too, but that Grandfather would have descendants, the right descendants; maybe He had foreseen already the descendants Grandfather would have, maybe He saw already in Grandfather the seed progenitive of the three generations He saw it would take to set at least some of His lowly people free—' and McCaslin

'The sons of Ham. You who quote the Book: the sons of Ham.' and he

'There are some things He said in the Book, and some things reported of Him that He did not say. And I know what you will say now: That if truth is one thing to me and another thing to you, how will we choose which is truth? You dont need to choose. The heart already knows. He didn't have His Book written to be read by what must elect and choose, but by the heart, not by the wise of the earth because maybe they dont need it or maybe the wise no longer have any heart, but by the doomed and lowly of the earth who have nothing else to read with but the heart. Because the men who wrote His Book for Him were writing about truth and there is only one truth and it covers all things that touch the heart.' and McCaslin

'So these men who transcribed His Book for Him were sometime liars.' and he

'Yes. Because they were human men. They were trying to write down the heart's truth out of the heart's driving complexity, for all the complex and troubled hearts which would beat after them. What they were trying to tell, what He wanted said, was too simple. Those for whom they transcribed His words could not have believed them. It had to be expounded in the everyday terms which they were familiar with and could comprehend, not only those who listened but those who told it too, because if they who were that near to Him as to have been elected from among all who breathed and spoke language to transcribe and relay His words, could comprehend truth only through the complexity of passion and lust and hate and fear which drives the heart, what distance back to truth must they traverse whom truth could only reach by word-of-mouth?' and McCaslin

'I might answer that, since you have taken to proving your points and disproving mine by the same text, I dont know. But I dont say that, because you have answered yourself: No time at all if, as you say, the heart knows truth, the infallible and unerring heart. And perhaps you are right, since although you admitted three generations from old Carothers to you, there were not three. There were not even completely two. Uncle Buck and Uncle Buddy. And they not the first and not alone. A thousand other Bucks and Buddies in less than two generations and sometimes less than one in this land which so you claim God created and man himself cursed and tainted. Not to mention 1865.' and he

'Yes. More men than Father and Uncle Buddy,' not even glancing toward the shelf above the desk, nor did McCaslin. They did not need to. To him it was as though the ledgers in their scarred cracked leather bindings were being lifted down one by one in their fading sequence and spread open on the desk or perhaps upon some apocryphal Bench or even Altar or perhaps before the Throne Itself for a last perusal and contemplation and refreshment of the Allknowledgeable before the yellowed pages and the brown thin ink in which was recorded the injustice and a little at least of its amelioration and restitution faded back forever into the anonymous communal original dust

the yellowed pages scrawled in fading ink by the hand first of his grandfather and then of his father and uncle, bachelors up to and past fifty and then sixty, the one who ran the plantation and the farming of it and the other who did the housework and the cooking and continued to do it even after his twin married and the boy himself was born

the two brothers who as soon as their father was buried moved out of the tremendously-conceived, the almost barn-like edifice which he had not even completed, into a one-room log cabin which the two of them built themselves and added other rooms to while they lived in it, refusing to allow any slave to touch any timber of it other than the actual raising into place the logs which two men alone could not handle, and domiciled all the slaves in the big house some of the windows of which were still merely boarded up with odds and ends of plank or with the skins of bear and deer nailed over the empty frames: each sundown the brother who superintended the farming would parade the Negroes as a first sergeant dismisses a company, and herd them willynilly, man woman and child, without question protest or recourse, into the tremendous abortive edifice scarcely yet out of embryo, as if even old Carothers McCaslin had paused aghast at the concrete indication of his own vanity's boundless conceiving: he would call his mental roll and herd them in and with a hand-wrought nail as long as a flenching-knife and suspended from a short deer-hide thong attached to the door-jamb for that purpose, he would nail to the door of that house which lacked half its windows and had no hinged back door at all, so that presently and for fifty years afterward, when the boy himself was big to hear and remember it, there was in the land a sort of folk-tale: of the country-side all night long full of skulking McCaslin slaves dodging the moonlit roads and the Patrol-riders to visit other plantations, and of the unspoken gentlemen's agreement between the two white men and the two dozen black ones that, after the white man had counted them and driven the home-made nail into the front door at sundown, neither of the white men would go around behind the house and look at the back door, provided that all the Negroes were behind the front one when the brother who drove it drew out the nail again at daybreak

the twins who were identical even in their handwriting, unless you had specimens side by side to compare, and even when both hands appeared on the same page (as often happened, as if, long since past any oral intercourse, they had used the diurnally advancing pages to conduct the unavoidable business of the compulsion which had traversed all the waste wilderness of North Mississippi in 1830 and '40 and singled them out to drive) they both looked as though they had been written by the same perfectly normal ten-year-old boy, even to the spelling, except that the spelling did not improve as one by one the slaves which Carothers McCaslin had inherited and purchased— Roscius and Phoebe and Thucydides and Eunice and their descendants, and Sam Fathers and his mother for both of whom he had swapped an underbred trotting gelding to old Ikkemotubbe, the Chickasaw chief from whom he had likewise bought the land, and Tennie Beauchamp whom the twin Amodeus had won from a neighbor in a poker-game, and the anomaly calling itself Percival Brownlee which the twin Theophilus had purchased, neither he nor his brother ever knew why apparently, from Bedford Forrest while he was still only a slave-dealer and not yet a general (It was a single page, not long and covering less than a year, not seven months in fact, begun in the hand which the boy had learned to distinguish as that of his father:

> *Percavil Brownly 26yr Old. cleark @ Bookepper. bought from N.B.Forest at Cold Water 3 Mar 1856 $265. dolars*

and beneath that, in the same hand:

> *5 mar 1856 No bookepper any way Cant read. Can write his Name but I already put that down My self Says he can Plough but dont look like it to Me. sent to Feild to day Mar 5 1856*

and the same hand:

> *6 Mar 1856 Cant plough either Says he aims to be a Precher so may be he can lead live stock to Crick to Drink*

and this time it was the other, the hand which he now recognised as his uncle's when he could see them both on the same page:

> *Mar 23th 1856 Cant do that either Except one at a Time Get shut of him*

then the first again:

> *24 Mar 1856 Who in hell would buy him*

then the second:

> *19th of Apr 1856 Nobody You put yourself out of Market at Cold Water two months ago I never said sell him Free him*

the first:

22 Apr 1856 Ill get it out of him

the second:

Jun 13th 1856 How $1 per yr 265$ 265 yrs Wholl sign his Free paper

then the first again:

1 Oct 1856 Mule josephine Broke Leg @ shot Wrong stall wrong niger wrong everything $100. dolars

and the same:

2 Oct 1856 Freed Debit McCaslin @ McCaslin $265. dolars

then the second again:

Oct 3th Debit Theophilus McCaslin Niger 265$ Mule 100$ 365$ He hasnt gone yet Father should be here

then the first:

3 Oct 1856 Son of a bitch wont leave What would father done

the second:

29th of Oct 1856 Renamed him

the first:

31 Oct 1856 Renamed him what

the second:

Chrstms 1856 Spintrius

) took substance and even a sort of shadowy life with their passions and complexities too as page followed page and year year; all there, not only the general and condoned injustice and its slow amortization but the specific tragedy which had not been condoned and could never be amortized, the new page and the new ledger, the hand which he could now recognise at first glance as his father's:

> *Father dide Lucius Quintus Carothers McCaslin, Cal-*
> *lina 1772 Missippy 1837. Dide and burid 27 June*
> *1837*
> *Roskus. rased by Granfather in Callina Dont know*
> *how old. Freed 27 June 1837 Dont want to leave. Dide*
> *and Burid 12 Jan 1841*
> *Fibby Roskus Wife. bought by granfather in Callina*
> *says Fifty Freed 27 June 1837 Dont want to leave.*
> *Dide and burd 1 Aug 1849*
> *Thucydus Roskus @ Fibby Son born in Callina 1779.*
> *Refused 10acre peace fathers Will 28 June 1837 Re-*
> *fused Cash offer $200. dolars from A.@ T. McCaslin*
> *28 Jun 1837 Wants to stay and work it out*

and beneath this and covering the next five pages and almost that many years, the slow, day-by-day accruement of
the wages allowed him and the food and clothing—the
molasses and meat and meal, the cheap durable shirts and
jeans and shoes and now and then a coat against rain and
cold—charged against the slowly yet steadily mounting sum
of balance (and it would seem to the boy that he could
actually see the black man, the slave whom his white owner had forever manumitted by the very act from which the
black man could never be free so long as memory lasted,
entering the commissary, asking permission perhaps of
the white man's son to see the ledger-page which he could
not even read, not even asking for the white man's word,
which he would have had to accept for the reason that
there was absolutely no way under the sun for him to test
it, as to how the account stood, how much longer before
he could go and never return, even if only as far as Jefferson seventeen miles away) on to the double pen-stroke
closing the final entry:

> *3 Nov 1841 By Cash to Thucydus McCaslin $200.*
> *dolars Set Up blaksmith in J. Dec 1841 Dide and*

> burid in J. 17 feb 1854
> Eunice Bought by Father in New Orleans 1807 $650.
> dolars. Marrid to Thucydus 1809 Drownd in Crick
> Cristmas Day 1832

and then the other hand appeared, the first time he had seen it in the ledger to distinguish it as his uncle's, the cook and housekeeper whom even McCaslin, who had known him and the boy's father for sixteen years before the boy was born, remembered as sitting all day long in the rocking chair from which he cooked the food, before the kitchen fire on which he cooked it:

> June 21th 1833 Drownd herself

and the first:

> 23 Jun 1833 Who in hell ever heard of a niger drownding him self

and the second, unhurried, with a complete finality; the two identical entries might have been made with a rubber stamp save for the date:

> Aug 13 1833 Drownd herself

and he thought *But why? But why?* He was sixteen then. It was neither the first time he had been alone in the commissary nor the first time he had taken down the old ledgers familiar on their shelf above the desk ever since he could remember. As a child and even after nine and ten and eleven, when he had learned to read, he would look up at the scarred and cracked backs and ends but with no particular desire to open them, and though he intended to examine them someday because he realised that they probably contained a chronological and much more comprehensive though doubtless tedious record than he would ever get from any other source, not alone of his own flesh and blood but of all his people, not only the whites but the black one too, who were as much a part of his ancestry

as his white progenitors, and of the land which they had
all held and used in common and fed from and on and
would continue to use in common without regard to color
or titular ownership, it would only be on some idle day
when he was old and perhaps even bored a little since what
the old books contained would be after all these years
fixed immutably, finished, unalterable, harmless. Then
he was sixteen. He knew what he was going to find before
he found it. He got the commissary key from McCaslin's
room after midnight while McCaslin was asleep and with
the commissary door shut and locked behind him and the
forgotten lantern stinking anew the rank dead icy air, he
leaned above the yellowed page and thought not Why
drowned herself, but thinking what he believed his father
had thought when he found his brother's first comment:
Why did Uncle Buddy think she had drowned herself?
finding, beginning to find on the next succeeding page
what he knew he would find, only this was still not it because he already knew this:

> Tomasina called Tomy Daughter of Thucydus @
> Eunice Born 1810 dide in Child bed June 1833 and
> Burd. Yr stars fell

nor the next:

> Turl Son of Thucydus @ Eunice Tomy born Jun
> 1833 yr stars fell Fathers will

and nothing more, no tedious recording filling this page
of wages day by day and food and clothing charged against
them, no entry of his death and burial because he had
outlived his white half-brothers and the books whichMc-
Caslin kept did not include obituaries: just *Fathers will*
and he had seen that too: old Carothers' bold cramped
hand far less legible than his sons' even and not much
better in spelling, who while capitalising almost every
noun and verb, made no effort to punctuate or construct
whatever, just as he made no effort either to explain or

obfuscate the thousand-dollar legacy to the son of an un-married slave-girl, to be paid only at the child's coming-of-age, bearing the consequence of the act of which there was still no definite incontrovertible proof that he ac-knowledged, not out of his own substance but penalising his sons with it, charging them a cash forfeit on the acci-dent of their own paternity; not even a bribe for silence toward his own fame since his fame would suffer only after he was no longer present to defend it, flinging almost contemptuously, as he might a cast-off hat or pair of shoes, the thousand dollars which could have had no more reality to him under those conditions than it would have to the Negro, the slave who would not even see it until he came of age, twenty-one years too late to begin to learn what money was. *So I reckon that was cheaper than saying My son to a nigger* he thought. *Even if My son wasn't but just two words. But there must have been love* he thought. *Some sort of love. Even what he would have called love: not just an afternoon's or a night's spittoon.* There was the old man, old, within five years of his life's end, long a wid-ower and, since his sons were not only bachelors but were approaching middleage, lonely in the house and doubtless even bored since his plantation was established now and functioning and there was enough money now, too much of it probably for a man whose vices even apparently re-mained below his means; there was the girl, husbandless and young, only twenty-three when the child was born: perhaps he had sent for her at first out of loneliness, to have a young voice and movement in the house, summoned her, bade her mother send her each morning to sweep the floors and make the beds and the mother acquiescing since that was probably already understood, already planned: the only child of a couple who were not field hands and who held themselves something above the other slaves not alone for that reason but because the husband and his father and mother too had been inherited by the white man from his father, and the white man himself had trav-

elled three hundred miles and better to New Orleans in a
day when men travelled by horseback or steamboat, and
bought the girl's mother as a wife for

and that was all. The old frail pages seemed to turn of
their own accord even while he thought *His own daughter
His own daughter. No No Not even him* back to that one
where the white man (not even a widower then) who
never went anywhere any more than his sons in their time
ever did and who did not need another slave, had gone all
the way to New Orleans and bought one. And Tomey's
Terrel was still alive when the boy was ten years old and
he knew from his own observation and memory that there
had already been some white in Tomey's Terrel's blood
before his father gave him the rest of it; and looking down
at the yellowed page spread beneath the yellow glow of
the lantern smoking and stinking in that rank chill midnight room fifty years later, he seemed to see her actually
walking into the icy creek on that Christmas day six months
before her daughter's and her lover's *(Her first lover's* he
thought. *Her first)* child was born, solitary, inflexible,
griefless, ceremonial, in formal and succinct repudiation
of grief and despair who had already had to repudiate belief and hope

that was all. He would never need look at the ledgers
again nor did he; the yellowed pages in their fading and
implacable succession were as much a part of his consciousness and would remain so forever, as the fact of his own
nativity:

> *Tennie Beauchamp 21yrs Won by Amodeus McCaslin
> from Hubert Beauchamp Esqre Possible Strait against
> three Treys in sigt Not called 1851 Marrid to Tomys
> Turl 1859*

and no date of freedom because her freedom, as well as that
of her first surviving child, derived not from Buck and
Buddy McCaslin in the commissary but from a stranger in
Washington and no date of death and burial, not only

because McCaslin kept no obituaries in his books, but because in this year 1883 she was still alive and would remain so to see a grandson by her last surviving child:

> *Amodeus McCaslin Beauchamp Son of tomys Turl @ Tennie Beauchamp 1859 dide 1859*

then his uncle's hand entire, because his father was now a member of the cavalry command of that man whose name as a slave-dealer he could not even spell: and not even a page and not even a full line:

> *Dauter Tomes Turl and tenny 1862*

and not even a line and not even a sex and no cause given though the boy could guess it because McCaslin was thirteen then and he remembered how there was not always enough to eat in more places than Vicksburg:

> *Child of tomes Turl and Tenny 1863*

and the same hand again and this one lived, as though Tennie's perseverance and the fading and diluted ghost of old Carothers' ruthlessness had at last conquered even starvation: and clearer, fuller, more carefully written and spelled than the boy had yet seen it, as if the old man, who should have been a woman to begin with, trying to run what was left of the plantation in his brother's absence in the intervals of cooking and caring for himself and the fourteen-year-old orphan, had taken as an omen for renewed hope the fact that this nameless inheritor of slaves was at least remaining alive long enough to receive a name:

> *James Thucydus Beauchamp Son of Tomes Turl and Tenny Beauchamp Born 29th december 1864 and both Well Wanted to call him Theophilus but Tride Amodeus McCaslin and Callina McCaslin and both dide so Disswaded Them Born at Two clock A,m, both Well*

but no more, nothing; it would be another two years yet

before the boy, almost a man now, would return from the
abortive trip into Tennessee with the still-intact third of
old Carothers' legacy to his Negro son and his descendants,
which as the three surviving children established at last
one by one their apparent intention of surviving, their
white half-uncles had increased to a thousand dollars each,
conditions permitting, as they came of age, and completed
the page himself as far as it would even be completed when
that day was long passed beyond which a man born in
1864 (or 1867 either, when he himself saw light) could
have expected or himself hoped or even wanted to be still
alive; his own hand now, queerly enough resembling neither his father's nor his uncle's nor even McCaslin's, but
like that of his grandfather's save for the spelling:

> *Vanished sometime on night of his twenty-first birth-
> day Dec 29 1885. Traced by Isaac McCaslin to Jackson
> Tenn. and there lost. His third of legacy $1000.00
> returned to McCaslin Edmonds Trustee this day Jan
> 12 1886*

but not yet: that would be two years yet, and now his father's again, whose old commander was now quit of sol-
diering and slave-trading both; once more in the ledger
and then not again and more illegible than ever, almost
indecipherable at all from the rheumatism which now
crippled him and almost completely innocent now even
of any sort of spelling as well as punctuation, as if the four
years during which he had followed the sword of the only
man ever breathing who ever sold him a Negro, let alone
beat him in a trade, had convinced him not only of the
vanity of faith and hope but of orthography too:

> *Miss sophonsiba b dtr t t @ t 1869*

but not of belief and will because it was there, written, as
McCaslin had told him, with the left hand, but there in
the ledger one time more and than not again, for the boy
himself was a year old, and when Lucas was born six years

later, his father and uncle had been dead inside the same twelve-months almost five years; his own hand again, who was there and saw it, 1886, she was just seventeen, two years younger than himself, and he was in the commissary when McCaslin entered out of the first of dusk and said, 'He wants to marry Fonsiba,' like that: and he looked past McCaslin and saw the man, the stranger, taller than McCaslin and wearing better clothes than McCaslin and most of the other white men the boy knew habitually wore, who entered the room like a white man and stood in it like a white man, as though he had let McCaslin precede him into it not because McCaslin's skin was white but simply because McCaslin lived there and knew the way, and who talked like a white man too, looking at him past McCaslin's shoulder rapidly and keenly once and then no more, without further interest, as a mature and contained white man not impatient but just pressed for time might have looked. 'Marry Fonsiba?' he cried. 'Marry Fonsiba?' and then no more either, just watching and listening while McCaslin and the Negro talked:

'To live in Arkansas, I believe you said.'

'Yes. I have property there. A farm.'

'Property? A farm? You own it?'

'Yes.'

'You dont say Sir, do you?'

'To my elders, yes.'

'I see. You are from the North.'

'Yes. Since a child.'

'Then your father was a slave.'

'Yes. Once.'

'Then how do you own a farm in Arkansas?'

'I have a grant. It was my father's. From the United States. For military service.'

'I see,' McCaslin said. 'The Yankee army.'

'The United States army,' the stranger said; and then himself again, crying it at McCaslin's back:

'Call aunt Tennie! I'll go get her! I'll—' But McCaslin

was not even including him; the stranger did not even
glance back toward his voice, the two of them speaking to
one another again as if he were not even there:

'Since you seem to have it all settled,' McCaslin said,
'why have you bothered to consult my authority at all?'

'I dont,' the stranger said. 'I acknowledge your authority
only so far as you admit your responsibility toward her as
a female member of the family of which you are the head.
I dont ask your permission. I—'

'That will do!' McCaslin said. But the stranger did not
falter. It was neither as if he were ignoring McCaslin nor
as if he had failed to hear him. It was as though he were
making, not at all an excuse and not exactly a justification,
but simply a statement which the situation absolutely re-
quired and demanded should be made in McCaslin's hearing whether McCaslin listened to it or not. It was as if he
were talking to himself, for himself to hear the words
spoken aloud. They faced one another, not close yet at
slightly less than foils' distance, erect, their voices not
raised, not impactive, just succinct:

'—I inform you, notify you in advance as chief of her
family. No man of honor could do less. Besides, you have,
in your way, according to your lights and upbringing—'

'That's enough, I said,' McCaslin said. 'Be off this place
by full dark. Go.' But for another moment the other did
not move, contemplating McCaslin with that detached
and heatless look, as if he were watching reflected in Mc-
Caslin's pupils the tiny image of the figure he was sustain-
ing.

'Yes,' he said. 'After all, this is your house. And in your
fashion you have. . . . But no matter. You are right. This
is enough.' He turned back toward the door; he paused
again but only for a second, already moving while he
spoke: 'Be easy. I will be good to her.' Then he was gone.

'But how did she ever know him?' the boy cried. 'I never
even heard of him before! And Fonsiba, that's never been
off this place except to go to church since she was born—'

'Ha,' McCaslin said. 'Even their parents dont know until too late how seventeen-year-old girls ever met the men
who marry them too, if they are lucky.' And the next morning they were both gone, Fonsiba too. McCaslin never saw
her again, nor did he, because the woman he found at last
five months later was no one he had ever known. He carried a third of the three-thousand-dollar fund in gold in
a money-belt, as when he had vainly traced Tennie's Jim
into Tennessee a year ago. They—the man—had left an
address of some sort with Tennie, and three months later
a letter came, written by the man although McCaslin's
wife Alice had taught Fonsiba to read and write too a little.
But it bore a different postmark from the address the man
had left with Tennie, and he travelled by rail as far as he
could and then by contracted stage and then by a hired
livery rig and then by rail again for a distance: an experienced traveller by now and an experienced bloodhound
too and a successful one this time because he would have
to be; as the slow interminable empty muddy December
miles crawled and crawled and night followed night in
hotels, in roadside taverns of rough logs and containing
little else but a bar, and in the cabins of strangers and the
hay of lonely barns, in none of which he dared undress
because of his secret golden girdle like that of a disguised
one of the Magi travelling incognito and not even hope to
draw him but only determination and desperation, he
would tell himself: *I will have to find her. I will have to.
We have already lost one of them. I will have to find her
this time.* He did. Hunched in the slow and icy rain, on a
spent hired horse splashed to the chest and higher, he saw
it—a single log edifice with a clay chimney which seemed
in process of being flattened by the rain to a nameless and
valueless rubble of dissolution in that roadless and even
pathless waste of unfenced fallow and wilderness jungle—
no barn, no stable, not so much as a hen-coop: just a log
cabin built by hand and no clever hand either, a meagre
pile of clumsily-cut firewood sufficient for about one day

and not even a gaunt hound to come bellowing out from
under the house when he rode up—a farm only in embryo,
perhaps a good farm, maybe even a plantation someday,
but not now, not for years yet and only then with labor,
hard and enduring and unflagging work and sacrifice; he
shoved open the crazy kitchen door in its awry frame and
entered an icy gloom where not even a fire for cooking
burned and after another moment saw, crouched into the
wall's angle behind a crude table, the coffee-colored face
which he had known all his life but knew no more, the
body which had been born within a hundred yards of the
room that he was born in and in which some of his own
blood ran but which was now completely inheritor of generation after generation to whom an unannounced white
man on a horse was a white man's hired Patroller wearing
a pistol sometimes and a blacksnake whip always; he entered the next room, the only other room the cabin owned,
and found, sitting in a rocking chair before the hearth, the
man himself, reading—sitting there in the only chair in
the house, before that miserable fire for which there was
not wood sufficient to last twenty-four hours, in the same
ministerial clothing in which he had entered the commissary five months ago and a pair of gold-framed spectacles
which, when he looked up and then rose to his feet, the
boy saw did not even contain lenses, reading a book in the
midst of that desolation, that muddy waste fenceless and
even pathless and without even a walled shed for stock to
stand beneath: and over all, permeant, clinging to the
man's very clothing and exuding from his skin itself, that
rank stink of baseless and imbecile delusion, that boundless rapacity and folly, of the carpet-bagger followers of
victorious armies.

'Dont you see?' he cried. 'Dont you see? This whole land,
the whole South, is cursed, and all of us who derive from
it, whom it ever suckled, white and black both, lie under
the curse? Granted that my people brought the curse onto
the land: maybe for that reason their descendants alone

can—not resist it, not combat it—maybe just endure and outlast it until the curse is lifted. Then your peoples' turn will come because we have forfeited ours. But not now. Not yet. Dont you see?'

The other stood now, the unfrayed garments still ministerial even if not quite so fine, the book closed upon one finger to keep the place, the lensless spectacles held like a music master's wand in the other workless hand while the owner of it spoke his measured and sonorous imbecility of the boundless folly and the baseless hope: 'You're wrong. The curse you whites brought into this land has been lifted. It has been voided and discharged. We are seeing a new era, an era dedicated, as our founders intended it, to freedom, liberty and equality for all, to which this country will be the new Canaan—'

'Freedom from what? From work? Canaan?' He jerked his arm, comprehensive, almost violent: whereupon it all seemed to stand there about them, intact and complete and visible in the drafty, damp, heatless, Negro-stale Negro-rank sorry room—the empty fields without plow or seed to work them, fenceless against the stock which did not exist within or without the walled stable which likewise was not there. 'What corner of Canaan is this?'

'You are seeing it at a bad time. This is winter. No man farms this time of year.'

'I see. And of course her need for food and clothing will stand still while the land lies fallow.'

'I have a pension,' the other said. He said it as a man might say *I have grace* or *I own a gold mine*. 'I have my father's pension too. It will arrive on the first of the month. What day is this?'

'The eleventh,' he said. 'Twenty days more. And until then?'

'I have a few groceries in the house from my credit account with the merchant in Midnight who banks my pension check for me. I have executed to him a power of attorney to handle it for me as a matter of mutual—'

'I see. And if the groceries dont last the twenty days?"
'I still have one more hog.'
'Where?'
'Outside,' the other said. 'It is customary in this country to allow stock to range free during the winter for food. It comes up from time to time. But no matter if it doesn't; I can probably trace its footprints when the need—'
'Yes!' he cried. 'Because no matter: you still have the pension check. And the man in Midnight will cash it and pay himself out of it for what you have already eaten and if there is any left over, it is yours. And the hog will be eaten by then or you still cant catch it, and then what will you do?'
'It will be almost spring then,' the other said. 'I am planning in the spring—'
'It will be January,' he said. 'And then February. And then more than half of March—' and when he stopped again in the kitchen she had not moved, she did not even seem to breathe or to be alive except her eyes watching him; when he took a step toward her it was still not movement because she could have retreated no further: only the tremendous fathomless ink-colored eyes in the narrow, thin, too thin coffee-colored face watching him without alarm, without recognition, without hope. 'Fonsiba,' he said. 'Fonsiba. Are you all right?'
'I'm free,' she said. Midnight was a tavern, a livery stable, a big store (that would be where the pension check banked itself as a matter of mutual elimination of bother and fret, he thought) and a little one, a saloon and a blacksmith shop. But there was a bank there too. The president (the owner, for all practical purposes) of it was a translated Mississippian who had been one of Forrest's men too: and his body lightened of the golden belt for the first time since he left home eight days ago, with pencil and paper he multiplied three dollars by twelve months and divided it into one thousand dollars; it would stretch that way over almost twenty-eight years and for twenty-eight

years at least she would not starve, the banker promising to send the three dollars himself by a trusty messenger on the fifteenth of each month and put it into her actual hand, and he returned home and that was all because in 1874 his father and his uncle were both dead and the old ledgers never again came down from the shelf above the desk to which his father had returned them for the last time that day in 1869. But he could have completed it:

> *Lucas Quintus Carothers McCaslin Beauchamp. Last surviving son and child of Tomey's Terrel and Tennie Beauchamp. March 17, 1874*

except that there was no need: not *Lucius Quintus @c @c @c,* but *Lucas Quintus,* not refusing to be called Lucius, because he simply eliminated that word from the name; not denying, declining the name itself, because he used three quarters of it; but simply taking the name and changing, altering it, making it no longer the white man's but his own, by himself composed, himself selfprogenitive and nominate, by himself ancestored, as, for all the old ledgers recorded to the contrary, old Carothers himself was

and that was all: 1874 the boy; 1888 the man, repudiated denied and free; 1895 and husband but no father, unwidowered but without a wife, and found long since that no man is ever free and probably could not bear it if he were; married then and living in Jefferson in the little new jerry-built bungalow which his wife's father had given them: and one morning Lucas stood suddenly in the doorway of the room where he was reading the Memphis paper and he looked at the paper's dateline and thought *It's his birthday. He's twenty-one today* and Lucas said: 'Whar's the rest of that money old Carothers left? I wants it. All of it.'

that was all: and McCaslin

'More men than that one Buck and Buddy to fumbleheed that truth so mazed for them that spoke it and so confused for them that heard yet still there was 1865:' and he

'But not enough. Not enough of even Father and Uncle Buddy to fumble-heed in even three generations not even three generations fathered by Grandfather not even if there had been nowhere beneath His sight any but Grandfather and so He would not even have needed to elect and choose. But He tried and I know what you will say. That having Himself created them He could have known no more of hope than He could have pride and grief but He didn't hope He just waited because He had made them: not just because He had set them alive and in motion but because He had already worried with them so long: worried with them so long because He had seen how in individual cases they were capable of anything any height or depth remembered in mazed incomprehension out of heaven where hell was created too and so He must admit them or else admit His equal somewhere and so be no longer God and therefore must accept responsibility for what He Himself had done in order to live with Himself in His lonely and paramount heaven. And He probably knew it was vain but He had created them and knew them capable of all things because He had shaped them out of the primal Absolute which contained all and had watched them since in their individual exaltation and baseness and they themselves not knowing why nor how nor even when: until at last He saw that they were all Grandfather all of them and that even from them the elected and chosen the best the very best. He could expect (not hope mind: not hope) would be Bucks and Buddies and not even enough of them and in the third generation not even Bucks and Buddies but—' and McCaslin

'Ah:' and he

'Yes. If He could see Father and Uncle Buddy in Grandfather He must have seen me too. —an Isaac born into a later life than Abraham's and repudiating immolation: fatherless and therefore safe declining the altar because maybe this time the exasperated Hand might not supply the kid—' and McCaslin

'Escape:' and he

'All right. Escape.—Until one day He said what you told
Fonsiba's husband that afternoon here in this room: *This
will do. This is enough:* not in exasperation or rage or
even just sick to death as you were sick that day: just *This
is enough* and looked about for one last time, for one time
more since He had created them, upon this land this
South for which He had done so much with woods for
game and streams for fish and deep rich soil for seed and
lush springs to sprout it and long summers to mature it
and serene falls to harvest it and short mild winters for
men and animals and saw no hope anywhere and looked
beyond it where hope should have been, where to East
North and West lay illimitable that whole hopeful continent dedicated as a refuge and sanctuary of liberty and
freedom from what you called the old world's worthless
evening and saw the rich descendants of slavers, females
of both sexes, to whom the black they shrieked of was
another specimen another example like the Brazilian ma-
caw brought home in a cage by a traveller, passing resolu-
tions about horror and outrage in warm and air-proof
halls: and the thundering cannonade of politicians earning votes and the medicine-shows of pulpiteers earning
Chautauqua fees, to whom the outrage and the injustice
were as much abstractions as Tariff or Silver or Immortality and who employed the very shackles of its servitude
and the sorry rags of its regalia as they did the other beer
and banners and mottoes redfire and brimstone and
sleight-of-hand and musical handsaws: and the whirling
wheels which manufactured for a profit the pristine re-
placements of the shackles and shoddy garments as they
wore out and spun the cotton and made the gins which
ginned it and the cars and ships which hauled it, and the
men who ran the wheels for that profit and established
and collected the axes it was taxed with and the rates for
hauling it and the commissions for selling it: and He
could have repudiated them since they were his creation

now and forever more throughout all their generations
until not only that old world from which He had rescued
them but this new one too which He had revealed and
led them to as a sanctuary and refuge were become the
same worthless tideless rock cooling in the last crimson
evening except that out of all that empty sound and bootless fury one silence, among that loud and moiling all of
them just one simple enough to believe that horror and
outrage were first and last simply horror and outrage and
was crude enough to act upon that, illiterate and had no
words for talking or perhaps was just busy and had no
time to, one out of them all who did not bother Him
with cajolery and adjuration then pleading then threat
and had not even bothered to inform Him in advance
what he was about so that a lesser than He might have
even missed the simple act of lifting the long ancestral
musket down from the deerhorns above the door, whereupon He said *My name is Brown too* and the other *So is
mine* and He *Then mine or yours cant be because I am
against it* and the other *So am I* and He triumphantly
Then where are you going with that gun? and the other
told him in one sentence one word and He: amazed: Who
knew neither hope nor pride nor grief *But your Associa-
tion, your Committee, your Officers. Where are your Minutes, your Motions, your Parliamentary Procedures?* and
the other *I aint against them. They are all right I reckon
for them that have the time. I am just against the weak because they are niggers being held in bondage by the strong
just because they are white.* So He turned once more to
this land which He still intended to save because He had
done so much for it—' and McCaslin

'What?' and he

'—to these people He was still committed to because
they were his creations—' and McCaslin

'Turned back to us? His face to us?' and he

'—whose wives and daughters at least made soups and
jellies for them when they were sick and carried the trays

through the mud and the winter too into the stinking cabins and sat in the stinking cabins and kept fires going until crises came and passed but that was not enough: and when they were very sick had them carried into the big house itself into the company room itself maybe and nursed them there which the white man would have done too for any other of his cattle that was sick but at least the man who hired one from a livery wouldn't have and still that was not enough: so that He said and not in grief either Who had made them and so could know no more of grief than He could of pride or hope: *Apparently they can learn nothing save through suffering, remember nothing save when underlined in blood—'* and McCaslin

'Ashby on an afternoon's ride, to call on some remote maiden cousins of his mother or maybe just acquaintances of hers, comes by chance upon a minor engagement of outposts and dismounts and with his crimson-lined cloak for target leads a handful of troops he never saw before against an entrenched position of backwoods-trained riflemen. Lee's battle-order, wrapped maybe about a handful of cigars and doubtless thrown away when the last cigar was smoked, found by a Yankee Intelligence officer on the floor of a saloon behind the Yankee lines after Lee had already divided his forces before Sharpsburg. Jackson on the Plank Road, already rolled up the flank which Hooker believed could not be turned and, waiting only for night to pass to continue the brutal and incessant slogging which would fling that whole wing back into Hooker's lap where he sat on a front gallery in Chancellorsville drinking rum toddies and telegraphing Lincoln that he had defeated Lee, is shot from among a whole covey of minor officers and in the blind night by one of his own patrols, leaving as next by seniority Stuart that gallant man born apparently already horsed and sabred and already knowing all there was to know about war except the slogging and brutal stupidity of it: and that same Stuart off raiding Pennsylvania hen-roosts when

Lee should have known of all of Meade just where Hancock was on Cemetery Ridge: and Longstreet too at Gettysburg and that same Longstreet shot out of saddle by his own men in the dark by mistake just as Jackson was. His face to us? His face to us?' and he

'How else have made them fight? Who else but Jacksons and Stuarts and Ashbys and Morgans and Forrests?—the farmers of the central and middle-west, holding land by the acre instead of the tens or maybe even the hundreds, farming it themselves and to no single crop of cotton or tobacco or cane, owning no slaves and needing and wanting none and already looking toward the Pacific coast, not always as long as two generations there and having stopped where they did stop only through the fortuitous mischance that an ox died or a wagon-axle broke. And the New England mechanics who didn't even own land and measured all things by the weight of water and the cost of turning wheels and the narrow fringe of traders and ship-owners still looking backward across the Atlantic and attached to the continent only by their counting-houses. And those who should have had the alertness to see: the wildcat manipulators of mythical wilderness townsites; and the astuteness to rationalise: the bankers who held the mortgages on the land which the first were only waiting to abandon and on the railroads and steamboats to carry them still further west, and on the factories and the wheels and the rented tenements those who ran them lived in; and the leisure and scope to comprehend and fear in time and even anticipate: the Boston-bred (even when not born in Boston) spinster descendants of long lines of similarly-bred and likewise spinster aunts and uncles whose hands knew no callus except that of the indicting pen, to whom the wilderness itself began at the top of tide and who looked, if at anything other than Beacon Hill, only toward heaven—not to mention all the loud rabble of the camp-followers of pioneers: the bellowing of politicians, the mellifluous choiring of self-styled men of God, the—' and

McCaslin

'Here, here. Wait a minute:' and he

'Let me talk now. I'm trying to explain to the head of my family something which I have got to do which I dont quite understand myself, not in justification of it but to explain it if I can. I could say I dont know why I must do it but that I do know I have got to because I have got myself to have to live with for the rest of my life and all I want is peace to do it in. But you are the head of my family. More. I knew a long time ago that I would never have to miss my father, even if you are just finding out that you have missed your son.—the drawers of bills and the shavers of notes and the schoolmasters and the self-ordained to teach and lead and all that horde of the semi-literate with a white shirt but no change for it, with one eye on themselves and watching each other with the other one. Who else could have made them fight: could have struck them so aghast with fear and dread as to turn shoulder to shoulder and face one way and even stop talking for a while and even after two years of it keep them still so wrung with terror that some among them would seriously propose moving their very capital into a foreign country lest it be ravaged and pillaged by a people whose entire white male population would have little more than filled any one of their larger cities: except Jackson in the Valley and three separate armies trying to catch him and none of them ever knowing whether they were just retreating from a battle or just running into one and Stuart riding his whole command entirely around the biggest single armed force this continent ever saw in order to see what it looked like from behind and Morgan leading a cavalry charge against a stranded man-of-war. Who else could have declared a war against a power with ten times the area and a hundred times the men and a thousand times the resources, except men who could believe that all necessary to conduct a successful war was not acumen nor shrewdness nor politics nor diplomacy nor money nor even integrity and simple arithmetic but just love of land and courage—'

'And an unblemished and gallant ancestry and the ability to ride a horse,' McCaslin said. 'Dont leave that out.' It was evening now, the tranquil sunset of October mazy with windless woodsmoke. The cotton was long since picked and ginned, and all day now the wagons loaded with gathered corn moved between field and crib, processional across the enduring land. 'Well, maybe that's what He wanted. At least, that's what He got.' This time there was no yellowed procession of fading and harmless ledger-pages. This was chronicled in a harsher book and McCaslin, fourteen and fifteen and sixteen, had seen it and the boy himself had inherited it as Noah's grandchildren had inherited the Flood although they had not been there to see the deluge: that dark corrupt and bloody time while three separate peoples had tried to adjust not only to one another but to the new land which they had created and inherited too and must live in for the reason that those who had lost it were no less free to quit it than those who had gained it were:—those upon whom freedom and equality had been dumped overnight and without warning or preparation or any training in how to employ it or even just endure it and who misused it not as children would nor yet because they had been so long in bondage and then so suddenly freed, but misused it as human beings always misuse freedom, so that he thought *Apparently there is a wisdom beyond even that learned through suffering necessary for a man to distinguish between liberty and license;* those who had fought for four years and lost to preserve a condition under which that franchisement was anomaly and paradox, not because they were opposed to freedom as freedom but for the old reasons for which man (not the generals and politicians but man) has always fought and died in wars: to preserve a status quo or to establish a better future one to endure for his children; and lastly, as if that were not enough for bitterness and hatred and fear, that third race even more alien to the people whom they resembled in pigment and in whom even the same blood ran, than to the people whom they did not,—that race three-fold in one and alien even among themselves save for a single fierce will for rapine and pillage, composed of the sons of middleaged Quartermaster lieutenants and Army sutlers and contractors in military blankets and shoes and transport mules, who followed the battles they themselves had not fought and inherited the conquest they themselves had not helped to gain, sanctioned and protected even if not blessed, and left their bones and in another generation would be engaged in a fierce economic competition of small sloven farms with the black men they were supposed to have freed and the white descendants of fathers who had owned no slaves anyway whom they were supposed to have disinherited and in the third generation would be back once more in the little lost county seats as barbers and garage mechanics and deputy sheriffs and mill- and gin-hands and powerplant firemen, leading, first in mufti then later in an actual formalised regalia of hooded sheets and passwords and fiery christian symbols, lynching mobs against the race their ancestors had come to save: and of all that other nameless horde of speculators in human misery, manipulators of money and politics and land, who follow catastrophe and are their own protection as grasshoppers are and need no blessing and sweat no plow or axe-helve and batten and vanish and leave no bones, just as they derived apparently from no ancestry, no mortal flesh, no act even of passion or even of lust: and the Jew who came without protection too since after two thousand years he had got out of the habit of being or needing it, and solitary, without even the solidarity of the locusts and in this a sort of courage since he had come thinking not in terms of simple pillage but in terms of his great-grandchildren, seeking yet some place to establish them to endure even though forever alien: and unblessed: a pariah about the face of the Western earth which twenty centuries later was still

taking revenge on him for the fairy tale with which he had
conquered it. McCaslin had actually seen it, and the boy
even at almost eighty would never be able to distinguish
certainly between what he had seen and what had been
told him: a lightless and gutted and empty land where
women crouched with the huddled children behind locked
doors and men armed in sheets and masks rode the silent
roads and the bodies of white and black both, victims not
so much of hate as of desperation and despair, swung from
lonely limbs: and men shot dead in polling-booths with
the still wet pen in one hand and the unblotted ballot in
the other: and a United States marshal in Jefferson who
signed his official papers with a crude cross, an ex-slave
called Sickymo, not at all because his ex-owner was a doctor
and apothecary but because, still a slave, he would steal
his master's grain alcohol and dilute it with water and
peddle it in pint bottles from a cache beneath the roots
of a big sycamore tree behind the drug store, who had attained his high office because his half-white sister was the
concubine of the Federal A.P.M.: and this time McCaslin
did not even say Look but merely lifted one hand, not
even pointing, not even specifically toward the shelf of
ledgers but toward the desk, toward the corner where it
sat beside the scuffed patch on the floor where two decades
of heavy shoes had stood while the white man at the desk
added and multiplied and subtracted. And again he did
not need to look because he had seen this himself and,
twenty-three years after the Surrender and twenty-four
after the Proclamation, was still watching it: the ledgers,
new ones now and filled rapidly, succeeding one another
rapidly and containing more names than old Carothers
or even his father and Uncle Buddy had ever dreamed of;
new names and new faces to go with them, among which
the old names and faces that even his father and uncle
would have recognised, were lost, vanished—Tomey's Terrel dead, and even the tragic and miscast Percival Brownlee, who couldn't keep books and couldn't farm either,

found his true niche at last, reappeared in 1862 during the
boy's father's absence and had apparently been living on
the plantation for at least a month before his uncle found
out about it, conducting impromptu revival meetings
among Negroes, preaching and leading the singing also
in his high sweet true soprano voice and disappeared
again on foot and at top speed, not behind but ahead of a
body of raiding Federal horse and reappeared for the
third and last time in the entourage of a travelling Army
paymaster, the two of them passing through Jefferson in
a surrey at the exact moment when the boy's father (it
was 1866) also happened to be crossing the Square, the
surrey and its occupants traversing rapidly that quiet and
bucolic scene and even in that fleeting moment and to
others beside the boy's father giving an illusion of flight
and illicit holiday like a man on an excursion during his
wife's absence with his wife's personal maid, until Brownlee glanced up and saw his late co-master and gave him
one defiant female glance and then broke again, leaped
from the surrey and disappeared this time for good and
it was only by chance that McCaslin, twenty years later,
heard of him again, an old man now and quite fat, as the
well-to-do proprietor of a select New Orleans brothel;
and Tennie's Jim gone, nobody knew where, and Fonsiba
in Arkansas with her three dollars each month and the
scholar-husband with his lensless spectacles and frock coat
and his plans for the spring; and only Lucas was left, the
baby, the last save himself of old Carothers' doomed and
fatal blood which in the male derivation seemed to destroy all it touched, and even he was repudiating and at
least hoping to escape it;—Lucas, the boy of fourteen whose
name would not even appear for six years yet among those
rapid pages in the bindings new and dustless too since
McCaslin lifted them down daily now to write into them
the continuation of that record which two hundred years
had not been enough to complete and another hundred
would not be enough to discharge; that chronicle which

was a whole land in miniature, which multiplied and
compounded was the entire South, twenty-three years after
surrender and twenty-four from emancipation—that slow
trickle of molasses and meal and meat, of shoes and straw
hats and overalls, of plowlines and collars and heel-bolts
and buckheads and clevises, which returned each fall as
cotton—the two threads frail as truth and impalpable as
equators yet cable-strong to bind for life them who made
the cotton to the land their sweat fell on: and he

'Yes. Binding them for a while yet, a little while yet.
Through and beyond that life and maybe through and
beyond the life of that life's sons and maybe even through
and beyond that of the sons of those sons. But not always,
because they will endure. They will outlast us because they
are—' it was not a pause, barely a falter even, possibly appreciable only to himself, as if he couldn't speak even to
McCaslin, even to explain his repudiation, that which to
him too, even in the act of escaping (and maybe this was
the reality and the truth of his need to escape) was heresy:
so that even in escaping he was taking with him more of
that evil and unregenerate old man who could summon,
because she was his property, a human being because she
was old enough and female, to his widower's house and
get a child on her and then dismiss her because she was of
an inferior race, and then bequeath a thousand dollars
to the infant because he would be dead then and wouldn't
have to pay it, than even he had feared. 'Yes. He didn't
want to. He had to. Because they will endure. They are
better than we are. Stronger than we are. Their vices are
vices aped from white men or that white men and bondage
have taught them: improvidence and intemperance and
evasion—not laziness: evasion: of what white men had set
them to, not for their aggrandisement or even comfort
but his own—' and McCaslin

'All right. Go on: Promiscuity. Violence. Instability
and lack of control. Inability to distinguish between mine
and thine—' and he

'How distinguish, when for two hundred years mine did not even exist for them?' and McCaslin

'All right. Go on. And their virtues—' and he

'Yes. Their own. Endurance—' and McCaslin

'So have mules:' and he

'—and pity and tolerance and forbearance and fidelity and love of children—' and McCaslin

'So have dogs:' and he

'—whether their own or not or black or not. And more: what they got not only not from white people but not even despite white people because they had it already from the old free fathers a longer time free than us because we have never been free—' and it was in McCaslin's eyes too, he had only to look at McCaslin's eyes and it was there, that summer twilight seven years ago, almost a week after they had returned from the camp before he discovered that Sam Fathers had told McCaslin: an old bear, fierce and ruthless not just to stay alive but ruthless with the fierce pride of liberty and freedom, jealous and proud enough of liberty and freedom to see it threatened not with fear nor even alarm but almost with joy, seeming deliberately to put it into jeopardy in order to savor it and keep his old strong bones and flesh supple and quick to defend and preserve it; an old man, son of a Negro slave and an Indian king, inheritor on the one hand of the long chronicle of a people who had learned humility through suffering and learned pride through the endurance which survived the suffering, and on the other side the chronicle of a people even longer in the land than the first, yet who now existed there only in the solitary brotherhood of an old and childless Negro's alien blood and the wild and invincible spirit of an old bear; a boy who wished to learn humility and pride in order to become skillful and worthy in the woods but found himself becoming so skillful so fast that he feared he would never become worthy because he had not learned humility and pride though he had tried, until one day an old man who could not have de-

fined either led him as though by the hand to where an
old bear and a little mongrel dog showed him that, by possessing one thing other, he would possess them both; and
a little dog, nameless and mongrel and many-fathered,
grown yet weighing less than six pounds, who couldn't be
dangerous because there was nothing anywhere much
smaller, not fierce because that would have been called
just noise, not humble because it was already too near the
ground to genuflect, and not proud because it would not
have been close enough for anyone to discern what was
casting that shadow and which didn't even know it was
not going to heaven since they had already decided it had
no immortal soul, so that all it could be was brave even
though they would probably call that too just noise. *'And
you didn't shoot,' McCaslin said. 'How close were you?'*

*'I dont know,' he said. 'There was a big wood tick just
inside his off hind leg. I saw that. But I didn't have the
gun then.'*

*'But you didn't shoot when you had the gun,' McCaslin
said. 'Why?' But McCaslin didn't wait, rising and crossing
the room, across the pelt of the bear he had killed two
years ago and the bigger one McCaslin had killed before
he was born, to the bookcase beneath the mounted head
of his first buck, and returned with the book and sat down
again and opened it. 'Listen,' he said. He read the five
stanzas aloud and closed the book on his finger and looked
up. 'All right,' he said. 'Listen,' and read again, but only
one stanza this time and closed the book and laid it on the
table. 'She cannot fade, though thou hast not thy bliss,'
McCaslin said: 'Forever wilt thou love, and she be fair.'*

'He's talking about a girl,' he said.

*'He had to talk about something,' McCaslin said. Then
he said, 'He was talking about truth. Truth is one. It
doesn't change. It covers all things which touch the heart—
honor and pride and pity and justice and courage and love.
Do you see now?' He didn't know. Somehow it had seemed
simpler than that, simpler than somebody talking in a*

*book about a young man and a girl he would never need
to grieve over because he could never approach any nearer
and would never have to get any further away. He had
heard about an old bear and finally got big enough to
hunt it and he hunted it four years and at last met it with
a gun in his hands and he didn't shoot. Because a little
dog—But he could have shot long before the fyce covered
the twenty yards to where the bear waited, and Sam Fathers could have shot at any time during the interminable
minute while Old Ben stood on his hind legs over them.
. . . He ceased. McCaslin watched him, still speaking, the
voice, the words as quiet as the twilight itself was:* 'Courage and honor and pride, and pity and love of justice and
of liberty. They all touch the heart, and what the heart
holds to becomes truth, as far as we know truth. Do you
see now?' and he could still hear them, intact in this twilight as in that one seven years ago, no louder still because
they did not need to be because they would endure: and
he had only to look at McCaslin's eyes beyond the thin
and bitter smiling, the faint lip-lift which would have
had to be called smiling;—his kinsman, his father almost,
who had been born too late into the old time and too
soon for the new, the two of them juxtaposed and alien
now to each other against their ravaged patrimony, the
dark and ravaged fatherland still prone and panting from
its etherless operation:

'Habet then.—So this land is, indubitably, of and by itself cursed:' and he

'Cursed:' and again McCaslin merely lifted one hand,
not even speaking and not even toward the ledgers: so
that, as the stereopticon condenses into one instantaneous
field the myriad minutia of its scope, so did that slight
and rapid gesture establish in the small cramped and clut-
tered twilit room not only the ledgers but the whole plantation in its mazed and intricate entirety—the land, the
fields and what they represented in terms of cotton ginned
and sold, the men and women whom they fed and clothed

and even paid a little cash money at Christmas-time in
return for the labor which planted and raised and picked
and ginned the cotton, the machinery and mules and
gear with which they raised it and their cost and upkeep
and replacement—that whole edifice intricate and complex and founded upon injustice and erected by ruthless
rapacity and carried on even yet with at times downright
savagery not only to the human beings but the valuable
animals too, yet solvent and efficient and, more than that:
not only still intact but enlarged, increased; brought still
intact by McCaslin, himself little more than a child then,
through and out of the debacle and chaos of twenty years
ago where hardly one in ten survived, and enlarged and
increased and would continue so, solvent and efficient and
intact and still increasing so long as McCaslin and his
McCaslin successors lasted, even though their surnames
might not even be Edmonds then: then he: 'Habet too.
Because that's it: not the land, but us. Not only the blood,
but the name too; not only its color but its designation:
Edmonds, white, but, a female line, could have no other
but the name his father bore; Beauchamp, the elder line
and the male one, but, black, could have had any name
he liked and no man would have cared, except the name
his father bore who had no name—' and McCaslin

'And since I know too what you know I will say now,
once more let me say it: And one other, and in the third
generation too, and the male, the eldest, the direct and
sole and white and still McCaslin even, father to son to
son—' and he

'I am free:' and this time McCaslin did not even gesture,
no inference of fading pages, no postulation of the stere-
optic whole, but the frail and iron thread strong as truth
and impervious as evil and longer than life itself and
reaching beyond record and patrimony both to join him
with the lusts and passions, the hopes and dreams and
griefs, of bones whose names while still fleshed and capable
even old Carothers' grandfather had never heard: and he:

'And of that too:' and McCaslin

'Chosen, I suppose (I will concede it) out of all your time by Him as you say Buck and Buddy were from theirs. And it took Him a bear and an old man and four years just for you. And it took you fourteen years to reach that point and about that many, maybe more, for Old Ben, and more than seventy for Sam Fathers. And you are just one. How long then? How long?' and he

'It will be long. I have never said otherwise. But it will be all right because they will endure—' and McCaslin

'And anyway, you will be free.—No, not now nor ever, we from them nor they from us. So I repudiate too. I would deny even if I knew it were true. I would have to. Even you can see that I could do no else. I am what I am; I will be always what I was born and have always been. And more than me. More than me, just as there were more than Buck and Buddy in what you called His first plan which failed:' and he

'And more than me:' and McCaslin

'No. Not even you. Because mark. You said how on that instant when Ikkemotubbe realised that he could sell the land to Grandfather, it ceased forever to have been his. All right; go on: Then it belonged to Sam Fathers, old Ikkemotubbe's son. And who inherited from Sam Fathers, if not you? co-heir perhaps with Boon, if not of his life maybe, at least of his quitting it?' and he

'Yes. Sam Fathers set me free.' And Isaac McCaslin, not yet Uncle Ike, a long time yet before he would be uncle to half a county and still father to none, living in one small cramped fireless rented room in a Jefferson boardinghouse where petit juries were domiciled during court terms and itinerant horse- and mule-traders stayed, with his kit of brand-new carpenter's tools and the shotgun McCaslin had given him with his name engraved in silver and old General Compson's compass (and, when the General died, his silver-mounted horn too) and the iron cot and mattress and the blankets which he would take each fall into

the woods for more than sixty years and the bright tin
coffee-pot

there had been a legacy, from his Uncle Hubert Beauchamp, his godfather, that bluff burly roaring childlike
man from whom Uncle Buddy had won Tomey's Terrel's
wife Tennie in the poker-game in 1859—'possible strait
against three Treys in sigt Not called'—; no pale sentence
or paragraph scrawled in cringing fear of death by a weak
and trembling hand as a last desperate sop flung backward
at retribution, but a Legacy, a Thing, possessing weight
to the hand and bulk to the eye and even audible: a silver
cup filled with gold pieces and wrapped in burlap and
sealed with his godfather's ring in the hot wax, which
(intact still) even before his Uncle Hubert's death and
long before his own majority, when it would be his, had
become not only a legend but one of the family lares.
After his father's and his Uncle Hubert's sister's marriage
they moved back into the big house, the tremendous cavern
which old Carothers had started and never finished, cleared
the remaining Negroes out of it and with his mother's
dowry completed it, at least the rest of the windows and
doors and moved into it, all of them save Uncle Buddy
who declined to leave the cabin he and his twin had built,
the move being the bride's notion and more than just a
notion and none ever to know if she really wanted to live
in the big house or if she knew before hand that Uncle
Buddy would refuse to move: and two weeks after his birth
in 1867, the first time he and his mother came down stairs,
one night and the silver cup sitting on the cleared dining-
room table beneath the bright lamp and while his mother
and his father and McCaslin and Tennie (his nurse: carrying him) —all of them again but Uncle Buddy—watched,
his Uncle Hubert rang one by one into the cup the bright
and glinting mintage and wrapped it into the burlap envelope and heated the wax and sealed it and carried it
back home with him where he lived alone now without
even his sister either to hold him down as McCaslin said

or to try to raise him up as Uncle Buddy said, and (dark times then in Mississippi) Uncle Buddy said most of the niggers gone and the ones that didn't go even Hub Beauchamp could not have wanted: but the dogs remained and Uncle Buddy said Beauchamp fiddled while Nero foxhunted

they would go and see it there; at last his mother would prevail and they would depart in the surrey, once more all save Uncle Buddy and McCaslin to keep Uncle Buddy company until one winter Uncle Buddy began to fail and from then on it was himself, beginning to remember now, and his mother and Tennie and Tomey's Terrel to drive: the twenty-two miles into the next county, the twin gateposts on one of which McCaslin could remember the halfgrown boy blowing a fox-horn at breakfast dinner and supper-time and jumping down to open to any passer who happened to hear it but where there were no gates at all now, the shabby and overgrown entrance to what his mother still insisted that people call Warwick because her brother was if truth but triumphed and justice but prevailed the rightful earl of it, the paintless house which outwardly did not change but which on the inside seemed each time larger because he was too little to realise then that there was less and less in it of the fine furnishings, the rosewood and mahogany and walnut which for him had never existed anywhere anyway save in his mother's tearful lamentations and the occasional piece small enough to be roped somehow onto the rear or the top of the carriage on their return (And he remembered this, he had seen it: an instant, a flash, his mother's soprano 'Even my dress! Even my dress!' loud and outraged in the barren unswept hall; a face young and female and even lighter in color than Tomey's Terrel's for an instant in a closing door; a swirl, a glimpse of the silk gown and the flick and glint of an ear-ring: an apparition rapid and tawdry and illicit yet somehow even to the child, the infant still almost, breathless and exciting and evocative: as though, like

two limpid and pellucid streams meeting, the child which
he still was had made serene and absolute and perfect
rapport and contact through that glimpsed nameless illicit
hybrid female flesh with the boy which had existed at that
stage of inviolable and immortal adolescence in his uncle
for almost sixty years; the dress, the face, the ear-rings
gone in that same aghast flash and his uncle's voice: 'She's
my cook! She's my new cook! I had to have a cook, didn't
I?' then the uncle himself, the face alarmed and aghast
too yet still innocently and somehow even indomitably of
a boy, they retreating in their turn now, back to the front
gallery, and his uncle again, pained and still amazed, in a
sort of desperate resurgence if not of courage at least of
self-assertion: 'They're free now! They're folks too just
like we are!' and his mother: 'That's why! That's why! My
mother's house! Defiled! Defiled!' and his uncle: 'Damn
it, Sibbey, at least give her time to pack her grip:' then
over, finished, the loud uproar and all, himself and Tennie
and he remembered Tennie's inscrutable face at the
broken shutterless window of the bare room which had
once been the parlor while they watched, hurrying down
the lane at a stumbling trot, the routed compounder of
his uncle's uxory: the back, the nameless face which he
had seen only for a moment, the once-hooped dress bal-
looning and flapping below a man's overcoat, the worn
heavy carpet-bag jouncing and banging against her knee,
routed and in retreat true enough and in the empty lane
solitary young-looking and forlorn yet withal still exciting
and evocative and wearing still the silken banner captured
inside the very citadel of respectability, and unforgettable.)

the cup, the sealed inscrutable burlap, sitting on the
shelf in the locked closet, Uncle Hubert unlocking the
door and lifting it down and passing it from hand to hand:
his mother, his father, McCaslin and even Tennie, insisting that each take it in turn and heft it for weight and
shake it again to prove the sound, Uncle Hubert himself

standing spraddled before the cold unswept hearth in
which the very bricks themselves were crumbling into a
litter of soot and dust and mortar and the droppings of
chimney-sweeps, still roaring and still innocent and still
indomitable: and for a long time he believed nobody but
himself had noticed that his uncle now put the cup only
into his hands, unlocked the door and lifted it down and
put it into his hands and stood over him until he had
shaken it obediently until it sounded then took it from
him and locked it back into the closet before anyone else
could have offered to touch it, and even later, when competent not only to remember but to rationalise, he could
not say what it was or even if it had been anything because
the parcel was still heavy and still rattled, not even when,
Uncle Buddy dead and his father, at last and after almost
seventy-five years in bed after the sun rose, said: 'Go get
that damn cup. Bring that damn Hub Beauchamp too if
you have to:' because it still rattled though his uncle no
longer put it even into his hands now but carried it himself from one to the other, his mother, McCaslin, Tennie,
shaking it before each in turn, saying: 'Hear it? Hear it?'
his face still innocent, not quite baffled but only amazed
and not very amazed and still indomitable: and, his father
and Uncle Buddy both gone now, one day without reason
or any warning the almost completely empty house in
which his uncle and Tennie's ancient and quarrelsome
great-grandfather (who claimed to have seen Lafayette
and McCaslin said in another ten years would be remembering God) lived, cooked and slept in one single room,
burst into peaceful conflagration, a tranquil instantaneous
sourceless unanimity of combustion, walls floors and roof:
at sunup it stood where his uncle's father had built it sixty
years ago, at sundown the four blackened and smokeless
chimneys rose from a light white powder of ashes and a
few charred ends of planks which did not even appear to
have been very hot: and out of the last of evening, the last
one of the twenty-two miles, on the old white mare which

was the last of that stable which McCaslin remembered, the
two old men riding double up to the sister's door, the one
wearing his fox-horn on its braided deerhide thong and
the other carrying the burlap parcel wrapped in a shirt,
the tawny wax-daubed shapeless lump sitting again and
on an almost identical shelf and his uncle holding the
half-opened door now, his hand not only on the knob but
one foot against it and the key waiting in the other hand,
the face urgent and still not baffled but still and even indomitably not very amazed and himself standing in the
half-opened door looking quietly up at the burlap shape
become almost three times its original height and a good
half less than its original thickness and turning away and
he would remember not his mother's look this time nor
yet Tennie's inscrutable expression but McCaslin's dark
and aquiline face grave insufferable and bemused: then
one night they waked him and fetched him still half-asleep
into the lamp light, the smell of medicine which was familiar by now in that room and the smell of something
else which he had not smelled before and knew at once
and would never forget, the pillow, the worn and ravaged
face from which looked out still the boy innocent and
immortal and amazed and urgent, looking at him and
trying to tell him until McCaslin moved and leaned over
the bed and drew from the top of the nightshirt the big
iron key on the greasy cord which suspended it, the eyes
saying Yes Yes Yes now, and cut the cord and unlocked
the closet and brought the parcel to the bed, the eyes still
trying to tell him even when he took the parcel so that
was still not it, the hands still clinging to the parcel even
while relinquishing it, the eyes more urgent than ever trying to tell him but they never did; and he was ten and his
mother was dead too and McCaslin said, 'You are almost
halfway now. You might as well open it:' and he: 'No. He
said twenty-one:' and he was twenty-one and McCaslin
shifted the bright lamp to the center of the cleared dining-
room table and set the parcel beside it and laid his open

knife beside the parcel and stood back with that expression of old grave intolerant and repudiating and he lifted it, the burlap lump which fifteen years ago had changed its shape completely overnight, which shaken gave forth a thin weightless not-quite-musical curiously muffled clatter, the bright knife-blade hunting amid the mazed intricacy of string, the knobby gouts of wax bearing his uncle's Beauchamp seal rattling onto the table's polished top and, standing amid the collapse of burlap folds, the unstained tin coffee-pot still brand new, the handful of copper coins and now he knew what had given them the muffled sound: a collection of minutely-folded scraps of paper sufficient almost for a rat's nest, of good linen bond, of the crude ruled paper such as Negroes use, of raggedly-torn ledger-pages and the margins of newspapers and once the paper label from a new pair of overalls, all dated and all signed, beginning with the first one not six months after they had watched him seal the silver cup into the burlap on this same table in this same room by the light even of this same lamp almost twenty-one years ago:

> *I owe my Nephew Isaac Beauchamp McCaslin five (5) pieces Gold which I.O.U. constitutes My note of hand with Interest at 5 percent.*
> *Hubert Fitz-Hubert Beauchamp*
> *at Warwick 27 Nov 1867*

and he: 'Anyway he called it Warwick:' once at least, even if no more. But there was more:

> *Isaac 24 Dec 1867 I.O.U. 2 pieces Gold H.Fh.B. I.O.U. Isaac 1 piece Gold 1 Jan 1868 H.Fh.B.*

then five again then three then one then one then a long time and what dream, what dreamed splendid recoup, not of any injury or betrayal of trust because it had been merely a loan: nay, a partnership:

> *I.O.U. Beauchamp McCaslin or his heirs twenty-five*

*(25) pieces Gold This & All preceeding constituting
My notes of hand at twenty (20) percentum compounded annually. This date of 19ih January 1873
                                        Beauchamp*

no location save that in time and signed by the single not
name but word as the old proud earl himself might have
scrawled Nevile: and that made forty-three and he could
not remember himself of course but the legend had it at
fifty, which balanced: one: then one: then one: then one
and then the last three and then the last chit, dated after
he came to live in the house with them and written in the
shaky hand not of a beaten old man because he had never
been beaten to know it but of a tired old man maybe and
even at that tired only on the outside and still indomitable,
the simplicity of the last one the simplicity not of resigna-
tion but merely of amazement, like a simple comment or
remark, and not very much of that:

> *One silver cup. Hubert Beauchamp*

and McCaslin: 'So you have plenty of coppers anyway.
But they are still not old enough yet to be either rarities
or heirlooms. So you will have to take the money:' except
that he didn't hear McCaslin, standing quietly beside the
table and looking peacefully at the coffee-pot and the pot
sitting one night later on the mantel above what was not
even a fireplace in the little cramped icelike room in
Jefferson as McCaslin tossed the folded banknotes onto
the bed and, still standing (there was nowhere to sit save
on the bed) did not even remove his hat and overcoat:
and he
   'As a loan. From you. This one:' and McCaslin
   'You cant. I have no money that I can lend to you. And
you will have to go to the bank and get it next month because I wont bring it to you:' and he could not hear Mc-
Caslin now either, looking peacefully at McCaslin, his
kinsman, his father almost yet no kin now as, at the last,

even fathers and sons are no kin: and he

'It's seventeen miles, horseback and in the cold. We could both sleep here:' and McCaslin

'Why should I sleep here in my house when you wont sleep yonder in yours?' and gone, and he looking at the bright rustless unstained tin and thinking and not for the first time how much it takes to compound a man (Isaac McCaslin for instance) and of the devious intricate choosing yet unerring path that man's (Isaac McCaslin's for instance) spirit takes among all that mass to make him at last what he is to be, not only to the astonishment of them (the ones who sired the McCaslin who sired his father and Uncle Buddy and their sister, and the ones who sired the Beauchamp who sired his Uncle Hubert and his Uncle Hubert's sister) who believed they had shaped him, but to Isaac McCaslin too

as a loan and used it though he would not have had to: Major de Spain offered him a room in his house as long as he wanted it and asked nor would ever ask any question, and old General Compson more than that, to take him into his own room, to sleep in half of his own bed and more than Major de Spain because he told him baldly why: 'You sleep with me and before this winter is out, I'll know the reason. You'll tell me. Because I dont believe you just quit. It looks like you just quit but I have watched you in the woods too much and I dont believe you just quit even if it does look damn like it:' using it as a loan, paid his board and rent for a month and bought the tools, not simply because he was good with his hands because he had intended to use his hands and it could have been with horses, and not in mere static and hopeful emulation of the Nazarene as the young gambler buys a spotted shirt because the old gambler won in one yesterday, but (without the arrogance of false humility and without the false humbleness of pride, who intended to earn his bread, didn't especially want to earn it but had to earn it and for more than just bread) because if the Nazarene had found

carpentering good for the life and ends He had assumed
and elected to serve, it would be all right too for Isaac
McCaslin even though Isaac McCaslin's ends, although
simple enough in their apparent motivation, were and
would be always incomprehensible to him, and his life,
invincible enough in its needs, if he could have helped
himself, not being the Nazarene, he would not have chosen
it: and paid it back. He had forgotten the thirty dollars
which McCaslin would put into the bank in his name
each month, fetched it in to him and flung it onto the bed
that first one time but no more; he had a partner now or
rather he was the partner: a blasphemous profane clever
old dipsomaniac who had built blockade-runners in
Charleston in '62 and '3 and had been a ship's carpenter
since and appeared in Jefferson two years ago nobody
knew from where nor why and spent a good part of his
time since recovering from delirium tremens in the jail;
they had put a new roof on the stable of the bank's president and (the old man in jail again still celebrating that
job) he went to the bank to collect for it and the president
said, 'I should borrow from you instead of paying you:'
and it had been seven months now and he remembered
for the first time, two-hundred-and-ten dollars, and this
was the first job of any size and when he left the bank the
account stood at two-twenty, two-forty to balance, only
twenty dollars more to go, then it did balance though by
then the total had increased to three hundred and thirty
and he said, 'I will transfer it now:' and the president said,
'I cant do that. McCaslin told me not to. Haven't you got
another initial you could use and open another account?'
but that was all right, the coins the silver and the bills as
they accumulated knotted into a handkerchief and the
coffee-pot wrapped in an old shirt as when Tennie's great-
grandfather had fetched it from Warwick eighteen years
ago, in the bottom of the iron-bound trunk which old
Carothers had brought from Carolina and his landlady
said, 'Not even a lock! And you dont even lock your door,

not even when you leave!' and himself looking at her as peacefully as he had looked at McCaslin that first night in this same room, no kin to him at all yet more than kin as those who serve you even for pay are your kin and those who injure you are more than brother or wife

and had the wife now, got the old man out of jail and fetched him to the rented room and sobered him by superior strength, did not even remove his own shoes for twenty-four hours, got him up and got food into him and they built the barn this time from the ground up and he married her: an only child, a small girl yet curiously bigger than she seemed at first, solider perhaps, with dark eyes and a passionate heart-shaped face, who had time even on that farm to watch most of the day while he sawed timbers to the old man's measurements: and she: 'Papa told me about you. That farm is really yours, isn't it?' and he

'And McCaslin's:' and she

'Was there a will leaving half of it to him?' and he

'There didn't need to be a will. His grandmother was my father's sister. We were the same as brothers:' and she

'You are the same as second cousins and that's all you ever will be. But I dont suppose it matters:' and they were married, they were married and it was the new country, his heritage too as it was the heritage of all, out of the earth, beyond the earth yet of the earth because his too was of the earth's long chronicle, his too because each must share with another in order to come into it and in the sharing they become one: for that while, one: for that little while at least, one: indivisible, that while at least irrevocable and unrecoverable, living in a rented room still but for just a little while and that room wall-less and topless and floorless in glory for him to leave each morning and return to at night; her father already owned the lot in town and furnished the material and he and his partner would build it, her dowry from one: her wedding-present from three, she not to know it until the bungalow was finished and ready to be moved into and he never know

who told her, not her father and not his partner and not
even in drink though for a while he believed that, himself
coming home from work and just time to wash and rest a
moment before going down to supper, entering no rented
cubicle since it would still partake of glory even after they
would have grown old and lost it: and he saw her face
then, just before she spoke: 'Sit down:' the two of them
sitting on the bed's edge, not even touching yet, her face
strained and terrible, her voice a passionate and expiring
whisper of immeasurable promise: 'I love you. You know
I love you. When are we going to move?' and he

'I didn't—I didn't know—Who told you—' the hot fierce
palm clapped over his mouth, crushing his lips into his
teeth, the fierce curve of fingers digging into his cheek
and only the palm slacked off enough for him to answer:

'The farm. Our farm. Your farm:' and he

'I—' then the hand again, finger and palm, the whole
enveloping weight of her although she still was not touching him save the hand, the voice: 'No! No!' and the fingers
themselves seeming to follow through the cheek the impulse to speech as it died in his mouth, then the whisper,
the breath again, of love and of incredible promise, the
palm slackening again to let him answer:

'When?' and he

'I—' then she was gone, the hand too, standing, her back
to him and her head bent, the voice so calm now that for
an instant it seemed no voice of hers that he ever remembered: 'Stand up and turn your back and shut your eyes:'
and repeated before he understood and stood himself with
his eyes shut and heard the bell ring for supper below
stairs and the calm voice again: 'Lock the door:' and he
did so and leaned his forehead against the cold wood, his
eyes closed, hearing his heart and the sound he had begun
to hear before he moved until it ceased and the bell rang
again below stairs and he knew it was for them this time
and he heard the bed and turned and he had never seen
her naked before, he had asked her to once, and why: that

he wanted to see her naked because he loved her and he
wanted to see her looking at him naked because he loved
her but after that he never mentioned it again, even turning his face when she put the nightgown on over her dress
to undress at night and putting the dress on over the gown
to remove it in the morning and she would not let him
get into bed beside her until the lamp was out and even
in the heat of summer she would draw the sheet up over
them both before she would let him turn to her: and the
landlady came up the stairs up the hall and rapped on the
door and then called their names but she didn't move,
lying still on the bed outside the covers, her face turned
away on the pillow, listening to nothing, thinking of nothing, not of him anyway he thought then the landlady went
away and she said, "Take off your clothes:' her head still
turned away, looking at nothing, thinking of nothing,
waiting for nothing, not even him, her hand moving as
though with volition and vision of its own, catching his
wrist at the exact moment when he paused beside the bed
so that he never paused but merely changed the direction
of moving, downward now, the hand drawing him and
she moved at last, shifted, a movement one single complete
inherent not practiced and one time older than man, looking at him now, drawing him still downward with the one
hand down and down and he neither saw nor felt it shift,
palm flat against his chest now and holding him away with
the same apparent lack of any effort or any need for
strength, and not looking at him now, she didn't need to,
the chaste woman, the wife, already looked upon all the
men who ever rutted and now her whole body had
changed, altered, he had never seen it but once and now
it was not even the one he had seen but composite of all
woman-flesh since man that ever of its own will reclined
on its back and opened, and out of it somewhere, without
any movement of lips even, the dying and invincible whisper: 'Promise:' and he
  'Promise?'

'The farm.' He moved. He had moved, the hand shifting from his chest once more to his wrist, grasping it, the
arm still lax and only the light increasing pressure of the
fingers as though arm and hand were a piece of wire cable
with one looped end, only the hand tightening as he pulled
against it. 'No,' he said. 'No:' and she was not looking at
him still but not like the other but still the hand: 'No, I
tell you. I wont. I cant. Never:' and still the hand and he
said, for the last time, he tried to speak clearly and he
knew it was still gently and he thought, *She already knows
more than I with all the man-listening in camps where
there was nothing to read ever even heard of. They are
born already bored with what a boy approaches only at
fourteen and fifteen with blundering and aghast trembling:* 'I cant. Not ever. Remember:' and still the steady
and invincible hand and he said Yes and he thought, *She
is lost. She was born lost. We were all born lost* then he
stopped thinking and even saying Yes, it was like nothing
he had ever dreamed, let alone heard in mere man-talking
until after a no-time he returned and lay spent on the
insatiate immemorial beach and again with a movement
one time more older than man she turned and freed herself
and on their wedding night she had cried and he thought
she was crying now at first, into the tossed and wadded
pillow, the voice coming from somewhere between the
pillow and the cachinnation: 'And that's all. That's all
from me. If this dont get you that son you talk about, it
wont be mine:' lying on her side, her back to the empty
rented room, laughing and laughing

—5—

He went back to the camp one more time before the
lumber company moved in and began to cut the timber.
Major de Spain himself never saw it again. But he made
them welcome to use the house and hunt the land whenever they liked, and in the winter following the last hunt

when Sam Fathers and Lion died, General Compson and
Walter Ewell invented a plan to corporate themselves, the
old group, into a club and lease the camp and the hunting
privileges of the woods—an invention doubtless of the
somewhat childish old General but actually worthy of
Boon Hogganbeck himself. Even the boy, listening, recognised it for the subterfuge it was: to change the leopard's
spots when they could not alter the leopard, a baseless
and illusory hope to which even McCaslin seemed to sub-
scribe for a while, that once they had persuaded Major de
Spain to return to the camp he might revoke himself,
which even the boy knew he would not do. And he did not.
The boy never knew what occurred when Major de Spain
declined. He was not present when the subject was
broached and McCaslin never told him. But when June
came and the time for the double birthday celebration
there was no mention of it and when November came no
one spoke of using Major de Spain's house and he never
knew whether or not Major de Spain knew they were going on the hunt though without doubt old Ash probably
told him: he and McCaslin and General Compson (and
that one was the General's last hunt too) and Walter and
Boon and Tennie's Jim and old Ash loaded two wagons
and drove two days and almost forty miles beyond any
country the boy had ever seen before and lived in tents for
the two weeks. And the next spring they heard (not from
Major de Spain) that he had sold the timber-rights to a
Memphis lumber company and in June the boy came to
town with McCaslin one Saturday and went to Major de
Spain's office—the big, airy, book-lined second-storey room
with windows at one end opening upon the shabby hinder
purlieus of stores and at the other a door giving onto the
railed balcony above the Square, with its curtained alcove
where sat a cedar water-bucket and a sugar-bowl and spoon
and tumbler and a wicker-covered demijohn of whisky,
and the bamboo-and-paper punkah swinging back and
forth above the desk while old Ash in a tilted chair beside

the entrance pulled the cord.

"Of course," Major de Spain said. "Ash will probably like to get off in the woods himself for a while, where he wont have to eat Daisy's cooking. Complain about it, anyway. Are you going to take anybody with you?"

"No sir," he said. "I thought that maybe Boon—" For six months now Boon had been town-marshal at Hoke's; Major de Spain had compounded with the lumber company—or perhaps compromised was closer, since it was the lumber company who had decided that Boon might be better as a town-marshal than head of a logging gang.

"Yes," Major de Spain said. "I'll wire him today. He can meet you at Hoke's. I'll send Ash on by the train and they can take some food in and all you will have to do will be to mount your horse and ride over."

"Yes sir," he said. "Thank you." And he heard his voice again. He didn't know he was going to say it yet he did know, he had known it all the time: "Maybe if you . . ." His voice died. It was stopped, he never knew how because Major de Spain did not speak and it was not until his voice ceased that Major de Spain moved, turned back to the desk and the papers spread on it and even that without moving because he was sitting at the desk with a paper in his hand when the boy entered, the boy standing there looking down at the short plumpish gray-haired man in sober fine broadcloth and an immaculate glazed shirt whom he was used to seeing in boots and muddy corduroy, unshaven, sitting the shaggy powerful long-hocked mare with the worn Winchester carbine across the saddlebow and the great blue dog standing motionless as bronze at the stirrup, the two of them in that last year and to the boy anyway coming to resemble one another somehow as two people competent for love or for business who have been in love or in business together for a long time sometimes do. Major de Spain did not look up again.

"No. I will be too busy. But good luck to you. If you have it, you might bring me a young squirrel."

"Yes sir," he said. "I will."

He rode his mare, the three-year-old filly he had bred and raised and broken himself. He left home a little after midnight and six hours later, without even having sweated her, he rode into Hoke's, the tiny long-line junction which he had always thought of as Major de Spain's property too although Major de Spain had merely sold the company (and that many years ago) the land on which the side-tracks and loading-platforms and the commissary store stood, and looked about in shocked and grieved amazement even though he had had forewarning and had believed himself prepared: a new planing-mill already half completed which would cover two or three acres and what looked like miles and miles of stacked steel rails red with the light bright rust of newness and of piled crossties sharp with creosote, and wire corrals and feeding-troughs for two hundred mules at least and the tents for the men who drove them; so that he arranged for the care and stabling of his mare as rapidly as he could and did not look any more, mounted into the log-train caboose with his gun and climbed into the cupola and looked no more save toward the wall of wilderness ahead within which he would be able to hide himself from it once more anyway.

Then the little locomotive shrieked and began to move: a rapid churning of exhaust, a lethargic deliberate clashing of slack couplings traveling backward along the train, the exhaust changing to the deep slow clapping bites of power as the caboose too began to move and from the cupola he watched the train's head complete the first and only curve in the entire line's length and vanish into the wilderness, dragging its length of train behind it so that it resembled a small dingy harmless snake vanishing into weeds, drawing him with it too until soon it ran once more at its maximum clattering speed between the twin walls of unaxed wilderness as of old. It had been harmless once. Not five years ago Walter Ewell had shot a six-point buck from this same moving caboose, and there was the

story of the half-grown bear: the train's first trip in to the
cutting thirty miles away, the bear between the rails, its
rear end elevated like that of a playing puppy while it
dug to see what sort of ants or bugs they might contain or
perhaps just to examine the curious symmetrical squared
barkless logs which had appeared apparently from nowhere
in one endless mathematical line overnight, still digging
until the driver on the braked engine not fifty feet away
blew the whistle at it, whereupon it broke frantically and
took the first tree it came to: an ash sapling not much bigger than a man's thigh and climbed as high as it could and
clung there, its head ducked between its arms as a man
(a woman perhaps) might have done while the brakeman
threw chunks of ballast at it, and when the engine returned
three hours later with the first load of outbound logs the
bear was halfway down the tree and once more scrambled
back up as high as it could and clung again while the train
passed and was still there when the engine went in again
in the afternoon and still there when it came back out at
dusk; and Boon had been in Hoke's with the wagon after
a barrel of flour that noon when the train-crew told about
it and Boon and Ash, both twenty years younger then, sat
under the tree all that night to keep anybody from shooting it and the next morning Major de Spain had the log-
train held at Hoke's and just before sundown on the second
day, with not only Boon and Ash but Major de Spain and
General Compson and Walter and McCaslin, twelve then,
watching, it came down the tree after almost thirty-six
hours without even water and McCaslin told him how for
a minute they thought it was going to stop right there at
the barrow-pit where they were standing and drink, how
it looked at the water and paused and looked at them and
at the water again, but did not, gone, running, as bears
run, the two sets of feet, front and back, tracking two
separate though parallel courses.

It had been harmless then. They would hear the passing
log-train sometimes from the camp; sometimes, because

nobody bothered to listen for it or not. They would hear it going in, running light and fast, the light clatter of the trucks, the exhaust of the diminutive locomotive and its shrill peanut-parcher whistle flung for one petty moment and absorbed by the brooding and inattentive wilderness without even an echo. They would hear it going out, loaded, not quite so fast now yet giving its frantic and toylike illusion of crawling speed, not whistling now to conserve steam, flinging its bitten laboring miniature puffing into the immemorial woodsface with frantic and bootless vainglory, empty and noisy and puerile, carrying to no destination or purpose sticks which left nowhere any scar or stump as the child's toy loads and transports and unloads its dead sand and rushes back for more, tireless and unceasing and rapid yet never quite so fast as the Hand which plays with it moves the toy burden back to load the toy again. But it was different now. It was the same train, engine cars and caboose, even the same enginemen brakeman and conductor to whom Boon, drunk then sober then drunk again then fairly sober once more all in the space of fourteen hours, had bragged that day two years ago about what they were going to do to Old Ben tomorrow, running with its same illusion of frantic rapidity between the same twin walls of impenetrable and impervious woods, passing the old landmarks, the old game crossings over which he had trailed bucks wounded and not wounded and more than once seen them, anything but wounded, break out of the woods, up and across the embankment which bore the rails and ties then down and into the woods again as the earth-bound supposedly move but crossing as arrows travel, groundless, elongated, three times its actual length and even paler, different in color, as if there were a point between immobility and absolute motion where even mass chemically altered, changing without pain or agony not only in bulk and shape but in color too, approaching the color of wind, yet this time it was as though the train (and not only the train but himself, not only his vision which had seen it and his memory which remembered it but his clothes too, as garments carry back into the clean edgeless blowing of air the lingering effluvium of a sick-room or of death) had brought with it into the doomed wilderness even before the actual axe the shadow and portent of the new mill not even finished yet and the rails and ties which were not even laid; and he knew now what he had known as soon as he saw Hoke's this morning but had not yet thought into words: why Major de Spain had not come back, and that after this time he himself, who had had to see it one time other, would return no more.

Now they were near. He knew it before the engine-driver whistled to warn him. Then he saw Ash and the wagon, the reins without doubt wrapped once more about the brake-lever as within the boy's own memory Major de Spain had been forbidding him for eight years to do, the train slowing, the slackened couplings jolting and clashing again from car to car, the caboose slowing past the wagon as he swung down with his gun, the conductor leaning out above him to signal the engine, the caboose still slowing, creeping, although the engine's exhaust was already slatting in mounting tempo against the unechoing wilderness, the crashing of draw-bars once more travelling backward along the train, the caboose picking up speed at last. Then it was gone. It had not been. He could no longer hear it. The wilderness soared, musing, inattentive, myriad, eternal, green; older than any mill-shed, longer than any spurline. "Mr Boon here yet?" he said.

"He beat me in," Ash said. "Had the wagon loaded and ready for me at Hoke's yistiddy when I got there and setting on the front steps at camp last night when I got in. He already been in the woods since fo daylight this morning. Said he gwine up to the Gum Tree and for you to hunt up that way and meet him." He knew where that was: a single big sweet-gum just outside the woods, in an old clearing; if you crept up to it very quietly this time of year and then ran suddenly into the clearing, sometimes you caught as many as a dozen squirrels in it, trapped, since there was no other tree near they could jump to. So he didn't get into the wagon at all.

"I will," he said.

"I figured you would," Ash said, "I fotch you a box of shells." He passed the shells down and began to unwrap the lines from the brake-pole.

"How many times up to now do you reckon Major has told you not to do that?" the boy said.

"Do which?" Ash said. Then he said: "And tell Boon Hogganbeck dinner gonter be on the table in a hour and if yawl want any to come on and eat it."

"In an hour?" he said. "It aint nine oclock yet." He drew out his watch and extended it face-toward Ash. "Look." Ash didn't even look at the watch.

"That's town time. You aint in town now. You in the woods."

"Look at the sun then."

"Nemmine the sun too," Ash said. "If you and Boon Hogganbeck want any dinner, you better come on in and get it when I tole you. I aim to get done in that kitchen because I got my wood to chop. And watch your feet. They're crawling."

"I will," he said.

Then he was in the woods, not alone but solitary; the solitude closed about him, green with summer. They did not change, and, timeless, would not, anymore than would the green of summer and the fire and rain of fall and the iron cold and sometimes even snow

the day, the morning when he killed the buck and Sam marked his face with its hot blood, they returned to camp and he remembered old Ash's blinking and disgruntled and even outraged disbelief until at last McCaslin had had to affirm the fact that he had really killed it: and that night Ash sat snarling and unapproachable behind the stove so that Tennie's Jim had to serve the supper and waked them with breakfast already on the table the next morning and it was only half-past one oclock and at last out of Major de Spain's angry cursing and Ash's snarling and sullen rejoinders the fact emerged that Ash not only wanted to go into the woods and shoot a deer also but he intended to and Major de Spain said, 'By God, if we dont let him we will probably have to do the cooking from now on:' and Walter Ewell said, 'Or get up at midnight to eat what Ash cooks:' and since he had already killed his buck for this hunt and was not to shoot again unless they needed meat, he offered his gun to Ash until Major de Spain took command and allotted that gun to Boon for the day and gave Boon's unpredictable pump gun to Ash, with two buckshot shells but Ash said, 'I got shells:' and showed them, four: one buck, one of number three shot for rabbits, two of bird-shot and told one by one their history and their origin and he remembered not Ash's face alone but Major de Spain's and Walter's and General Compson's too, and Ash's voice: 'Shoot? In course they'll shoot! Genl Cawmpson guv me this un'—the buckshot—'right outen the same gun he kilt that big buck with eight years ago. And this un'—it was the rabbit shell: triumphantly—'is oldern thisyer boy!' And that morning he loaded the gun himself, reversing the order: the bird-shot, the rabbit, then the buck so that the buckshot would feed first into the chamber, and himself without a gun, he and Ash walked beside Major de Spain's and Tennie's Jim's horses and the dogs (that was the snow) until they cast and struck, the sweet strong cries ringing away into the muffled falling air and gone almost immediately, as if the constant and unmurmuring flakes had already buried even the unformed echoes beneath their myriad and weightless falling, Major de Spain and Tennie's Jim gone too, whooping on into the woods; and then it was all right, he knew as plainly as if Ash had told him that Ash had now hunted his deer and that even his tender years had been forgiven for having killed one, and they turned back toward home

*through the falling snow—that is, Ash said, 'Now whut?'
and he said, 'This way'—himself in front because, although
they were less than a mile from camp, he knew that Ash,
who had spent two weeks of his life in the camp each year
for the last twenty, had no idea whatever where they were,
until quite soon the manner in which Ash carried Boon's
gun was making him a good deal more than just nervous
and he made Ash walk in front, striding on, talking now,
an old man's garrulous monologue beginning with where
he was at the moment then of the woods and of camping
in the woods and of eating in camps then of eating then
of cooking it and of his wife's cooking then briefly of his
old wife and almost at once and at length of a new light-
colored woman who nursed next door to Major de Spain's
and if she didn't watch out who she was switching her tail
at he would show her how old was an old man or not if
his wife just didn't watch him all the time, the two of them
in a game trail through a dense brake of cane and brier
which would bring them out within a quarter-mile of
camp, approaching a big fallen tree-trunk lying athwart
the path and just as Ash, still talking, was about to step
over it the bear, the yearling, rose suddenly beyond the
log, sitting up, its forearms against its chest and its wrists
limply arrested as if it had been surprised in the act of covering its face to pray: and after a certain time Ash's gun
yawed jerkily up and he said, 'You haven't got a shell in
the barrel yet. Pump it.' but the gun already snicked and
he said, 'Pump it. You haven't got a shell in the barrel
yet.' and Ash pumped the action and in a certain time the
gun steadied again and snicked and he said, 'Pump it?'
and watched the buckshot shell jerk, spinning heavily,
into the cane. This is the rabbit shot: he thought and the
gun snicked and he thought: The next is bird-shot: and
he didn't have to say Pump it; he cried, 'Dont shoot! Dont
shoot!' but that was already too late too, the light dry
vicious snick! before he could speak and the bear turned
and dropped to all-fours and then was gone and there was*

*only the log, the cane, the velvet and constant snow and
Ash said, 'Now whut?' and he said, 'This way. Come on.'
and began to back away down the path and Ash said, 'I got
to find my shells.' and he said, 'Goddamn it, goddamn it,
come on.' but Ash leaned the gun against the log and returned and stooped and fumbled among the cane roots
until he came back and stooped and found the shells and
they rose and at that moment the gun, untouched, leaning
against the log six feet away and for that while even forgotten by both of them, roared, bellowed and flamed, and
ceased: and he carried it now, pumped out the last mum-
mified shell and gave that one also to Ash and, the action
still open, himself carried the gun until he stood it in the
corner behind Boon's bed at the camp*

—; summer, and fall, and snow, and wet and saprife
spring in their ordered immortal sequence, the deathless
and immemorial phases of the mother who had shaped
him if any had toward the man he almost was, mother and
father both to the old man born of a Negro slave and a
Chickasaw chief who had been his spirit's father if any
had, whom he had revered and harkened to and loved and
lost and grieved: and he would marry someday and they
too would own for their brief while that brief unsub-
stanced glory which inherently of itself cannot last and
hence why glory: and they would, might, carry even the
remembrance of it into the time when flesh no longer talks
to flesh because memory at least does last: but still the
woods would be his mistress and his wife.

He was not going toward the Gum Tree. Actually he
was getting farther from it. Time was and not so long ago
either when he would not have been allowed here without
someone with him, and a little later, when he had begun
to learn how much he did not know, he would not have
dared be here without someone with him, and later still,
beginning to ascertain, even if only dimly, the limits of
what he did not know, he could have attempted and carried it through with a compass, not because of any in-

creased belief in himself but because McCaslin and Major de Spain and Walter and General Compson too had taught him at last to believe the compass regardless of what it seemed to state. Now he did not even use the compass but merely the sun and that only subconsciously, yet he could have taken a scaled map and plotted at any time to within a hundred feet of where he actually was; and sure enough, at almost the exact moment when he expected it, the earth began to rise faintly, he passed one of the four concrete markers set down by the lumber company's surveyor to establish the four corners of the plot which Major de Spain had reserved out of the sale, then he stood on the crest of the knoll itself, the four corner-markers all visible now, blanched still even beneath the winter's weathering, lifeless and shockingly alien in that place where dissolution itself was a seething turmoil of ejaculation tumescence conception and birth, and death did not even exist. After two winters' blanketings of leaves and the flood-waters of two springs, there was no trace of the two graves anymore at all. But those who would have come this far to find them would not need headstones but would have found them as Sam Fathers himself had taught him to find such: by bearings on trees: and did, almost the first thrust of the hunting knife finding (but only to see if it was still there) the round tin box manufactured for axle-grease and containing now Old Ben's dried mutilated paw, resting above Lion's bones.

He didn't disturb it. He didn't even look for the other grave where he and McCaslin and Major de Spain and Boon had laid Sam's body, along with his hunting horn and his knife and his tobacco-pipe, that Sunday morning two years ago; he didn't have to. He had stepped over it, perhaps on it. But that was all right. *He probably knew I was in the woods this morning long before I got here,* he thought, going on to the tree which had supported one end of the platform where Sam lay when McCaslin and Major de Spain found them—the tree, the other axle-grease

tin nailed to the trunk, but weathered, rusted, alien too
yet healed already into the wilderness' concordant gen-
erality, raising no tuneless note, and empty, long since
empty of the food and tobacco he had put into it that day,
as empty of that as it would presently be of this which he
drew from his pocket—the twist of tobacco, the new bandanna handkerchief, the small paper sack of the pepper-
mint candy which Sam had used to love; that gone too,
almost before he had turned his back, not vanished but
merely translated into the myriad life which printed the
dark mold of these secret and sunless places with delicate
fairy tracks, which, breathing and biding and immobile,
watched him from beyond every twig and leaf until he
moved, moving again, walking on; he had not stopped, he
had only paused, quitting the knoll which was no abode
of the dead because there was no death, not Lion and not
Sam: not held fast in earth but free in earth and not in
earth but of earth, myriad yet undiffused of every myriad
part, leaf and twig and particle, air and sun and rain and
dew and night, acorn oak and leaf and acorn again, dark
and dawn and dark and dawn again in their immutable
progression and, being myriad, one: and Old Ben too, Old
Ben too; they would give him his paw back even, certainly
they would give him his paw back: then the long challenge and the long chase, no heart to be driven and outraged, no flesh to be mauled and bled—Even as he froze
himself, he seemed to hear Ash's parting admonition. He
could even hear the voice as he froze, immobile, one foot
just taking his weight, the toe of the other just lifted behind him, not breathing, feeling again and as always the
sharp shocking inrush from when Isaac McCaslin long yet
was not, and so it was fear all right but not fright as he
looked down at it. It had not coiled yet and the buzzer had
not sounded either, only one thick rapid contraction, one
loop cast sideways as though merely for purchase from
which the raised head might start slightly backward, not
in fright either, not in threat quite yet, more than six feet

of it, the head raised higher than his knee and less than his knee's length away, and old, the once-bright markings of its youth dulled now to a monotone concordant too with the wilderness it crawled and lurked: the old one, the ancient and accursed about the earth, fatal and solitary and he could smell it now: the thin sick smell of rotting cucumbers and something else which had no name, evocative of all knowledge and an old weariness and of pariah-hood and of death. At last it moved. Not the head. The elevation of the head did not change as it began to glide away from him, moving erect yet off the perpendicular as if the head and that elevated third were complete and all: an entity walking on two feet and free of all laws of mass and balance and should have been because even now he could not quite believe that all that shift and flow of shadow behind that walking head could have been one snake: going and then gone; he put the other foot down at last and didn't know it, standing with one hand raised as Sam had stood that afternoon six years ago when Sam led him into the wilderness and showed him and he ceased to be a child, speaking the old tongue which Sam had spoken that day without premeditation either: "Chief," he said: "Grandfather."

He couldn't tell when he first began to hear the sound, because when he became aware of it, it seemed to him that he had been already hearing it for several seconds—a sound as though someone were hammering a gun-barrel against a piece of railroad iron, a sound loud and heavy and not rapid yet with something frenzied about it, as the hammerer were not only a strong man and an earnest one but a little hysterical too. Yet it couldn't be on the log-line because, although the track lay in that direction, it was at least two miles from him and this sound was not three hundred yards away. But even as he thought that, he realised where the sound must be coming from: whoever the man was and whatever he was doing, he was somewhere near the edge of the clearing where the Gum Tree was and where he was to meet Boon. So far, he had been hunting as he advanced, moving slowly and quietly and watching the ground and the trees both. Now he went on, his gun unloaded and the barrel slanted up and back to facilitate its passage through brier and undergrowth, approaching as it grew louder and louder that steady savage somehow queerly hysterical beating of metal on metal, emerging from the woods, into the old clearing, with the solitary gum tree directly before him. At first glance the tree seemed to be alive with frantic squirrels. There appeared to be forty or fifty of them leaping and darting from branch to branch until the whole tree had become one green maelstrom of mad leaves, while from time to time, singly or in twos and threes, squirrels would dart down the trunk then whirl without stopping and rush back up again as though sucked violently back by the vacuum of their fellows' frenzied vortex. Then he saw Boon, sitting, his back against the trunk, his head bent, hammering furiously at something on his lap. What he hammered with was the barrel of his dismembered gun, what he hammered at was the breech of it. The rest of the gun lay scattered about him in a half-dozen pieces while he bent over the piece on his lap his scarlet and streaming walnut face, hammering the disjointed barrel against the gun-breech with the frantic abandon of a madman. He didn't even look up to see who it was. Still hammering, he merely shouted back at the boy in a hoarse strangled voice:

"Get out of here! Dont touch them! Dont touch a one of them! They're mine!"